"WONDERFUL...
The Mourning Sexton shows what
the law is really supposed to be about—
morality, atonement, responsibility,
and redemption."—Nelson DeMille

"The author imbues David with a
complexity and intelligence that
could make *The Mourning Sexton*
the start of a fine series."
—*Sun-Sentinel* (Florida)

THE
MOURNING
SEXTON

MICHAEL BARON

JOVE BOOKS, NEW YORK

THE BERKLEY PUBLISHING GROUP
Published by the Penguin Group
Penguin Group (USA) Inc.
375 Hudson Street, New York, New York 10014, USA
Penguin Group (Canada), 90 Eglinton Avenue East, Suite 700, Toronto, Ontario M4P 2Y3, Canada
(a division of Pearson Penguin Canada Inc.)
Penguin Books Ltd., 80 Strand, London WC2R 0RL, England
Penguin Group Ireland, 25 St. Stephen's Green, Dublin 2, Ireland (a division of Penguin Books Ltd.)
Penguin Group (Australia), 250 Camberwell Road, Camberwell, Victoria 3124, Australia
(a division of Pearson Australia Group Pty. Ltd.)
Penguin Books India Pvt. Ltd., 11 Community Centre, Panchsheel Park, New Delhi—110 017, India
Penguin Group (NZ), Cnr. Airborne and Rosedale Roads, Albany, Auckland 1310, New Zealand
(a division of Pearson New Zealand Ltd.)
Penguin Books (South Africa) (Pty.) Ltd., 24 Sturdee Avenue, Rosebank, Johannesburg 2196,
South Africa

Penguin Books Ltd., Registered Offices: 80 Strand, London WC2R 0RL, England

This is a work of fiction. Names, characters, places, and incidents either are the product of the author's imagination or are used fictitiously, and any resemblance to actual persons, living or dead, business establishments, events, or locales is entirely coincidental. The publisher does not have any control over and does not assume any responsibility for author or third-party websites or their content.

THE MOURNING SEXTON

A Jove Book / published by arrangement with The Doubleday Broadway Publishing Group, a division of Random House, Inc.

PRINTING HISTORY
Doubleday hardcover edition / May 2005
Jove mass market edition / March 2006

Copyright © 2005 by Michael Baron.
Text design by Kristin del Rosario.

ISBN: 0-515-14146-1

JOVE®
Jove Books are published by The Berkley Publishing Group,
a division of Penguin Group (USA) Inc.,
375 Hudson Street, New York, New York 10014.
JOVE is a registered trademark of Penguin Group (USA) Inc.
The "J" design is a trademark belonging to Penguin Group (USA) Inc.

PRINTED IN THE UNITED STATES OF AMERICA

10 9 8 7 6 5 4 3 2 1

To Margi—
again, and always

ACKNOWLEDGMENTS

To write a novel is to set off on a trek through an uncharted wilderness. If you want to reach the other side, you'd better have a compass. I had two superb ones—in my agent, Maria Carvainis, and my editor, Stacy Creamer.

Part One

—

On the highest throne in the world, we still sit only on
our own bottom.

MICHEL DE MONTAIGNE

1

JUST before sunrise on a cold December weekday, the morning *gabbai* unlocks the front door of Anshe Emes. He steps inside the small foyer and turns on the light. Squinting in the sudden brightness, he unbuttons his overcoat. The *gabbai* is a tall, handsome man in his late fifties with strong features, salt-and-pepper hair, and somber blue eyes.

He pauses in the main sanctuary to adjust the thermostat and continues along the back corridor to the small shul, the place of worship used for weekday services. He opens the door, turns on the light, and waits as the fluorescent tubes flicker overhead, making the contents of the room seem to jiggle. There are three rows of benches on either side of a narrow center aisle. Seating for eighteen, maybe twenty. He checks to make sure that there is a prayer book and a *chumash* in each of the slots along the backs of the seats and extras in the first row. A wide podium up front is draped with a blue felt cloth. It faces forward, or east, toward the small ark against the front wall. Mounted along the side walls are several heavy brass memorial plaques, each with two columns of names and a small commemorative lightbulb next to each name, some turned on.

Along the north wall is a window facing the parking lot that the small synagogue shares with a 7-Eleven, a dry cleaner, and a Little Caesar's Pizza. The sky has begun to lighten. Through the window he watches a large Dodge pickup pull into a spot in front of the 7-Eleven. Two construction workers step down from the pickup cab, each carrying a big, plastic coffee mug, their breath vaporing in the cold air. Down in the synagogue basement, the furnace rumbles to life. He moves over to the window and closes the shades.

Back in the foyer, he hangs his coat on the rack and places his gray fedora on the shelf above it. Reflexively, his right hand moves to his head to check that his *kippah* is in place. In his left hand he holds a small blue velvet bag embroidered with gold Hebrew letters. He unzips the bag and removes his *tallit*. Unfurling the silk prayer shawl, he inspects the ends to make sure that none of the fringes is tangled. As he does this, he quietly recites the Hebrew prayer thanking God for commanding him to wrap himself in the garment. Holding the *tallit* by the collar, he kisses each end and places it over his shoulders.

Just then the front door opens. He turns as Hyman Kantor enters, his walking cane hooked over his forearm. Kantor is in his late seventies—strong nose, hawk eyes, bald head splotched with brown age spots, posture slightly hunched by age.

"Good morning, Mr. Kantor."

"And a good morning to you, *Gabbai*."

He waits for the question as he watches the old man hang up his coat and arrange his belongings.

Mr. Kantor turns to him. "Will we have a *minyan* today?"

"There should be twelve."

Mr. Kantor nods, pleased. "Well done."

The *gabbai* smiles to himself. Mr. Kantor is the first to arrive each weekday morning, and each morning he asks the same question about the *minyan*, which is the quorum of ten Jewish men required to pray as a community and recite the mourner's *Kaddish*.

Mr. Kantor thrusts his cane forward and starts toward the shul. "I shall see you inside, sir."

The other men are arriving now, many in their sixties and seventies. They welcome one another as they take off their gloves and unbutton their overcoats and stamp their feet and rub their hands together for warmth. The men greet him warmly—several giving his first name the Yiddish pronunciation, *Doovid*. A few call him *Gabbai*.

The lofty title embarrasses him. Unlike the evening *gabbai* and the *Shabbas gabbai* of Anshe Emes—and their counterparts in Conservative and Orthodox synagogues around the world—he is not fluent in Hebrew, is not well versed in the Torah, does not call men up to the *bima* to read from the Torah, does not stand next to them to correct pronunciation and chanting errors, and never himself reads from the Torah. Nor is he a member of long standing or in any way deserving of the great honor normally associated with the title *Gabbai*. The men gave it to him out of appreciation for the tasks he's performed since joining the small congregation two years ago. Winter, summer, rain, or shine, he opens the building at sunrise each weekday morning and makes sure there is a *minyan* for the morning service. On snowy days, he shovels the front walk. These duties place him somewhere closer to custodian than *gabbai*. He'd prefer no title, but if forced to take one, he'd choose the humbler designation of sexton.

Inside the shul, Mr. Kantor is in his customary preservice position up at the podium facing the front wall. Bent over, forehead resting on his palms, *tallit* covering his head, he is softly reciting the preliminary prayers. The other men are scattered among the three rows, each in his usual seat. Some are going through the prayer shawl ritual. Others have progressed to the donning of the *tefillin*.

The *tefillin* had intrigued the *gabbai* at first. Raised a Reform Jew, he'd never heard of the leather contraptions, which, on first impression, seemed almost kinky. Now, though, he couldn't imagine the morning prayers without them.

He rolls his left shirtsleeve above the elbow, unwraps the leather strap of the arm *tefillin*, places the black leather box on his left bicep, and silently recites the first prayer. He tightens the *tefillin* and winds the leather strap seven times around his forearm, ending near his wrist. Next he places the leather box of the head *tefillin* in the middle of his forehead at his hairline. He recites the second prayer and tightens the straps behind his neck. Each of the leather boxes—the one on his left arm and the one on his forehead—contains a tiny scroll with the four scriptural passages that command Jews to put on the *tefillin*. As he does every morning, he quietly recites in English one of those passages—today the one from Exodus where God explains to Moses the observance of Passover.

"And you shall tell your son on that day, saying, 'It is because of this that Hashem acted on my behalf when I left Egypt.' And it shall serve you as a sign on your arm and as a reminder between your eyes—so that Hashem's Torah may be in your mouth; for with a strong hand Hashem removed you from Egypt."

He moves to his seat in the second row against the north wall near the window. Mr. Kantor has finished his preliminary prayers and moves to his aisle seat in the front row. Rabbi Zev Saltzman, a slender man in his early forties with a neatly trimmed beard and a wry smile, stands to the side of the podium, his left sleeve rolled up, softly reciting the prayers as he dons his *tefillin*. Most of the regulars are here this morning, all in their usual spots. In the second and third rows on the far side of the aisle is the group of elderly men who call themselves the *Alter Kocker* Brigade: Saul Birnbaum, Morris Cohen, Benny Abrams, Sid Shalowitz, Heshie Lipsitz, and Mendel Klein—all retired, all in their seventies, all mumbling the preliminary prayers as they rock back and forth, prayer books open on their laps, *tallit* covering their heads like shawls on elderly widows. In the front row on the left are the two *minyan* volunteers for today: a podiatrist in his forties named Bob Finkel and a CPA in his thirties named Gerald Brown. Both are yawning. He had called them last night to confirm that they would be here this morning. Seated behind the *gabbai* in the back row on his side of the aisle are the two mourners: Sam Gutman, whose seventy-three-year-old wife, Sadie, died two months ago, and Kenny Rosenberg, whose mother, Shirley, died of lung cancer seven months ago. They are here today—as they were yesterday, and the day before, and the day before that—to say *Kaddish*, the special prayer recited every morning during the first eleven months following the death of a loved one and thereafter on every anniversary of the death, known as the *yahrzeit*.

Rabbi Saltzman glances over at Mr. Kantor and nods. The old man clears his throat and calls out in his reedy quavering voice, "Page twenty-four, the *Akeidah*."

The rabbi reads the first several Hebrew words aloud and then lowers his voice to a mumble as the rest of the men join in.

This aspect of the service had perplexed the *gabbai* at first, since it was such a contrast to the Reform services he'd attended a lifetime ago. In temple, every member of the congregation is literally on the same page—indeed, the same line and word, reciting prayers aloud together, doing responsive readings on cue from the rabbi. In shul, each man proceeds at his own pace—gathered together in prayer but praying alone, the only guidance coming from Mr. Kantor, who occasionally calls out the page and prayer.

During his first weeks, the service seemed chaotic, especially on crowded Saturday mornings in the main sanctuary, surrounded by dozens of men chanting and mumbling and rocking and reciting—all at different paces and places in the *siddur*, or prayer book. But, gradually, the chaos melded into comfort, the mumbling into meditation—a protective cocoon that allowed many to gather while each spoke to God on his own.

The *gabbai* follows along, reading a Hebrew passage here or there, otherwise silently mouthing the English translation on the facing page. During a pause in the prayers, he glances around the room. He is surprised to see Abe Shifrin in the back row on the other side of the aisle, seated close to the door. He must have arrived after the service started. Shifrin rarely attended weekday services, showing up only on the *yahrzeits* of his wife and his daughter. Yesterday had been his daughter's third *yahrzeit*, and thus he had been there to stand for the mourners' *Kaddish*. But here he is again, a distracted look on his face, the prayer book closed on his lap. Their eyes meet for a moment before Shifrin turns away with a frown.

"Page ninety-four, the *Shema*."

The *gabbai* stands with the others and recites the prayer aloud. As the rest of the men continue in Hebrew, he skims through the English translations of the various texts and commandments that follow the Shema, his eyes catching, as always, on the warning from Deuteronomy:

Beware lest your heart be seduced and you turn astray and serve gods of others and bow down to them. Then the wrath of Hashem will blaze against you.

Head lowered, he stares at the warning. Some mornings the words sting. Some mornings they make him sad. Today, they blur into dark squiggles on the page.

"Page one hundred two," Mr. Kantor announces. He grunts as he pushes up from the bench. "Rise for the *Shemoneh Esrei*."

The men stand and silently recite the devotional prayer. The *gabbai* reads along in English. *Blessed are you, Hashem, our God and God of our forefathers, God of Abraham, God of Isaac, and God of Jacob.*

As the men rock back and forth, Mr. Kantor moves down the center aisle, using his cane for support. He stops before each man and holds out the *pushke*, the small tin box used to collect money for Jewish charities. One of the *gabbai*'s memories from childhood was the blue *pushke* that his mother's parents—his *bobba* and *zayde*—kept on the lace doily in the center of their small kitchen table next to the heavy crystal salt-and-pepper shakers. Their *pushke* had a Jewish National Fund logo on the side and a coin slot on top, like a piggy bank. Each night his grandfather emptied his loose change into it. When he had dinner with his grandparents at their house, his *zayde* would hand him the coins to drop into the slot, one by one.

He sustains the living with kindness, resuscitates the dead with abundant mercy, supports the fallen, heals the sick, releases the confined, and maintains. His faith to those asleep in the dust.

At Anshe Emes, the *pushke* is silver, and Mr. Kantor removes the lid to allow paper currency as well. The *gabbai* folds and stuffs a five-dollar bill inside.

Forgive us, our Father, for we have erred. Pardon us, our King, for we have wilifully sinned; for You are the good and forgiving God. Blessed are You, Hashem, the gracious One Who pardons abundantly.

* * *

"PAGE one seventy-six," Mr. Kantor calls out. He glances over at the *gabbai*. "The Mourner's *Kaddish*."

The men of Anshe Emes insist that their *gabbai* have a role in the service, and this is it. As Mendel Klein likes to joke, "Better a mourning *gabbai* than a silly *shammas*."

He moves up the aisle toward the podium, where the rabbi is reading aloud the names of those who died in the last eleven months and those whose death occurred at this time in years past.

"Good morning, Sexton," the rabbi whispers, giving him a friendly wink.

"Good morning, Rabbi."

He turns to face the *minyan*. All are seated but Sam Gutman and Kenny Rosenburg. The two mourners stand side by side, heads bowed over their prayer books. Abe Shifrin stares at him from his seat in the back row, eyes blinking rapidly.

The *gabbai* knows the words by heart, as does every man at the service. The *Kaddish* is the most familiar prayer in Judaism, and the most peculiar—a memorial prayer in which there is no mention of death or loss or grief.

"Yit-ga-dal v'yit-ka-dash sh'may ra-baw," he begins as the two mourners join in. *"B'ol-mo dee-v'ry hir-u-say v'yam-lech mal-hu-say . . ."*

Glorified and sanctified be God's great name throughout the world which He has created according to His will . . .

"Yit-bawrach, v'yishtaback, v'yitpaw-ar, v'yit-romaim . . ."

Blessed, praised, glorified, exalted, extolled, mighty, upraised and lauded be the Name of the Holy One . . .

The prayer closes on a gentler note with a simple plea:

"O-se sha-lom bim-ro-mov" he recited, *"hu ya-a-se sha-lom o-lay-nu v'al kol yis-ro-ayl v'im-ru o-mayn."*

He who makes peace in his high holy places, may he bring peace upon us, and upon all Israel; and let us say Amen.

THE *gabbai* is walking across the parking lot toward his car when Abe Shifrin hales him.

"Oh, Mr. Hirsch!"

He turns to see the older man approaching.

"May I beg a moment of your time, sir?"

He smiles. "Of course."

"I apologize for bothering you, sir, but I can't stop myself from thinking about it."

"About what?"

"My daughter, Judith. She died, you know. My only child."

"I know. I'm sorry."

Shifrin stares up at him, squinting in the morning sun. He is a short, stocky man in his late sixties with a round nose, a pencil-thin mustache, heavy bags under his eyes, and sagging jowls. His gray eyes seem to swim behind the thick lenses of his oversized horn-rimmed glasses. His mouth is moving as he struggles for the words.

"In an accident," Shifrin says. "She died in an automobile accident."

The *gabbai* nods. He knows about the accident. Many people do. Judith Shifrin had been a law clerk to U.S. District Judge Brendan McCormick. After the courthouse Christmas party three years ago, Judge McCormick decided that he'd had too much to drink and gave his car keys to Judith. She drove him out to his home on the country club grounds so he could pick up the gifts he planned to present that evening at his annual staff Christmas dinner. When the two of them left his house for the restaurant, the back of the Judge's Ford Explorer was loaded with gifts.

Judith was driving down the icy road when a small animal dashed across the road in front of them. She swerved to avoid the animal, lost control of the car, and drove head-first into a tree. The intoxicated judge survived. The sober driver did not. Wasn't it Leo Durocher who once said that God watches over third basemen and drunks?

"Some of the other men," Shifrin says, "they told me you were once a famous lawyer."

The *gabbai* says nothing.

"A real big shot, they said. Head of a law firm, cases in the Supreme Court, the whole shmear. They tell me you were one of the best."

The *gabbai* knows what's coming.

"Well, Mr. Hirsch, I could use a lawyer."

"Why is that?"

"I've decided I should file a lawsuit."

"For what?"

"For my Judith." He hesitates. "For the accident that killed her."

"I'm sorry, Mr. Shifrin. I handle bankruptcy matters these days."

"But before?"

"Once upon a time."

"So? Isn't it like riding a bike?"

"Not exactly. And back then, I was a defense lawyer. I can ask around for you. I'll find you a good plaintiff's lawyer."

"A plaintiff's lawyer? Never." Shifrin wrinkles his nose in disgust. "*Goniffs* is what they are. Ambulance-chasing *goniffs*. I'd like to flush every one of them down a toilet. I owned my own business for forty-two years, Mr. Hirsch. Shifrin Plumbing Supplies. I spent half of my time fighting those miserable shysters. Never paid one of them a penny, either. Ask around and you'll find that's true."

He doesn't need to ask around. Although Shifrin sold his business a few years ago and supposedly has mellowed since his daughter's death, he's still known around the synagogue for his quick temper and imperious manner. Hirsch once saw him snapping orders at the caterers during a *bar mitzvah kiddush*—a function at which Shifrin was merely a guest. Mendel Klein refers to him, out of earshot, as the Little Emperor.

"No, Mr. Hirsch," he continues, "I want a real lawyer. Understand, sir, that it's not money I'm after. To tell you the truth, I couldn't care less about the money. Blood money is what it is. You can keep it all yourself or donate it to charity, whatever you want. This for me is not about money."

"Then what is it about?"

Shifrin stares up at him, his eyes watering from the cold. "Justice, Mr. Hirsch. That's what this is about. Nothing else. My only child is dead, sir. I am all that's left to say *Kaddish* for her. My little girl skids off the road in that crappy car and dies, and those rich bastards in Detroit go on like nothing happened." He shakes his head angrily. "That's not right. They should remember her *yahrzeit*, too."

Not this, he thinks. *Not now*.

A sudden gust of wind snaps at their overcoats.

"Last month, Mr. Hirsch . . ." Shifrin hesitates. "Last month my doctor sent me to a specialist. For some tests. He was worried, thought something maybe was wrong with my head, something besides old age. Well, guess what happened, Mr. Hirsch? They took all these tests and they studied the results and now they tell me I have that Alzheimer's situation. Early stage, they say, but that's for now. What about next month? Next year? I read the newspapers, sir. I watch the news. I know what's waiting for me and my brain right around the corner."

Shifrin pauses to shake his head.

"She was an only child, Mr. Hirsch. No brothers or sisters to mourn her. No husband, no children. Her mother—*aleya ha'sholem*—is dead and buried."

He gives the *gabbai* a sad smile.

"It's a funny thing, Mr. Hirsch. I used to worry that when I died, the memory of my daughter would go into the grave with me. But now—My God, now, Mr. Hirsch, her memory is going to die *before* I do."

Shifrin's lips quiver slightly.

"Even her own father is going to forget she ever lived on this earth. That's why I come to you, sir. Not for money. I spit on their money and I spit on them. Help me, Mr. Hirsch. Help me save my Judith's memory."

They face each other in silence. Shifrin stares up at Hirsch, the wind flapping his coat, his hand holding his hat in place.

Finally, Hirsch asks, "Do you have a file?"

"Oh, this I have." Shifrin is grinning. "Absolutely, sir. Don't move. I'll be right back."

Hirsch watches him scurry over to his car, open the trunk, and rush back with a thick folder under his arm.

"Here you are, sir." Shifrin holds out the file. "In here is everything I could put my hands on."

"I'll review it. No promises."

"That's fine—no, that's excellent. I'm so relieved, Mr. Hirsch. Judith and I, we had our fights, you know, but what family doesn't, eh? Oy, listen to me talking away like it's a Sunday in the park. I'm making you late for work standing out here."

He reaches out his gloved hand and they shake. Shifrin has little hands—rigid little hands. He grasps Hirsch's right hand with both hands. "God bless you, sir."

The *gabbai* is still standing by his car as Shifrin pulls out of the parking lot, pausing at the exit to tap his horn three times and wave.

The *gabbai* does not hear the horn. He is staring down at the file, the wind riffling the pages. Off in the distance a train whistle sounds—a long, mournful wail. As the sound fades, the *gabbai* lifts his face toward the gray sky.

2

IS plan was barely an hour old when it started unraveling. The first sign of trouble arrived in the form of Dick Brandon's scheme to sell his dead father. It was, to say the least, an unusual proposal for repaying your creditors.

Hirsch had driven downtown after his parking lot encounter with Abe Shifrin and gone directly to bankruptcy courtroom C for Chapter Thirteen day. He had nine debtors on the docket that morning. One was Dick Brandon, whose original repayment plan had cruised through the creditors meeting two months ago. A week later, he lost his job as second-shift manager at the Denny's in Sunset Hills, and with it the funding source for the plan. With seventy grand in debt and no job, he was facing a motion to convert his Chapter Thirteen repayment plan into a Chapter Seven liquidation.

Judge Shea was running late, which gave Brandon a chance to explain his bizarre scheme to Hirsch in the hallway outside the courtroom. He told him about a plaintiff's lawyer named Hildebrand across the river in Belleville who supposedly had a group of investors—"Deep pockets," Brandon called them—willing to buy personal injury claims.

"Cash on the barrelhead," Brandon told him with a wink.

He was a burly guy in his late fifties with thinning brown hair slicked across his forehead, deep-set eyes, a ski-slope nose splotched with red veins, and a ragged mustache.

His plan, he explained, was to sell his father's claim.

"His claim for what?"

"For getting himself killed, that's what."

"Who killed him?"

"Bastards that run that nursing home. We're talking gross negligence. We're talking crappy food. We're talking filthy rooms and broken air conditioners and a staff of damn morons. We're talking food poisoning and pneumonia and a staph infection—and all in his last year. Staph infection killed him. It'll be four years this February."

Brandon explained that a drinking buddy of his had a big cousin who'd sold her back injury to the Belleville lawyer and his deep pockets for sixty thousand dollars.

"So I says, shit, if that gal could parlay a bad back into sixty grand, I oughta be able to sell my daddy for triple that. Me and my brother Paul split the take fifty-fifty and I still got enough to pay off the debt." He grinned. "It's a great country ain't it?"

BACK in the courtroom, Hirsch approached Rochelle Krick, the bankruptcy trustee. She was in her usual spot up front, seated alone at counsel's table.

She frowned as she listened to his request for a continuance of the hearing on the Brandon motion. Krick was a serious young woman with short curly black hair and wire-rimmed glasses. Her lips pursed in concentration as she paged through the court papers in one of the three accordion files on the table in front of her. She removed a folder and read the court order on top.

"He's already had one." She looked up at Hirsch. "You know how much Judge Shea hates a second continuance."

"He'd go along if you recommend it."

"Tell me why I should."

"My client has an idea that could generate enough money to fund his repayment plan, but he'll need more time to put it together."

She sighed. "How many times have I heard that? Okay, Counselor, I'm all ears."

Hirsch kept his expression neutral. "Mr. Brandon believes he has a strong claim for wrongful death against the nursing home where his father died. He believes he can raise some money by finding an investor for the claim."

She pulled out the debtor's schedules of assets and liabilities and ran her index finger down the columns. "He didn't list it. Where is the case pending?"

"He hasn't filed suit yet."

"When does he plan to file?"

"Soon, I believe."

"Soon?" She looked up at him. "When did his father die?"

"Almost four years ago."

And the moment he said the number it clicked.

"Four years?" she said.

He knew what was coming.

"Did his father die in Missouri?"

How could he have forgotten something that basic? How could he be so out of it?

He thought back to Abe Shifrin in the parking lot that morning—the morning *after* his daughter's third *yahrzeit*—the old man staring up at him, a gust of wind tugging at his coat. The third *yahrzeit*. And yet he'd remained oblivious.

"Mr. Hirsch, the statute of limitations for wrongful death is three years. I'm afraid your client is out of luck."

Three stately raps of the gavel, and then the clerk's deep voice:

"All rise."

BUT he hadn't considered the significance of lunar time versus solar time. The moon's rotation around the earth controls the Jewish calendar while the earth's rotation around the sun controls the Gregorian calendar. As a result, the two are never in synch. On the Jewish calendar, each month begins on the first day of the new moon. One moon cycle multiplied by twelve equals roughly 355 days, which means that each year the Jewish calendar falls another ten days behind the Gregorian one. To keep the days in harmony with the seasons, the Jewish calendar inserts a leap month every third year, which is why Hanukkah and the other holidays seem to jump around the Gregorian calendar.

The Jewish calendar governed the *yahrzeit* for Judith Shifrin while the Gregorian calendar governed the statute of limitations for her wrongful death claim. On the Jewish calendar, Judith Shifrin died on the twenty-eighth day of Kislev, which meant that her *yahrzeit* would be on the twenty-eighth of Kislev each year no matter where in December that date fell that year on the Gregorian calendar. This year, the twenty-eighth day of Kislev happened to fall on the sixteenth day of December. Three years ago, when the attending physician at St. John's Hospital pronounced Judith Shifrin dead on arrival at 10:14 P.M., the date on the death certificate was December 18.

All of which meant that her death claim was still alive. Just barely.

Good news for Judith's father, bad news for Hirsch.

When he'd taken the file from Abe Shifrin that morning, he'd had no intention of actually handling the lawsuit. None whatsoever. His plan was to play the limited role of go-between—to review the file, perhaps hire an investigator to poke around for evidence of defects in the vehicle or the tires, make a preliminary assessment of liability, and find Shifrin an experienced personal injury lawyer. He wasn't concerned about the old man's aversion to plaintiff's lawyers—an aversion no doubt based on a few unpleasant encounters with bottom fishers. The top plaintiffs lawyers had an extraordinary ability to connect with people, to inspire trust and empathy from complete strangers. That's why juries awarded their clients millions of dollars. When he took the file, Hirsch had no doubt that he could find Shifrin such a lawyer.

But today was December 17, which meant tomorrow was D-Day for the wrongful death claim. No time for investigators, no time for careful analysis, and surely no time for screening interviews with personal injury lawyers. There wasn't even time to figure out whether Judith Shifrin's death merited a lawsuit; although he had to make that decision anyway since there was no one else.

Shifrin's folder included copies of the accident report and the medical examiner's report, a spec sheet on the Ford Explorer for the model year involved, various news clippings (including Judith's obituary), and several photographs of her, ranging from a fifth-grade Sears portrait through her law school graduation picture.

Seated at his desk that afternoon, Hirsch shuffled slowly through the photos, watching her grow from a pudgy, rosy-cheeked eleven-year-old girl with pigtails, glasses, and braces into an earnest young woman with shoulder-length black hair and a slender, almost wiry figure. Gone were the glasses and braces—the former giving way to contacts (he assumed), and the latter having helped create a lovely smile. He studied the photos, trying to connect with the dead woman, forcing back thoughts of his own two daughters. Judith Shifrin was somewhere along that continuum between attractive and plain.

In her high school graduation picture, she was posed with her father. He stood at least a head taller than his daughter, which meant that she was quite short. Her father stood at attention next to her, his shoulders back, his expression stern, while Judith looked the role of submissive daughter. She reminded Hirsch of the quiet girls from his high school—the ones who turned in all their homework assignments on time, never raised their hands in class, and served as the recording secretaries for one of those earnest high school clubs for Russian studies or future nurses. By the time of her law school photograph, there were subtle changes. She stood alone, her diploma in one hand and her cap in the other, looking a bit more intense, a bit less submissive—the determined young lawyer marching off into the world.

He picked up the accident report, which included a three-page statement from the sole witness, Judge Brendan McCormick. McCormick's statement, taken at the hospital the following morning by one of the officers from the scene of the accident, generally confirmed Hirsch's recollections, probably because the statement had been quoted and paraphrased in the news stories that Shifrin had clipped for the file and that Hirsch must have originally read in the prison library. McCormick's memory of the accident was somewhat fuzzy, in part because it happened so quickly and in part because he'd been fiddling with the car radio at the time and in part because he was drunk. He recalled Judith giving a surprised gasp. He'd looked up from the dashboard to see a small animal—a fox perhaps, or maybe a large cat, he wasn't sure—dart across the road in front of the vehicle, moving left to right. Judith swerved hard to the left to avoid the animal and centrifugal force shoved him against the door. He felt a slight acceleration, and then a tree seemed to leap out of the forest at them as she cried, "No!" The next thing he remembered was the sound of rapping on the window and a male voice shouting, "Are you okay, sir?"

That voice belonged to a high school senior named Charlie Peckham, whose 911 call that night was logged in at 8:43 P.M. According to Peckham's statement, he was driving home after a concert band practice and had taken a shortcut through the country club grounds when he spotted the rear lights of what turned out to be a Ford Explorer almost hidden in the trees off the side of the road. He got out of his car to check it out. The driver's side of the front end of the Explorer was crushed against the trunk of a large tree, but the engine was still running. The headlights were angled in crazy directions, spotlighting tree trunks and bare limbs dusted with snow. He peered inside the vehicle and saw a large man in the front passenger seat and a small woman behind the wheel. Both air bags had deployed. The man was moaning and moving his head slightly. The woman was motionless, her face pressed against the partially deflated air bag.

McCormick's sensation that the vehicle had accelerated before the collision seemed consistent with the physical evidence. The tire tracks suggested that Judith Shifrin had not applied the brakes. The investigating officer concluded that a combination of panic and unfamiliarity with the vehicle had caused her to mistakenly step on the gas instead.

Hirsch turned to the medical examiner's report. There had been no autopsy. The assisting technician had taken X-rays and photographs of the corpse and samples of blood, urine, and vitreous fluid. The results of the toxicology tests revealed a small amount of alcohol (below the legal limit, indicating perhaps one drink, the pathologist's notes stated). Judith Shifrin was tiny—just five feet tall, ninety-two pounds.

The X-rays and photographs were contained in a sealed envelope labeled "Forensic Materials—Duplicates," which Shifrin must have obtained in his efforts to put together a complete file on his daughter's death. Understandably, he'd never broken the seal to view the contents.

Hirsch did.

But the X-rays were meaningless to him, anonymous skeleton sections. He flipped through the morgue shots, disturbed by the stark white flesh, the frail naked body, the gray lips, the vacant eyes.

Even though the driver's side air bag deployed, the impact from the collision had killed her. Hirsch was not familiar with much of the medical terminology in the report, but he understood the medical examiner's conclusion: "*Cause of Death*: Blunt force trauma with asphyxia, apparently caused by motor vehicle accident and deployment of air-bag system."

To that conclusion Hirsch added his own: an unfortunate accident with no one to blame but fate.

3

SEYMOUR Rosenbloom closed the file folder and slid it across his desk toward Hirsch. "This is a no-brainer."

"What's that mean?"

"Sue the bastards."

"Which ones?"

"All of them. Ford Motor, the tire manufacturer, the outfit that made the air bags, anyone who had anything to do with that car. Sue them all."

"On what ground?"

"On the ground she's fucking dead. On the ground that drunk knucklehead survived and she didn't. What's that all about, huh?"

Rosenbloom backed his wheelchair away from the desk and wheeled himself toward the window. He peered out at the lights of downtown and then turned toward Hirsch with a grin.

"Come on, Samson. If you're going to play the personal injury game, you're going to need the proper mind-set.

You're going to need to cleanse your system of all those defense attorney toxins. You're going to need a brand-new mantra."

"And I suppose you have one for me?"

"This is your lucky day, *boychik*. Place your hand over your heart and solemnly recite after me. Hey, I'm serious. Hand over your heart."

"Cut it out, Sancho."

"Come on. This is important."

Hirsch sighed and placed his hand over his heart.

"That's better. Now, recite after me. Ready? 'If you've been hurt in an accident'—go ahead, say it."

Hirsch gave him a look.

"Come on."

" 'If you've been hurt in an accident.' "

"Good. 'If you've been hurt in an accident, someone somewhere owes you a boatload of money?' "

"That is a profoundly spiritual mantra."

"Right out of the goddamn sacred Hindu texts."

Rosenbloom rolled his wheelchair back over to his desk. He reached for the file. "Who'd you say made the air bags on that Ford?"

"A company called OLM."

"Never heard of them, but they sound ripe for the picking. She was a little thing, right?"

"Just five feet. Weighed ninety-two pounds."

"I read somewhere how dangerous those damn bags can be with kids in the front seat. What about the tires? Goodyear?"

"Peterson."

"Peterson?" Rosenbloom chuckled with delight. "Oh, my God. That's beautiful. Absolutely beautiful."

"This is different."

"Who cares? You gotta love it. I assume he knows."

Hirsch shrugged. "Probably."

"Peterson Tire." Rosenbloom was grinning. "I offer a hearty salute to the god of irony."

The Peterson Tire Corporation was currently enmeshed in *In re Turbo-XL Tire Litigation*, a massive consolidated tort case arising out of allegedly defective tires on various models of sport-utility vehicles, including Ford Explorers. Not only was the case pending in St. Louis federal court, but the presiding judge was Brendan McCormick. On the night of the fatal accident, Judith Shifrin was driving Judge McCormick's Ford Explorer, which, according to the accident report, was equipped with four Peterson Turbo-XL tires.

Hirsch shook his head. "I don't see any evidence of tire malfunction."

"Who cares? For chrissake, Samson, that's no reason *not* to include those bastards in the suit. Hell, the words *Peterson* and *defective* are practically synonyms. Sue 'em all. Let them figure out who gets to pick up the tab. If you can survive the first round of motions, one of those defendants is going to start waving money at you. Most of these cases settle."

"Probably not this one. Abe Shifrin has no interest in settlement. He sees it as a battle of principle. But even if he didn't, this case"—he gestured toward the file—"it's a weak one, Sancho. If one or more of these companies feel they need to fight one of these claims, they could do worse than pick this case."

"Never say never, Samson, especially when you're up against fancy corporate litigators. You used to eat their livers for sport."

To others, they were Seymour and David. To each other, they were still Sancho and Samson. Hirsch had been Rosenbloom's junior counselor at an overnight camp in Minnesota for three summers during his college years. The fat and jovial Rosenbloom, a few years Hirsch's senior and nearly bald even then, had been a passionate fan of *Don Quixote*. He'd nicknamed himself Sancho, after Sancho Panza, and claimed to be waiting for his Knight of the Sad Face. He nicknamed his junior counselor Samson after Samson Carrasco, the clever university student in the novel. That was back when Hirsch's plans for the future included a stint in the Peace Corps and a career teaching Shakespeare to inner-city kids. Back before his ambition metastasized at Harvard Law School and devoured his idealism and, according to his ex-wife, his heart and soul.

They followed different career paths in the law and eventually lost touch with each other, although not by Rosenbloom's choice. It was Hirsch who became too busy with important people and weighty matters to make time for his old camp buddy. Nevertheless, it was Rosenbloom who reached out to Hirsch in prison—one of the few who did. That first year at Allenwood, Hirsch received a package from Sancho containing a leather-bound edition of *Don Quixote* and a harmonica. He read the novel in jail—read it twice, in fact—his first work of fiction in more than a decade. And he even took up the harmonica again, although not quite the way Sancho had assumed from their summer nights around the campfire when Hirsch entertained the campers with cowboy tunes.

A year ago last November, when the Missouri Supreme Court provisionally restored Hirsch's law license with the stipulation that he could practice only under the direct supervision of an attorney who'd been a member of the bar in good standing for at least twenty years, there had been only one choice for him.

He'd worked up the nerve to call Rosenbloom and ask him to lunch at an Italian restaurant on the Hill. Rosenbloom was delighted. It had been a long time since he'd seen his old junior counselor.

Hirsch had been startled when Rosenbloom arrived using a walker. During all those years apart, Hirsch's image had reverted to the Sancho of their camp counselor youth—to the burly, sweaty, vigorous guy who'd hauled the biggest backpack on the camping trips and helmed the tug-of-war team during color wars and roughhoused with the campers in the lake, tossing them into the water while a half dozen other kids hung from his arms and neck and climbed on his back. Although Hirsch had heard somewhere that Rosenbloom had multiple sclerosis, he'd never accepted the debilitating reality until he saw his Sancho hauling himself through the doorway of the restaurant on the walker.

Over a platter of linguini with red clam sauce, Rosenbloom had read through the terms of the Missouri Supreme Court's reinstatement order. When he finished, he wiped his chin with a napkin, broke off a piece of Italian bread, and shrugged.

"There must be an empty chair somewhere in my office. Until Sharon Stone passes the bar, I might as well stick your sorry ass in it."

These days, Rosenbloom was confined to a wheelchair from the disease that gradually, inexorably, whittled away his bulk and darkened his moods. As courtroom appearances became more difficult, Hirsch had increasingly become his legs. He handled about half of the firm's bankruptcy docket, representing debtors at the creditors meetings and at the hearings to approve their wage-earner plans.

Hirsch said, "It's easier to eat your opponent's liver when you have the facts on your side."

"Don't worry. As Don Quixote teaches, 'Fortune always leaves some door open to come at a remedy.'"

"As I recall, he also teaches that many go out for wool and come home shorn themselves."

Rosenbloom was grinning. "So? Just keep your eyes peeled for badass shepherds toting shears."

4

HIS Honor's secretary had a prim moon face, penciled eyebrows, and gray hair gathered in a neat bun. A pair of reading glasses hung from a gold cord around her neck. The scent of talcum powder reminded him of his grandmother.

She gave him a tidy smile. "The judge is still in his three o'clock pretrial. I shouldn't think it will be much longer."

Hirsch took a seat, opened his briefcase, and removed some of the files for the next day's creditors meetings. He tried to focus.

He'd been edgy ever since the judge's secretary called two days ago to schedule the meeting. Given that Hirsch had no case before Judge McCormick and hadn't spoken with him in more than a decade, the request had seemed almost out of the blue.

Almost.

But not quite.

He'd been thinking about setting up his own meeting

with McCormick. Even though he kept putting it off, he knew a meeting was inevitable.

The first time he'd almost called McCormick was an hour before he filed the lawsuit. His secretary had just finished the final revisions to the petition and come in with the original, three copies, and the check for the filing fee. He'd stared at the petition, shaking his head over the slapdash nature of it all. Cobbling together a lawsuit on the very last day was contrary to everything he'd learned and everything he'd practiced during all those years as a federal prosecutor and a partner at Marder McFarlane—years when nothing was done slapdash, when every court filing, no matter how routine, was carefully vetted.

He'd checked his watch that afternoon. Quarter to four. The courthouse was just a ten-minute walk, which meant he still had almost an hour's leeway. Paging through the petition, he'd wondered whether there was anything else he should do—could do—before the deadline. He'd read Abe Shifrin's file, of course, and he'd done a quick review of the case law and researched the identities of the registered agents for each of the defendants. He'd done all that and he'd drafted the lawsuit and suddenly the mad blur of preparation had slowed to the sharp focus of the telephone on his desk.

He'd stared at the phone—stared and mulled over whether to call Brendan McCormick.

Minutes had passed in silence.

And then he'd gathered the court papers and headed for the elevator.

The docket clerk stamped the date and time on the first page of the petition: December 18, 4:37 P.M. As of that moment, his meeting with the only eyewitness in the case became inevitable. He'd be conducting an interview of Brendan McCormick, and eventually he'd be taking his deposition. It was no longer if, but when.

Nevertheless, as he'd told himself again just last week, there was still time.

And there was. The lawsuit was barely three weeks old. There'd been no press coverage of its filing. No attorney for any of the defendants had yet to enter an appearance.

All of which meant that it was possible the judge had another reason for the meeting. The two of them did have a shared past, although their four years together as young assistant U.S. attorneys dated back more than a quarter of a century.

He closed his briefcase and strolled over to the windows. McCormick's chambers were on the seventeenth floor of the federal courthouse. He looked down at the Civil Courts Building, where he'd filed the wrongful death case a few weeks ago. The structure looked even more bizarre from above. What was otherwise a staid 1930s fourteen-story limestone office building veered into the surreal at the "roof," which consisted of a Greek temple crowned by an Egyptian step pyramid crowned by two sphinxlike creatures seated back to back. He'd read somewhere that the hodgepodge replicated some ancient structure, although what it was doing on top of a St. Louis government building was a mystery.

"His Honor will see you now."

Hirsch turned as four lawyers emerged from the judge's office—three men and a woman, chatting quietly, seriously, all carrying leather briefcases. Following behind was a young man in khakis, white shirt, and dark tie, carrying a legal pad filled with notes. Presumably one of the judge's law clerks. As Hirsch stepped toward the judge's office, the young man glanced back at him before turning into a side office.

Seated behind a large desk at the far end of the imposing room was the Honorable Brendan R. McCormick, United States District Judge for the Eastern District of

Missouri. The judge was frowning and scribbling something onto a yellow legal pad. As Hirsch approached, he looked up and the frown vanished.

"Hello, David." The familiar, hearty voice.

Capping his fountain pen, the judge stood, grinning broadly.

As they shook hands, Hirsch noted that McCormick's taste in clothing had gone upscale in the decades since their AUSA days together. Back then, he bought wash-and-wear suits off the racks at JCPenney and picked up shirts from the irregular bins at the discount houses. These days, Hirsch guessed, McCormick's clothiers knew him by name and kept his measurements and current wardrobe on file. Today's outfit included a monogrammed dress shirt, gleaming gold cuff links, an elegant silk tie, and a navy pinstripe suit perfectly tailored to his large frame. The crisp white shirt contrasted nicely with the deep tan, which, if Hirsch recalled correctly, he'd likely picked up playing golf over Christmas in Bermuda, where he had a second home.

"Good afternoon, Judge."

" 'Judge?' Christ, David, cut that formal crap. Outside my courtroom I'm just Brendan. Grab a seat. How 'bout something to drink? Soda? Coffee?"

"I'm fine." Hirsch settled into the chair facing the desk.

"So I hear you're a bankruptcy lawyer these days."

"Mostly Chapter Thirteens."

"Do you enjoy them?"

Hirsch shrugged. "They have their challenges."

"Not exactly the fast lane."

"I spent enough time in the fast lane for one lifetime."

They talked a bit about the bankruptcy practice and a bit about the whereabouts of some of their colleagues from the U.S. Attorney's Office and a bit about a recent football recruiting brouhaha at Mizzou and a bit about the contrasts between the college football players these days versus the real men of their era. This was Brendan McCormick's meeting. Eventually, he'd get around to the reason he called it.

He hadn't seen McCormick for maybe twenty years. Time had taken its toll. Back in his college linebacker days, Brendan McCormick had carried a strapping 240 pounds on his six-foot-four-inch frame. He'd stayed in shape at the U.S. Attorney's Office, but the years since then had changed him into a bulky slab of a man with a neck and torso that seemed too big for his legs. The chiseled features that once stirred women jurors had starting eroding—the jutting chin receding into a puffy neck and jowls, the strong nose beginning to bulge, the eyelids sagging over the corners of his blue eyes. Even the hair—still jet black, though likely from dye—had thinned into a comb-over.

Eventually, the chitchat petered out. McCormick paused, and leaned forward, his expression grave.

"David, I want you to know how relieved I am that you filed that lawsuit for Judith."

"How did you find out?"

He gestured out the window toward the Civil Courts Building. "I sent someone over there to check on the filings.

"Why?"

"Why?" McCormick's features softened. "Because I wanted to know. I had to know. I assumed you'd understand why."

"You were there that night."

"It was more than just that. She was my law clerk, David. That's a special relationship, and she was a special gal. Loyal, hardworking, dedicated. I had great affection for her. Great affection, and great respect." He leaned back. "And yes, she was in my car. Died in my car. Even worse, died behind the wheel because I had too much to drink at that damn Christmas party. Judith Shifrin would be here today if I'd been driving."

"You don't know that."

"Don't tell me what I know. An icy road? Hell, I drove that Explorer through the Rocky Mountains in a snowstorm. I could have handled that road dead drunk." He paused. "You know me, David. You know I'm no fan of personal injury litigation. Even so, I raised the possibility of a lawsuit with Judith's father a few weeks after the funeral. I wanted to have something done. He wouldn't hear of it. Talk about a tough old bird. I tried again after the first anniversary of her death. What's the name you people have for it?"

"Yahrzeit."

"Right. I went to his synagogue that Saturday. Spoke with him after the service. He still wanted nothing to do with a lawsuit. Even so, I couldn't forget about it. I knew the exact day the statute of limitations would expire. I have that date etched in my memory. As the deadline approached, I couldn't stop thinking about it. On December nineteenth—the day after—I sent one of my clerks over to state court. Had him check on the filings. I expected nothing, but when he came back carrying a copy of your petition I almost called to thank you."

"For filing the lawsuit?"

"And for giving me a chance to do something for her, or at least for her memory." He paused and leaned forward. "That night, well, by the time we left my house that night I was feeling pretty okay, but she wanted to drive. Said she loved being behind the wheel of such a big car. Jesus Christ."

McCormick turned sideways in his chair to stare out the window, his eyes watering. Off in the distance to the east, a long line of barges slowly passed under the Poplar Street Bridge heading upriver.

Hirsch waited.

Mounted along one wall of the office were stuffed trophy heads of an elk, a bobcat, and a grizzly, each with a little brass plaque stating the date and spot where McCormick shot the animal. Another wall had a gun cabinet that displayed, in addition to some of McCormick's rifle collection, the cowboy hat, spurs, and vintage Colt '45 given to him by the St. Louis county police when he became a state circuit judge. During his years as the county's chief prosecutor, one of the local newspaper columnists dubbed him McCowboy because he liked to ride with the cops on big raids. The alternative weekly gave him a second nickname, McCrazy, after he pistol-whipped a cocaine dealer arrested in a drug bust. The dealer, handcuffed at the time, had made the mistake of calling McCormick a "pussy," or at least that's what the alternative paper reported. The prisoner spent a week in the hospital, but nothing came of the incident. The cops stayed mum, the doctors declined to comment, and McCormick's spokesman quoted him as "refusing to stoop to respond to the paranoid fantasies of a crackhead."

The incident hadn't hurt McCormick's standing within the GOP, since shortly thereafter the Republican governor appointed him to a judicial opening on the Circuit Court of St. Louis County—a position he would hold for nearly two decades, until a Republican president elevated him to federal district court.

McCormick turned back to Hirsch with a resigned smile. "We both know I'm the only eyewitness. That makes me an important witness at trial. That's why I called you here today. To tell you that I'll be a good witness. I'm going to tell the truth, of course. I'm going to tell it like it is, but," he paused, "it's been more than three years now. Exactly what happened that night may not be totally clear until your accident reconstruction experts have a chance to

examine the evidence and reach their own conclusions."
He contemplated Hirsch for a moment. "It might help if I
know what their conclusions are before I testify."

Hirsch nodded.

"I have a crazy schedule this month." He reached for his
personal calendar and started paging. "Let's see."

On the credenza behind his desk sat a battered black
football helmet with a gold *M* emblazoned on each side.
Framed above the credenza was a large color photograph
from his football days at Mizzou. It was a telephoto shot
taken an instant before the snap. In it, he towered above the
crouching lineman, his breath vaporing in the chilly air,
mud smeared on his arms and pants and jersey. He'd
earned a reputation on the gridiron as a headhunter.

Hirsch almost smiled at the memories triggered by the
helmet and the photo. He, too, had played linebacker for a
college team, the Tigers, and he, too, had worn the same
number on his jersey. But as McCormick often taunted
back in their assistant U.S. attorney years, especially in
crowded singles bars after hours, the level of competition
in the Ivy League was a far cry from Saturday warfare on
the gridirons of the Big Eight.

"Like tiger lilies to tigers," he used to shout at Hirsch
over the din.

Not anymore, pal, Hirsch thought as he eyed Mc-
Cormick's puffy face. But he caught himself, irritated by
his own cockiness. There were, he reminded himself, far
more reputable places to get in shape than the weight room
of a federal penitentiary, and far more respectable workout
programs then the so-called Eminem Regimen, which got
its name not from the rap star or the little candies but from
the disgraced junk bonds prince Michael Milkin, whose
personal trainer supposedly wrote the program for his
client's stay at the federal prison camp in Pleasanton. Photocopies of the program had spread throughout the federal

correctional system and were posted on the gym walls of most minimum-security facilities, including Allenwood.

"Looks like I should have a break in my trial docket the middle of next month," McCormick said, studying his calendar. "Assuming I don't get a preemptive criminal setting, I'll have Betty set up a time for you to come in here for a witness interview. Hopefully, you'll have some feedback from your experts by then. Do you have them all retained?"

"Almost."

Actually, not even close. One of Rosenbloom's paralegals had put together a list for him of possible experts, but he'd contacted none of them. Indeed, he'd done little work on the lawsuit. The file had sat unopened on his credenza since the afternoon he came back from the clerk of the court with the file-stamped petition.

McCormick chuckled. "We do have one crazy quirk here, don't we?"

"What's that?"

"One of your defendants is Peterson Tire. Until I read your petition, I'd forgotten they made the tires on that Explorer."

"I'm not optimistic about that claim."

"Really? Why not?"

"I haven't retained a tire expert yet, but I didn't see any indication of tire failure."

"Don't give up on Peterson, David. That's my advice. I've had those fellows in my courtroom for five years now. Believe me, they have the litigation equivalent of shell shock. Of all your defendants, they'll be the most susceptible to settlement overtures. You've got Ford Motor in your lawsuit. I've had them before me in a couple of cases. They can be tough as nails. Don't know about that air-bag manufacturer. Never had them before me. But Peterson, well, that's a different story." He leaned forward and lowered his voice. "Let's not b.s. each other, David. We both know what you're going to be up against when the lawyers for the defendants start ramping up. You're no slouch, of course. Hell, back in your heyday you were one of the best. But you're not Gary Cooper and this sure as hell won't be High Noon. You're going to find yourself outgunned once the defense lawyers arrive. You've been on the other side, and you know what I'm talking about. Just you against a pack of lawyers. They're going to do their best to grind you into the ground, and they'll try to smear you with shit in the process. Maybe you do have a lousy case." McCormick held up his hands and shrugged. "Hell, I have no idea. But I do know that most death cases settle. Even the crappy ones. So hang in there. You mark my words. If any of those defendants are going to blink, it'll be Peterson."

5

LITTLE Walter was on the stereo but Hirsch didn't hear the music. He was leaning forward, elbows on his knees, staring at the harmonica as he rotated it in his hands.

I am so pleased that you're the lawyer on this case, David.

Two days later and the words still rang hollow.

Not to Rosenbloom, though. He'd been waiting for Hirsch late that afternoon when he returned from his meeting with McCormick. Together, they took the elevator down to the building garage as Hirsch described the conversation and his misgivings.

"So what?" Rosenbloom had said as he wheeled himself toward his black Cadillac. "What's so odd about knowing when the statute of limitations expires?"

He'd watched as Rosenbloom folded the wheelchair, slid it into the back, and winched himself into the driver's seat, which had been modified to accommodate his condition. Hirsch knew better than to offer to help.

"*Nu?*" Rosenbloom said between gasps. He wiped his face with a handkerchief. "Am I right?"

"Maybe."

"Maybe? What's with the maybe? He was in the fucking car when it crashed. He may not be Felix Frankfurter, but even a knucklehead would remember that date."

Rosenbloom started the engine and closed the door. He rolled down the window and looked up at Hirsch. "The judge told you he was happy you filed the lawsuit, right? Even told you he was happy to find out that you were the lawyer on the case, right?"

"Right."

"That means that *you're* the lawyer who gets to curry favor with a federal judge, right?" He gave Hirsch a wink. "I can think of worse things to happen in a legal career."

HE turned the harmonica in his hands as he thought back again to the way McCormick had ended their meeting—the firm handshake, the earnest look, the parting words: "I am so pleased that you're the lawyer on this case, David."

Maybe Sancho was right. Maybe he shouldn't be so skeptical.

But he knew enough about his standing in the legal community to know that he was on no one's short list of personal injury lawyers.

He was on no one's list—short or long.

Period.

The silence pulled him back to the present, back to the small living room of his apartment. He stared at the scraped skin on the back of his right hand, where he'd slammed into the wall during the handball game earlier that night at the Jewish Community Center. Times had changed, he thought with a smile. Ten years ago it would have been squash at the country club, followed by a drink in the club's bar. Now it was handball at the JCC, followed by a drink at the water fountain on the way out. He'd learned squash at Princeton. He'd learned handball on the outdoor courts at Allenwood.

He glanced over at the stereo just as the quick drumroll and opening bars of Little Walter's "My Babe" began. He was lifting the harmonica to his mouth when the phone rang.

"The Eagle has landed."

It was Rosenbloom.

"Oh?"

"Yep, and a big prick stepped out."

"What's that mean?"

"I got a call from Channel Five. They wanted a statement on the lawsuit."

"Which lawsuit?"

"Which one do you think?"

"The Shifrin case? You?"

"Don't forget my name's first on the pleadings."

Under the reinstatement order, Rosenbloom had to jointly sign all court filings with Hirsch.

"Apparently," Rosenbloom said, "Ford Motor's lawyers filed their appearance today."

"So?"

"So they held a press conference."

"A press conference. Who would care enough to cover it?"

"Channel Five, for starters. They're running a story at ten tonight."

Hirsch frowned. "That makes no sense."

"Never underestimate the self-promotion skills of Jack Bellows."

"Bellows," Hirsch repeated.

"I hear he's a prick."

"He is—or at least he was."

"There's no such thing as a former prick." In a gentler voice, he said, "I think he took a shot at you in the press conference."

Hirsch said nothing.

"The guy from Channel Five said he called the lawsuit frivolous. He wanted a response from one of us. I told him you were the sole spokesman on the case. I also told him that you preferred to do your talking in court papers instead of public relations events. He wanted your phone number."

Hirsch's number was unlisted.

"I told him I didn't know it."

"I wouldn't talk to him anyway."

"Yeah, but you may want to check out the news at ten."

"I will. Thanks."

"Well, Samson," Rosenbloom said with a grim chuckle, "fasten that seat belt. I think we're in for a little turbulence."

H IRSCH adjusted the antenna on the portable TV. He hadn't watched the ten o'clock news since he'd been a recurring lead item a decade ago.

The show opened with a three-alarm fire at a warehouse in north St. Louis. Then came a series of stories apparently culled from the day's events based upon the quality of the visuals. Thus a rogue alligator caught in a mall parking lot in Fort Lauderdale and a Yorkshire terrier stranded atop a mailbox in an Arizona flash flood trumped a hostile takeover bid in the cable television industry and the congressional defeat of a major health-care reform bill. Hirsch was beginning to question Rosenbloom's heads-up when the male anchor, a balding, middle-aged black man with tortoiseshell eyeglasses, looked into the camera with furrowed brow and announced, "A new lawsuit over an old death."

Cut to a silent video of Jack Bellows talking at a lectern.

The anchor, in voice-over. "But a lawyer for the defense claims it's all much ado about nothing."

Back to the news desk, this time on the female anchor, a woman in her fifties with short hair, pearls, and a black dress. She gave the camera a solemn look. "More on the lawsuit when we come back."

Cut to a commercial for Taco Bell.

The quick shot of Jack Bellows had jolted Hirsch. Back when he'd been managing partner of Marder McFarlane, Hirsch had blocked the firm's efforts to recruit Bellows. Although Bellows had a good book of business and the backing of the chairman of the litigation department, Hirsch controlled the vote on the executive committee, and that's precisely where Bellows's candidacy died. The reason was simple: Hirsch couldn't stand him. Bellows was an arrogant blowhard who'd earned the nickname Jack the Ripper for his back-alley litigation techniques. There were lawyers in town who refused to discuss anything with him without a court reporter present. Eventually, Bellows discovered that Hirsch had been the one to block his bid to join the firm. According to someone who'd overheard him in the locker room at the Missouri Athletic Club, Bellows had vowed to "nail that Jewish prick to the cross some day."

That was eleven years ago. Since then, Bellows's book of business had apparently grown to irresistible proportions because he was now a senior partner at Hirsch's old firm. Although Bellows's nastiness and holier-than-thou attitude enraged his opponents, Hirsch knew that Jack the Ripper was one formidable adversary.

Back from commercials.

The male anchor: "Three winters ago, a law clerk to United States District Judge Brendan McCormick died in a tragic one-car accident while driving the judge to his annual staff Christmas dinner."

Cut to a head shot of Judge McCormick.

The male anchor continued in voice-over: "That young clerk, Judith Shifrin—"

Cut to a photo of Judith, the one from her law school yearbook.

"—lost control of the car on an icy road and rammed into a tree. The force of the collision killed the twenty-five-year-old woman. Judge McCormick, seated in the passenger seat at the time of the accident, escaped serious injury but spent the night in the hospital."

Cut to the first page of the file-stamped petition that Hirsch had filed four weeks ago.

The male anchor, in voice-over: "That was three years ago. News Channel Five has learned that a wrongful death action has recently been filed on behalf of the deceased woman. The lawsuit seeks an unspecified amount of damages against Ford Motor Company and two other corporations."

Cut to the male anchor. "Today, the lawyers for Ford Motor entered their appearance in the case, and our own Rob Drennan was there."

The camera pulled back to reveal a bearded guy in his late thirties seated in the chair next to the male anchor. The anchor turned to him with an avuncular smile. "Rob?"

Drennan nodded and faced the camera, which moved in tight. "That's correct, Mel."

His grin faded. "This is no ordinary case."

Grave expression. "The victim was a law clerk to a powerful federal judge. The defendants include some of the nation's largest corporations. And the plaintiff's lawyer himself is no stranger to controversy. Ten years ago, attorney David Hirsch was the managing partner of one of this city's oldest and most powerful law firms and a rising star in Democratic politics."

Cut to a head shot of Hirsch, taken about fifteen years ago as he addressed a bar association group.

"But in a turn of events as swift as it was bizarre, Hirsch was first implicated in the drug-related death of a prostitute—"

Cut to a front-page headline from the *St. Louis Post-Dispatch*:

PROMINENT ST. LOUIS ATTORNEY UNDER ARREST

Found in East Side Motel with Dead Prostitute

Police Say Wild Night Ended in Fatal Drug Overdose

"And then, at the end of that same week, FBI agents raided his law firm's offices, seizing two years of billing records on his clients."

Cut to a shot of the imposing lobby of Hirsch's former law firm—the legend MARDER McFARLANE LLP carved in marble over the entranceway—as men wearing FBI windbreakers loaded boxes of records onto a freight elevator.

"Federal agents had acted on a tip from one of Hirsch's riverboat casino clients, whose audit of its legal bills uncovered more than forty thousand dollars in phony charges by nonexistent court reporters, copy services, and the like. Hirsch was indicted on various federal charges for the embezzlement of more than a million dollars from clients of his law firm."

Cut to a shot of a U.S. marshal leading a handcuffed Hirsch up the stairs of the federal courthouse.

"And finally, at the end of that same month, nine women—all current or former secretaries and paralegals at his firm—filed suit against him for sexual harassment. By the time David Hirsch entered prison one year later, he was divorced, disbarred, and about to become destitute. That final blow landed three weeks after he entered prison—"

Cut to front-page headline from the *St. Louis Post-Dispatch:*

JAILED ATTORNEY HIT FOR
$10 MILLION VERDICT

Jury Finds Him Guilty of Sexual Harassment

"He would serve seven years in a federal penitentiary for the embezzlement crimes."

Cut to generic shot of a prison interior—a long hallway lined with prison cells.

"But Hirsch is out of jail these days, his license to practice law has been reinstated, and now he has filed suit over the death of that young law clerk Judith Shifrin. Among the targets of the suit: Ford Motor Company. Today—"

Cut to a mid-range shot of Jack Bellows behind the lectern, squinting into the television lights.

"—the lawyer for Ford had his say."

The camera zoomed in for a close-up. Bellows had a good TV face—craggy features, unruly shock of reddish-gray hair, bushy eyebrows. His name appeared at the bottom of the screen as *Attorney for Ford Motor Company*.

"There's one word for this lawsuit," Bellows said in his gruff voice, "and that word is 'frivolous.' I am confident that we will dispose of this ridiculous case in short order, and once we do, I intend to focus my attention on the lawyer behind this outrage."

A reporter in the crowd called out, "Why do you say that?"

Bellows's mouth curled into a smirk. "Because David Hirsch has proven again that he's a disgrace to the legal profession."

Cut back to Drennan at the anchor desk. "The lawsuit may only be starting, but"—dramatic pause, puckish smile—"it's already shaping up to be a real barn burner."

The female anchor shook her head in wonder. " 'Disgrace to the legal profession.' Those are strong words, Rob."

Drennan nodded. "And they weren't the strongest. After the press conference, Mr. Bellows told me that one of his goals was to get Mr. Hirsch's law license, and I quote, 'yanked and shredded.' "

The male anchor said, "Thanks, Rob. We'll be sure to keep an eye on that lawsuit. Meanwhile, meteorologist Dan Webber has been keeping an eye on that winter storm developing to our west."

Cut to a bald man with a goofy grin and protruding ears posed in front of a weather map. "That's right, Mel. The latest from the National Weather—"

Hirsch turned off the television. The phone rang. It was Rosenbloom.

"That miserable cocksucker."

"Vintage Jack Bellows."

"I hope you drill him a new asshole. That stuff he said, it's bullshit, Samson. Nasty, below-the-belt bullshit."

"I'm okay with it."

"Totally uncalled for—way, way out of bounds. I am so pissed right now I can't see straight. If I had a baseball bat—"

"Sancho."

"I'm not kidding. If I had—"

"Sancho."

A pause. "What?"

"I'm okay with it."

"Ah, come on. How can you—"

"I've heard worse. Get some sleep. We'll talk in the morning."

Hirsch walked over to the window of his apartment. It

was starting to snow, the big flakes briefly illuminated as they floated through the light of the streetlamps.

Hirsch understood, of course. This wasn't rocket science. Bellows's goal was intimidation, to demoralize him, maybe undermine his commitment to the case. The execution was over the top, but everything about Bellows was over the top. Nevertheless, the strategy was sound and based on two reasonable assumptions. First, that Hirsch knew that he was alone and facing three platoons of big-firm litigators, and second, that Hirsch knew that many in his profession viewed him as a pariah.

No, the strategy was simple and sound. Rub his nose in it, and do so publicly.

What surprised Hirsch was his reaction.

He wasn't intimidated.

He wasn't demoralized.

And his commitment to the case hadn't lessened.

Quite the contrary.

Once upon a time, he had loved a good courtroom battle. Indeed, he had craved a trial the way others craved gambling or mountain climbing or cocaine. He used to joke that a good cross-examination was better than good sex—and he spoke from experience, having had plenty of both. He needed trials. He sought them. He never felt more alive than inside a courtroom in the middle of a trial.

He understood that side of himself. Not back then, but he'd had time to mull it over. He'd had time to realize that the drive that made him a success had also destroyed him. He now understood that as his duties as managing partner began cutting into his litigation time, he'd started looking for those highs elsewhere. But there was a crucial difference between life inside and outside the courtroom—a difference he failed to grasp at the time. The rush he'd sought within the controlled environment of a courtroom was far riskier to seek outside. During trial, that shot of adrenaline helped him carve up a hostile witness with icy precision. Outside the courtroom, it pushed him ever closer to the edge, from after-hours quickies with young paralegals on his office couch to forty-eight-hour gambling marathons in Vegas to his final night of infamy—a night that shifted into high gear as he staggered off the *Casino Queen* at two in the morning with six grand in his pocket and six shots of Jack Daniel's in his bloodstream. First stop was a strip club on the east side, where he had two more bourbons and a lap dance from a red-haired Cuban girl named Juanita. Standing outside the club, the world around him slightly off kilter, he'd flagged a cab and told the driver to cruise the streets of East St. Louis for some action. The sequence of events got fuzzy from that point until he awoke later that day. It wasn't the first time events had gotten fuzzy, but it's one thing to awaken in a canopied bed in a suite at the Bellagio with the sated glow of a big night at the craps table topped by a session with an A-list call girl. It's another to awaken facedown in your own vomit on the frayed carpet of a hot-sheets motel room while a streetwalker named LaTavia is on her back on the bed with a crack pipe and drug paraphernalia scattered on the mattress, her naked body already in the early stage of rigor mortis.

The life he'd constructed since his release from prison was designed to steer him clear of anything that might resurrect the old David Hirsch.

Hirsch pressed his forehead against the icy window. He could feel the change within him. Nothing dramatic, of course. He wasn't about to rise from the basement laboratory table, yank off the electrical cords, lurch through the forest toward the sleeping villagers. But he could feel a change nevertheless.

After a moment, he turned away from the darkness.

As he undressed for bed, he forced himself to forget about Jack Bellows and the lawsuit and to focus instead on tomorrow's details. He'd already made the necessary calls to confirm the morning *minyan*. He'd already skimmed through the client files in preparation for the creditors committee meetings that started at ten A.M.

He turned on the reading light and lifted *The Guermantes Way* off the nightstand. For the past few months, he'd been reading Marcel Proust's masterwork. He opened the book, glad to return to the fashionable salon of the Guermantes and leave, at least for the night, the wage-earner plans and wrongful death action and general wreckage of his life. But even as he rejoined his narrator among the snobs and the wits and the hypocrites and the phonies of Parisian society at the time of the Dreyfus Affair, he found himself remembering similar evenings at his own country club, at a time almost as distant and a place almost as nasty as the salon of the Guermantes.

6

THE other lawyers arrived without the Jack the Ripper fanfare.

Counsel for the air-bag manufacturer entered silently. No press release and no hype. Just a one-sentence entry of appearance stating: "Now come Bruce A. Conroy and Elizabeth Ann Purcell of the law firm of Egger & Thomas and hereby enter their appearance as counsel for Defendant OLM, Inc." Hirsch received his copy of the court filing in the next day's mail. He'd heard of Egger & Thomas. It was an insurance defense firm that dated back to World War Two. He'd never heard of Bruce Conroy or Elizabeth Purcell, but that meant nothing. He'd been gone for a while.

Counsel for Peterson Tire Corporation entered softly as well, but with an invitation to lunch. Hirsch received it two days after Jack Bellow's performance on the ten o'clock news. He was at his desk in the late afternoon when his secretary buzzed to tell him that there was a Mr. Guttner on line three.

"Good afternoon, David." The voice smooth as silk. "Marvin Guttner, at Emerson, Burke. How are you?"

"Fine."

"We entered our appearance today, David, on behalf of Peterson Tire in the Shifrin matter."

Hirsch was not surprised. Guttner had represented Peterson Tire for years, and his firm was lead defense counsel in the massive tire litigation pending before Brendan McCormick.

"As we were preparing our court papers this morning, David, I realized that I have never had the pleasure of litigating against you."

"I certainly hope it won't be a pleasure for you."

That earned a rumbling chortle. Even if you'd never seen Marvin Guttner, you could tell from his voice that the body generating it was ample.

"Well put, David. Spoken like a true warrior. And speaking of combat, I thought perhaps that it would make sense for the two of us to chat a bit about your case before we don our battle gear and heft our cudgels."

Hirsch shook his head, amused. As if Guttner would ever get within a mile of a litigation brawl. Although he controlled more than ten million dollars in litigation business and held an important committee chairmanship of the litigation division of the American Bar Association, Guttner had not tried a case in more than a decade and had never done a jury trial. He was the litigation equivalent of a Pentagon general—good at the politics and the meetings and "the big picture," glad to let the troops and tacticians fight the battle.

"Okay," Hirsch said, "I'm listening."

"Oh, not over the telephone, David. I had in mind a real chat. An opportunity for the two of us to get to know one another, to bandy about the issues in your case. How does lunch tomorrow sound? I can arrange a private room at my club. Shall we say noon?"

AND thus at noon the following day, Hirsch stood alone at the east window of a private dining room at the St. Louis Club in Clayton. Off in the distance, the Gothic spires and turrets of Washington University jutted over the bare trees as if from some walled town in medieval France.

He was intrigued to finally meet Marvin Guttner, rumored to be the highest paid partner at the venerable Emerson, Burke & McGee, a six-hundred-attorney law firm that traced its St. Louis roots to the Civil War era and represented many of the region's largest corporations. To be the highest paid partner at that firm was no mean feat even for someone with the correct pedigree, but it was extraordinary for a man who not only had *not* attended the proper prep school in St. Louis but whose prominent involvement in St. Peter's Episcopal Church in snooty Ladue did nothing to dispel rumors of his less-than-Episcopal origins in Youngstown, Ohio.

Hirsch turned to the sound of the door opening.

"Ah, yes. Greetings, David."

Guttner's detractors dubbed him Jabba the Gutt, and there was a family resemblance. He was fat and bald, with heavy-lidded eyes, broad nose, bulging double chin spilling over his collar, and liver-colored lips that sagged open. Even so, as he approached to shake hands, Hirsch was struck by how gracefully the big man moved. He seemed to glide across the room in his elegant gray suit, starched white shirt, and gleaming black shoes.

"Delighted to finally meet you, David."

Guttner's lips pulled back into a grimace meant to pass as a smile. He gestured toward the dining table, which was large enough to accommodate eight but was set that day for two.

"Please make yourself comfortable. I shall have Julian bring us menus."

The elderly black man named Julian arrived, departed with their drink orders, returned with iced teas, departed quietly, returned to take their lunch orders, and departed again—and all the while Guttner kept the conversation moving smoothly from one innocuous topic to the next, from the Blues game last night to the latest sex scandal in Washington, from the current episode of *The Sopranos* to the recent litigation tussle between Microsoft and one of the cable companies, and not once did he allude to the lengthy gap in Hirsch's legal career or to the events giving rise to that gap.

Even though Hirsch had heard that Guttner could be charming, he was taken by how engaging the man could be in person. Taken, but not taken in. Guttner's reputation preceded him. He could be charming when it served his purpose, but charm did not often serve his purpose. Clients treasured him as someone who would implement whatever litigation strategy they desired, no matter how harsh or oppressive or outrageous. Attorneys on the other side despised him as a brutal opponent who never apologized but was never vulnerable because he appeared in court only on ceremonial or procedural occasions, and even then was always surrounded by an entourage. Subordinates feared him as a cold taskmaster who expected obedience to whatever the client desired or he demanded. He bullied attorneys within his firm, including those who were years his senior, and regularly issued commands on Friday afternoons to underlings who knew that weekend plans were no excuse. Over the years, Guttner had summoned many a junior partner back from vacation for this or that "crisis," most of which seemed to get resolved just about the time the harried lackey returned from Hawaii or Aspen or Tuscany. They put up with this abuse, these ambitious young and not-so-young attorneys; because Guttner had the power within the firm to shower money and resources and perks on those who pleased him and to banish those who did not.

Julian brought their lunch orders—broiled trout for Hirsch, an off-menu hamburger for Guttner that consisted of nearly a pound of chopped sirloin topped with a thick slice of Bermuda onion and a large scoop of soft cheddar cheese. Juice oozed down into the enormous bun as the room filled with the tangy odor of ketchup and the sharp scents of cheese and sliced onion. Hirsch eyed it with amazement. The logistics of getting the thing into your mouth seemed every bit as daunting as consuming it all in one sitting. Guttner, transformed by the sight and smell of his lunch, attacked it with a feral intensity.

Hirsch was only halfway through his trout when Guttner pushed back from an empty plate and removed the napkin from under his chin. There were beads of sweat on his face. He patted his forehead dry with his cloth napkin, dropped it onto his plate, and stifled a belch. His appetite sated, he settled back in his chair and resumed his genial aura.

"If not for the fatality, David, one could almost be amused by the irony."

Hirsch gave him a puzzled look. "What irony?"

"Your lawsuit, David." He stifled another belch. "My client has been in front of Judge McCormick for nigh on five years in what is now our nation's largest product liability case. At issue in that lawsuit is the performance of my client's Turbo XL tires. And what should happen? The very law clerk that the judge assigns to the case dies in an automobile accident while driving a vehicle equipped with Turbo XL tires. Even worse, her passenger that night, indeed, the owner of the vehicle, is none other than the Honorable Brendan McCormick. That, my good man, is irony on a grand, almost absurd scale. More fitting for one of those legal thrillers that are all the rage these days. Grist for the Grisham mill, eh?"

Hirsch said nothing.

"With one crucial difference. This is the real world, and in the real world we both know one thing about that accident."

Guttner paused, a sheen of perspiration on his face, a faint glimmer in his dull eyes.

Hirsch waited. Guttner stared at him.

Hirsch asked, "What is the one thing we both know?"

"That there was not a damn thing wrong with any of those tires."

"I assumed that would be your position, Marvin."

"Hardly just mine, David. I had one of our accident reconstruction experts review the evidence. She sees no indication of tire malfunction."

"She needs to look closer."

"Come, come, David. We can be frank with one another. This lunch is off the record. Whatever is said here goes no further. You know, and I know you know, that there is no evidence of culpability on the part of my client."

"I've lost cases I should have won, Marvin, and I've won cases I should have lost."

"This is one case you are not going to win."

Hirsch shrugged. "Juries can be unpredictable."

"Assuming you even get to a jury. What if the judge throws the case out before trial?"

"As you said, Marvin, let's be frank with one another. No city of St. Louis judge is going to toss this case before trial. We'll be picking a jury a year from now."

"So what? Let us imagine that you get your chance to play Clarence Darrow to a typical city jury of troglodytes. That's only chapter one. We both know that the existence of St. Louis juries is the reason why we have a court of appeals. I am quite confident that my client will prevail at the end of this lawsuit."

Hirsch smiled. "And this is why you asked me to lunch?"

Guttner chuckled. "Touché."

The fat man leaned forward, his smile fading.

Finally, Hirsch thought.

"As so often is the case, David, the economics of the lawsuit bear little relation to its merits. Although my client will no doubt prevail in the end, the price of victory will be substantial. That same calculus applies for the other two defendants, each of whom can expect to incur legal fees well above their liability exposure in the case."

"You make a lot of assumptions for a lawsuit that's a month old."

"I think not, David. Even if you could win, where are your damages? This is a wrongful death claim on behalf of a woman who had no husband, no children, no siblings, and no financial dependents. There is no claim for lost income or lost support. As for loss of companionship, the only possible claimant is her father. While we will no doubt learn a great deal more about that relationship during discovery, our preliminary investigation suggests that the father and daughter were not especially close. Indeed, some might say they were estranged at the time of her death. But even if they were close—indeed, even if the elder Shifrin takes the stand and tells a tale of paternal devotion worthy of a Hallmark greeting card—this is not a big damage case."

"And your point is?"

"My point is that these defendants are corporations, David. From their perspective, this is nothing more than a routine one-car fatality on an icy road. Is her death regrettable? Certainly. Does that make them blameworthy? Certainly not. Does the case have any significance as a future precedent for them? Hardly. A courtroom victory advances no master strategy for any of them, and defeat establishes no harmful precedent. That suggests certain possibilities, David, including that these defendants might be willing to explore a resolution that would rid them of the case *now* for an amount less than their anticipated litigation costs in the future. Especially my client, in light of the decedent's connection to the judge."

"Did you know Judith Shifrin?"

"Not really. I tend to leave the daily grind of my cases to those more interested in the procedural minutiae of litigation. She was present at one of the pretrial conferences I attended. I recall a little wisp of a girl with dark hair and keen eyes. The attorneys who dealt with her on a regular basis spoke favorably of her diligence and ability." He puckered his lips thoughtfully. "By all accounts, the judge thought highly of her."

"So I understand."

"And that, my good man, is the wild card here. My client can safely assume that Judge McCormick has at least a passing interest in your lawsuit. I should think His Honor would be pleased if your case reached a swift and satisfactory conclusion, and if he is pleased, then perhaps some of that good karma will spill over to other cases involving my client. Conversely, if your case becomes difficult and unpleasant, which it most certainly will if we do not settle early on, then who knows what else that unpleasantness might befoul? But I must emphasize, David, that the settlement window is narrowing even as we speak."

"Why?"

"Because every dollar I spend on defense is a dollar less I can spend on settlement. I have five lawyers and two paralegals assigned to this case. Think of them as my pack of Dobermans growling and clawing at their cage doors. At some point soon, I will have no choice but to unlock those cages. When that happens, the settlement window slams shut. Quite simply, David, if you would like to settle your case, now is the time. Ah, here's Julian, hopefully bringing us news of today's dessert offerings."

The elderly black man smiled down at them. "Yes, sir, Mr. Guttner."

"Has Maurice made my favorite today?"

"Chocolate cheesecake? He certainly has, sir."

"Ah," he said, leaning back in his chair. "Superb, Julian. Superb."

7

ABE Shifrin stood in the doorway, a dab of brown mustard on his chin. From somewhere inside the house came the sounds of the evening news. He studied Hirsch with a frown.

"Hirsch?" he repeated.

"I'm the attorney who filed the case over your daughter's death. I called you this afternoon to see if I could drop by after work."

The frown changed to an embarrassed grin. "Oh, of course. Come in, Mr. Hirsch. *Oy*, this brain of mine. Come in from the cold."

Shifrin's home was a redbrick two-bedroom bungalow with a small living room to the right of the front door and a smaller dining room to the left. The living room looked old and tired—the couch sagging in the middle, the fabric frayed, the blond coffee table and end tables scarred by water rings and cigarette burns, the lampshades faded to a yellowish gray.

Hirsch followed Shifrin toward the little kitchen, moving around a dining room table strewn with newspapers and unopened junk mail and magazines still in shrink-wrap. The kitchen sink was piled with dirty dishes, pans, and silverware. So was the countertop. A faint odor of rotting food filled the room.

"Excuse the mess," Shifrin said, waving his hand vaguely. "The *schvartza* comes tomorrow."

On the small kitchen table was a chipped dinner plate with a half-eaten salami on rye and a handful of potato chips. Near the plate sat an open jar of pickle spears and a large plastic cup with a red Wal-Mart logo. The cup was half filled with dark soda, presumably from the plastic liter bottle of store-brand diet cola on the kitchen counter. The noise came from a portable black-and-white television that sat on a TV tray facing the table. The little television had a bent shirt hanger for an antenna. Hirsch recognized one of the local sports reporters on the fuzzy screen.

Shifrin turned off the TV and turned to Hirsch. "Can I fix you something to eat, sir?"

"No, thanks."

He gestured toward the other kitchen chair as he took his seat. "Make yourself comfortable. If you don't mind, I'll finish my dinner while we talk."

Shifrin listened intently as Hirsch gave him a status report, which ended with yesterday's lunch meeting with Marvin Guttner. When Hirsch finished, Shifrin grunted and reached for a toothpick.

"So they want us to think about a settlement?"

"They do."

Shifrin pointed the toothpick at Hirsch. "But only if the settlement is for less than their defense costs. I've heard that one before." He paused to pick at his side teeth with the toothpick. "I was in a lawsuit once where my lawyer told me to make that kind of offer. What did he call it? 'Nuisance value,' right?"

"That's what some people call it, but that number could be quite high here."

Shifrin leaned back in his chair and studied the toothpick. "So that's what my Judith's death means to those miserable bastards, huh? Just a nuisance?"

"It's only a word, Mr. Shifrin."

"Only a word? I have a word for them, Mr. Hirsch. My word is 'guilty.' About the money I couldn't care less. This is my daughter they killed. Money is nothing here. What I want is for a court to tell the world they're guilty."

"Our settlement demand could include an expression of regret."

Shifrin crossed his arms over his chest. "No confession, no deal."

"If the defendants pay enough, Mr. Shifrin, the money becomes an admission. Sometimes a person makes an admission with his actions."

He snorted. "Money talks, eh?"

"Occasionally."

"It's got to do more than just talk, sir. What did you have in mind?"

"That's one of the reasons I came over here. We need to talk about that."

"Let's go in the living room."

HIRSCH leaned forward to study the framed portraits that hung side by side on the living room wall across from the couch. One was a high school photograph of Judith Shifrin—a standard yearbook shot of a smiling young woman with a pale airbrushed complexion, straight dark hair, and dark eyes. The other was of her mother—one of those Sears specials with a flowery background and artificial light. Mrs. Shifrin was a washed-out version of her daughter—a thin, pallid woman with sad eyes and limp hair streaked with gray.

From the couch Shifrin said, "That was my Harriet, *aleya ha 'sholem*."

Hirsch turned toward him. "When did she pass away?"

"Almost fourteen years ago. *Oy*, she had so many problems, but in the end it was the cancer that killed her. Ovaries, the doctors said." Shifrin shook his head. "It was very hard."

"I can imagine."

"You have no idea, Mr. Hirsch. No one said life would be easy, of course, and no one said life would be fair. Even so, those were difficult times for me. She was bedridden for years."

"How old was Judith when her mother died?"

"Just fifteen. Think about that, why don't you. There I was, burying a wife and trying to raise a teenage daughter. Believe me, Mr. Hirsch, those were not easy years for me."

"Were you and your daughter close?"

"I thought so back then, but what did I know?"

"Why do you say that?"

Shifrin stiffened. "And why should this be any business of yours, my daughter and I?"

Hirsch came over and sat down across from him. "These are difficult subjects to discuss, Mr. Shifrin, but they're important for the lawsuit. We need to talk about them."

"Why?"

"Because the lawyers for the defendants will. They are going to ask you lots of questions about your relationship with your daughter."

"*My* relationship?" He blinked his eyes. "How can they do that?"

"One of the ways a jury determines damages in these

cases," he explained, "is to place a dollar value on the loss of a loved one. You're the only living member of Judith's family. Under the law, you're the only one who will suffer the loss of her companionship. That means that your relationship with your daughter is an important factor for the jury to consider in determining the damages in this case."

"So what does that mean then? I become like one of those rape victims? All of a sudden I'm on trial?" Shifrin crossed his arms over his chest. "All of a sudden they're staring at me instead of the bastards who killed my daughter, those sons of bitches. This is what you call justice?"

"You won't be on trial, Mr. Shifrin. I won't let them put you on trial. But your relationship with your daughter is part of the lawsuit. This is a wrongful death case. That means that you are one of the victims of the wrongdoing. You've lost a loved one. That's one of the reasons I'm here tonight. I need to learn more about you and her. Were you close? Did you spend time together?"

"When? When she was little? She lived here, for God's sake. Of course we spent time together."

"What about later? What about her last few years?"

Shifrin turn and stared at the base of the lamp, a tense little man with his arms crossed over his chest.

Still looking away, he said, "We had our ups and downs. What father and daughter don't?" He gave a resigned shrug. "They become teenagers, Mr. Hirsch, and everything gets crazy, and then they decide that they're adults and all of a sudden the whole world turns topsy-turvy, and then on top of all that her mother dies." Shifrin turned toward him, his face flushed with anger. "I do not like this, sir. I do not like this one bit. This lawsuit should be about those bastards killing my only child. It's not about whether I took her to the zoo on Sunday or read her a bedtime story.

I had a business to run and a dying wife in my bedroom, and then I had a dead wife and a daughter who—" He shook his head and then patted his chest. "Believe me, sir, I had plenty of *tsouris*."

Hirsch suggested that they look at family albums, hoping that old photographs might help ease them into a discussion of his relationship with his daughter. Shifrin went back to one of the bedrooms and returned with three worn albums.

The old photographs worked for a while. Shifrin grew sentimental over pictures spanning Judith's toddler and elementary school days—shots of him pushing her in a stroller at the zoo, of the two of them seated together on a picnic blanket in the park, of him holding her on a merry-go-round, of him and his wife standing proud at a piano recital with their grade school daughter seated at the piano in a starched white dress and black patent leather shoes. But the later photos, especially the ones that included cousins and family friends, seemed to highlight the widening gaps in his memory. His mood shifted from teary nostalgia to teary frustration as he tried to remember the names of the people in the photos. He slammed the album closed and squeezed his eyes shut.

"I'M sorry," Shifrin told him at the front door. "I get upset with my brain. Maybe we can try again in a few days."

Hirsch adjusted the two photo albums under his arm. "Sounds good."

Shifrin forced a smile. "So what's our next step?"

"I'm meeting with an expert tomorrow."

"What kind?"

"Medical."

"A doctor? Why a doctor?"

"To go over some matters related to the accident." He shook the old man's hand. "I'll be back in touch, Mr. Shifrin. Have a good evening."

"You, too, sir."

HIRSCH sat in his car in front of Shifrin's bungalow, letting the engine warm up. Tomorrow's meeting with Dr. Granger had suddenly become key. He hadn't learned all the details that night, but it was clear that Shifrin's relationship with his daughter had been troubled, especially toward the end. Somehow, Guttner had discovered that as well.

Which didn't mean that he couldn't patch together a claim for loss of companionship. Enlargements of the best of those father-daughter photos, placed on an easel in front of the jury would help. But pretty pictures alone would never make the loss of companionship claim worth big money, especially at the settlement stage.

And that left him with one last angle for boosting damages. When Shifrin asked him why a medical expert, he'd been vague. He wanted to spare the old man the anguish that any father would feel if told that the expert was a pathologist who might be able to determine from the medical records whether his daughter had been conscious for at least a few seconds after the impact. If so, the jury would be allowed to award damages for pain and suffering, and that would significantly increase the settlement value. If not, well, he'd be left with those childhood photos and whatever dirt he might be able to dig up on the defendants.

He shook his head.

Digging for dirt.

As if he were some knight errant preparing to battle an evil empire instead of just another personal injury lawyer scrabbling for purchase in a one-car accident case.

This is your brave new world, he told himself. *A world where you hope an expert will tell you that the nice young woman survived long enough to experience the anguish of her own death. Welcome.*

He glanced over at the house. The living room shades were pulled back on a gloomy tableau. Shifrin sat on the threadbare couch and stared at the wall across the room, at the framed photographs of his dead wife and his dead child.

Hirsch put the car in gear and pulled away.

8

DR. Henry Granger was over at the window again, squinting at an X-ray he was holding up to the light.

Hirsch watched, intrigued. He was seated at the round table in the sunny breakfast room of Dr. Granger's two-story colonial in suburban Webster Groves. The room was as snug and cheerful as the doctor himself, who was in his seventies now—a spry man with ruddy cheeks, a shock of white hair, and clear blue eyes. The only hint of time's un-kindness was the tremor in his hands.

Hirsch took another sip of the fresh coffee that Mrs. Granger had insisted upon brewing when she'd returned from the grocery store and found the two of them in the breakfast room. She was in the den now, listening to the Brandenburg Concertos on the stereo as she knitted a sweater for one of her grandchildren. All six of those grandchildren were in the family portrait that hung on the breakfast room wall. In the photograph, she and Granger were seated on a loveseat, surrounded by their adult chil-dren and spouses and grandchildren, who ranged in age from elementary school to college. It was a vision of domestic happiness that underscored the wreckage of his own life. There were no family portraits in his apartment.

"Intact," the doctor mumbled as he studied the X-ray. "No question."

With his reading glasses perched on the end of his nose and a cardigan sweater buttoned over his blue dress shirt, Henry Granger could have stepped out of a Norman Rockwell painting of a Vermont country doctor. Actually, though, the first twenty-five years of his career more closely resembled a Charles Addams cartoon. He spent those years cutting up corpses in the subbasement morgue of one of the city's major hospitals. As the hospital's chief pathologist, he occasionally testified in criminal cases, and in the process developed a yen for the courtroom. He spent the final decade of his career as a plaintiff's expert witness and earned big fees testifying in a wide assortment of injury and death cases.

They'd met years ago when Granger served as a medical expert in a case Hirsch was defending. He'd been a formidable opponent—intelligent, well-organized, articulate, unflappable, good courtroom demeanor. When Hirsch decided, after his lunch meeting with Marvin Guttner, that he needed to retain a medical expert with a background in pathology, Granger was his first choice. The doctor had been retired for several years, but he was intrigued enough by the request from an old adversary to agree to meet him. The timing was good, since Granger and his wife were leaving at the end of next week to spend a month in Tucson with their eldest daughter and her family.

Now he was holding up another X-ray to the sunlight. This one appeared to be a front shot of the head and upper torso. The doctor was thorough, no question about that.

Hirsch had assumed that Granger would be able to review the file in ten minutes. After all, the accident report (including witness statements) was just six pages long, the medical examiner's report was another two pages (plus six X-rays, three morgue photos, and a half page of lab results), and there was no autopsy report.

But Granger was still at it after, Hirsch checked his watch, forty minutes. He'd made two pages of notes on a legal pad. He'd carried the X-rays over to the window three times and held them up to the light, studying them one by one. He'd used a magnifying glass to examine each of the morgue shots. A pair of medical textbooks on pathology were open on the kitchen table.

Although Granger had hoped to see an autopsy report, he hadn't been surprised by its absence. Autopsies, he'd explained to Hirsch, were no longer routine in traffic fatalities. The procedure had become so expensive that it was only performed on a traffic accident victim if there were suspicious circumstances.

Granger returned to the table. He lifted his notes and studied them with a frown.

"Fascinating case," he said, more to himself than Hirsch. "Troubling case."

"What's the bottom line?" Hirsch braced himself for the worst.

"Hard to say for sure."

"Do you think she was conscious after the collision?"

"Oh, no."

Hirsch's shoulders sagged. "Are you sure?"

Granger pondered the question. "I suppose I am about as sure as one could be without an autopsy. Do I believe that this lady was conscious after the collision? No. Does the available evidence support my conclusion? Yes. Is it possible that an autopsy could refute my conclusion?" He leaned back and crossed his arms over his chest, lowering his head to peer at Hirsch over the top of his reading glasses. "Possibly, but probably not."

Hirsch leaned back in his chair and exhaled slowly. "So we can forget pain and suffering."

"I wouldn't say that. There certainly was pain and suffering."

After a moment, Hirsch said, "I'm not following you, Doc."

Granger stared at Hirsch, his lips pursed. "I do not believe that the young lady died in the accident."

Hirsch tried to parse the sentence but couldn't. "What do you mean?"

"I would surmise that she was dead before she got in the car."

Hirsch stared at him. "I'm lost."

"The medical examiner concluded that she died of asphyxia. Based on the observations in his report, I would agree with his conclusion. I would disagree, however, with his determination of the cause of that asphyxia. Of course, this is hardly the first time I've disagreed with Sam Avery."

"Was he the medical examiner?"

Granger nodded and pointed to the signature line on the report.

"You don't like him?"

"To the contrary, Sam is a charming man. Just last fall, in fact, the two of us went duck hunting in Illinois. On a professional level, however, Sam is second-rate. In medical school, David, some students gravitate toward pathology because they are fascinated with the study of various diseases and the changes they produce in the organs they attack. Other students are steered toward pathology because their professors believe they will inflict less harm if their patients are already dead. Sam Avery was one of the latter. Still, I shouldn't be too harsh on him here. This case arrived with all the earmarks of a routine traffic fatality. On a busy night, a better pathologist than Sam could have missed it."

"Missed what?"

He pointed to the bottom line on the medical examiner's report. "Sam describes the cause of death as 'blunt force trauma with asphyxia, apparently caused by motor vehicle accident and deployment of air bag system.'" Granger looked up from the report. "In a front-end collision, David, there are only two ways asphyxia could be the cause of death. Either the victim suffocated while jammed against the air bag, or the force of the impact broke her spinal cord and she lost the ability to breathe. The X-rays eliminate the latter scenario." He held up one of the X-rays he'd been studying by the window. "Her spinal cord was intact."

"What about the air bag? She was a small woman."

"Her size has little to do with it. To suffocate, the air bag would have to have remained fully inflated for longer than thirty seconds." Granger shook his head. "That is not possible."

"Why do you say that?"

"Several years back, I worked on two infant fatality cases involving rear-facing seat restraints in the front seat. As a result, I became somewhat of an expert on air-bag design. There are not many of us, and Sam Avery most certainly is not one. I learned that all air bags have multiple vents in the back. Without exception. The vents are an essential design element that ensures that the bag stays inflated for less than half a second. Which is not to say they can't cause injury. Air bags inflate with explosive force—explosive enough to have knocked this young lady unconscious, perhaps even given her a concussion. But the bag would have deflated a fraction of a second later." He shook his head. "She did not suffocate against an air bag."

"But you still believe that she suffocated?"

"That's my opinion."

"How? And when?"

Granger picked up the medical examiner's report and

adjusted his reading glasses. "Do you see this observation?"

He turned the page toward Hirsch and pointed to a line of text.

"Petechial hemorrhages," Hirsch read aloud.

"Exactly. Petechial hemorrhages in the eyes."

"What are they?"

"Red splotches in the whites of the eyes. The usual cause is the restriction of blood flow in the head area. Here, I would venture to say that the cause of that blood flow restriction is linked to this observation."

He pointed to the phrase *slight compression of soft tissue of neck*.

"What does that mean?" Hirsch said.

"I can't be one hundred percent certain without an autopsy, but in my judgment the most likely cause of death was manual strangulation." He shook his head sadly. "I'm afraid there would have been plenty of pain and suffering."

Hirsch tried to grasp the implications.

Granger leaned over one of the morgue shots with the magnifying glass, studying her neck. "It's barely detectable in the picture," he said, frustrated. "They should have taken a close-up."

He sat back and gazed at Hirsch.

"David, based on what I've reviewed here, I'd say that it is more likely than not that someone strangled that poor girl. Strangled her, stuck her behind the wheel of that car, and then drove it into a tree. You wouldn't need much of an impact to trigger the air bag. Moreover, if you were seated in the passenger seat and could brace yourself for the moment of impact, you could actually run the speed up high enough to do some impressive damage to the front end of the vehicle without seriously injuring yourself."

Granger removed the reading glasses and studied Hirsch. "I suppose one could try to construct another scenario out of this evidence, but this is the one that seems most likely to me."

He put his glasses back on and peered at the front page of the medical examiner's report.

"Judith Shifrin. The name sounds familiar." He looked up. "Who was she?"

Part Two

———

Take care, your grace, those things
over there are not giants but windmills.

SANCHO PANZA TO DON QUIXOTE

9

"**D**OOVID?"

The hoarse whisper registered somewhere along the edge of his consciousness.

"Doovid."

Louder this time.

Hirsch looked up from his prayer book. Mr. Kantor stood before him, eyebrows raised. He was holding out the *pushke*. Hirsch fumbled for his wallet, removed a pair of dollar bills, and stuffed them into the silver box. Mr. Kantor nodded and moved down the aisle.

Hirsch tried to focus on the service, but his thoughts kept returning to yesterday's meeting. Granger refused to elevate his cause-of-death scenario above hypothesis. Nor would any competent pathologist, he assured Hirsch. Without an autopsy, no one could be certain that Judith Shifrin had been murdered. The existing evidence was strongly suggestive but incomplete. The only potentially conclusive evidence would have been a fractured hyoid. Manual strangulation occasionally fractured the hyoid, which was a small bone in the neck area near the base of the tongue. Even a pathologist as second-rate as Sam Avery would have checked the hyoid, Granger said. Moreover, Judith's X-rays indicated no such fracture.

In many cases, Granger explained, exhumation of the body, even years later, could provide the necessary confirming (or refuting) evidence. But not here. As the copy of the death notice in Judith Shifrin's file confirmed, a Jewish mortuary prepared her body for interment, Rabbi Zev Saltzman of Anshe Emes officiated at the funeral, and she was buried (next to her mother) in an Orthodox cemetery. Observant Jews do not embalm their dead, believing that the soul's return to God is dependent upon the body's swift return to the earth.

For dust you are and to dust you shall return.

Three years after her burial, Judith Shifrin's corpse would have no remaining relevant soft tissues to examine.

So now what?

The day after Jack Bellows's press conference, Hirsch had shifted his focus to the Ford Motor Company. If Jack the Ripper wanted to throw down the gauntlet, he was prepared to pick it up and smash him in the face with it. He'd assigned one of Rosenbloom's brightest paralegals to research accidents involving Ford Explorers. She'd already found him an Explorer accident database at a Web site maintained by a national organization of plaintiffs' personal injury lawyers specializing in SUV crash cases. Each day, he'd called another two or three of the lawyers listed on the site who'd handled accident cases against Ford. Although he didn't have much yet, he'd come across a few promising leads, or what had seemed to be promising leads before yesterday's meeting with Henry Granger.

Strangled her?

Was it even conceivable?

He tried to visualize Brendan McCormick—six foot

four, at least two hundred sixty pounds these days—
choking little Judith Shifrin.

Strangulation was a crime of passion.

Obviously.

No one committed a premeditated murder by strangulation.

What could have set off that type of rage in McCormick?
An affair gone bad? Announcement that she was pregnant?
He tried to imagine a scenario that would end in her death.

Nothing.

He thought back to the rumors he'd heard during their
assistant U.S. attorney days together. Vague rumors about
McCormick's sexual antics at Mizzou. About rough stuff
with football groupies—some involving McCormick alone,
others involving several players at once. Rumors about one
such incident that ended with the young woman in intensive care.

Just rumors, though. McCormick was never charged.
None of them were. Which didn't prove a thing, of course.
Back then, athletic departments of the major football
schools tended to view sexual assaults as a cost of running
a successful program. Boys would be boys, and when
something got out of hand, there were influential alumni
standing by to help keep things quiet.

Just rumors.

Then again, he'd once witnessed McCormick's rage up
close. Almost twenty-five years ago. Several of the assistant U.S. attorneys had gone over to Broadway Oyster Bar
for drinks after work. There'd been a blues band playing
that night, and the place was jammed. Bodies jostling
against one another, a haze of cigarette smoke in the air,
waitresses squeezing through the crowd with drink trays
held aloft, the blues harp wailing and the electric bass
thumping. He'd been standing directly behind McCormick
when it happened. A skinny guy with long hair and a

scraggly mustache was working his way through the crowd
toward the men's room. A mug of beer in his hand, a lit cigarette dangling from his lips. Someone bumped him from
behind. He staggered against McCormick, beer slopping
over the edge of his mug, cigarette burning a hole in his
shirt. McCormick stepped back, shirt wet, clearly pissed
off. He shouted something at the skinny guy, who said
something back—Hirsch couldn't hear over the din. Mc-
Cormick suddenly punched the guy in the stomach. As he
doubled over in pain, McCormick grabbed him by his hair,
jammed his head under his left arm, and started pounding
him with uppercuts. By the time several of them pulled
him away, the guy was unconscious and bleeding from his
nose and mouth and ears. McCormick would have killed
him if they hadn't intervened.

"Page one sixty-nine," Mr. Kantor called out. "The
psalm of the day."

Hirsch looked down at his *siddur* and turned to the correct page. He silently read the English translation:

*O God of vengeance, Hashem: O God of vengeance ap-
pear! Arise, O Judge of the earth, render recompense to the
haughty. How long shall the wicked, O Hashem, how long
shall the wicked exult? Your nation, Hashem, they crush
and they afflict. Your heritage. The widow and the stranger
they slay, and the orphans they murder. And they say, "God
will not see and God will not understand."*

The words blurred.

He lifted his head. The men on either side of him continued chanting. He stared at the ark, his thoughts roiling.

What in God's name had happened that night?

ROSENBLOOM glared at him from behind his desk, his
hands gripping the handles of his wheelchair. "Are you
fucking insane?"

Hirsch shrugged. "I don't know what else I can do."

"I'll tell you what else you can do, you crazy bastard. You can settle that goddamn case right now and walk the fuck away."

Hirsch shook his head.

"What?" Rosenbloom demanded.

"I can't do that. Not after what I've learned."

"After what you've learned? What exactly do you think you've learned? You got some guesswork from a retired Quincy. What's he call it? A working hypothesis. Guess what? His goddamn working hypothesis has already been refuted by the actual goddamn medical examiner who examined her body on the night of the goddamn accident. You don't have any *hard* evidence to contradict those findings. You got no autopsy. You got no body. All you got is *bupkes*, my friend. *Bupkes*."

"That's because I haven't started looking yet."

Rosenbloom rolled his eyes heavenward. "Oh, my God, Samson, listen to yourself. You're actually thinking about trying to build a three-year-old murder case against a federal district judge? And from scratch? Talk about insane. No, it's worse than insane. It's suicidal."

"If Dr. Granger is right, this really is a wrongful death case. I can't just walk away from that."

"Of course you can. This is a free country, pal. Start walking."

"It's not the right thing to do."

"What's right have to do with it? It's the smart thing to do."

"You sound like a lawyer."

"Because I am one. And so are you. We're talking about a lawsuit here, not an Elizabethan revenge play. This ain't *Hamlet*, *boychik*, and you ain't Prince Hal."

Rosenbloom paused and sighed.

"Come on, Samson. Get real. You'll never prove he

killed her. Never. And even if you could, which you can't, so what? That's not going to bring her back to life. She's dead, and no matter what you do she's going to stay dead. Forever."

Rosenbloom shook his head.

"Listen to me, Samson. The old man wants to preserve her memory, right? You can do that, and you can do it now, before he loses the rest of his own goddamn memory. Squeeze a nice settlement out of that fat piece of shit, pocket our fee, and tell the old man to use the money to build her a memorial."

The receptionist buzzed on the speakerphone.

"What is it?"

"I have a call for Mr. Hirsch on line four."

Rosenbloom said, "Take a message, Lois. Tell them he's in a meeting."

"It's a judge, sir."

"Which one?"

"Judge McCormick."

Hirsch and Rosenbloom stared at one another across the desk. After a moment, Rosenbloom pressed the intercom button. "He'll take it in here."

Rosenbloom looked at Hirsch and nodded toward the phone.

Hirsch leaned over the desk, lifted the receiver, and depressed the blinking light. "Hello?"

"Mr. Hirsch?"

"Yes."

"Hold for Judge McCormick."

A short pause.

"David?"

"Yes."

"Bet you thought I'd forgotten all about your lawsuit."

"I assumed you were busy."

"You can say that again." A grim chuckle. "I've been on

a killer pace, but that doesn't mean I'm not thinking about you and poor Judith. How's the case going?"

Hirsch held Rosenbloom's gaze. "It's still early."

"I caught Jack Bellows's circus act on the tube last week. Off the record, David, he was way out of line. He ever tries a stunt like that in one of my cases, I'll wring his neck. Anyway, I'm calling because I should finally have a break in my schedule the week after this one. How 'bout we get together that Friday afternoon and talk about your case?"

Hirsch took out his pocket calendar and checked the date. "Okay."

"Say about two?"

"That works."

"I'll see you then."

10

HIRSCH didn't need a psychic to figure out the cause of the professor's attitude. When he'd phoned her that morning, she'd been pleasant enough until he told her his name, at which point her voice turned cold. He had soldiered on, explaining that he had filed a wrongful death claim on behalf of Judith Shifrin and needed to talk to her about the case. She'd been reluctant to meet but finally agreed, telling him that she had office hours that afternoon between two and four. He told her those times didn't work, pretending to have a conflicting appointment, not wanting to explain the real reason. He'd suggested they could meet somewhere on her way home. Anywhere. Perhaps for a cup of coffee. He told her it was important. He promised it wouldn't take long. Eventually, she relented. Kaldi's at five, she told him. He told her thanks. She hung up.

He arrived there ten minutes early, wanting to be sure they would have a table with some privacy. He ordered a cup of coffee and carried the steaming mug over to the table. He took a chair facing the door. The coffeehouse was half empty, its late-afternoon patrons consisting mostly of college students hunched over textbooks, one per table.

After the telephone conversation that morning, he'd gone to the law school's Web site to look up Professor Adelaide Lorenz—partly so he'd recognize her when she came through the door, partly to find out who she was, and partly to figure out why her name sounded familiar. She'd certainly reacted to him as if they had a history, and not a pleasant one at that. Maybe she'd been in private practice before going into academia. If so, perhaps they'd had a professional confrontation years ago, maybe a skirmish in some lawsuit. She'd hardly be the only adversary he'd pissed off back then. Then again, the chill in her voice might not be tied to a particular lawsuit. It could be general disdain for the conduct that put him in jail. She'd hardly be the only member of the profession to shun him.

Or perhaps her frostiness was truly personal. That was his real fear. He didn't remember any conquest named Adelaide Lorenz, but the names and faces blurred together. During those final years, coked up or boozed up, he'd been the king of the one-night stands, a serial seducer of dozens and dozens of young women. Paralegals, junior associates, secretaries. Quickies on his office couch at night, stand-ups in bathroom stalls at bars, trysts in their little studio apartments as he pretended to admire their taste in art or books or music while maneuvering them toward the fold-out couch. Pumped 'em and dumped 'em—that was his modus operandi. If there was a Hell, that part of his life guaranteed him a miserable spot several levels down.

But the photograph on the Web site hadn't rung a bell. He would have thought that he'd remember someone that attractive.

Her biography didn't ring any bells, either. Professor Adelaide Lorenz had earned her bachelor of arts magna cum laude from Wellesley College and her juris doctor with honors from Stanford University, where she'd been an editor of the law review. She'd clerked for a federal circuit court judge for two years and then gone into private practice, mainly representing plaintiffs in employment discrimination cases. She'd joined the law school faculty of Washington University in St. Louis seven years ago.

He'd run a search on her in Nexis, which turned up three articles from the *Post-Dispatch*, all on a nasty custody battle with her ex-husband. She'd married a Stanford classmate the summer after graduation. They divorced eight years ago, back when she was still in private practice. During the dissolution proceedings, her ex-husband—ironically, a divorce lawyer himself—launched a nasty custody battle over their son, Benjamin, who was six at the time. She didn't back down, and eventually prevailed.

The search also picked up a feature article on the Family Justice Legal Clinic that she ran as part of the law school's clinical program. Dozens of law student volunteers, mostly women, staffed her clinic, which provided legal services to the victims of domestic violence and child abuse. The article gave her age as thirty-nine. That was two years ago. According to the article, everyone at the clinic—students, staff, and clients—called her Dulcie.

That's what Judith had called her as well. The Hanukkah card she'd sent to Judith a week before her death was signed, "Love, Dulcie."

H E was sipping his coffee when she stepped inside the coffeehouse a few minutes after five. He stood and offered a friendly smile. She nodded in acknowledgment, glanced at his coffee mug on the table, and stepped toward the counter, her manner clearly telling him to not even bother offering to pay.

He studied her as she placed her order. She was dressed in black—*Vogue* magazine black. Black leather jacket, black turtleneck sweater, black wool skirt hemmed above the knees, black tights, and black leather boots. The color seemed to highlight her striking Mediterranean features—strong nose, curly dark hair down to her shoulders, high cheekbones, olive skin. He definitely hadn't slept with Adelaide Lorenz. Even in the fog of alcohol and cocaine that swirled around those quickies, he would have a remembered a woman that striking.

She paused at the sideboard to pour milk in her coffee and then came over to the table. They shook hands. She had a firm grip.

"Professor, I'm David Hirsch. Thank you for meeting me here."

She placed her mug on the table. "You can call me Dulcie, Mr. Hirsch."

Her tone was cool, professional.

"And you can call me David."

As she hung her jacket on a hook on the wall, he noticed the swell of her breasts beneath the turtleneck, the elegant sweep of her neck. She had the aura of an athlete, of someone who worked out regularly. She also had the aura of determination, of someone who'd be a formidable adversary in the courtroom or the boardroom.

She took the seat opposite him. Lifting the mug with both hands, she studied him over the rim as she sipped her coffee. Her eyes, dark and enormous, seemed to blaze with intensity.

She said, "You have some questions for me about Judith Shifrin?"

"I do."

"I have some questions for you first."

"Fire away."

"Did you know Judith?"

"No."

In the background came the sudden gurgle and hiss of the espresso machine.

"How did you get the case?"

"Her father approached me."

Her eyes narrowed slightly. "Are you a friend of her father?"

"Not really."

"What does that mean?"

"We belong to the same synagogue. He approached me after services one morning last December. He wanted to hire me to file a lawsuit on his daughter's behalf. All I agreed to do was look at the file. Unfortunately, I discovered that the statue of limitations was about to expire." He gave a shrug. "I filed the lawsuit."

"But you don't believe in it."

"I didn't back then."

"But now?"

He gazed at her. "I do."

She took a sip of coffee. "What's my connection?"

"You were close to her."

"What makes you say that?"

He described the results of his search yesterday afternoon. After Judith's death, her personal belongings had been boxed and stored in Abe Shifrin's basement. In one of those boxes he'd found a shoebox filled with birthday and holiday cards that Judith had received over the years going all the way back to high school.

"I went through the cards one by one," he said. "During the last three years of her life, she received a few cards from some out-of-town friends, but the only people in St. Louis who sent her cards were you and her aunt Hannah. I matched the names on the cards with the birthday reminders on her personal calendars for the last several years of her life. The only two St. Louis birthdays on there all three years were yours and her aunt Hannah's. She had Judge McCormick's birthday on her calendar two years before she died, but not the last year."

"No one else?"

There was a touch of sadness in her voice.

Hirsch said, "There are others if you go back farther. She listed someone named Reggie Jordan for several years. Saved his birthday cards, too. Judging by what he wrote on them, I'd guess he was a boyfriend."

"He was."

"There was nothing from him for the last three years of her life. I assume they broke up."

"They did."

"During law school?"

She nodded. "They met in college. He was a year older. After graduation, he got a job as a stockbroker. They broke up toward the end of her first year of law school."

"Did you know him?"

"Not really. I met him once or twice on campus, but I didn't know Judith that well at the time. It wasn't until the spring of her second year that she started volunteering at the clinic. Reggie was history by then."

"Does he still live in St. Louis?"

"I have no idea."

He glanced at his notes. "Do you know Judith's father?"

"Never met him. Never want to."

He let that one sink in. He'd heard the spike of anger in her voice. She must have as well, because she was staring at her coffee mug.

He asked, "Did she talk to you about her father?"

She studied him as she sipped her coffee. "What does that matter?"

"Her mother is dead. She had no siblings. That means her father is her closest surviving relative."

"So?"

"So their relationship is relevant for damages."

She pursed her lips. After a moment, she nodded. "Okay."

Hirsch picked his words carefully. "I've spoken with her father about their relationship. I got the sense that it was somewhat troubled. He refused to go into any details. I'm not sure that he could even if he wanted to. He's been diagnosed with Alzheimer's. Although the disease is in an early stage, his memory is already erratic. What little he told me, though, is consistent with what I found—or didn't find. There were no birthday or Hanukkah cards from him. His birthday wasn't on any of her calendars. It was as if he didn't exist for her."

"Oh, he existed for her"—her nostrils flared—"that was the problem. Her father was a narcissistic bastard."

She shook her head in disgust. "What do you know about her mother?"

"I know that she died when Judith was in high school."

"Her mother was an invalid. She was bedridden from the time Judith was in fifth grade and died when Judith was in high school. By then, Judith was cooking her father's meals, washing and ironing his clothes, darning his socks, cleaning his house, and listening to him whine every night and every morning about what a hard life he had."

She paused and shook her head sadly. "That was her junior year of high school. Think about what you were doing your junior year, and then think about Judith. He wouldn't let her go away to college, of course. Wouldn't hear of it. She attended Washington U, but she lived at home. While her college friends were partying or hanging out at coffeehouses or gathering in dorm rooms to talk into the wee hours about life, she was stuck at home cooking his meals and washing his clothes and cleaning up after him. He kept her trapped at home." She paused and then smiled.

"Until the great escape. It happened after her sophomore year of college."

"That's when she met Jordan?"

"Yes. Reggie was everything her father wasn't. He was tall and sweet and bighearted and African American. Two weeks before the start of her junior year she moved out of her father's house and into Reggie's apartment."

"Oh."

"Oh is right. Her father went berserk. Literally cut her out of his life—emotionally, financially, every way. He refused to see her or have anything to do with her. Total rejection."

"Did they ever reconcile?"

"Never." She sighed. "It so pained Judith. She used to talk to me about it. That's how I know all this. The poor thing was confused. One day she'd feel sorry for him, and the next day she'd hate him. She'd have these terrible waves of guilt and depression. She worked up the nerve to reach out to him when she was in law school, but he totally rebuffed her. She didn't give up, though. The last time she tried—" Dulcie paused, her eyes suddenly watering.

She took a deep breath and seemed to will herself back from tears. "That last time was about a week before she died. It was the first night of Hanukkah. She made a plate of potato *latkes* and homemade applesauce and took them over to his house. She rang the doorbell. He opened the door, stared at her, and then closed it in her face. *In her face.*"

The memory clearly infuriated Dulcie.

"She called me that night sobbing. She was devastated. Absolutely devastated." Dulcie stared at him. "Some father, eh?"

He said nothing, letting the story sink in.

After a moment, she gestured at his empty coffee mug. "You want a refill?"

"Sure. Thanks."

The story of Judith and her father made him sad. He thought of the terrible remorse that must have haunted Abe Shifrin. He was well acquainted with that emotion. As he thought of that final confrontation between father and daughter, he could almost hear the sound of that front door closing. He thought of that sound reverberating in Abe Shifrin's mind. Echoing through the years. Echoing as he stood over her open grave as the dirt from his shovel clattered down onto her coffin. Echoing in the flare of the match as he lit that first *yahrzeit* candle in his empty home. Echoing in the clatter of bare tree branches in the winter winds as he lay awake in bed. There was an echo to hound you to your grave—or at least until the Alzheimer's finally silenced it.

"Why me?" Dulcie asked.

He looked up from his reverie, regrouping his thoughts.

"Because I'm representing someone I never met," he said. "I need to learn more about her. I need to find out what she liked and didn't like. Who her friends were. Whether she had any enemies. Did she have hobbies? Did she have dreams? Did she have plans for the future?"

"That's a lot of information."

"For one life?" He shook his head. "Not really."

"What do you have so far?"

"I have two photo albums from her childhood, a few graduation portraits, a box or so of personal papers. I have a packet of morgue shots and another one of postmortem X-rays. I have a list of names I copied down from her calendars and holiday cards and personal papers."

Dulcie leaned back in her chair. After a moment, she said, "She loved Eva Cassidy."

"Who's that?"

"A jazz singer. She's dead, too. Died in her thirties. Her favorite movie was *Sleepless in Seattle*." She smiled at the memory. "Her second favorite movie was *Cinderella*. She owned both on videotape."

She crossed her arms over her chest as she thought back, her lips pursed in thought. "She loved Charles Dickens. I never met anyone who loved Dickens the way Judith did. Especially *Great Expectations* and *Bleak House*. She'd read each at least a half dozen times. Her favorite song was 'Fields of Gold'—the version by Sting. Actually, she loved just about anything by Sting."

Dulcie's eyes seemed to go distant as she thought back.

"Did she have a boyfriend after Reggie?"

"No one special."

"How about anyone at all?"

"She had a few dates. Nothing serious."

"Girlfriends?"

She thought it over. "She never talked about anyone else to me, but that doesn't mean she didn't have other friends. I do know that she spent a lot of time on her own. Especially her last year. Or at least I didn't see her as often. But through it all, she never cut back on her time at the family justice clinic. Right up to the end. That was unusual."

"How so?"

"I've had many dedicated student volunteers, but students tend to view the clinic as a law school thing. Once they graduate, they move on. But not Judith. She was there two evenings every week and all day every Saturday—summer, winter, spring, and fall."

"What did she do at the clinic?"

"We provide legal services to abused women and their children. The real challenge is to gain their trust when they first come in. Judith had a wonderful ability to connect with the women, to gain their confidence and serve as a link between them and the lawyers who would deal with their legal problems. She was an incredibly valuable asset at the clinic. I miss her anyway, but I miss that part of her, too."

"Was she as close with anyone else as she was with you?"

"I don't know. I never heard of anyone else. But you need to understand that we weren't friends in the typical sense."

"What do you mean?"

"I began as her professor, and then I was her supervisor at the clinic. There was the age difference and the authority difference. We'd have a cup of coffee together maybe once a week. Occasionally we'd go out to lunch. I'd do a lot of listening."

"To what?"

"To her life. Judith talked about her life almost obsessively. Especially about her father. It was really quite sad. I suppose we're all hung up to a certain degree on our parents and on what we think they did or didn't do to us. But most of us are able to get on with our lives. Not Judith."

He handed her a photocopy of the list of names he'd copied down from Judith's personal papers. "Do you know any of these people?"

She took a moment to scan down the list. There were thirty-seven names on it, including hers. "I recognize a few students. Barry Embry's one. He was in her class. I think he clerked for an Eighth Circuit judge after graduation. Linda Hartstein. I had her in a class. Bonnie Ross, too. A few other names look familiar." She shrugged. "Maybe they were law students." She looked up at him. "Maybe not."

"Could you check? You can keep the list. It's an extra copy."

She gave him a curious look. "Why do these names matter?"

"I'm looking for connections."

"To what?"

"To Judith," he said, keeping it general, trying to convey through his tone and manner that he'd fully answered the question. "To her life."

She studied him a moment. "Okay."

"Thanks."

She folded the list in half and dropped it into her purse. "I won't be on campus tomorrow. I'll have time to check the school records the following morning. We can touch base later that day. I'll be at the clinic the entire afternoon. You can call me there." She closed her purse and glanced at her watch. "Is that it?"

"One more thing. How would you describe her relationship with Judge McCormick?"

"Her relationship? She was his law clerk."

"Did she talk about him?"

She leaned back in her chair. "Yes and no. The first year of her clerkship she talked about him all the time."

"Good or bad?"

"All good. She worshipped the man. Thought he was a genius." She shook her head in disbelief. "You worked with him, right? I had a couple of cases before McCormick back when he was a state court judge. We both know that when it comes to judges, he's no Learned Hand. But not to Judith that first year. You'd have thought she was clerking for Moses."

Hirsch nodded, surprised that she knew that part of his own history. Had she looked him up or known it all along?

"The whole thing was strange that first year of her clerkship. Like she'd become a Moonie. Never complained about his temperament on the bench, even though it's awful. Never complained about working for him, even though he's supposed to be one of the worst judges to clerk for in this district."

"Really?"

"Absolutely. Former clerks I've talked to tell me he's arrogant and impatient and irritable. But to hear Judith talk about him that first year, you would have thought she was working for Mister Rogers."

"But that changed?"

"Oh, yes."

"What happened?"

"I never found out. Around the middle of her second year, she stopped talking about him. Completely. A few times I tried to ask her how the clerkship was going, but she'd just deflect the question, telling me she didn't want to talk about work."

Hirsch asked, "Do you think they had an affair?"

She stared at him. "The thought crossed my mind."

"Why do you say that?"

She shrugged. "Pure conjecture. She didn't have a boyfriend, and he was divorced. The first year she adored him, and then all of sudden she wouldn't talk about him. He was a skirt chaser even when he was married. He had a reputation." She leveled her gaze at him, her eyes cool. "Not unlike some other powerful men."

He met her gaze, a hint of a smile on his lips. "Maybe he changed. Sometimes that happens."

"Usually not."

She checked her watch, reached into her purse, took out a business card, and handed it to him. "I need to go. This has my office number and the number at the clinic. I should have something on those names the day after tomorrow."

He stood as she did. She slipped on her coat and turned to him as she buttoned it.

"Thank you, Dulcie."

She shook her head. "No need to thank me. I'm not doing this for you. Judith was a wonderful person. If her death is someone else's fault, and if I can help make the case against that someone, I'm happy to do so. But not for you. And not for me. And not for her father. Just for her."

She turned and left.

Just like that.

He watched through the coffeehouse window as she stepped through the snow toward her car. He felt the ache of desire, something he hadn't felt in years. But he also felt the sting of knowing that she detested him.

11

MISSY Shields looked up from her milk shake and gave him an exaggerated eye roll. "What-*ev*-er."

She had that sorority thing down pat. French manicured nails, perfect makeup, eyes a vivid contact-lens blue, shoulder-length hair too blond and too puffy. Facial expressions announcing emotions like Kabuki masks—wide eyes, O-shaped mouth, hands pressed to cheeks, eyebrows arched. Prada bag on the seat beside her in the booth. BGBG suit with a frilly blouse unbuttoned at the throat to reveal a David Yurman platinum choker.

But what made the persona noteworthy was what it hid. While Missy Shields might still affect the perky princess crowned Sweetheart of SAE's Spring Fling her junior year, she was now a young partner at Drahner Cortez LLC, known in the legal community as Drawn & Quartered. It was an aggressive litigation boutique headquartered in West Palm Beach with a nationwide class-action practice. Missy Shields had earned her stripes in the Enron class actions down in Houston and in tobacco litigation in several states. Drawn & Quartered was one of six law firms serving as lead cocounsel for the plaintiffs in *In re Turbo-XL Litigation*, and Missy Shield was one of three attorneys from the firm on the case.

Hirsch found her the same way he found Dulcie Lorenz, during that long afternoon of digging through boxes of Judith's personal belongings in Abe Shifrin's basement. Unlike Dulcie, though, he didn't actually find Missy by name. He'd come across two recurring telephone numbers on Judith's phone bills, both in the 561 area code. The first call was on November 9 of the year before Judith died. The calls continued on and off for about seven weeks—three calls one week, four the next, one the following week, eight the week after, and then gradually tapering off. There were no calls after the first of the year.

He had dialed both phone numbers that evening. The first was answered on the fourth ring.

"You have reached the law firm of Drahner Cortez LLC. Our office is closed now. If you know the extension of the party—"

He had hung up, mystified. He recognized the law firm name but didn't make the connection to the Peterson Tire case.

He had checked the front pages of his telephone directory, found the map of area codes, and confirmed that 561 was indeed West Palm Beach, Florida.

Why did Judith call a south Florida law firm, he paused to count, thirteen times over a two-month period? A personal legal matter? Something else?

He called the second number, also answered on the fourth ring:

"Hi there," a cheerful woman's voice said. "You've reached Rob and Missy. We'd love to talk but we can't come to the phone right now, so like please leave us a message at the beep and we'll—"

He tried again an hour later, got the recording, hung up, tried back a third time, and Missy answered. He told her who he was and explained why he was calling.

"Oh, poor little Judith," she'd said. "I miss her so."

From her tone of voice and the number of calls Judith had made to her home number, he'd assumed the two had been dear friends. Instead, he learned that they'd been merely casual acquaintances in college who'd gone their separate ways after graduation. They met freshman year in Political Science 101, a lecture class with assigned seats in alphabetical order. Thus Shifrin found herself next to Shields. They became friendly that semester and occasionally had lunch together. The relationship went nowhere, though. Judith was living at home, and Missy was pledging a sorority. They lost touch after that first semester. Both were poli-sci majors, though, and they got reacquainted senior year when they shared the same faculty adviser and took the same honors seminar on the Vietnam War. After graduation, Missy moved back home to south Florida. She didn't see or talk to Judith again until a Peterson Tire hearing in St. Louis nearly five years later.

When she'd mentioned that hearing during their first phone call, Hirsch had been surprised, wondering what she'd been doing in that courtroom, never even imagining from her "whatevers" and "for sures" that she was an attorney, thinking instead that perhaps she was related to one of the claimants, or maybe she was someone's paralegal.

But when he asked her if there would be a good time for them to talk about Judith, she answered, "How 'bout like over lunch the day after tomorrow?"

"Down there?"

"No, silly. In St. Louis. I've got to be up there in the morning to argue a motion before Judge McCormick. I'll be done by noon. We can talk then, but only if it's over lunch at Crown Candy Kitchen."

"Crown Candy?"

"For sure. Their BLTs and shakes are to die for."

She was working on that milk shake now—a peanut butter one, her head bent over the tall glass, lips puckered around the straw.

As he'd learned over lunch, there'd been no grand reunion when the two women spotted each other that first time during a court hearing. It had been about a week after Halloween the year before Judith's death. Judith had been seated in the empty jury box, a yellow legal pad on her lap, taking notes as Missy argued the motion. Although she looked familiar, Missy couldn't connect the face with a name or a history. After the hearing, Judith approached and introduced herself. She suggested maybe they could meet that afternoon for a cup of coffee. Missy said absolutely yes.

"It was like a totally awesome opportunity for me," she explained to Hirsch.

Missy knew that a relationship with her old college acquaintance would give her unique access, since Judith was the sole law clerk assigned to *In re Turbo XL Litigation*. That meant that Missy could giggle with her over college memories and gossip about former classmates and catch up on their lives since graduation and along the way try to pick up some insights into the judge's attitude and perspective on the case, especially specific claims. She just had to be careful not to cross the line and place Judith in an awkward position by initiating any conversation about the case.

But Judith had no interest in giggling over college memories or gossiping about former classmates or catching up on their lives since graduation. And Judith hadn't invited Missy for coffee to reminisce. She wanted to talk about the case, but not the merits. Instead, she wanted to talk about the discovery materials, namely, the documents produced, the answers to interrogatories, the testimony at depositions.

Missy quickly saw that Judith's focus was not on the topics Missy had expected. Judith had no interest in the physics of tire tread separations or the testimony of the engineering experts concerning manufacturing defects or the economic losses to the victims' loved ones or any of the other issues that Missy viewed as the heart of the case. Instead, Judith was fascinated by the corporate structure of the Peterson Tire Corporation—the chain of command, who did what, who was there now, who'd been there before but was now gone, what positions each person had held while employed at the company's headquarters. And not just the top executives. She was interested in everyone within the organization, including secretaries and filing clerks and mailroom employees. Anyone and everyone who'd worked at the headquarters.

"Is that in Knoxville, Tennessee?" Hirsch asked.

"That's right."

He was thinking of all the calls on Judith's phone bills to the 423 area code. Unlike the pair of phone numbers in the 561 area code—one for Missy's home phone and one for her office phone—at least three dozen different phone numbers in the Knoxville area code had appeared over a five-month period beginning in April of Judith's last year. She'd called the same number more than once only four times, and none more than twice.

Hirsch asked Missy about her telephone conversations with Judith. What did they talk about? What did Judith want?

Judith's first call was just a few days after they'd met for coffee in St. Louis. She wanted to know: 1. What kinds of discovery materials existed, 2. How much of it there was, and 3. how much had been converted into computer files.

The answers were: 1. every kind, 2. tons, and 3. all.

As Missy explained, over three hundred witnesses had been deposed. Transcripts of those depositions totaled almost four hundred thousand pages. As for documents, Peterson Tire alone had produced more than one million pages of them. With numbers that high, computer storage-and-retrieval systems were indispensable. Missy's firm had all of the deposition transcripts entered into a searchable database. You typed in a keyword or phrase, pressed the search key, and the computer retrieved every reference by every witness to, say, the March 4 memo from Terry Fitzgerald to Jim Hedstrom. So, too, Missy's firm had used imaging software to replicate, one by one, the entire warehouse of documents produced by Peterson Tire. Those documents were also in a searchable electronic database. Thus, if you wanted to see all memos between Terry Fitzgerald and Jim Hedstrom, you could type in the search request and the computer would retrieve an image of that March 4 memo along with dozens of others between the two men.

Judith called back a few days later to ask for copies of those databases to load onto her computer. Missy was taken aback by the request. She'd never had a court ask for the raw discovery data; instead, the court only addressed those discovery materials that became an issue, either before or during trial. Judith assured her that she wanted nothing of an attorney-client nature, and certainly nothing privileged. She explained that as the sole law clerk on the case, she needed an efficient way to access the voluminous discovery records. That way, whenever certain testimony or category of documents became the subject of a motion filed in the case, Judith could quickly retrieve the relevant materials and, if necessary, print off copies for the judge.

The request sounded reasonable to Missy. Even better, it would give her firm a chance to do a favor for the judge's law clerk at little cost, since it simply involved copying existing electronic files onto CD-ROMs.

Hirsch asked, "Was she getting similar materials from lawyers for the other parties?"

"I have, like, no idea. I didn't ask, and she didn't volunteer."

"Were you able to get her what she wanted?"

"Totally. Next time I went to St. Louis, I brought along the disks."

"What about your subsequent phone calls with her?"

"She had lots of questions."

"About what?"

"Like I said, mostly about employees at the headquarters. Who was this guy? Was he still there? If not, did I know where he lived now? What did he do for the company? That sort of thing."

"Anyone specific?"

She thought about it. "No one stands out. Just lots of names and lots of questions."

"Did you get all her questions answered?"

"I guess, but it took awhile. Judith was an e-mail fanatic. Sometimes I'd have five from her in one day."

"Same types of questions?"

"Pretty much, but she started having specific questions about documents, too. I finally put her in touch with Becky, who was one of our document paralegals. Judith kept poor Becky busy answering questions."

"How long did that last?"

"I think like a couple months. I guess she finally got all her questions answered,'cause it was like, poof, and then no more."

"No more?"

"No more e-mails, no more questions."

"When did that happen?"

She thought about it. "March maybe."

"You mentioned her e-mails. Do you still have any of them—the ones to you or to your paralegal?"

"I'll ask Ray tomorrow. He's our systems guy. If they're still in there, Ray will know how to find them."

"If he finds any, could you ask him to print out a copy for me? I'm interested in the ones she sent to you, the ones she sent to your paralegal, and the replies."

"For sure."

"One last thing. Did Judith ever talk to you about Judge McCormick?"

Missy gave him a curious look. "Talk about him? In what way?"

"In any way—personally or professionally."

She thought about it as she poked her straw around the bottom of her empty milk shake glass.

"Not exactly . . . well, there was this one time. It was several months later. I was up for some mini-trials that summer. We were riding down the courthouse elevator over the lunch break, just Judith and me. She asked what we thought about the mini-trial procedure. If we were satisfied with the outcomes."

"How'd you answer?"

"I told her we were generally happy, which was pretty much true. We had issues, but I didn't want to cross any line with her."

"What kind of issues?"

"That was what was so weird. Our main issue was the size of the damage awards. And that's the very next thing she asked me. I was, like, 'Whoa.' I wasn't sure how to answer. I mean, she was his law clerk, and he's the one handing out the awards. I finally said that some of us thought some of the awards were on the low side, and she asked, 'By how much?' I told her it varied case by case. Sometimes the numbers were real good, but other times they were, like, low. I was careful not to sound like I was whining."

"How did she react?"

"She wanted specific examples. I was like so uncomfortable, but I finally mentioned a couple recent cases. Like we'd submitted this case the month before that was worth nine hundred and twenty thousand dollars and the judge awarded only seven seventy-five."

"What did she say?"

"Nothing really. She mostly just listened and thanked me. Then the elevator doors opened, we stepped off, and we never talked about it again."

She thought back. "That was like our last conversation. Ever."

12
_____

HIRSCH leaned back in his office chair, laced his fingers behind his head, and stared out his office window into the night. Silhouetted against the dark sky to the north were the factories and warehouses along the Mississippi River, smokestacks pointing to the stars.

So what had he learned? he asked himself.

And where exactly was he now?

He'd spent the last three hours dialing the thirty-eight telephone numbers in the 423 area code—the numbers that had begun showing up on Judith's phone bills in March of the year she died. Eight numbers were disconnected. Twelve were picked up by answering machines, and on each he'd left a short message: his name, telephone number, and a request that they call him collect. Four other numbers rang and rang until he hung up. Three were answered by people who'd had the telephone number less than three years, and thus not at the time of Judith's call. The final eleven were answered by someone who'd had that telephone number back at the time Judith called it. Seven of them had been employees of the Peterson Tire Corporation back then. The other four were wives of employees.

None of the four wives remembered Judith's call, but each promised to ask her husband that night. Five of the seven employees he spoke with remembered the call; the other two didn't. Of the five who did, none recognized the name Judith Shifrin. Three of them couldn't remember any name, but two recalled that the woman had identified herself as—and Hirsch had written it down to be sure—"Esther Summerson." All of the five remembered that she had told them she was a private investigator looking into matters surrounding the handling of the Turbo-XL litigation. Not into matters surrounding the litigation itself, but into matters surrounding *the handling* of the litigation. He wasn't sure whether the distinction made a difference, but the last of the five, and one of the two who'd specifically remembered the name Esther Summerson, insisted on the distinction. His name was Ralph Kindle.

"No, sir," Kindle told him, "the lady said she was investigating the *way* the case was being handled. That was why she wanted them other names."

Hirsch leaned back in the chair and mulled over what Kindle had said. Off in the distance, beyond the factories and warehouses, he could make out the lights of a towboat pushing a double row of barges upriver.

"What the hell are you still doing here?"

He turned from the window as Rosenbloom wheeled himself into his office. He had on his overcoat, unbuttoned, and his fedora was resting on his briefcase on his lap.

"Working," Hirsch said.

"Something profitable, I hope."

Hirsch gave him a shrug. "Maybe some day."

"Not that goddamn Shifrin case again. Talk about piss-ing up a rope." He gave him a jaded look. "*Nu?* You mak-ing any headway?"

"Hard to say. I spent the afternoon calling people in Knoxville."

"Tennessee?"

Hirsch explained about the phone bills and Missy Shields and his thirty-eight calls.

"What do you think she was she looking for down there?" Rosenbloom asked.

"Sounds like she was trying to find someone in the ex-ecutive offices who could talk to her about the tire case. None of the five who remembered her call worked in that area. They were all in sales or marketing or production."

"Isn't Peterson a publicly held company?"

Hirsch nodded. "New York Stock Exchange."

"So why would she bother calling those people? She could find that information on her own. The head honchos are listed in their annual report and in their ten-Ks."

"She wasn't looking for head honchos. She wanted to talk to the people who worked for the head honchos. Sec-retaries, file clerks, office personnel."

"Why?"

Hirsch shrugged. "She didn't say—or at least the ones I talked to don't recall her saying."

"Did they give her any names?"

"Only one of them did. Guy named Kindle. Retired last year. He was a sales manager when Judith called him. She promised to keep his identity confidential if he would give her some names. He did."

"How many?"

"Two. His secretary was friends with the CFO's secre-tary. A woman named Ruth. He couldn't remember her last name. The other was a guy on the accounting staff named

Ron Gammons. Gammons had been Kindle's fraternity brother at the University of Tennessee."

"Did you try to call them?"

Hirsch shook his head. "Gammons is a dead end. Literally. He died of a heart attack about a year ago. As for Ruth, I don't have a last name yet. I'm hoping her telephone number is one of the others on Judith's list. If not, maybe one of those people will know."

Rosenbloom scratched his neck. "There could be a completely innocent explanation to her phone calls."

"Such as?"

"Maybe there was a pending discovery motion in the case. Something having to do with getting access to documents at the company's headquarters."

"I checked the court docket. No such motions."

"The whole time?"

"There were motions. Lots of them. But none that would have caused her to make those calls."

"Nothing's easy, eh?"

Hirsch nodded wearily.

"Hang in there, Samson. You're my man."

Hirsch felt a surge of affection. The bond between them was as intense as it was illogical, and even without the age difference. They had nothing in common but three luminous summers in Minnesota as Sancho and Samson. Hirsch had grown up in the comfort of a middle-class Jewish family of the 1950s—father a mildly successful optometrist, mother a housewife, little sister an annoying presence in the background. Rosenbloom had grown up on the fringe—the only child of a struggling accountant who committed suicide when Rosenbloom was nine, forcing his mother to get a job at the perfume counter at Famous-Barr to put food on the table. Hirsch had a car at sixteen; Rosenbloom rode the bus until he was twenty-five. Hirsch's high school class voted him "Most Likely to Succeed." Rosenbloom's high school class remembered him as the fat kid with the infectious laugh who couldn't do a single pull-up in gym but who regularly corrected the errors Mr. Kohler made at the chalkboard while writing out solutions to calculus problems. Hirsch went to Princeton with a monthly allowance from his father. Rosenbloom went to Washington University with a scholarship and a night job. Hirsch was the golden boy of the law, a Harvard grad who became the youngest chairman in his law firm's history. Rosenbloom, despite an honors degree from the University of Chicago Law School, was deemed "too Jewish" by the major St. Louis firms. Like other brilliant lawyers of his generation deemed "too ethnic," he fashioned a remarkable career handling collection matters and bankruptcy cases, often on referral from the very firms that had rejected him.

Hirsch glanced at his watch. Quarter after seven.

"Me? What are you doing here so late?"

"I was talking with Nathan. It's his birthday."

"Mazel tov." Hirsch felt a pang. "How's he doing?"

Nathan was Rosenbloom's only child—a florist living in Seattle and sharing a condo with his boyfriend, an architect named Todd.

Rosenbloom beamed. "Life is good for my little boy. The shop is doing well. He's playing the piano again. Jazz, God bless him. Even gets an occasional gig at one of the coffeehouses. He and Todd are going up to Vancouver this weekend to celebrate his birthday."

"That's wonderful."

"Oh, he's a good boy, Samson. A good boy."

The mere mention of Nathan's name made Rosenbloom smile. For Hirsch, though, the mere mention of Nathan's name made him wince with shame. He'd skipped Nathan's *bar mitzvah* to attend the *bar mitzvah* of a prominent real estate developer whose business he'd been hustling at the time. He'd missed Nathan's high school graduation party to attend a fund-raiser for a state senator who'd agreed to help his riverboat casino client.

And the neglect extended beyond Nathan. The year the bankruptcy bar honored Rosenbloom as man of the year at their annual banquet, he'd bought a ticket and sent a telegram but hadn't attended. On the morning of the funeral for Rosenbloom's beloved wife, Sarah, dead of breast cancer just two months before their twenty-fifth anniversary, he'd been in a hotel room in the Central West End fucking a lissome paralegal named Stephanie. He showed up on the second night of *shiva*, and assumed that his reliable secretary had made the appropriate donation to an appropriate charity in memory of Sarah.

"She didn't use her own name?"

Hirsch looked up. "Huh?"

"Judith. You said when she made her calls she used another name."

"Oh, right. She told people her name was . . ." he paused to check his notes, "Esther Summerson."

Rosenbloom chuckled. "Nice touch."

"You know her?"

"In a way. You ever read *Bleak House*?"

"No." He remembered his conversation with Dulcie. "It was one of Judith's favorite books."

"Makes sense."

"Why?"

"*Bleak House* is Charles Dickens's version of a legal thriller—and believe me, Charles Dickens could kick John Grisham's ass. Then again, Dickens could kick just about any writer's ass. At the heart of *Bleak House* is this massive lawsuit—a humongous probate matter called Jarndyce and Jarndyce. By the time the novel opens, the case has been pending in chancery court for decades. It's so complex that none of the lawyers or litigants is even sure what it's about anymore. Esther Summerson is this sweet innocent girl who finds herself trapped somewhere in the middle of the case."

"Just like Judith."

"I suppose." After a moment, Rosenbloom added, "An ugly, messy case."

"Peterson Tire?"

"No, Jarndyce and Jarndyce. Lots of waste and corruption."

"Happy ending?"

Rosenbloom smiled. "It's Dickens, man. He loved happy endings."

"Must be nice."

Rosenbloom nodded. "Yeah, to have that kind of control. You don't get that in real life. Bummer, eh?"

13

THE Family Justice Legal Clinic occupied a storefront in an older brick building along Delmar Boulevard about a mile east of Skinker. If you stared hard at the faded letters chiseled into the concrete slab above the storefront, you could just make out the words *CHOSID KOSHER POULTRY*. This area had once been the heart of the Jewish business district. David's father grew up in a three-flat just a few blocks away, went to services at the synagogue around the corner, and met his mother at nearby Soldan High School.

Since then, the three-flat had been razed to make way for public housing, the synagogue became a Baptist church, Soldan hadn't graduated a Jewish student for more than half a century, and his parents were dead.

He stepped into the small reception area of the clinic. Seated behind the metal desk was a heavyset young black woman with braided cornrows. She was on the phone.

"We're open Tuesday through Saturday," she was saying.

He nodded at her and she smiled back, holding up the thumb and forefinger of her free hand to show that the phone call was almost over. Behind her spread the main office area of the clinic, which had been divided into a half dozen cubicles, each large enough to accommodate a desk and three chairs. He could see the tops of heads in several of the cubicles.

A baby was crying. A phone rang in one of the cubicles. A cell phone sounded in another. A mother scolded a child: "Put that down, Demetrius."

On the right side of the room along the storefront window was a law library with several low bookshelves and a rectangular table with four chairs. On the other side was a row of filing cabinets. Along the back wall was a conference table with seating for eight. He could see Dulcie back there, seated alongside a young Hispanic woman who was taking notes on a yellow legal pad. A student, he assumed. Dulcie was paging through a file and making comments to the Hispanic woman, who was jotting them down.

"Can I help you, sir?" the receptionist asked.

"I'm here to see Professor Lorenz. My name is David Hirsch."

A warm smile. "Just a moment, Mr. Hirsch."

She got up and walked toward the back of the office. The front door opened, and Hirsch turned to see a slight black woman in her twenties enter. She was holding the hand of a little black girl, maybe three years old. The woman glanced up at him with tired eyes and then averted her gaze. She took one of the seats in the reception area, pulled the little girl onto her lap, and began unbuttoning her coat as the girl squirmed. In the back of the room, the receptionist was leaning over talking to Dulcie. Then she turned toward the front, and both of them looked at Hirsch. The receptionist gestured for him to come back.

Dulcie stood as he approached. She was wearing brown corduroy slacks, a tan turtleneck sweater, and hiking boots. The colors contrasted nicely—well, strikingly—with her dark curly hair and dark eyes. The look was academic but alluring. Very alluring.

"Welcome to our clinic," Dulcie said.

There was a drop more warmth in her voice today, although just barely.

She turned toward the student, who was gathering her things. "Gloria, this is Mr. Hirsch. He's an attorney in town. Gloria is a third-year from Chicago."

They shook hands. The young woman excused herself, explaining that she had to get back to school to work on a paper.

"Make yourself comfortable," Dulcie said, nodding toward the chairs around the conference table.

He took a seat across from her.

She opened her briefcase. "I was able to match several of those names," she said, "although I doubt whether I found anything worth a special trip to the clinic."

"I had a meeting in Clayton this afternoon," he lied. "Since I was already in the vicinity, I thought I'd drop by."

She was sorting through her papers. "I had the alumni office run your list of names against their lists."

She pulled out a few sheets of paper.

"You had twelve names. There were nine hits. Four were in law school with her. Five were in the same undergraduate class. The alumni offices had current addresses for all nine." She shrugged. "Not much else."

"It's a start. Maybe one of them knows something."

"Something?" She frowned. "Something about what?"

As he weighed his response, he noticed her gaze shift above his left shoulder.

From behind him a young woman said, "Professor Lorenz?"

The voice was familiar. As he started to turn toward the speaker, he made the connection—and the room suddenly seemed to tilt.

He struggled to his feet. She followed him up with her eyes. He took a small step backward as he gazed down at her—at those big green eyes, at the freckles sprinkled over her nose and cheeks, at that red curly hair.

He'd thought about this moment for years. Yearned for it. Worried about it. Wondered how he should handle it if ever given the chance.

"Lauren," he said finally, his voice hoarse.

She lowered her eyes.

He gazed at his baby girl, nearly grown now.

He wanted to hug her to him, to tell her how much he loved her, to apologize. But he didn't. He knew it would startle her, maybe upset her, definitely embarrass her, especially here.

She looked toward Dulcie, her lower lip quivering. "I'll talk to you later."

Turning away, she hurried toward the front, head down. He watched her grab her coat off the rack and push open the front door, stepping into the winter air with her coat only half on, moving now at almost a jog.

He watched her disappear into the night.

And then he turned back. Dulcie was staring at him.

14

SHE shook her head. "I never made the connection."
   "Why would you?" he said.
   "Same last name."
   "Lots of same last names. I went to high school with a
guy named Lorenz. Ted Lorenz. Any relation?"
   She put her hand over her heart in mock surprise. "You
knew Great-grandpa Ted?"
   He smiled and lifted his pint of beer toward her in appreciation. She touched her martini glass in acknowledgment and gave him back a smile. It was a lovely smile.
   Back at the clinic, Dulcie broke the silence by suggesting they go have a drink. She phrased it diplomatically,
mentioning that this terrific jazz trio played down the block
at the Delmar Lounge every Thursday during happy hour
and wouldn't it be nice to catch a session or two before going home.
   The trio was playing when they arrived. The two of
them nursed their first drink without a word, listening to
the remainder of the session, or at least pretending to. By

the time the piano player announced a break, Hirsch had regained control of his emotions.

But just barely.

He hadn't seen either of his daughters in a decade. He missed them both keenly, but his estrangement from Lauren was the most painful. At the time of his arrest, Melissa had been a seventeen-year-old princess immersed in her own world. Lauren had been the baby sister in every respect. The softer one. The vulnerable one. Daddy's little girl, worshipping a daddy who was seldom at home and who rarely had time for her. When he left for prison, Lauren had been an awkward, plump eighth grader with braces and pimples and none of the charm and self-assurance and good looks of her older sister, now an account executive in a Seattle ad agency.

Dulcie asked him about his daughters. He gave her the abridged version. Liza divorced him during his first year in prison and moved back home to Chicago with the girls. Two years later she became Mrs. Ronald Greenbaum, complete with a Gold Coast condominium featuring a breathtaking view of Lake Michigan. Liza made sure he knew that Lauren had gone into therapy shortly after his imprisonment and continued twice a week until she went off to college. She also made sure he understood he was to have no contact with his daughters during his incarceration, claiming it would scar them, driving the point home with a hammer letter from her lawyer.

When he finished, Dulcie said, "Divorce can be cruel."

"I put them through more than a divorce."

He took a sip of beer. They were silent for a while.

He finally said, "I need you to solve a personal mystery."

She gave him a bemused look. "Okay."

"Let me start by narrowing the possibilities. Can I assume that I've never slept with you?"

She laughed. "That's a safe assumption."

He nodded. "Even as boozed up as I occasionally got, I would have remembered someone as remarkable as you."

"That's quite an unusual compliment. Thank you. I think."

He studied her. "If sex wasn't the reason, it must have been an old lawsuit."

"What must have been a lawsuit?"

"The reason you hate me."

She gazed at him. "I don't hate you."

"But once upon a time?"

She thought about it. "Maybe."

"Even so, I'm surprised I don't remember you."

"We never met. We talked on the phone once, but mostly I dealt with your henchmen."

"Which ones?"

"Brian Morgan and Gino Vitale."

"So it was an employment case."

She nodded.

Back then, Brian Morgan had been a junior partner and Gino Vitale an associate at the firm. The two specialized in defending companies sued for employment discrimination. They handled all of the discrimination cases for Hirsch's clients, who loved them. They were a pair of bullies who relished the mismatch of such cases—the big corporation with its litigation war chest versus the lone wage-earner plaintiff and his contingent-fee attorney.

"Who were the parties?" he asked.

"My client was Willie Freeman. Yours was Arch Shipping."

The case didn't ring a bell.

She shook her head in wonder. "You have no idea, do you?"

"That was a long time ago."

"Not for Willie."

He could hear the anger in her voice.

"Refresh my recollection," he said.

"My client almost died in your conference room."

"Oh, that one."

"Yes, that one."

"You were there?"

"I was the one giving him CPR when the paramedics arrived."

He nodded, trying to find the appropriate words. "You saved his life."

"But not his lawsuit."

"His life is more important."

"His job was his life."

Willie Freeman had been a fifty-four-year-old black man who'd sued Hirsch's client for age and race discrimination when his position as loading-dock foreman was eliminated and his duties transferred to the warehouse foreman, a thirty-eight-year-old white male. Hirsch's litigation platoon waged a war of attrition that ended when Willie suffered a massive heart attack seven hours into the fourth straight day of his videotaped deposition.

Hirsch later viewed the moment on videotape. Brian Morgan had just asked him a question about a negative statement by one of Freeman's coworkers. The court reporter was waiting for his answer, fingers poised above the keyboard. Freeman scowled, his breathing shallow. The silence lengthened. Off-screen, the sound of Morgan leafing through his notes stopped. The court reporter leaned toward the witness.

"Sir," she asked, "are you feeling—"

Suddenly, Freeman grimaced and lurched backward. He grabbed his chest as he fell sideways off his chair and disappeared from the screen. The court reporter cried, "Oh, my God!"

Hirsch had been across town at a board meeting when his secretary called to tell him what had happened. He hurried back in time to see them loading the black man into the ambulance parked in front of the building.

Ten days later, while still in the intensive care unit of Barnes Hospital, Willie dropped his lawsuit. Or rather, Dulcie filed the necessary court papers for him.

After their initial shock, Morgan and Vitale milked the victory, entertaining others in the firm with the play-by-play of what came to be known as the Demolition Depo. Hirsch's client had been quite pleased with the result, especially, according to the company's general counsel, with the "deterrence value" of the finale.

Looking back now, of course, he felt sympathy for Dulcie. It was hard to imagine a more crushing defeat. But as he sat there in the bar, the details of the case gradually coming back, he remembered how thin her client's case had been. The court would likely have thrown it out before trial anyway. She would have lost.

Which proved what?

That there were two sides to the story?

There were always two sides.

She had good reason to be angry with him. He'd been lead counsel on the case, the first name on all the pleadings, and thus the person ultimately responsible for everything his firm did in that case, including the implementation of a macho litigation strategy that nearly killed her client and did kill his case.

"If it makes you feel any better," he finally said, "the wheel has turned."

"What's that mean?"

"Judith's case. I'm on the receiving end this time around."

She took a sip of her martini. They were on their second round.

She asked, "How many defendants?"

"Three."

"Represented by big firms?"

"Of course. My old law firm represents Ford. Emerson, Burke represents Peterson Tire."

"Who at Emerson, Burke?"

"Lead counsel is Marvin Guttner."

"He's a creep."

"But a prince compared to Jack Bellows. He's lead counsel for Ford."

"I wouldn't call Bellows a creep," she said. "I'd call him a miserable prick."

"I wouldn't disagree."

"Who's the third defendant?"

"The air-bag manufacturer. They're represented by two lawyers at Egger and Thomas. They've been fairly low key so far."

"Even so, that's three law firms plus one creep and one prick. Do you have any backup?"

"I have an excellent paralegal. She's been helping me with some of the factual research. Once we get into discovery, I'll have her help with the documents."

"One paralegal? That's it?"

"Not quite," he said, smiling. "I have this brilliant law school professor. She's been helping me identify some of Judith's former classmates."

That drew a grudging smile. "Brilliant, yes. But that still doesn't even the odds."

"It gets me closer."

"Speaking of those names, I don't want you to get your hopes up. I don't remember Judith talking to me about any of them. I doubt whether any will have been close enough to qualify."

"Qualify for what?"

"For a loss of companionship claim."

"I'm not looking for that."

She gave him a puzzled look. "Then what are you looking for?"

He chose his words carefully. "I am looking for someone that Judith confided in."

"About what?"

"About her judge."

"What about her judge?"

"I'm not sure. You told me her attitude toward her judge changed that last year."

She nodded. "It did."

He took a sip of beer. "From what I've learned so far, she seemed to have some concerns about the Peterson Tire case."

"What kind of concerns?"

"I don't know, yet. But maybe they included the judge."

"Why would that matter?"

"That's what I'm trying to find out."

Dulcie leaned back in her chair and shook her head. "I'm lost."

The jazz trio was back from break. They opened the set with "Giant Steps," an old John Coltrane number.

He listened to the music, trying to decide how far to bring her inside. In the process, he tried to decipher his motives for doing so.

Dulcie leaned forward so he could hear her over the music. "I'm not following you, David. You've got a wrongful death case on behalf of Judith. I understand that Peterson Tire is a defendant in your case and it's also a defendant in the case before Judge McCormick. So what? Where's the connection between your case and that case?"

"Possibly the judge."

"Which judge?"

"McCormick."

She stared at him. "What does that mean?"

"Abe Shifrin got a copy of the medical examiner's file on Judith. I showed it to a retired pathologist. I was hoping that he could determine whether she'd been conscious after the crash. I was looking for pain and suffering."

She nodded. "Good way to increase the damages."

"There was no autopsy, so I knew there'd be some uncertainty. Still, I thought it was worth a shot."

"And?"

He leaned closer and lowered his voice. "He was fairly sure she was dead before the crash."

She frowned. "What does that mean?"

Leaning even closer, he explained.

When he finished, she leaned back in her chair.

He took a sip of his beer.

She crossed her arms over her chest and stared down at her empty martini glass.

He waited.

She looked up, eyes wide.

"My God, David."

He nodded.

15

IF this had been the deposition of a hostile witness, he would have stopped the line of questioning right there and moved on. He already had the witness staked out, each limb securely fastened down. All of which meant he could save that final killer question for trial. Hit him with it on cross-examination and let the jury look on as he gave you one of those startled-deer-in-a-headlight stares.

But this wasn't a deposition, and Brendan McCormick wasn't a hostile witness. Or at least not for sure.

As he reminded himself yet again, McCormick might be a friendly witness. Judith could have been driving that car that night. She could have lost control on the ice and died in a genuine accident. That's certainly what the police at the scene concluded. And the medical examiner had confirmed. And Henry Granger had emphasized that he couldn't be certain of the cause of death without an autopsy.

But hostile or friendly, Brendan McCormick had locked himself into a time line that began at 6:00 P.M. and ended at 8:43 P.M., which is when the emergency operator logged in the 911 call from Charlie Peckham, the high school kid who found the Explorer half in the woods, jammed against that tree.

And in the process, McCormick had locked himself into a time line that included a critical gap of more than an hour.

6:00 P.M.: That's when McCormick and Judith left the Christmas party at the courthouse downtown. It's what McCormick told the police on the night of the accident, and it's what he'd just confirmed during their witness interview.

7:00 P.M.: That's the latest they would have arrived at McCormick's house. McCormick said that the drive to his house at that time of night took twenty minutes, thirty tops. Hirsch agreed. He'd done that drive himself at six o'clock to be sure—the last four nights in a row, in fact. Nineteen minutes the first time, twenty-five the second, twenty-three the third, twenty the fourth. Toss in an extra ten minutes on the night in question. And then add another fifteen for wintry conditions. But even with all that padding, they would have reached his house no later than seven o'clock.

7:15 P.M.: That's when they supposedly departed from his house with the gifts. McCormick said they loaded the gifts into the back of the Explorer, and then Judith asked if she could drive to the restaurant.

How long to load the gifts?

Ten minutes, McCormick estimated.

"You're sure?"

McCormick had leaned back in his chair and rubbed his chin, mildly amused by Hirsch's question.

They were in McCormick's chambers. Just the two of them.

McCormick had pushed their meeting back from two to five-thirty, and now it was after six. Everyone else in his chambers had gone home for the day, and for the week.

It was Friday night. At least thirty minutes past sundown.

Shabbas, Hirsch thought ruefully.

He should be home lighting the Sabbath candles and saying the blessings. He should have said no when McCormick moved the meeting to five-thirty. An observant Jew—a good Jew—would have said no. *Remember the Sabbath and keep it holy.* Couldn't get much clearer than that. But he hadn't said no. He couldn't. He needed this meeting, and the thought of postponing it even a day had been unbearable. Now was the time.

"Fifteen minutes tops," McCormick finally said, "but I'd say ten. There were only a half dozen gifts. It took us each only one trip from the house to the car."

Hirsch nodded and jotted it down on his legal pad.

No more than 15 minutes to load gifts. Latest departure time: 7:15 P.M.

He stared at the departure time, face deadpan.

Almost ninety minutes after they supposedly left the house.

Hirsch ran through that final scene in his imagination, stretching it out to be sure—Peckham staring at the accident, getting out of the car, tentatively approaching the SUV, peering through the windows, first on the driver's side, then on the passenger's side. Seeing McCormick move, hearing the moan. Peckham reaching for his cell phone, punching in the numbers. How long from the moment he stopped his car until he dialed 911? Ten minutes? Slow it down by five to be safe. Fifteen minutes. That meant he'd arrived at the scene of the accident no later than eight-thirty.

McCormick told the police that he remembered nothing after the crash until the sound of knocking on the window. He didn't know how long he'd been unconscious, and he was still groggy when the paramedics lifted him out of the Explorer.

Left the house at seven-fifteen, discovered by Peckham one hour and fifteen minutes later.

Locked in.

Actually, and fortunately, locked in since the moment he gave his original witness statement to the police more than three years ago.

Hirsch pretended to study his notes, flipping back a page to study something written there.

He looked up with a frown. "So you stopped at your house, got the gifts, and left."

"That's what happened."

"You're sure you didn't hang around the house for a while, maybe have a drink, or perhaps a bite to eat?"

McCormick chuckled. "I hardly think so, David. The holiday dinner at Cardwell's was scheduled for seven-thirty. I was the host. That meant I had to be there at the start, greet my guests. That's why we left the courthouse party early. Had to haul ass out to my house, pick up the gifts, and haul ass over to the restaurant. No time to dawdle over drinks."

Nice, Hirsch thought, jotting down a quick note to make sure he remembered McCormick's words.

"Well," he said, feigning uncertainty, "okay."

"Well? Well what?"

Hirsch shrugged. "Probably nothing."

"Don't pull that shit with me. What's bothering you?"

"Judith's wristwatch was shattered. Presumably in the accident."

"Makes sense."

"But the time doesn't."

"What do you mean?"

"Her watched stopped at eight-fourteen."

"So?"

"So the accident occurred less than half a mile from

your house. According to the time line we just went over, the two of you left your house no later than seven-fifteen."

McCormick pursed his lips and squinted. "I'm not following you."

"Based on the time on her wristwatch, the accident occurred almost an hour after you left the house. That means either the time line is off or her wristwatch is off."

"Maybe the damn thing kept ticking after the accident."

"Maybe," Hirsch said, pretending to consider the suggestion.

He'd actually seen the watch. It was among the personal effects the hospital gave to Abe Shifrin in the large, sealed plastic bag, which also included her wallet and jewelry and purse. The watch had been smashed—the crystal shattered, the face pushed in. He'd shown it to a jeweler, and the jeweler confirmed that the watch would have stopped functioning immediately upon impact. That was because some of the inner workings were crushed as well.

Hirsch wasn't going to tell that to McCormick. His goal wasn't to cross-examine him. That would come later. The goal today was to rattle McCormick's cage a bit. Observe how he handled it.

"Hell, maybe I was drunker than I realized."

"How so?"

"Maybe it took a lot longer at the house than I thought."

"Maybe."

"Even so, what's it matter when we got back in the Explorer? The key is what happened *after* we got in it."

"Your housekeeper had the night off."

McCormick gave him a baffled look. "Huh?"

"Your housekeeper. You gave her the night off."

"Did I?"

Hirsch nodded. "My investigator interviewed her."

"Interviewed her? You're kidding? My housekeeper? Which one?"

"Judy Gonzalez. She was your housekeeper back then."

"Why did you have someone talk to her?"

"I was hoping she could help us fill that time gap, tell us how long the two of you were in the house. She couldn't, though. She wasn't there. She said her normal nights off were Sunday and Monday, but that week you gave her Thursday night off as well."

McCormick shook his head, amused. "David, I'm not here to tell you how to prepare your case, but I doubt whether the jury will give two shits whether we left the house at seven-fifteen or seven-thirty. This lawsuit is all about what happened after we got back in the vehicle."

"You might be right."

"Trust me on this one. The timeline doesn't matter. Maybe I went back in the house to take a leak. Maybe she had to make a phone call. It must not have seemed important at the time, because I honestly don't remember. All I know is that Judith asked to drive, I let her have the keys, we got back in the vehicle, and a minute later we crashed head-on into that goddamn tree. The only part that counts is that last part, the damn crash."

"Then let's talk about the crash."

"Finally," McCormick said.

Hirsch expected nothing new, and that's exactly what he got. Whether McCormick's narrative was based on actual memory or rehearsed fiction, the sequence of events tracked the account he'd given to the police officer at the hospital the morning following the accident: fiddling with the radio, Judith's surprised gasp, looking up from the dashboard, a small animal scurrying across the road, Judith turning hard to the left, the slight acceleration, the tree suddenly jumping in front, her cry of "No!"

"Do you remember anything after the moment of impact?"

McCormick shook his head. "Not a thing."

"No memory of Judith?"

"I'm not following you?"

"Any sound from her after the impact? Groans? Moans? Any movement?"

McCormick frowned up at the ceiling and rubbed his chin. Eventually, he looked at Hirsch and shook his head. "Afraid not. I must have blacked out immediately."

Hirsch smiled. "Nothing's easy."

McCormick gave him a sympathetic look. "That's why settlement might be the best option."

"Probably not here."

"Why?"

"Her father isn't interested."

"Everyone has a price. Even her father."

"I don't know. He's looking for things beyond money."

"Such as?"

"Vindication. A finding of guilt."

"That's just money, David. Get him enough shekels and it'll translate into vindication and guilt."

"Jack up the numbers, eh?"

"Sure. That's the key."

"It's also the problem," Hirsch said, pleased at how McCormick was wandering into the trap.

"What do you mean?"

"I think the defendants might be willing to talk settlement. At least Marvin Guttner suggested as much. But before I meet with him again, I need to be able to jack the numbers up. The best way to do that is with pain and suffering. But that means I need Judith to be conscious after the accident. Even if it's just for a few seconds."

"Ah," McCormick said, grasping the purpose off the prior questions. "Unfortunately, I'm no help there."

"But there's still hope."

"How so? Did that boy see her moving?"

"Oh, no. And she had no vital signs when the paramedics arrived."

"So where's the hope?"

"I just need her to survive for a few seconds. I'll have to find a top medical examiner. I'll have him examine Judith's file—the morgue photos, the X-rays, the medical examiner's report."

"Was there an autopsy?"

"No, but I've done some calling around on that issue. From what I've been told, a top forensic pathologist can often tell the cause of death even without an autopsy."

McCormick gazed at him, eyes neutral. "We know the cause of death."

"Right. But if he can pinpoint the actual medical cause of death, he might be able to determine whether she was conscious after the accident."

"I'm not following you."

"Her death certificate's a little ambiguous. It states the cause of her death was 'blunt force trauma with asphyxia.' Asphyxiation is a nasty way to die. If she was conscious while she was suffocating, there'd be plenty of pain and suffering."

"You think these defendants will pay you more if you can prove a few seconds of pain and suffering?"

"Absolutely. If Judith was conscious as she choked to death, we're talking much bigger numbers. That's why I need a top pathologist."

McCormick studied him. "I guess you'll do whatever you feel you need to do."

Hirsch stood up to go. "That's my job."

16

WHEN Hirsch finished, Rosenbloom leaned back in his wheelchair and shook his head.

"You're nuts."

"Maybe not," Hirsch said.

"*Maybe* not?" Rosenbloom frowned in disbelief. "Maybe isn't enough. You two aren't exactly in the same weight class anymore, Samson. He's a federal district judge, invested with all the powers of article three of the U.S. Constitution. And you, *boychik*, are just a bankruptcy schlub standing there with nothing but your *putz* in your hand. Not"—he turned toward Dulcie, who had just returned to the dining room carrying a bottle of red wine, a corkscrew, and three wineglasses—"that I am suggesting that David's penis is anything less than imposing." He placed his hand over his heart. "Heaven forfend. By all accounts, it is a most noteworthy appendage—a handsome and imposing instrument."

"How nice for you, David." She handed him the wine bottle and corkscrew. "Pour us some wine."

"My point is," Rosenbloom said to Hirsch, "that all you got is your noteworthy appendage. Brendan McCormick may be a knucklehead, but he's an article three knucklehead, and that means he's virtually untouchable. Worse yet, you don't have hard evidence of anything beyond the fact that he is a knucklehead."

Hirsch twisted down the corkscrew. He looked up at Rosenbloom and smiled. "It's still early."

They were having dinner at Dulcie's house, an arrangement Hirsch learned of just twenty minutes before they arrived. Rosenbloom had been waiting for him in front of Anshe Emes when the Saturday afternoon services ended. As Hirsch emerged from shul, he heard the familiar tap of a horn. He turned, surprised to see Rosenbloom seated in his Cadillac, engine idling. Rosenbloom gestured him over, lowering the driver's-side window as he approached.

"Hop in, Samson. We got a dinner date."

"With who?"

"Your professor pal."

On the ride over, Rosenbloom explained that Dulcie had called him at the office that morning, anxious to hear about Hirsch's meeting with the judge.

"I told her she wasn't the only one, but that we'd have to wait till Saturday night to find out because the Reb Hirsch doesn't answer his phone until sundown."

During Rosenbloom's telephone conversation with Dulcie that morning, he'd mentioned that Federal Express had just dropped off a delivery for Hirsch from someone in Florida named Shields. The package contained what appeared to be several dozen printed e-mails. Dulcie recognized Missy's name from her conversation with Hirsch. She asked if she could drop by his office that afternoon, explaining that she was curious to look at the e-mails. She didn't mention that she was also curious to finally meet Rosenbloom, whom she'd seen only in the photograph on the back cover of the metropolitan St. Louis telephone directory, staring into the camera under the caption. "THE ROSENBLOOM FIRM: TOUGH LAWYERS FOR TOUGH TIMES."

She arrived at his office shortly after noon and spent an hour reviewing the packet of materials from Missy Shields. On her way out, she suggested that Rosenbloom and Hirsch come by her house for dinner that night. That way she could hear what happened with Judge McCormick, too. Rosenbloom accepted the invitation with delight. As became apparent to Hirsch during the short drive from shul to her house, Rosenbloom's enthusiasm was less about Missy's documents and more about Dulcie's good looks.

Hirsch yanked the cork out of the wine bottle.

"Okay." Rosenbloom held up his hands in a gesture of appeasement. "Let's assume McCormick really did do something nasty to that poor girl. If so, what was the purpose in telling him about the time gap and the pathologist? All you're doing is poking a stick at a snake."

"Exactly," Hirsch said.

"Exactly what?" Rosenbloom frowned. "If he's actually guilty, what's the point of fucking with him?"

"An old litigation ploy." Hirsch paused to fill each of their wineglasses. "When your case is stalled, you lob a hand grenade into the middle of the lawsuit and wait for people to scramble. If you watch carefully, sometimes you get an opportunity."

"And sometimes you get blown up."

Hirsch took a sip of wine. "But not often."

"Not often. *Oy.*" Rosenbloom gave Dulcie an exasperated look and turned back to Hirsch. "This is no ordinary lawsuit. If he really killed her, now he knows you've discovered a hole in his story. A one-hour hole. He also knows you just might find a forensic pathologist who could raise a genuine issue about the cause of death. You get blown up here, *boychik*, it'll be no metaphor. They'll need a new *gabbai* to say *Kaddish* for the old one."

Hirsch smiled and shook his head. "No one's getting blown up yet." He turned to Dulcie. "What about Missy Shields's e-mails? What did you find?"

"Let me get our food ready and we can talk over dinner."

Hirsch stood. "I'll help."

The aromas of garlic and fresh tomatoes and basil and oregano and Parmesan cheese filled her kitchen. A savory tomato sauce bubbled in the pan. Garlic bread warmed in the oven. Spaghetti noodles were churning in the boiling water. She'd omitted the meat from her sauce in deference to his dietary restrictions. Not easy to find kosher Italian sausage, she explained as she chopped anchovies for the Caesar salad. He tested one of the spaghetti strands and then poured the pot of boiling water and noodles into the colander. Shaking out the extra water, he turned out the spaghetti into the serving bowl.

It felt good to be in a real house again, to be in a real kitchen helping prepare a real homemade dinner. He glanced over at Dulcie, who was scraping the chopped anchovies off the cutting board into the wooden salad bowl. She looked lovely tonight in a navy turtleneck and snug faded jeans.

From the den came the sound of a televised basketball game.

"Is your son in there?" he asked.

She glanced over and nodded. "His name is Ben."

BEN was slouched on the couch facing the television. He was leaning against an oversized throw pillow, the remote in hand, staring at the screen, unaware of Hirsch watching from the doorway. The boy was maybe fourteen— slender, on the verge of puberty, still more child than man. Baggy cargo pants, oversized black-and-tan-checked shirt, orange T-shirt beneath, floppy white socks.

Hirsch glanced at the television screen long enough to take in the teams and game situation—Lakers and Celtics, early in the second quarter, Lakers up by eight. Now ten.

He waited for a commercial break.

"You a Celtics fan?"

Ben turned, surprised to see him standing there. He shrugged. "Not really."

"They were good when I was your age."

"You like them?"

"Not really, but I never liked the Lakers, so I guess that makes me a Celtics fan tonight."

After a moment, the boy said, "I like Shaq."

"Me, too. I'm just tired of them winning every year."

The boy smiled. "Like the Yankees, huh?"

"Tired of them, too."

"My mom likes the underdogs."

"How 'bout you?"

"I like the Cardinals. And the Blues."

The basketball game resumed. They watched in silence— Ben on the couch, Hirsch leaning against the doorjamb, arms crossed over his chest.

"Do you play basketball?" Hirsch asked during the next break in the action.

The boy shrugged. "Not very good."

He was a cute kid, this Ben. Big brown eyes, long eye-lashes, his mother's strong nose, curly hair.

Hirsch came around the couch and sat alongside Ben.

"I'm David," he said.

Ben glanced at him and nodded. "Hi."

They watched the game side by side, their conversation consisting of random comments on the action:

"Nice shot."

"Why isn't that traveling?"

"He called that a foul?"

Just two guys watching a game on the tube. Nothing forced.

He could hear Rosenbloom and Dulcie talking in the other room. He glanced over at the boy.

He loved his daughters. Adored them. Still, a boy would have been a nice addition. Someone to teach how to shoot a layup. How to hit a baseball to the opposite field.

Dulcie poked her head into the den. "Dinner's ready, boys."

Ben looked over at Hirsch.

Hirsch said, "You'll be able to catch the fourth quarter after dinner."

The boy pointed the remote at the TV and pressed the Power Off button.

T HEY didn't talk about the case during dinner, or at least until Ben finished his dinner. Dulcie let him go back to watch the end of the basketball game and told him she'd call him for dessert.

She'd made a copy of the printed e-mails that Missy Shields had sent Hirsch. She retrieved the copies from her briefcase in the front closet. As she sorted through them she explained that they confirmed Missy's recollections, namely, that Judith had been focused on the names of the people who staffed the executive offices of Peterson Tire. For the most part, the e-mails were queries about the whereabouts of specific Peterson Tire employees mentioned in depositions or shown as recipients on interoffice memoranda. Several e-mails asked Missy's paralegal how to retrieve certain documents from the database. All of her queries seemed to tie back to the identities, job titles, and job descriptions of employees in the executive offices in Knoxville.

"Someone better start checking the rest of those Knoxville numbers," Rosenbloom said. "Find out if she ever reached anyone important at headquarters. Find out what the hell she was looking for."

"Speaking of telephone numbers," Dulcie said to Hirsch, "I tried calling her classmates."

"Classmates?" Rosenbloom asked.

Hirsch explained how Dulcie had matched several of the names in Judith's personal papers with actual students who were at Washington University during her undergraduate or law school years.

"I talked with some," she said.

"And?" Rosenbloom asked.

"Not much. Judith mainly kept in touch by e-mail, usually by way of a short note at the holidays or on their birthdays. One or two remember a phone call on a happy occasion, but mostly it was e-mail. Occasionally she'd forward by e-mail something she thought they'd be interested in—maybe an article she'd found on the Internet, an opinion she'd worked on for McCormick, an essay from an online newspaper, a joke someone had sent. One of her classmates, a girl named Sharon Berger, saved an e-mail Judith sent her after the birth of her first child. I had her forward it to me." She smiled. "It's classic Judith—warm and thoughtful."

"Do you have it here?" Hirsch asked.

"Back in my study." Dulcie stood. "I'll bring it out."

Rosenbloom gazed at her rear end as she walked down the hall. "My goodness," he said with appreciation. "You think the professor gives private tutorials?"

Hirsch flipped through the batch of Judith's e-mails that Missy Shields had sent. Most were brief questions:

> *p 58 of pierce depo. witness mentions someone in executive offices named eva. who is she? what else do u have on her? thanks!*

> *remington depo 218—letter from korte, v/p marketing. typist's initials at bottom read "btr" do u know who that is?*

> *is there a secretary in exec offices named ruth? last name? u have address?*

And so on.

He noted her e-mail address: judith_shifrin@moed.uscourts.gov.

He flipped back through the other e-mails to make sure they all had that address.

Dulcie returned with the e-mail from Judith to her friend Sharon. She handed it to Hirsch. In it, Judith congratulated her friend on the birth of a little girl, wished her much joy, and ended with a poem Judith described as her favorite blessing for a new baby. The poem was "For the Child" by Fannie Stearns Davis and included the following stanza:

> And you shall run and wander,
> And you shall dream and sing,
> Of brave things and bright things,
> Beyond the swallow's wings.

He looked at the top of the page. Same e-mail address. The time on the e-mail showed that Judith had sent it at 6:52 P.M.

"She only had the office computer," Hirsch said.

"What do you mean?" Rosenbloom asked.

"There was no computer among her personal belongings. I've looked through her canceled checks and credit card bills. I didn't see any payments to an Internet service provider." He held up the e-mail he'd just read. "This is clearly personal. She sent it at night from her office e-mail address."

"So?" Rosenbloom said. "I only have one computer. So do you."

Dulcie said, "What David means is that everything she wrote and every e-mail she sent and every e-mail she received was on that computer."

Hirsch said, "And if she was as methodical as you say she was, then whatever she was looking for—"

"And whatever she found," Dulcie added.

"Will be on that computer," Hirsch said.

"Unless it was erased," Rosenbloom said.

"It's hard to erase anything from a computer," Dulcie said. "There are data recovery firms that specialize in retrieving deleted files. When it comes to hard drives, nothing's gone forever."

"First things first," Rosenbloom said. "You have to find the computer. She's been gone for more than three years. That means her computer has long since been reassigned to someone else in the courthouse."

"Most likely to the next law clerk to occupy her office," Hirsch said.

"Even so," Dulcie said, "you'll need to get access to it to find out what's on the hard drive."

"How are you going to do that?" Rosenbloom asked.

"Russ Jefferson," Hirsch said.

Rosenbloom said, "You really think Jefferson is going to stick his neck out like that for you? That guy is strictly by the book."

"He might," Hirsch said. "We used to work together."

"That was a long time ago."

Hirsch shrugged. "It's worth a shot."

17

WHEN he'd arrived, he paused to stare at the legend over the entrance:

OFFICE OF THE UNITED STATES ATTORNEY
EASTERN DISTRICT OF MISSOURI

RUSSEL T. JEFFERSON
UNITED STATES ATTORNEY

United States Attorney.

To call it ironic didn't capture the embarrassment and the remorse. Of course, Russ Jefferson was hardly the first person to trigger that brew of emotions, a recurrent feature of his postincarceration life.

And now, as he sat in Russ Jefferson's large office and watched his former colleague page through the documents he'd given him, he couldn't help but think how improbable this meeting would have seemed to both of them back in their days together as assistant U.S. attorneys. They'd joined the same day in June twenty-six years ago. There'd been four rookie AUSAs that year—Hirsch, Jefferson, Gloria Dowd, and the big ex-jock from Mizzou named Brendan McCormick.

Although none of them had much in common, the contrast between Hirsch and Jefferson had been the most striking. Hirsch the hotshot Harvard grad, Jefferson the unassuming black man who'd gone to night law school at St. Louis University while working days as a claims adjuster for an auto insurer. One smooth and assured, the other awkward; one quick, the other a plodder; one treating the job as a mere stepping-stone, the other as a calling; one taking every opportunity to schmooze his superiors for high-profile cases, the other working late hours on the dregs of the office's criminal docket.

Back then, Hirsch thought of Jefferson, if he thought of him at all, as a drudge. During the years they worked together in that office, he spoke to Jefferson no more than a dozen times, and rarely longer than a stop at the watercooler or a ride in the elevator. They had lunch maybe once. It wasn't that he snubbed the black attorney. It was just that Jefferson wasn't relevant to Hirsch's ambitions.

Russell Jefferson's contemporaries left the U.S. Attorney's Office one by one for lucrative jobs in the private sector or prestigious jobs in government. Hirsch left for a prosecutor gig in the Justice Department's elite antitrust division in Washington, D.C. McCormick left to become county prosecutor. Gloria Dowd left to join the litigation department of Chicago's Kirkland & Ellis. But Jefferson continued to plug away. Gradually, he came to be recognized—first by the other AUSAs, eventually by each succeeding U.S. attorney—as *the* indispensable member of the staff. Three years ago, the new president opted for merit over politics and appointed Jefferson to the top job.

And thus, as the farce of Hirsch's life continued unfurling, the man he'd once considered irrelevant was now his best hope. And despite their nonrelationship in the past, and despite whatever snubs Jefferson may have felt from him, Hirsch knew that Jefferson would give him a fair shake. He was, as Hirsch's grandfather would have said, a real *mensch*.

Jefferson shook his head. "I have to tell you, David, you have not given this office much to go on."

"I'm not asking for a search warrant, Russ. You don't need probable cause to find out who has her computer."

"But you want access to that computer as well."

"Not to any current files. I'm just looking for data on the hard drive that goes back to when she was alive. You could probably have one of your computer guys download that stuff in an hour. Nothing current. Nothing created by anyone else. Just her stuff."

"On what grounds, David? On the basis of a conversation with a retired pathologist who raised a question about the medical examiner's determination of cause of death? I am supposed to seek authority for a search and seizure on that ground?"

"Not a search and seizure. Forget that aspect. Forget the entire criminal element. Pretend I never mentioned it. Let's assume that this is just an ordinary wrongful death case. And who knows? Maybe that's all it will turn out to be. I still need to give the jury a sense of Judith Shifrin in her final days, if for no other reason than to let them know what she was like. I can't do that by myself. I didn't know her, and what little her father may have known is fading fast. But she happened to be someone who used her computer to keep in touch with friends and loved ones. Access to those files might just give me access to the Judith I need to show the jury."

Jefferson tugged at the edge of his thin mustache as he listened. Except for the bald spot on top and the deep lines in his face, he looked the same as he had back in their AUSA days together, right down to his outfit. Jefferson was the antithesis of funky and cool. Hirsch had never seen him in jeans or even khakis. He'd always projected the look of the hardworking, sober African-American prosecutor: close-cropped hair, no sideburns, pencil-thin mustache, starched white shirt, thin tie, dark suit, shiny black wingtips.

Jefferson drummed the fingers of his right hand on the top of his desk as he studied Hirsch.

"This is highly irregular, David."

"But legal."

"Perhaps."

Hirsch smiled. "Does that mean you'll do it?"

"It means that I shall take this one small step at a time. I shall speak with the court administrator. His office should have a record of the whereabouts of the computer in question. Once I obtain that information, I will consider allowing a review of the files contained therein. The older files, that is. Nothing since the time of the young lady's passing."

"I really appreciate that, Russ. And if I happen to find anything of interest to your office in those files, I will—"

"No." Jefferson held up his hand. "There can be no quid pro quo here, David. You are an officer of the court. If there are materials in those files of a potentially incriminating nature, I shall assume that you will fulfill your professional responsibilities in connection therewith."

"Your assumption is correct."

Jefferson nodded. "Then I shall be in touch once we locate the computer."

Hirsch stood and extended his hand. "Thank you, Russ."

Jefferson stood and shook his hand. "Miss Shifrin was a fine young lady, David. Diligent and hardworking. Respectful of the office and of her role therein. Although I only had a few occasions to deal with her, I was impressed.

I had even mentioned to her that she should consider our office after the conclusion of her clerkship. If anything untoward occurred, well . . ." He paused. "But first things first. Good to see you, David."

18

TWO sentences into the argument, Jack Bellows had revved himself up to Full Smug Mode—face flushed, bushy eyebrows arched, almost sneering as he presented his position to Judge Kalnitz, who was rubbing his goatee while he listened to the argument.

"Your Honor," Bellows said, shaking his head in disgust, "Mr. Hirsch's motion is merely another example of his utter disrespect for the rule of law. Even if we assume that this database Mr. Hirsch so ardently seeks is somehow relevant to this lawsuit, which it surely is not, the court that is in charge of that database has entered a protective order stating that no one else can have access to it. My client, the Ford Motor Company, is a party to that case and is bound by the terms of that order. We understand the rule of law, Your Honor, and we respect the rule of law. If Mr. Hirsch did as well, he wouldn't dare attempt this end run around that court's jurisdiction. Instead, he'd go up there and try to present his meritless motion to the court in charge of that database. Instead, he's trying to sneak those documents out through the back door."

"That's the Enlow case?" Judge Kalnitz asked, looking through the file.

"Correct, Your Honor," Bellows answered. "That was a class action against my client and General Motors in Springfield, Massachusetts. I have a copy of the protective order entered in that case right here."

Bellows handed the judge a copy of the four-page order and glanced toward Hirsch with a smirk.

They were in court this morning on Hirsch's motion to compel Bellows's client to produce an elaborate computer file of information compiled by the plaintiff's expert witness in the *Enlow* class action. He'd learned of the file through one of the Web sites maintained by plaintiffs' personal injury lawyers specializing in SUV crash cases. Indeed, he'd learned far more about the *Enlow* case and the protective order than Bellows apparently suspected.

Standing at the podium with Hirsch and Bellows were Beth Purcell, one of the attorneys for OLM, Inc., the airbag manufacturer, and Marvin Guttner. The four of them waited for Judge Kalnitz to finish reading through the protective order.

Hirsch had been surprised to see Guttner. He rarely appeared in court, preferring, as he told Hirsch at their private lunch, to have his minions handle the "procedural minutiae" of his cases. This motion to compel would seem to qualify as procedural minutia. It was just one of the scores of motions in various cases set for hearing that morning as part of the motion docket in Division One.

There were close to a hundred lawyers scattered throughout the large courtroom. Some were reading newspapers or reviewing court papers or chatting quietly as they waited for the clerk to call their motions. The low hum of voices had ceased during Bellows's bombastic presentation. Many in the crowd were watching now, mildly interested in the proceeding.

"Counsel," Judge Kalnitz said to Hirsch, peering over his reading glasses, "this order seems fairly clear to me. It says the contents of that database are strictly confidential and can be disclosed to no one other than the attorneys in that case. It further states that all motions to modify that order must be brought before that court." He looked at Bellows. "Is that accurate?"

"One hundred and ten percent." Bellows grinned and ran his fingers through his shock of reddish-gray hair.

Kalnitz looked back at Hirsch. "Well, Counsel?"

"Your Honor," Hirsch said, "I believe Mr. Bellows stated that his client intends to abide by the orders of the *Enlow* court." He turned to Bellows. "Is that accurate?"

Bellows frowned slightly. "Certainly."

"One hundred and ten percent, right?" Hirsch asked him.

There were a few chuckles from the gallery.

Bellows stiffened. "I informed His Honor that my client was a party to the *Enlow* case and was bound by orders entered in that case."

Hirsch turned to the judge. "The protective order that Mr. Bellows provided the Court was entered in that case two years ago. On April third, I believe."

He waited for the judge to flip to the back page to confirm the date. "Yes. April third."

"As the Court knows, the database compiled in that lawsuit contains a variety of information on more than two hundred traffic accidents involving sport-utility vehicles on icy roads. This is also an accident case involving a sport-utility vehicle on an icy road. There's no question that the information is relevant. The only issue is whether we can have access to it. What Mr. Bellows has failed to disclose to this court is that courts in at least fifteen other cases around the country involving SUV accidents on icy roads have already faced the issue before the court today. The plaintiffs in the first three of those fifteen cases filed their motions with the *Enlow* court in Massachusetts asking for access to the database. The *Enlow* court granted all three of those motions and allowed those plaintiffs access to the database. I've obtained certified copies of those three court orders."

He handed the originals to the judge and copies to Bellows and the other lawyers.

"This simply proves my point, Judge," Bellows announced, waving his copies of the orders. "If Mr. Hirsch thinks he's entitled to this database, let him hop on a plane and make his pitch to the judge in Massachusetts who entered the order sealing that evidence."

Hirsch said, "That is precisely what the fourth plaintiff did, Your Honor." He turned to Bellows. "Would you care to tell the Court what happened that time?"

Bellows's eyes narrowed. "I'm not an attorney in that case," he snapped.

"But your client is a party in that case."

Hirsch turned back to the judge. "The *Enlow* judge did more than simply grant that fourth motion, Your Honor. He entered an order modifying his protective order—the one that Mr. Bellows handed you earlier. Curiously, Mr. Bellows decided not to provide you with a copy of the second order, or even tell you about it. Fortunately, I have a certified copy of it here. As you will see, it specifically refers to the protective order that Mr. Bellows handed to you."

He handed the judge the two-page order and passed out copies to the other attorneys.

"In this order," he continued, "the judge in the *Enlow* case specifically empowered *every other judge* in the country to allow parties in accident cases before them to have access to that database so long as those parties are bound by the same confidentiality terms of the protective order in the *Enlow* case."

He waited until the judge finished reading and looked up.

"Therefore," he said, "I don't need to hop on a plane to Massachusetts, and I don't need to present this motion to the *Enlow* court. Instead, I can present that motion to this Court, just as each of the other eleven plaintiffs in similar SUV accident cases have presented their motions to compel to their courts. I have copies of all of those orders granting those motions to compel if this Court would like to see them. As the *Enlow* court stated in its order modifying the protective order, and I quote, 'There is no reason to prevent victims of similar accidents from having access to this database so long as they agree to abide by the confidentiality restrictions.' Your Honor, I can assure the Court that we agree to abide by those restrictions. Surely, Mr. Bellows has no problem with that. As he told this Court in no uncertain terms, his client intends to abide by the orders of the *Enlow* court." He turned to Bellows. "I assume that is still one hundred-and-ten-percent accurate?"

A few more chuckles from the gallery. Bellows glared back at him.

"I've heard quite enough, gentlemen," Judge Kalnitz said. He peered over his reading glasses at Bellows for a long moment and then shook his head.

"Motion granted. Mr. Hirsch, prepare an order for me to sign." He turned to his clerk. "Call the next case."

THE reason for Guttner's presence became clear when the four of them stepped into the hallway outside Division One. Normally, they would have dispersed, the defendants' counsel talking among themselves as the lone plaintiff's counsel headed for the bank of elevators. Instead, Guttner turned to him with a smile as the other two lingered in the background, watching.

"David," Guttner said, "I thought perhaps that the four of us could talk for a moment."

"About what?"

"There is an empty jury room across the hall," Guttner said. "Why don't we step in there and I can explain?"

The jury room seemed even older than the rest of the 1930s-era Civil Courts buildings. The ceiling tiles were splotched with brown water stains, the long, wood table was gouged and scarred and spotted black with cigarette burns, and the high-backed wooden chairs were rickety and uncomfortable. The wind rattled the tall window, which had a transom operated by a brass crank handle.

Guttner took the seat at the head of the table, his bulk making the chair creak ominously. He gestured to Hirsch to take the seat next to him. Beth Purcell, a prim woman in her thirties who dressed as if she were in her fifties, sat on the other side of the table two chairs from the head, apparently in deference to Jack Bellows. Bellows, though, stood by the far window and glared down at the park across the street.

"David," Guttner began, "I am reminded of that wonderful aphorism attributed to Yogi Berra, who purportedly said that when you come to a fork in the road, you should take it. Well, sir, we have come to that fork. Two paths diverge before us, and each leads to a very different form of closure—one in a final judgment, the other in a settlement. Your motion today signals the start of discovery. If we take that fork, we will soon be generating substantial legal fees, and you, David, will soon be devoting large portions of your days and nights and resources to a case for which you may never be compensated. That is the discovery path. It will lead inexorably, and expensively, to final judgment. The other path leads to settlement. It is a much shorter journey, and a far different form of closure. That's the fork we've come to, David, and Mr. Berra advises that we take it."

Bellows had turned to watch Guttner. The expression on his face suggested that he was unimpressed with his co-counsel's presentation.

"As you will recall, David," Guttner continued, "just a little over a month ago we spoke in general terms of the possibility of an amicable resolution of your lawsuit. As I told you then, I believe that an attorney owes a duty to his client to explore settlement issues in earnest at an early point in the lawsuit. I hope by now that you have had an opportunity to raise the issue with your client. I have with mine, and I know that Ms. Purcell and Mr. Bellows have with theirs."

Guttner paused.

Hirsch said nothing.

Guttner said, "My client is willing to consider a settlement upon reasonable terms. Ms. Purcell and Mr. Bellows advise that their respective clients are also open to discussion of an equitable resolution of the matter." Guttner raised his eyebrows and smiled at Hirsch. "How does Mr. Shifrin view the possibility of settlement?"

"Guardedly," Hirsch said.

"Why is that?" Guttner asked.

Hirsch allowed his gaze to shift to Purcell and then to Bellows, who stood by the window with his arms crossed over his chest.

Turning back to Guttner, Hirsch said, "My client dislikes lawyers, and he dislikes lawsuits. It took him almost three years to file this lawsuit. He filed it because he is haunted by his daughter's death. He filed it because he wants justice and believes he can find it in a courtroom. You may think him naive to seek justice there. You may think he's old enough to know better." Hirsch shrugged. "But you're not him, and you're not haunted by the death of your daughter, and you're not the one determined to seek justice."

They were silent. The only sound was the syncopated clang of the steam radiator.

Hirsch waited. He wasn't going to make it easy for them.

"But what about settlement, David?" Guttner finally said. "What does your client want?"

"He wants justice. He's afraid he won't get it in a settlement."

Bellows snorted. "Cut the crap, David. Your guy may try to delude himself into believing he's filed an action for justice, but have him read his court papers. All he's filed is a civil lawsuit for money. I think it's a bullshit claim, and so does my client. I think you're going to lose, but I didn't call this meeting. Peterson Tire wants to talk settlement, so let's cut the crap here. How much money does he want?"

"I just told you, Jack. He wants justice."

"Good for him. And I want a blow job from Julia Roberts, but how 'bout we talk some reality here?"

Beth Purcell flinched.

"Please, Jack," Guttner said, holding up his hand and shaking his head in reproach.

He turned to Hirsch. "David, we are not engines of justice here. We are merely corporate defendants. All we can offer your client by way of settlement is money."

"You can also give him an admission of liability," Hirsch said.

Bellows burst into laughter. "Are you out of your fucking mind?"

Hirsch waited until Bellows was quiet.

"I didn't call this meeting, Jack," he said. "I'm simply answering your questions." He turned to Guttner. "Do you have any more?"

"David, I can assure you that we understand your client's desire for some measure of justice in this case, for an acknowledgment that someone is responsible for his daughter's tragic death. I truly believe that this will not be an insurmountable hurdle here. We are all creative lawyers. Among the four of us we must be able to devise a way to satisfy your client's desire without prejudicing our clients' interests. So let us assume, at least for now, that we can accomplish that task. That still leaves us with the monetary issue. Rather than review the facts pertinent to liability and damages, facts I daresay we are all conversant with by now, I suggest that we cut to the chase. Even assuming what none of the defendants will concede, namely, that you could actually establish liability, this is not a big-money case. You have virtually no hard damages, and very little in the way of persuasive soft damages. I should think you would be lucky to get fifty thousand dollars out of a jury. Be that as it may, in the interest of getting this case behind us and thereby avoiding significant legal expense, we are prepared to offer you seventy-five thousand dollars to settle the case."

Hirsch shook his head. "Not even close."

"What?" Bellows said. "Are you crazy?"

And that's when it clicked. He tried to remember which Japanese martial art it was. The one that had you use your opponent's strength to disarm himself. The name didn't matter. The concept did.

Hirsch gazed at Bellows, pretending to consider his question. "I'll discuss the offer with my client, but I won't recommend it. Not at this stage of the litigation."

"I don't understand," Beth Purcell said to him. "Why does it matter what stage we're in?"

"It's too early. At least one area of damages is still uncertain."

"What area is that?" she asked.

"Pain and suffering."

"Jesus Christ," Bellows said, "what the hell are you talking about? I saw the medical examiner's report. We all did. She died instantly."

"Not necessarily." Hirsch kept his tone matter-of-fact.

"What's that mean?" Bellows asked.

"The report mentioned asphyxia as part of the cause of death. If she was conscious after the impact, that would have been a horrible way to die. The pain and suffering would be substantial, and so would be your exposure."

"Oh, come on," Bellows snapped. "How are you ever going to prove pain and suffering here? There wasn't even an autopsy."

"But there were X-rays," Hirsch said, "and morgue shots. I understand a good forensic pathologist can do wonders with that stuff."

"Do you believe this guy?" Bellows asked the others, amused. "He's going to tell his client to reject seventy-five grand because a forensic pathologist *might*—not *will*, mind you, just might—opine that this gal was conscious for a few seconds after the accident." He turned to Hirsch. "I got some news for you, pal. Believe it or not, this isn't Ford's first wrongful death case, and this certainly isn't the first time some shyster has tried to inflate his case with this bullshit tactic. Ford has access to the best pathologists in the nation, and you can be sure I'll get one assigned to this case pronto."

Hirsch shrugged. "Fine."

Bellow chuckled. "You've got to understand something, Hirsch. Peterson Tire is the only defendant with any reason to try to suck up to Brendan McCormick here. But even they have their limits. We're sure as hell not holding back much longer. If I were you, I'd jump at Guttner's seventy-five grand like it was a lifesaver,'cause once it's off the table, pal, you're going down. And you're going down hard."

19

HIRSCH was on the sagging couch in Abe Shifrin's living room, his overcoat still on, his briefcase on the floor between his feet. The smell of rotting garbage filled the house.

Abe Shifrin stopped pacing, clutched his hands in front of his chest, and sighed. "Oh, my God."

He gave Hirsch a woeful look and started pacing again, head down, hands now clasped behind his back. The old man hadn't shaved in days. His clothes were wrinkled and stained.

He stopped and turned toward Hirsch, his face a mix of pain and anger.

"Seventy-five thousand? That's what they call an offer? And then what? I'm supposed to forget? Pretend like it never happened? And also I'm supposed to forgive her? Forgive and forget? After what she's done to me? To me?"

He stared at Hirsch. A tear rolled down his cheek. "Never. Tell her forget it."

He started pacing again, head down, mumbling to himself.

Hirsch tried to parse what he'd just heard.

"I don't understand."

Shifrin glanced at him as he paced. "You don't understand? That's because you're not me. You haven't lived with this torment."

Shifrin gestured toward the framed photographs of his wife and daughter on the wall. "Why would she do that to me?"

"Do what?"

"Leave me. And for a *schvartza*, yet. It's a *shanda*, I tell you. It wasn't enough she should leave me. Oh, no. She had to disgrace me as well."

"Are you talking about Judith?"

He held up his hands. "Never say that name around me."

"After what she did"—he made a dismissive gesture—"she's dead to me. I was good to her, sir. A good provider. A nice home. Money for clothes and for jewelry and for whatever else a woman might want. And was she grateful? Did she show respect? Ha! She walked out on me. Left me for another man. For a *schvartza*. And now her lawyers want to buy me off for seventy-five grand?" He shook his fist. "Tell them to shove it. I won't take their bribe money."

Hirsch stood up. "I think you might be confused, Mr. Shifrin."

The old man looked up at him, eyes blinking. "What? What are you saying?"

Hirsch walked over to the framed photos on the wall.

"This is Judith;" he said, pointing. "She was your daughter. This is your wife. Her name was Harriet."

"Harriet? What are you talking Harriet? I think I know who I was married to, sir."

Hirsch shook his head. "No, Mr. Shifrin. Judith was your daughter."

Shifrin looked back and forth between the pictures, a puzzled frown on his face.

Hirsch continued in a gentle voice. "Your wife Harriet died of cancer, Mr. Shifrin. Many years ago. You loved her very much. After she died, your daughter took over many of her chores. She cooked your meals and washed your clothes and cleaned the house. Her name was Judith." He pointed to her photograph on the wall. "That's Judith. She was a good girl, Mr. Shifrin. Judith was killed in an automobile accident three and a half years ago. That's why I am here tonight. I am your lawyer. We filed a lawsuit against the makers of the car and the tires and the air bags. I am here tonight because the defendants have made an offer to settle that lawsuit. They have offered you seventy-five thousand dollars. I have come here to discuss it with you."

Shifrin moved closer to the photograph of Judith. He leaned forward and squinted at it for a moment. He turned to Hirsch, baffled.

"What are you trying to tell me? She's dead? When did this happen?"

20

HIRSCH stood at the picture window of Rosenbloom's high-rise condo and stared into the night sky over Forest Park. In the distance, silhouetted atop Art Hill, were the outlines of the Art Museum and the statue of the city's namesake, King Louis IX astride his horse. Directly over the museum hung a crescent moon.

The living room was dark. A light in the hall cast just enough illumination for him to see the reflection of Rosenbloom in his wheelchair, staring at Hirsch's back.

Hirsch had phoned from his car after leaving Shifrin's house. "Sancho, we need to talk."

"Then get your ass over here."

Rosenbloom's condo, with its parquet floors and graceful fixtures and elegant lines, reminded Hirsch of the Park Avenue and Upper East Side apartments of the New York City lawyers he'd worked with back in his glory days. It was the last place you'd expect to find Seymour Rosenbloom, who seemed far better suited for a two-flat in a middle-class neighborhood. Two years ago, after his M.S.

reached the stage where life in a two-story house was no longer an option, he sold the beloved family home in University City, where he and Sarah had raised Nathan and a menagerie of pets, and moved into West Park Towers, with its all-important elevator running from the underground garage to his condo on the sixteenth floor.

Hirsch had helped him pack his personal belongings over two weekends back then. That had been a difficult journey into the past for Sancho—made especially so by his disease, which seemed to have stripped the protective layer between his memories and his emotions. Plenty of tears those two weekends.

"I have an idea."

Hirsch turned from the window. "Pardon?"

Rosenbloom rolled himself into the living room. "Let's play a game of pretend. Indulge me."

"Go ahead."

"Let's pretend that she really died in the crash. No foul play. No loose ends. Let's pretend it happened exactly the way McCormick and the cops and the medical examiner said it did. You with me so far?"

"So far."

"And let's also pretend that she died instantly. No pain, no suffering. Okay?"

"Okay."

"That's our scenario. Now, let's pretend that the other side offers seventy-five grand. What do you do?"

"I talk to my client."

"What do you tell him?"

"I tell him the offer is too low, but it's a good start."

"What's your counter?"

Hirsch shrugged. "Two fifty, maybe three."

"What's your bottom line?"

"One fifty."

"Maybe less?"

"Maybe."

"What about your client's desire for retribution?"

"You mean the admission of guilt?"

"Think any of the defendants will give you that?"

"No."

"So how do you deal with that?"

"I try for an expression of sorrow, assuming it was really just an accident. I'd let them deny liability but include a paragraph in the settlement agreement stating their deep sadness over what happened to his daughter."

"I like it." Rosenbloom nodded. "They might go for it. You'll be a hero."

"Maybe in your game of pretend. I'm stuck with reality."

"Wait. I'm not done with our game. Let's compare fantasies. If we make mine real, you settle the case, and probably for a nice pile of money. Don't knock that part, my friend. Between the restitution order in your criminal case and child support for Lauren, you're barely one rung above our Chapter Thirteen clients. Be glad your older daughter's out of school. And don't forget old Jack the Ripper, who is about to cry havoc and let slip his dogs of war. There's a pleasant thought, eh? Two years of trench warfare with that cretin. But a settlement, well, a settlement solves everything. It eliminates the litigation death march, earns you a big payday, and maybe even gets you a little positive spin in the press, which wouldn't be such a bad thing. Let's face it, Samson, your media profile could use a little buffing."

Hirsch smiled. "It's tempting."

"Tempting? That's an understatement. Especially if we compare my fantasy to yours, also known as Samson's Last Stand. Our first problem with your fantasy is that this ain't Hollywood and you ain't Luke Skywalker. Our second problem is that before you can catch a killer you need a murder. But let's set those pesky little problems to one side, okay? What if McCormick actually killed her? And let's not forget how big of an 'if' that if is. But let's assume he did. What's that mean for you? It means you're going to be trying to build a circumstantial case for murder against a federal district judge. Even worse, you're going to be trying to build it in the face of a determination by the medical examiner on duty that night that the cause of death was the accident. And just to add one other tiny hitch, she died more than three years ago and wasn't embalmed. That means that key physical evidence—probably the only physical evidence—has decomposed."

Rosenbloom shook his head.

"In the face of all that, Samson, you want to try to gather enough evidence to convince a prosecutor to charge a federal district judge with first-degree murder? That's the equivalent of hunting a Bengal tiger with a BB gun. The only thing worse than missing him is hitting him."

"I know all that, Sancho. So what? That doesn't mean we just walk away."

"Wait." Rosenbloom was staring at him. A grin spread over his face and he shook his head in amusement.

"What?"

"You slick bastard."

"Huh?"

Rosenbloom chuckled. "I just realized what's going on."

"What are you talking about?"

"It's Dulcie, right?"

"Pardon?"

"You're trying to impress that foxy professor."

Hirsch gave him a weary smile. "There are far easier ways to do that than rejecting a settlement offer in this case."

"Ah, but none so noble. Especially for her. Hell, it's what she does for a living. Look at her clinic. Defender of abused and exploited women. Champion of the underdog.

And along comes Mr. Former Male Chauvinist Pig Felon Seeking Redemption. You're a goddamn chick-flick come to life."

Hirsch shook his head. "To quote a wise man, this isn't Hollywood and I'm no Luke Skywalker. Moreover, she's been through her own version of hell with an ex-husband. Her clinic is a lot more grit than glory. I wouldn't call her a romantic."

"Call her whatever you want, but you have to agree she's a total babe."

"No dispute there. But that's no reason to turn down that settlement."

"And this fantasy of yours is?" Rosenbloom gave him a sad smile. "*Oy*, Samson, look at us. We're not the Hardy Boys. Be sensible. Judith Shifrin is dead. She's going to stay dead no matter what you do. If you can squeeze a six-figure settlement out of those bastards, you're going to be a genuine American hero."

"This isn't about us, Sancho. You know that. Her father didn't hire me to broker a deal. The least I can do is to try to find out the truth about his daughter's death. I owe it to him—and to her, too."

"Why?"

"You know the answer as well as I do. I'm a lawyer and he's the client. I'm doing what he hired me to do."

Rosenbloom rolled his wheelchair across the floor to the other picture window. He stared out at Forest Park.

After a moment, he turned to Hirsch. "Speaking of lawyers, you do recall that I am actually the lead lawyer on this case, don't you?"

"I do."

Rosenbloom rolled his eyes. "If I had any sense, I'd yank your ass off this case and settle it myself."

He leaned back in his wheelchair and sighed. He smiled at Hirsch.

"You're crazy, Samson. You understand that, right? Fucking nuts."

Hirsch was smiling. "I hope not."

"Oh, trust me on this one, Samson. You're completely irrational. Off your rocker. But guess what? If you're crazy enough to take on a goddamn federal district judge, I can't let you do that on your own."

"Of course you can. This is my client. This is none of your business."

"Hey, you're my business, *boychik*. And I'm yours." He patted the side of his wheelchair. "She ain't much of a donkey, but she'll do."

21

"RUSS Jefferson called me this morning."

Dulcie put down her fork. "About her computer?"

He waited until the waitress refilled their iced teas and left.

"They can't find it," he said.

"How can that be?"

"The court administrator has no record of her computer after her death."

They were having lunch at the Chez Leon bistro in the Central West End. Dulcie had called that morning to say she'd been able to reach a few more of the people whose Knoxville phone numbers were on Judith's phone bills. Hirsch had been thinking about her at the time she called— as he had been, off and on, for most of the morning. He'd suggested they talk about it at lunch, and she agreed.

On the way to the restaurant he tried to temper his anticipation, reminding himself that Dulcie's involvement in the case was due to her relationship with Judith and not him.

She'd been seated alone in a booth along the side wall

with a legal pad on the table in front of her. Reading glasses were perched on the end of her nose and the top of her pen was pressed against her lower lip as she studied her notes. She was wearing a black wool vest over a white cotton turtleneck, a tartan plaid skirt, and high leather boots. She'd looked up as he scooted into the booth across from her. When she smiled, he felt like he was back in junior high sitting next to the cutest girl in the class.

But she was frowning now. "It wasn't a laptop computer, was it?"

"Nope. Just a standard desktop model."

"Then what about the law clerk who replaced her? Why didn't he receive her computer?"

"Good question. Lousy answer. There was a six-month gap between Judith's death and the arrival of McCormick's new clerk, a guy named Hernandez. His computer had a different serial number than Judith's."

"They're sure?"

"That's what Russ told me. He even had the court administrator send someone over to McCormick's chambers yesterday afternoon to physically check the serial number on the current law clerk's computer."

"Is the clerk in her old office?"

"Yes."

"So where did her computer go?"

Hirsch shrugged. "All the court administrator could say was that it was probably a clerical error."

"No pun intended."

It took Hirsch a moment. "Right."

"You think McCormick knew what she had on her computer?"

"Who knows? Remember, we don't even know if she had *anything* incriminating on her computer. And if she did"—he shook his head in frustration—"we have no idea what it could be. We're assuming that if he killed her, he had a dark motive. But maybe they were having an affair. Maybe it was just a crime of passion, assuming there was any crime at all. If so, there wouldn't be much on her computer besides maybe a few romantic e-mails."

Dulcie leaned back in her chair. "Shit."

Hirsch took a sip of iced tea and then another forkful of his grilled salmon. He watched Dulcie eat her pesto pasta. She looked up and met his gaze.

She gave him a curious look. "What?"

"Have you talked with Lauren?"

He'd been thinking about his daughter constantly since their encounter at Dulcie's clinic last week.

She nodded. "This morning. She wanted to know how I knew you. I told her. We talked some about your case."

"What did you tell her?"

"Don't worry, David. I told her nothing beyond the facts of the wrongful death claim you filed. Nothing beyond the public documents in the court file. She knows nothing about your suspicions."

"How's she doing?" he asked.

"She's dealing with it. She told me you send her a letter every year on her birthday. And another one on the High Holidays."

"Does she read them?" Hirsch asked.

"Yes." Dulcie smiled. "And she's saved them all."

Hirsch nodded, momentarily unable to speak.

Dulcie said, "She was pleased to hear about the lawsuit. Maybe even a little proud of her father."

Hirsch shook his head. "She's still young."

Dulcie gave him a sympathetic look. "It'll take time."

He wasn't there for therapy. "Tell me about your Knoxville calls."

"I reached six more people. One still works at Peterson. Guy named Finch. He's in risk management. Spends most of his time on workmen's comp claims. The other five," she paused to check her notes, "two are retired and three work for other companies. Most of them barely even remembered her phone call. But one of the five, a woman named Carmen Moldano, actually met Judith."

"In person?"

Dulcie nodded. "She came to Knoxville."

"In September, right?"

Dulcie looked surprised. "How did you know?"

"Judith's credit card records. They included one roundtrip airline ticket in September. I checked with the airline for the flight information. She flew into Knoxville on the afternoon of September eleventh. That was a Friday. She flew home two days later."

"She saw Carmen that weekend. Carmen remembers that she was planning to meet with two others the same weekend."

"Did she know who?"

Dulcie shook her head. "Judith wouldn't tell her."

"Why not?"

"She told Carmen that all of the meetings were strictly confidential."

"Did she tell her why?"

"Something vague about investigating something related to the lawsuit in St. Louis."

"How did she set up the meeting?"

"She talked to Carmen on the phone a couple times. The first time was pretty general, but the second time she explained that she was real interested in the names of people at the company involved with the tire case. Carmen was a file clerk in the legal department back then, so she knew a lot of names. About two weeks after their second telephone conversation, Judith sent her an e-mail telling her she was coming to Knoxville and wanted to meet with her. They e-mailed back and forth to set up the meeting. By the way, Judith didn't use her own name."

"Esther Summerson?"

"Yep. She must have set up another e-mail account for that name."

"So what happened when they met?"

"It was basically a more detailed version of their second telephone call. Judith had Carmen walk her through all of the legal department personnel, from the general counsel down to the guy who worked in the copy center. She took careful notes, asking her about each of the people and what they did."

"You said Carmen was a file clerk?"

"Right."

"Did she work on the tire case?"

"No. She worked mainly with the environmental lawyers. She was aware of the tire case. Everyone in the legal department was. But she had no involvement in it."

"She's no longer with Peterson Tire?"

"Right. She's a paralegal with a Knoxville law firm."

Hirsch leaned back in his seat, pondering the information. "Did she think it was unusual to get a visit like that from the law clerk for the judge in that tire case?"

"Judith didn't tell her she was a law clerk. She told her she was a lawyer—a lawyer representing a third party who was interested in certain aspects of the case."

"Interested in what way?"

"Judith never told her."

"So what did Carmen think?"

"She thought it was a little odd. But she told me that Judith's, or rather Esther's, visit wasn't the only odd thing about the case."

"How so?"

"She said that there was a lot of top-secret stuff with the case, which seemed strange to her because so much of what was happening *in* the case was public knowledge. But the lawyers and staff on the case never talked about any aspect of it with anyone in the department. Never. The files were kept in a separate locked room. Everything was highly confidential."

"Anything else about the visit?"

"She said Judith asked her about Ruth Jones."

"That was the CFO's secretary?"

"How'd you know?"

Hirsch said, "One of the Knoxville people I talked to was a retired sales manager named Kindle. He told Judith that his secretary had a friend in the executive suite named Ruth. He couldn't remember her last name, but he said she was the CFO's secretary."

"According to Carmen," Dulcie said, "Judith was very interested in finding out more about Ruth."

"What did Carmen know about Ruth?"

"She knew that Ruth had left the company earlier the summer Judith visited. Judith told Carmen that she'd been trying to locate Ruth but couldn't find her. Carmen agreed to look for her new address. She assumed that Personnel would have it, and they did. About a week after their meeting in Knoxville, she sent Judith an e-mail with the new address."

"Does she remember it?"

Dulcie shook her head. "All she remembered was that Ruth lived somewhere in Chicago."

"Chicago." Hirsch nodded. "Judith must have gone to visit her. Maybe twice."

"Why do you say that?"

"Credit card bills. She paid for gas in Chicago once in late September and again in mid-October. There's also a motel bill from up there as well. The Hyatt Lincolnwood. That's from the October visit."

"Did she travel anywhere else that last year?"

"Just the one trip to Knoxville and the two to Chicago."

Dulcie signed. "This is maddening. What was she looking for?"

"And whatever it was, did she find it?"

22

CHAPTER Thirteen Day, and once again Judge Shea was running late.

All the usual players were in all the usual positions. Rochelle Krick, the bankruptcy trustee, was alone at counsel's table, seated erect, facing the judge's bench, her color-coded accordion files on the table before her. Hirsch was in the front row, his trial bag on the floor at his feet as he leafed through his notes for today's debtors.

The gallery behind them hummed with voices. Scattered around the courtroom were lawyers and debtors—the two easy to distinguish. The lawyers were mostly male and mostly white, while the debtors were a motley assortment—black and white, male and female, city and suburb, young and old, waitresses and auto mechanics, riverboat casino pit bosses and department store floor managers, computer technicians and used car salesmen. Many wore the uniforms of their trades, some with their names stitched above the breast pockets.

Among the lawyers, there were two breeds, debtor lawyers and creditor lawyers, and the keen observer could tell them apart. Most of the debtor lawyers were in sports jackets and slacks, and most were clutching jumbled batches of files. Many stood along the side walls, peering around the crowd as they called out names, trying to locate their clients. By contrast, the creditors' lawyers were the suits. Not a plaid jacket among them. All with meters running, paid by the hour by their corporate and banking and public utility clients. These weren't country-club suits, of course. The five-hundred-dollar-an-hour swells worked the big Chapter Elevens, the ones covered by the *Wall Street Journal*. No, these were the second-tier suits, the Chapter Thirteen boys from the smaller firms, the ones who snagged the work by cutting their hourly rates and then making it back in volume. The suits waited calmly, some chatting together, others seated on the benches, paging through their papers or doing the crossword puzzle in the *Post-Dispatch*, one or two drifting up to confer with Rochelle Krick, others talking on their cell phones.

Not a big-firm lawyer in the lot. Hirsch had been handling Chapter Thirteen dockets for nearly a year now and had yet to run into a single lawyer he'd known from before. Parallel universes with little overlap, in or out of court. The Jewish lawyers in the bankruptcy bar tended to be in the Jewish Community Center crowd, while their counterparts in the big law firms tended to be in the country-club crowd. In his former life, he'd never run into any of these bankruptcy lawyers in court, at his country club, or at any social function. And now he never saw any of the lawyers from that life, while the bankruptcy faces were getting familiar. Two of his regular handball opponents at the JCC represented secured creditors, and one of the debtor attorneys was often in the JCC weight room on the nights Hirsch did his lifting.

"Hey, David?"

Vinny Manoli. He represented GMAC, a creditor in at least a third of Hirsch's Chapter Thirteens. Vinny was in his mid-thirties, a stocky guy with a dark complexion and thick black hair slicked straight back, highlighting a deep widow's peak.

"Guy out there wants to see you." He gestured toward the back of the courtroom with his thumb, reminding Hirsch of an umpire signaling an out.

"Who is he?"

Vinny shrugged. "Didn't say. Fat guy, expensive threads."

A description that fit Vinny, too, although Hirsch knew who it was.

MARVIN Guttner stood by the window facing east toward the Arch and the Mississippi River. His entourage that morning consisted of a junior partner and two associates. They were huddled farther down the hall, just out of earshot. All of their eyes followed Hirsch as he approached Guttner, who turned to greet him.

"Good morning, David. A happy coincidence, eh?"

"How so?"

"I had a hearing upstairs."

The district court courtrooms were on the upper floors. This was, Hirsch assumed, the first time Guttner had ever found himself down here with the bankruptcy riffraff.

Guttner said, "We were before Judge McCormick at nine. A short hearing. In the Peterson Tire case, in fact. I noticed on the schedule in the lobby that Judge Shea had a Chapter Thirteen docket at ten this morning. I took a chance that you might be here, and so you are."

Hirsch waited.

As usual, Guttner was elegantly attired: a gray chalk-striped suit, crisp white shirt, silk tie, gleaming black Guccis. Hirsch marveled at the skills of the tailor who could drape that frame so gracefully, as if Omar the Tentmaker had earned an advanced degree from Saville Row.

Guttner's smile faded, replaced by a concerned frown. "Jack Bellows is chomping at the bit, David. For that matter, so is my litigation team. I can hold them back only so long. Bellows told me yesterday that if you haven't responded by the close of business today, he's withdrawing from the settlement discussions and serving you with his written discovery."

Guttner leaned forward, lowering his voice. "Frankly, David, I get the sense that Bellows has some personal agenda here. Something with you in the past. In any event, time is of the essence. I cannot emphasize that enough. Explain to your client that we need his response as soon as possible. Today, if possible. Talk to him."

"I have."

"Ah, good. And?"

"He rejects your offer."

"I suppose I am not shocked. I understand that he was a tenacious businessman in his day. Not an easy man to bargain with, they say. I must warn you, however, that I do not have much wiggle room here, David. Nonetheless, you might as well let me hear it."

"There's nothing to let you hear."

"Surely he has a counteroffer?"

"He didn't give me one."

"How can that be?"

"He rejected your offer, Marvin. He has not asked me to make a counteroffer."

Guttner pursed his lips. "That is unwise."

"To you, perhaps."

"What about to you?"

Hirsch shrugged. "I'm just the lawyer. If my client

wants to settle, fine. If not, that's his prerogative. He didn't retain me to force him to do something against his will."

"But he did retain you to give him legal advice."

"Actually, he retained me to sue your client. That's what I've done."

Guttner tugged at a loose fold of skin on his massive neck. "This is imprudent. For him and for you."

"It is what it is, Marvin. Your clients made an offer. My client turned it down. Away we go."

"Yo, David."

Hirsch turned.

Vinny Manoli was leaning out of the courtroom. "He's on the bench."

Hirsch nodded at Vinny and turned back. "See you in court, Marvin."

Guttner stared at him for a moment and then turned away, shaking his head.

23

WHEN he got back from court, Hirsch found Rosenbloom in the office manager's cubicle. For the umpteenth time, the unflappable Molly Hamilton was listening to her boss grumble about receivables and billable hours and out-of-control overhead and declare, loudly enough for all to hear, that he could earn more and sleep better working the drive-thru window at McDonald's. Acting in short, as if he were in it only for the money.

Hirsch knew better. So did Molly.

They all did—right down to the receptionist and the mailroom clerks. They all knew that Seymour Rosenbloom relished his skirmishes with the banks and finance companies that hounded his clients. They'd all heard him cackling over the way he'd outfoxed yet another smug creditor. They all knew he loved drubbing the law firms that once rejected him.

GMAC or First National might have a *contractual* right to repossess that car or foreclose on that mortgage, but Rosenbloom's clients had the next best thing, namely, a lawyer with a Talmudic skill for finding ambiguities and loopholes in the fine print of form contracts drafted by lawyers with a fraction of his brainpower. He regularly came up with ways to halt foreclosures and derail repossessions that left his opponents slack-jawed.

All I do, he liked to say, *is try to level the playing field.*

As if it were no big deal to put his forklift driver from Fenton on equal footing with, say, Bank of America.

"I'm getting too old for this," he groaned as he wheeled himself down the hallway.

Hirsch followed him into his office, sneaking a look back at Molly, who stood watching them with her hands on her hips. She smiled and rolled her eyes.

Rosenbloom moved behind his desk and turned to face Hirsch. *"Nu?"*

"I ran into Guttner outside Judge Shea's courtroom today."

"Really? Why was Jabba slumming?"

"Looking for me."

"Blimpie is getting a little antsy, eh?"

"Seems to be."

Rosenbloom chuckled. "Can't figure out why you won't take his money."

"He does seem perplexed."

"Curious, eh? That pompous motherfucker is eager to throw money at you this early in the case? Suggests to me that Jabba's hands may not be lily white."

"Maybe not."

"Trying to settle a case this soon? Before his shock troops get a chance to bill some hours? That greedy bastard would no more pass up a fat fee than pass up a dozen jelly doughnuts." He paused. "By the way, you ever find that gal? The one who moved to Chicago? What's her name?"

"Ruth Jones. I'm still looking. If she's in the phone book, she has plenty of company."

"Lots of them, eh?"

"Twelve listings for Ruth Jones and more than a hundred listings for R. Jones. I tried several last night, several more this morning." He sighed. "Slow process."

T WENTY minutes later, back in his own office, he stared at the phone and shook his head. He'd just concluded a short conversation with yet another R. Jones from Chicago—this one named Roshanda, who was convinced that he was the same Hirsch who represented her ex-husband Cletis, and who slammed down the phone after suggesting that he perform an unnatural act, first upon her ex-husband, then upon the divorce judge, and finally upon himself.

He thus eyed the phone warily as it started ringing moments later. Could Roshanda have Caller ID?

He picked it up after the fourth ring.

"How's it hanging, Rebbe?"

Hirsch leaned back in his chair and smiled. "Hey, Jumbo. What's up?"

"Not me, dude. I'm down here in hillbilly heaven and it feels like the third level of hell."

"I thought you loved Nashville."

"Hell, man, I ain't calling from Nashville. I'm in friggin' Branson, Missouri."

"Branson? Doing what?"

"Going so stir-crazy I'm contemplating a parole violation. There's this dang industry conference on computer security they put on here every year. My company sent three of us to attend."

"Bet you're loving the music."

"Oh, man, if I hear one more steel guitar playing twangy chords, I may just go postal."

"How much longer does the conference run?"

"We finish tomorrow at noon."

"You flying home?"

"Nah. I drove my pickup over. I was thinking I might drive back on forty-four, maybe stop by to see you."

"Great. I'll buy you dinner."

"Been awhile for us, ain't it."

"Too long."

"I'll second that."

Neither said anything for a moment.

"You still a bankruptcy lawyer, Rebbe?"

"Mostly."

"Mostly, eh? What else you got going on?"

"Just a wrongful death case."

"Big bucks?"

"Hard to say."

"What's wrong?"

"It's kind of complicated."

"That don't sound good."

"It's a long story."

"So we'll have ourselves a long dinner and talk it out."

Hirsch smiled. "That sounds good. Actually, I almost had something up your alley."

"Computers or pussy?"

"The former."

"What do you mean by 'almost?'"

"We can't find it."

"The computer?"

"Yep."

"Whose was it?"

"The government's, actually. But the dead girl used it at her job."

"Why'd you need her computer?"

"She sent some e-mails that might be relevant. And she may have written some documents as well."

"I hear you. Same question."

"What do you mean?"

"Why do you need her computer?"

"To review that stuff."

"You got her e-mail address?"

"Yes."

"What's the ass end?"

"What's the *what*?"

"The part after the 'at' symbol."

He found his notes. "M-O-E-D," he read, "dot-U-S-Courts-dot-G-O-V."

Jumbo chuckled. "This might be your lucky day, Rebbe."

"Why?"

"Sound to me like that gal's computer was hooked into the courthouse network."

"Which means?"

"Which means you and me gonna have an interesting conversation tomorrow night. What time's dinner?"

24

He crumpled the sheet of stationery and tossed it into the wastebasket with the other five crumpled sheets. He took out a fresh sheet, set it in front of him on the kitchen table, and wrote, *Dear Lauren:*

He stared at the page.

You'll be turning 24 this Sunday, he wrote.

A few days before his release from prison, his ex-wife's attorney delivered a letter to him warning that neither of his daughters wanted anything to do with him again. Ever. The hammer letter ended with a vague warning about unfortunate consequences if he ignored the express desires of his daughters. Nevertheless, he wrote each of them letters—always on their birthdays and on Rosh Hashanah, and occasionally one or two other times during the year. Lengthy letters. Always upbeat. Always supportive. None were ever answered. That didn't matter. Well, it did, but at least the letters didn't come back stamped "Return to Sender." He'd wondered whether they read them. According to Dulcie, Lauren said she did.

He stared at the page, thinking how to phrase it. This time it was different.

Although every one of your birthdays is special for those who love you, this one is particularly special for me. Until last week at Professor Lorenz's clinic I hadn't seen you since your fourteenth birthday. I've thought about you, of course, and I've dreamed about you and prayed for you. But after all those years, it was difficult to picture you in my mind. I could still see you as you were on your fourteenth birthday, but what did you look like now? How had you grown? What had you become?

He paused, remembering again their brief encounter at the clinic, seeing again the young woman who'd last been his awkward eighth-grade daughter.

Now I know, and I am so proud.

He stared at that sentence, fighting the urge to crumple the sheet.

As if his being proud meant anything to her.

But maybe it did. He was still her father.

Shift the focus. This is her birthday, her special day.

Professor Lorenz told me about your work at the clinic. She thinks highly of you, Lauren.

Twenty-four, he thought.

He tried to remember his own twenty-fourth birthday.

When I turned 24, I was in law school, too. But I had little interest in helping the types of people you serve at your clinic. That was my failing—just the first of many.

He stared at that last sentence for a moment and then ran his pen through it:

This was his daughter, and this was her birthday. He was debris from her past. She didn't need to be reminded of his failings, and he certainly didn't need to wallow in them for sympathy.

He set down the pen.

What the hell was the purpose of this letter? All of his

prior birthday letters had been chatty and carefully unde-
manding. No guilt trips, no pleas for forgiveness, no at-
tempts to force himself upon her or her big sister. Just an
innocuous I'm-thinking-of-you. For her birthday two years
ago he'd congratulated her on her acceptance to Washington University School of Law—a fact he'd learned from
his ex-wife's attorneys, who'd sent him a payment schedule for tuition for Lauren's first year. For her last birthday,
he'd included a few reminiscences from his first year of
law school and offered some advice about things he'd
wished someone had told him when he was going into law
school. Of course, he wouldn't have paid any attention to
such advice, and he assumed she didn't, either.

But now, well, now he'd finally seen her. He'd been
close enough to touch her. Everything had changed. The
shame, the reticence, the uncertainty—they'd all given
way to a simple longing to see her again. To sit with her. To
talk with her about her day, about her plans, her hopes, her
dreams.

Just to be with her.

Powerful feelings.

And, he reminded himself, feelings she might not share.

Who could blame her?

So don't come on strong.

*I've gotten to know Professor Lorenz because she was
friendly with another law student who worked at her clinic.
That young woman died in an automobile accident a few
years after graduation. I've filed a wrongful death action
on her behalf. Professor Lorenz has been nice enough to
help me with certain aspects of the case. She is an impressive person, and thus the fact she thinks so highly of you
should make you proud.*

The letter was getting away from him. They always
seemed to.

I apologize if this seems disjointed, Lauren. I keep

thinking how much I miss you and how much I love you and how sorry I am that I was such a lousy dad for you.

Too intense.

He glanced at the wastebasket and back at the letter.

Just bring it to a close, he told himself. He'd spent nearly an hour on a letter that would take her less than a minute to read.

What's done is done, of course, and people move on with their lives, but that doesn't change the facts or make them any better. I'm proud that you haven't let that stuff get in your way. You were a wonderful little girl, Lauren, and you've become a wonderful young woman.

He toyed with suggesting they meet for coffee somewhere—nothing big, just to talk.

Not yet. Don't overwhelm her.

I hope you have a happy 24th birthday, Lauren. May this be a good year and a sweet year for you.

Love, Dad

After a moment, he folded the letter, slid it into the envelope, and opened the drawer to get a stamp.

25

HIRSCH stayed after the morning service to help the rabbi straighten up.

"You seem distracted," Zev Saltzman said.

Hirsch was putting the prayer books into the slots along the backs of the seats. He turned toward the rabbi.

"I've been busy at work," he said.

The rabbi nodded sympathetically. "A father's *yahrzeit* is never easy."

"I suppose."

He hadn't considered it. His mourning sexton function had become so routine that the list of names read aloud by the rabbi before he led the *minyan* in *Kaddish* didn't always register with him. Yesterday the list had included Hirsch's father, who'd died that day years ago. He'd known it was his father's *yahrzeit*, of course—indeed, he'd lighted a *yahrzeit* candle at his apartment—but he hadn't allowed himself to linger over the memories. There'd had been too much else on his mind.

The rabbi turned off the shul lights, and they walked down the hall side by side.

Hirsch smiled as he thought of his father. It had sometimes seemed that Milton Hirsch spent most of his final two decades bragging to his friends and his optometry patients and even the checkout ladies at the supermarket about his son David-the-Harvard-lawyer. If Hirsch won an important case or landed a big client or delivered a speech at some bar association function, he would eventually hear about it from someone who'd spoken with his father. Although his father's continuous bragging was no doubt a bore, people seemed to tolerate it from someone as good-natured and modest as Milton Hirsch.

But the bragging ended with Hirsch's arrest, and a year after Hirsch entered prison, a massive heart attack sealed his father's lips forever. His mother, never one to miss an opportunity, wrote him in prison the day after the funeral. She wrote that his father died of a broken heart. She was dead as well, killed five years ago in an automobile accident in Florida.

We're orphans now, his sister had written him after that funeral.

"David," the rabbi said, pausing near his office, "I had a visit yesterday from a lawyer. He was asking questions about Abe Shifrin."

That snapped him back to the present.

"A lawyer."

The rabbi nodded. "I thought you should know."

"What kind of questions?"

"Mainly about his mental state."

Hirsch tensed. "Who was the lawyer?"

"Felts, I think. Or maybe Folts. Something like that. He gave me his card."

"Do you still have it?"

"In my desk. Come with me."

He followed Saltzman into his cluttered, book-lined office. The rabbi walked behind his desk, pulled open the top drawer, and lifted out a business card.

"Here you go."

He handed the card to Hirsch.

KENNETH M. FELTS, ESQ.
ATTORNEY AT LAW

According to the address, his office was in Clayton, a busy suburb of St. Louis and the county seat.

Hirsch asked, "What did he want to know about Abe Shifrin's mental condition?"

"He asked if I'd observed any decline in his mental functions. Did he seem more forgetful than before? Less focused? Less organized? That sort of thing."

"What did you tell him?"

"I told him that I hadn't observed any big changes. I explained that Abe didn't come to services as often as he once had, and thus we didn't have an opportunity to spend much time together. I suggested that he talk with you. I explained that you were representing him in a lawsuit. He seemed to know about your lawsuit already."

"Did he tell you why he was asking these questions?"

"I asked him that very question. He told me he was representing Abe's sister, Hannah. Hannah Goldenberg. He said she was worried about her brother, especially his mental condition. He said he'd been retained to help her out."

"That's how he put it? 'Been retained'? Not retained by her?"

Saltzman thought back. "I'm pretty sure he said 'been retained.'"

Hirsch stared at the business card as he mulled it over.

He didn't know for sure, of course, but he'd been in enough of these litigation chess matches to sense what

might be afoot on the other side of the board. Marvin Guttner may have just moved another dangerous piece into
position. He ran through his options—none of them promising. Just a matter of time now.

He handed the card back to Saltzman and stood up.
"Thanks, Rabbi."

"You're welcome, David. I thought you might want to
know about it."

Saltzman walked him to the front door.

"David," he said as Hirsch put on his coat, "is there anything else bothering you?"

Hirsch concentrated on buttoning his coat as he weighed
his response.

Anything else? he said to himself. *How much time do
you have?*

He glanced at the rabbi, and suddenly he was too weary
to be sardonic. Saltzman was a good man, a gentle rabbi
who studied the Talmud and visited the sick and worked
patiently with the bar mitzvah students. But he was no
Pinky. Hirsch knew he would never find another Pinky.

"David?"

"I'm okay," Hirsch said. "Just a lot going on."

Walking across the parking lot toward his car, he smiled
as he thought again of Pincus Green. It was a sad smile.

Oh, Pinky, he thought, *I could use some of your guidance.*

Pinky had been the Allenwood Jewish chaplain—a
young Conservative rabbi who made the three-hour drive
from Philadelphia once a week to meet with the handful of
Jewish inmates. At the warden's urging, Pinky scheduled a
session with Hirsch, who'd been stuck in what the prison
psychiatrist diagnosed as a mild depression.

Hirsch had entered that first session with low expec-
tation, made even lower when he saw the young rabbi,
who perfectly matched Hirsch's stereotype: short, pudgy,

bearded, thick eyeglasses, wrinkled dark suit. Hirsch told him right off that he was wasting his time. He didn't believe in God, he used to observe the High Holidays on his country club golf course, and the closest he'd ever come to a spiritual experience inside a synagogue was when his wife's cousin Arlene from Scottsdale gave him blow job in a darkened classroom down the hall during the *kiddush* luncheon following his eldest daughter's bat mitzvah. He'd intentionally used the phrase *blow job*, determined to repel the young rabbi.

But Pinky had listened with an expression of mild amusement. When Hirsch finished, Pinky assured him that God was losing no sleep over whether David Hirsch believed in Him, that there were worse venues than a gold course for confronting your shortcomings on the Day of Atonement, and that a blow job from a casual acquaintance was nothing compared to one from the woman you loved.

"But enough about *shtupping*, David. They tell me you're from St. Louis. Let's talk about those Cardinals of yours."

Which is exactly what they did for the first few sessions. Pinky Green was a consummate sports fan whose encyclopedic knowledge far exceeded Hirsch's. Although the rabbi was not even born in 1964 when the Cardinals slid the pennant out from under the slumping Phillies, he knew the game-by-game details of the late-season swoon of his beloved team.

Gradually, the rabbi steered the focus of their meetings from sport to Judaism, and Hirsch, to his surprise, responded. Within a year, he was lighting the candles on Friday night and reciting the *Shabbas* blessings. By the time of his parole, he was keeping kosher, wearing a *kippah*, and studying Hebrew. For reasons he couldn't quite articulate, he'd found solace in the rituals and the teachings of the religion. Even so, he was troubled by his continuing doubts in God's existence.

"God is patient," Pinky had assured him during their final session, just two days before Hirsch's release. "He'll wait for you to come home, David."

A year later, while in Israel visiting his sister and her family, Pinky was killed when a suicide bomber blew himself up inside a Jerusalem café.

Hirsch unlocked his car door.

Well, Pinky, he thought, glancing upward, *is God still waiting for me?*

26

JIMMY Beau Redding.

Known to all as Jumbo Redding.

They'd been the least likely twosome in the entire prison population: the national trial lawyer with the Harvard law degree and the small-town deputy with the GED. But by the end they were inseparable. Hirsch dearly loved the man. Loved him like the brother he never had.

At first glance, Jumbo Redding seemed to fit a rather distinct stereotype. Southern drawl, scraggly goatee, enormous bald head, tattoos, fifty pounds overweight. A mouth breather as a result of a nose broken that was never reset. If you were asked where to find him at dinnertime, you'd guess perched on a stool at the counter of a diner hunched over a platter of grits and fried catfish, big spoon in that big fist, shoveling food into that big mouth.

Indeed, even the solemn Japanese waiter was taken aback when Jumbo asked, without bothering to open his menu, "Y'all got some of that chutoro tonight?"

"Uh, yes, sir. We do, yes."

"Glad to hear. What about your kanpachi? How's that lookin' tonight, pal?"

"Very fresh, sir. Very fresh."

"Then give me some of them, too. And some tekka-maki, a little of that edomai-zushi, maybe couple of them hotategai, and, oh yeah, how about some nice pieces of that sawara." He'd looked over at Hirsch and sighed with pleasure. "Sawara is Spanish mackerel, Rebbe, and that's some fine shit. Gives me a chubby just thinking about it."

Hirsch couldn't help but grin as he watched Jumbo eat his sushi, clearly savoring each piece. One might not expect *deft* to have any descriptive relevance to a three-hundred-pound ex-con, but there was no better way to describe Jumbo's skills with chopsticks.

If told that he was presently employed, you'd conjure an image of him driving a forklift on a loading dock or hanging off the back end of a garbage truck. You'd be wrong. You'd be wrong about a lot when it came to Jumbo Redding. If told he'd served time, you'd guess a county jail for drunk and disorderly, and not a club fed for an embezzlement scam based on a software program he'd created—a program so innovative that he'd earned big bucks in prison selling the copyright to a major software company.

You'd never guess he'd turned Hirsch on to *In Search of Lost Time*. His recommendation had been, well, classic Jumbo. "Give ol' Marcel a shot, Rebbe,'cause ah swear that little French faggot can write like a motherfucker."

Despite fingers the size of knockwursts, he was a banjo virtuoso, as Hirsch learned during their prison jam sessions. Jumbo would soar off on elaborate riffs, his fingers a blur, and then glide back into the melody just at the right beat.

And he was a blues fan, with a passion that extended far beyond a personal blues library of nearly five hundred CDs covering the greats from all periods and regions of the country. He'd made the pilgrimage to John Lee Hooker's birthplace in Clarksdale, Mississippi. He'd played "Come on in My Kitchen" with T-Model Ford in a juke joint in Water Valley, Mississippi. And the week after his release from prison, he'd driven south past Tunica to the crossroads of Highway 49 and Old Highway 61, gotten out of his car at midnight, and stared up at the full moon while imagining another midnight seventy years earlier when Robert Johnson stood at that same spot beneath that same moon and sold his soul to the devil for the guitar skills that made him father of the blues.

"So how's your job?" Hirsch asked.

"Indoor work, no heavy lifting."

Jumbo was chief of computer security for a Fortune 500 company that had recruited him from prison. On the morning of his release, a limo waiting outside the prison gate had whisked him to an airport near Allenwood, where his new employer had chartered a jet to fly him to its headquarters in Nashville. Heady stuff for a high school dropout.

Jumbo shrugged. "It's that old theory in action, I guess. Hire a thief to catch a thief."

"But it must feel good to have their trust."

Jumbo chuckled. "Come on, Rebbe. Them Nashville boys trust me 'bout as fer as they can throw me, and those sumbitches can't even lift me."

"What makes you think they don't trust you?"

"They hired a specialist to shadow me. Fellow named Ernie Strahan. Works for an outfit called eZone Security. Ol' Ernie checks in on me once or twice a week. Makes sure I'm not siphoning off the company's assets to some Swiss bank account."

"At least they told you about him."

"They didn't tell me jack."

"How'd you find out?"

Jumbo smiled and took a chug of his Kirin beer. "Guy with my record, I figured they'd have someone shadowing me. Hell, wouldn't you? So I wrote me up this reverse shadow program that lets me know whenever Ernie is out there in cyberspace peering over my shoulder. He has no idea, of course. In fact, he has no idea my program's been monitoring his e-mails as well. Figure I might as well know what he's telling my bosses. Guess what else I found out? Turns out ol' Ernie's getting a little strange on the side. Her name is Sherry. Been tempted once or twice to send ol' Ernie an e-mail suggesting I might just tell his old lady 'bout lovely Sherry if he gets out of line. But I figure what the hell, no reason to rattle the poor bastard. They pay me good money and give me nice benefits and I ain't tempted. At all. You got to remember, Rebbe, I'd have never strayed if it weren't for Amber, God bless her perky little butt."

Jumbo had been deputy chief of the Jonesboro Police Department—a position he reached in just six years because of his astonishing computer skills, all self-taught. Among other things, he had redesigned the department's computer network and written a software program (eventually licensed to a major player in Silicon Valley) that enabled his department's computers to communicate with computers from other police departments around the state and across the Mississippi River into Tennessee. That feat brought him to the attention of three Memphis officials who'd been nosing around for a computer wizard to implement their scheme to embezzle money from the city's health insurance fund. To lure him into the conspiracy, they enlisted the services of a drop-dead-gorgeous hooker named Amber. Although she was expensive, they got their money's worth.

So did Jumbo.

"Amber done things to me that month," he told Hirsch in prison, "that nearly make this jail time worth it."

The waiter removed their empty sushi platters and placed down Jumbo's order of shrimp and vegetable tempura. The man could eat.

"So, Rebbe, let me hear 'bout this big case you got yourself into."

Hirsch started with Abe Shifrin's parking lot plea and brought him up to date.

Jumbo pondered the situation as he chewed on a shrimp.

"If that pathologist fellow is right, then the big question is 'Why.' You think she was banging the judge, or you think she caught him in a compromising position in that big tire case?"

"The latter. She was bothered about something having to do with the case. Whatever it was, it seemed to have soured her view of the judge as well."

"What makes you think she had anything worthwhile on her computer?"

"She had no computer at home. She sent personal e-mails from her office. Maybe she used her computer for other purposes, too."

"If so, that stuff may still be floating around in that network. Judith Shifrin, eh?" he said, jotting her name down on a napkin.

"You think you can get in the network?"

"Can I get in? Come on, Rebbe. Does the wild pope shit in the woods?" He took a long pull on his Kirin beer, set the bottle on the table, and gave Hirsch a wink.

"Let's just say, 'Been there, done that.' "

"You already found a way in?"

Jumbo smiled as he chewed on another piece of tempura.

"When?" Hirsch asked.

"This morning."

"From where?"

"From Branson. Before checking out."

"You broke into the federal court Web site from your hotel room?"

"I wouldn't exactly call it breaking in. That makes it sound kind of, well, intrusive, if you know what I mean. I just poked around a little on the outside, found me an unlocked door, and sort of poked my head inside and took a gander."

Hirsch shook his head in disbelief. "I thought the FBI was in charge of Internet security for the federal courts."

"That's what I hear."

"Will they be able to figure out you got in?"

"I don't think so."

"What if they do?"

"I suppose they'll try to plug the hole."

"But aren't you worried?"

"I'll find another way in."

"No, I mean about them connecting you to the, uh, to the security breach?"

Jumbo gave him a puzzled expression. "Connecting me?"

"What if they trace it back to your hotel room?"

Jumbo smiled. "Oh, I doubt that'll ever happen."

"How can you say that?"

"They gotta first find some fingerprints in their network, and then they gotta figure out them fingerprints belong to someone who was in there without permission, and then they gotta figure out how to trace that someone back to his origin. That's a whole lotta figurin' for a federal employee, Rebbe. But even if they do all that figurin', they'll end up at a computer in the Justice Department in Washington, D.C. That oughta stop 'em. But if some smart guy figures out that maybe somebody was accessing that computer from a remote location and then figures out how to track down that remote location, he's gonna learn the meaning of remote. He's gonna find hisself inside the computer network of a Nigerian telephone company. Believe me, Rebbe, the trail dies right there."

Hirsch smiled. "I guess you're good."

Jumbo shrugged. "Everyone's good at something. I just thank the Lord for giving us Bill Gates,'cause if weren't for computers, Rebbe, I'd be pumping gas at the Sinclair back home. Listen, I got one more day before I got to be back at work. How 'bout I drop by your office tomorrow morning with my laptop and take another look around that courthouse network, this time with your gal in mind?"

"That would be great. Thanks."

"My pleasure." He finished off his beer and stifled a belch. "So how you and Marion getting along?"

Hirsch smiled. "I'm still having trouble keeping up."

"You ain't the only one, Rebbe. Marion done things with that harp that still leaves 'em scratching their heads."

Jumbo's arrival at Allenwood had coincided with Hirsch's decision to take up the harmonica again. During the quiet hour after lunch, while his cell mate played bridge in the common area, Hirsch had worked on his old camp repertoire. One afternoon he was seated on his bed with his back to the door playing "Streets of Laredo." As the final chord faded, a voice behind him said, "Ain't bad, Tex."

He turned to see Jumbo filling up the doorway. The big man was beaming as he held up a banjo, which looked like a toy instrument in his massive hands. Hirsch had avoided him since Jumbo's arrival, assuming from his appearance and rasping breath that he was the nightmare spawn of a backwoods coupling of siblings.

"Mind if I sit in?" Jumbo had asked.

He started dropping by at the same time each afternoon.

They'd been playing together for a few weeks when he asked Hirsch, "You really a fan of this hillbilly music, Rebbe?"

He'd taken to calling him "Rebbe" after learning about Hirsch's sessions with Pinky Green.

"Reason I ask is y'all don't seem like much of a country boy. Guy been through what you been through and lost what you done lost and coming from a people that's been taking it in the shorts since the time of ol' Ramses, well, jes' seem to me that Marion Jacobs makes a whole lot more sense than Camptown Races."

"Marion who?"

"Jacobs."

"Who's she?"

"Him. His stage name was Little Walter."

"Who's that?"

Jumbo shook his head patiently. "You best come on back to my cell. Time we begun your education."

Lesson One was Little Walter's "Sad Hours," a 1952 cut from of one of Jumbo's collection of Chess Records. Lesson Two was "We're Ready" by Junior Wells. Lesson Three was "Help Me" by Sonny Boy Williams. By then, he was hooked on blues.

Hirsch paid the bill, and the two of them headed toward the front of the restaurant.

As they stepped outside, Jumbo said, "I got my banjo out in the car. I was thinking maybe we could drop by your apartment, see if we're as good outside of prison as we used to be inside."

Hirsch smiled and nodded. "That sounds good."

"Sure do, don't it?"

27

THE following morning, Jumbo came down to the office and spent several hours on the computer before heading back to Memphis. Unfortunately, Hirsch never saw him. That's because the emergency motion to appoint a guardian for Abe Shifrin arrived about an hour before Jumbo did.

The court papers stated that the preliminary hearing was set for eleven o'clock that morning, which gave them just two hours to prepare. There was no question that Rosenbloom had to be there. Although Abe Shifrin's mental capacity might be the ostensible subject of the proceeding, they both knew the real objective was to get Hirsch removed from Judith's lawsuit. Indeed, paragraph eight of the Emergency Motion of Petitioner Hannah Goldenberg for Appointment of Guardian Ad Litem alleged:

8. The risks of irreparable harm to Respondent Abraham Shifrin and his heirs caused by said mental incapacity are/or disablement of Respondent are exacerbated by

the fact that the principal attorney handling said wrongful death action and advising Respondent concerning settlement of same is David M. Hirsch, a felon who has already been convicted of the crimes of embezzling client funds and otherwise defrauding clients, all in willful violation of his fiduciary and professional duties to his clients.

"Nasty little cocksucker, eh?" Rosenbloom had said after reading that paragraph.

When he finished reading the petition, he stared at the signature block. "Who the fuck is Ken Felts?"

That was the first of the two questions they sought to answer in the two hours before the hearing. The second question was who could they propose as cocounsel for the wrongful death action?

Rosenbloom found out the answer to the first question by calling a few colleagues around town. He learned that Kenneth M. Felts was a solo practitioner in his fifties with a specialty in real estate law. After law school, Felts went to work for Emmanuel Castleman & Associates, Attorneys at Law. Back then, Manny Castleman had the largest condemnation practice in St. Louis County. He and his three associates represented a wide variety of property owners in proceedings that challenged the monetary value placed on their property by the city, county, or state government authority in the condemnation proceedings. About fifteen years ago, when Manny was in his sixties, the chairman of Emerson, Burke & McGee convinced him to join the law firm and bring along his lucrative book of business. Ken Felts decided to go off on his own, but the other two associates went with Manny to the new firm. One of them was Marvin Guttner.

"There's your connection," Rosenbloom said to Hirsch. "I'll bet Felts is Jabba's bitch on this one."

Hirsch had the answer to the second question the moment they found out that the judge assigned to hear the guardianship proceeding was Ann Burke.

"YOUR Honor," Rosenbloom said, cutting off Ken Felts in midsentence, "we will stipulate that Mr. Hirsch has been convicted of those crimes. I will remind opposing counsel that Mr. Hirsch has been punished for those crimes, has served his time, and has returned not merely to society but to the practice of law under my direct supervision. Unless Mr. Felts would now like to impugn my character as well, perhaps he could move on to something remotely relevant to these proceedings."

"I object to that statement," Felts said, glaring at Rosenbloom in outrage, his fists clenched on his hips.

Hirsch was seated back at counsel's table watching the proceedings. Felts and Rosenbloom were up at the bar facing Judge Burke, who listened to them with her arms crossed over her chest, her lips pursed in concentration.

Even standing, Felts was only slightly taller than Rosenbloom seated in his wheelchair. Physically, they were opposites—Rosenbloom big and hulking and bald, Felts short and scrawny and hairy enough to be called furry, with kinky brown hair on his head and his neck and the backs of his hands and above his collar and sprouting from his nostrils and ears. There was an aura of decay about him—discolored teeth, a dusting of dandruff on the shoulders and down the back of his suit jacket, gray eyes distorted behind the thick lenses of horn-rimmed glasses.

"Ah, forgive me." Rosenbloom placed his hand over his heart in a burlesque of remorse. "We must not forget that Mr. Felts claims to come before the Court on behalf of Mr. Shifrin's beloved sister Hannah Goldenberg. He claims that his client has deep concerns about the mental state of her brother and the propriety of her brother's attorney-client relationship with Mr. Hirsch. We must not allow ourselves to wonder about the cause for these sudden concerns of Mrs. Goldenberg, who has not spoken with her brother for more than two months and who has never spoken with him about the wrongful death action that brings us all together today in court—indeed, that even brings us the attorneys representing the defendants in that case, all of whom are perched here along the front row like, well, like birds of prey."

He turned and gestured toward Marvin Guttner, Jack Bellows, and Elizabeth Purcell, all seated along the front row, their associates arrayed in the row behind them. All had been served with notice of the hearing, as required under the rules. Bellows flinched slightly at the phrase "birds of prey," and his face reddened. Guttner was unperturbed.

"No," continued Rosenbloom, turning back to the judge, "we must endeavor to keep focused on what Mr. Felts tells us are the relevant issues. We must not ask ourselves how his client was able to gather sufficient information about her brother and his lawsuit to decide that she should commence this guardianship action. Nor must we ask ourselves how she was lucky enough to find Mr. Felts to represent her. May I remind the Court that Mr. Felts's client, unlike Mr. Shifrin, presently resides in a nursing home."

"This is slanderous and outrageous," Felts said to the Court.

"Mr. Rosenbloom," Judge Burke said with a mix of amusement and impatience, "is there some proposal buried within this discourse of yours?"

Rosenbloom smiled. "Forgive me, Your Honor. Although I am a mere bankruptcy hack, I respectfully suggest that our adversary system, especially as arrayed before the Court this morning in all its litigious glory, may not be the best mechanism for determining Mr. Shifrin's mental competency. We suggest that if the Court has genuine concerns about Mr. Shifrin's state of mind, then the Court should appoint an impartial medical expert to examine him and report directly to the Court. This seems far preferable to the dueling doctors scenario that Mr. Felts's motion contemplates. As for Mr. Felts's concerns about Mr. Shifrin's principal counsel, may I first remind the Court that by the express terms of the Missouri Supreme Court's order reinstating Mr. Hirsch's law license, I am ultimately responsible for all matters on which he works. I can assure the Court that Mr. Hirsch has acted at all times at the highest level of professional responsibility on this case. Even so, Mr. Felts correctly points out that wrongful death actions are not within my legal area of expertise. Of course, I could point out that questions of mental competency are not within Mr. Felts's legal area of expertise, either, but instead, Your Honor, I believe I can put Mr. Felts and the Court at ease on this matter. The decedent was especially close with one of her law school professors. I believe Your Honor is familiar with Professor Adelaide Lorenz?"

Judge Burke raised her eyebrows in surprise. "I am indeed, Mr. Rosenbloom. As a matter of fact, I serve on the board of the legal clinic that Professor Lorenz supervises."

"So I understand, Your Honor. That's why I am pleased to report that, if the Court permits, Professor Lorenz is prepared to enter her appearance as additional counsel for the plaintiff in the wrongful death action. That way the Court *and* Mr. Felts *and* Mr. Felts's client *and*, lest we forget"— and here he paused to gesture toward the front row—"our colleagues from the wrongful death case, can all rest assured that the case will proceed under the watchful eye of an attorney that not even Mr. Felts has the audacity to vilify."

"That is an excellent proposal." Judge Burke turned to Felts. "Any problems, Counsel?"

Hirsch saw Felts's head jerk slightly toward the three

lawyers seated in the front row. "It's an interesting concept, Your Honor, although I obviously haven't had sufficient time to consider all of its ramifications. I'd request a day or so to consult with my client and to advise the Court of our informed position on the matter."

Rosenbloom snorted. "Come on, Kenny Boy. This ain't rocket science. Your client will be relieved to know that her brother will be examined by a neutral medical expert and that the legal team on his wrongful death lawsuit will include an esteemed law school professor who was close to your client's niece."

"I have the right to consult with my client," Felts responded testily.

"You certainly do, Counsel," Judge Burke said, "and you may take as much time as you need, and you are free to come back to the Court with any concerns you may have. In the interim, however, I will adopt Mr. Rosenbloom's excellent suggestions. I will appoint a medical expert, and I will grant Professor Lorenz leave to file her appearance. Thank you, gentlemen."

She nodded at her clerk, who rapped his gravel three times and announced, "All rise."

"HOLD on," Rosenbloom said to Hirsch, stopping his wheelchair outside the courtroom.

He nodded toward Jack Bellows, who was farther down the hallway speaking on his cell phone. An associate from his firm, a young dark-haired male in an expensive pinstriped suit, stood nearby, trying to look important while waiting for his boss's next order.

Rosenbloom said, "Give me a minute alone with that *schmuck*."

Hirsch stepped back to the side wall near the bank of pay phones and watched as Rosenbloom wheeled himself forward until he was in Bellows's path to the elevators. He took some papers out of his briefcase and studied them as he waited.

Bellows's call ended. He slipped the cell phone into the front pocket of his suit jacket and started toward the elevators, his young associate in tow.

"Hey, Jack," Rosenbloom called.

Bellows stopped. "What?"

"I have to tell you, tough guy, I'm a little disappointed."

"Pardon?"

"I thought you were supposed to be a real macho man. A big swinging dick."

Bellows's eyes narrowed. "I'm not following you."

"This chickenshit proceeding." Rosenbloom shook his head. "Doesn't seem your style."

"What are you talking about?"

"I caught your press conference on TV. The one about our wrongful death case. Man, you sounded ready to rumble. I thought I'd have a ringside seat to a real heavyweight bout. As you no doubt recall, my boy was once a helluva courtroom fighter."

"That was a long time ago."

"Oh, he's still got a nasty haymaker. But what's this? You're backing down before the opening bell. As soon as things get a little rough, you wimp out with a competency proceeding."

"That's bullshit." Bellows's face was flushed.

"Call it whatever you want to call it, Jack, but this pussy move was yours."

"I had nothing to do with this proceeding. This is Guttner's deal one hundred percent. You can tell Hirsch he's one lucky bastard. But you better tell him to get his deal finalized quick, because I gave Guttner one week to get it done. After that, the wraps come off, and I'm going to drill David Hirsch a new asshole. Tell him that."

"Tell him yourself, Dirty Harry."

Bellows was glaring down at Rosenbloom as Hirsch stepped out from the pay phones. Bellows looked up, his entire body tensing, fists clenching. For a moment, Hirsch thought Bellows was going to charge—and during that tense moment, even as he shifted his weight to get ready, Hirsch flashed on the absurdity of two lawyers in their late fifties tussling in a courthouse hallway.

"For chrissake, Jack," Rosenbloom said, "don't be a horse's ass. This isn't the WWF, you *putz*, and you sure as hell ain't Hulk Hogan."

Bellows looked at Rosenbloom and then back at Hirsch.

Staring at Hirsch, Bellows said, "I sure hope you fuck up that settlement, because once this case is back on track, you're dead meat."

He turned and marched off toward the elevators.

Rosenbloom called after him, "Then you better line up a good pathologist."

The elevator doors slid open and Bellows and his associate got on. Bellows turned back to face them and held the door open.

"Don't worry about my experts," he called, as the elevator doors began to close. "We've have the top two pathologists in the nation."

Rosenbloom turned his wheelchair toward Hirsch. "Let's hope he's right." He chuckled. "What a goober. Guess we smoked them out, eh?"

Hirsch nodded. "Guttner's running the show."

"Let's get back to the office and let Dulcie know what happened."

Hirsch checked his watch. "I have a meeting with the U.S. trustee in ten minutes."

"I'll give her a call. See if she can drop by later."

28

THE three of them—Dulcie, Rosenbloom, and Hirsch—were seated around the table in a small conference room in Rosenbloom's offices.

"How did he take it?" Dulcie asked Hirsch.

"Abe doesn't remember seeing or talking with her," Hirsch said. "I don't know if he even remembers he has a sister named Hannah, or if he understands anything that's going on in the case anymore. He did remember that he had a daughter named Judith this time, but he seems to think she's alive."

Dulcie winced. "Oh, no."

Hirsch shook his head. "His mind is getting worse."

It was a quarter to five. Dulcie had arrived just a few minutes before Hirsch, who'd been out of the office the whole day, having gone directly from probate court to a bankruptcy court meeting and from there to a debtors exam out in Jefferson County and then back to meet with Abe Shifrin.

The old man had seemed almost angelic that afternoon.

His anger and irritation had vanished, replaced by an eerie serenity. The house was even messier than before. His shirt and pants were wrinkled and stained. Even so, he was calm and amiable. The television was on in the kitchen when he'd opened the door and looked up at Hirsch, giving him a pleasant smile. Hirsch introduced himself, not wanting to make Shifrin strain his memory. Shifrin beckoned Hirsch to join him in the kitchen, where he was watching a Roadrunner cartoon. Hirsch stood by the sink and watched Shifrin watch the cartoon, watched him laugh with delight as Wiley E. Coyote smashed into the image of a railroad tunnel that the Roadrunner had painted onto the side of the mountain before disappearing into it.

The cartoon ended, a laxative commercial came on, and Shifrin had turned to him. "So how can I help you, young man?"

Dulcie and Rosenbloom listened quietly to Hirsch's account of the meeting with Shifrin. Rosenbloom winced as Hirsch described his attempt to make Shifrin understand that his daughter was actually dead and not down at the supermarket picking up a head of lettuce.

When Hirsch finished, Dulcie asked, "When will the judge appoint a physician to examine him?"

"Already happened," Rosenbloom said. He turned to Hirsch "We got the order by fax this afternoon. Doctor named Nemes. On the faculty at Wash U. Solid reputation."

Hirsch nodded. "Good. Abe needs help. The sooner we get it for him, the better."

"But what happens to the lawsuit?" Dulcie asked.

Hirsch looked at each of them. "We don't need the lawsuit."

Dulcie frowned. "What?"

"I did some thinking on the drive back from Jefferson County. The lawsuit has served its purpose. We can't count on it anymore as a tool for developing the kind of information I'm looking for. If something's not kosher in the Peterson Tire litigation, I'm never going to find out what it is through a formal document request or a deposition. I'll have to do that investigation outside the rules of procedure."

"So what do we do with the case?" Dulcie asked.

"Settle it," Hirsch said.

"Settle it?" she repeated.

Hirsch nodded. "And you should be the one to settle it."

"David's right," Rosenbloom said. "You've been cast in the role of guardian angel. You should be the one to make the contact with Marvin Guttner. Tell him you'd like to explore the possibility of a settlement."

"Guttner will be delighted," Hirsch said. "Just as important, the mere act of making that overture will immunize you."

"Guttner doesn't trust you now," Rosenbloom said to Dulcie. "We're the ones who suggested your name to the judge. He'll assume you're tainted. But if you contact him early on to explore settlement, those suspicions are going to disappear."

"Or at least get diluted," Hirsch added.

"I don't get it." She stared at Hirsch. "You really want me to settle this case?"

Hirsch nodded. "This is the right moment. Abe is going to end up in a nursing home, and probably sooner rather than later. It's going to be expensive. Might as well get Peterson Tire to help pay the bills." He paused. "But the settlement can't be just for money."

"What do you mean?" she asked.

Hirsch glanced at Rosenbloom. "We owe him that much, Sancho."

Rosenbloom gave him a weary shrug.

Hirsch turned to Dulcie. "Abe never cared about the

cash. He called it blood money." Hirsch leaned back in his chair. "It took him three years of brooding before he decided to bring a lawsuit. He told me he wanted to make sure that the people responsible for her death would be forced to remember her. He wanted them to accept responsibility."

He paused and shook his head. "He doesn't remember that anymore, but I do. That's why the settlement has to be for more than money. We need to get him some justice, too."

"What do you have in mind?" Dulcie asked.

Hirsch sighed. "I'm not sure anymore. Even if they agreed to put some kind of an admission in the settlement agreement, and they'd never agree to, how do we know if they're guilty of anything? How does a false admission honor her memory? Still, we need to get something out of them. We need to be realistic. We need to admit to ourselves that we may never find anything on McCormick. This could be our only chance to do something for Judith." He shrugged. "Maybe we ask them for an expression of regret." He glanced over at Rosenbloom. "Not much, but it's something."

Dulcie nodded. "I'll see what I can get."

"And while you're at it," Rosenbloom said, "be sure you squeeze Jabba's nuts for some more cash. Seventy-five grand isn't enough. Make Blimpie squirm a little."

She smiled. "It'll be my pleasure."

Hirsch checked his watch. Ten minutes after five.

"Did Jumbo come by today?" he asked.

Rosenbloom said, "For a few hours this morning. While we were in court. He was heading out just as I got back. He told me to tell you he's still trying to find her e-mails but he was able to locate most of the documents she created on her computer."

"Really?" Hirsch said. "Can he get us access to them?"

Rosenbloom chuckled. "Oh, yeah. I don't understand the connection he hooked up, but he told me he made sure that no one could ever trace it back to this office. He's got the print command routed through a computer in the admissions office at the University of Nebraska. The guy is goddamn amazing. Anyway, he told me it might take awhile for our printer to kick in, and he was right. But it's been printing like a bastard for the last hour."

"Printing what?"

"Go in your office and check it out. You got a big stack of shit, and it's growing by the minute. That little gal could write."

29

THE sheer quantity was astounding. And daunting.

Thousands of documents. Thousands and thousands of pages. The written detritus of more than two years of a district court clerkship. A half dozen different documents a day, each ranging in length from one to twenty pages, most in the three- to five-page range. There were research memos and letters and draft orders and interoffice communications and draft opinions and internal memos and notes and outlines of legal issues and status reports and so on and so on and so on.

Each document included a document-profile cover page, with the date and time of its creation and the date and time of each edit. Jumbo had arranged for the documents to print in chronological order, beginning with what appeared to be a sample file memo created on her first day on the job as part of a computer training class at the courthouse.

He started in on the pile at 5:30 that night. He moved through them slowly and deliberately, not sure what he was looking for, not wanting to miss something subtle buried on page three of an otherwise irrelevant memorandum.

For the period covering her first months on the job, he read every word of every document. He needed to understand the clerkship of Judith Shifrin, and, as he gradually realized, the world of Judith Shifrin. He'd seen photographs of her—the childhood snapshots, the posed graduation photos, the final morgue shots. And he'd heard the words of others about her—the words of her father, of Dulcie, of Missy Shields, of even Marvin Guttner. But finally, here in this pile of documents, he had access to her words.

And at last, he began to hear her voice. It was a younger voice than he'd imagined. Almost naive. A voice lacking self-confidence. But an earnest voice. And an intelligent one, too.

For every day during her first few months on the job, Judith created at least two multipage documents, one entitled Court Notes and the other entitled Chambers Notes. Each was a distillation of the copious notes she took during court proceedings and conferences in her judge's chambers. According to the date and time notations on the document profile pages, she apparently returned to her office at the end of the day and typed up her notes, sometimes working as late as ten or eleven at night, especially during the early days, back when she was unsure of the significance of what had occurred.

In those early Court Notes and Chambers Notes, she seemed to write down everything—objections, arguments of counsel, evidentiary rulings, oral motions, scheduling matters, testimony summaries, the judge's comments on anything and everything. She was especially careful to record whatever McCormick said, surrounding his banalities and hackneyed expressions with quotation marks, as if recording gems of wisdom for the ages. Thus her first Court Notes recorded McCormick's observation that "Close only counts in horseshoes, Counselor." The following Monday, her Conference Notes quoted McCormick advising the defendant's counsel, "That dog won't hunt, Deirdre." At the end of that same week, McCormick denied the defendants' motion for summary judgment, explaining, "I understand Oliver Wendell Holmes said that the law is a seamless web. Maybe so, Mr. Abrams, but your motion is a defective mess." Afterward, she had written, in parenthesis: "(Touché!)"

Hirsch was amused and touched by her innocence. Had he ever been that young and impressionable?

Gradually, the Peterson Tire litigation consumed more and more of her working hours. Although she continued to split the judge's criminal docket with his other law clerk— identified in a few of her Chambers Notes as "Julian"—by the end of her first six months on the job the Peterson Tire case had become her sole civil matter. Indeed, the *In re Turbo XL Tire Litigation* grew so large so quickly that the presiding judge of the Eastern District of Missouri entered an order removing Brendan McCormick's name from the assignment wheel for new civil cases. From that point on, Julian was the law clerk on the rest of the judge's gradually dwindling civil docket while Judith had principal responsibility for the myriad matters comprising *In re Turbo XL Tire Litigation*.

And myriad they were. It was hard to imagine one law clerk having enough time to handle just the administrative burden of tracking more than a thousand claims, each moving toward resolution at its own pace and in its own way and with its own set of attorneys and its own set of witnesses and issues. But the administrative tasks were only part of her job. Procedural and substantive legal issues kept popping up—some involving just one claim, others affecting entire groups of claims—and the initial responsibility for dealing with those issues fell on her shoulders as well.

And hers alone. Her fellow clerk, the guy named Julian, was completely isolated from the case. Eventually, according to one of her memos, he was moved to an office on another floor in order to make way for more storage space in the massive case.

Judith seemed to relish the challenges and didn't mind the long hours. What came through in her papers that first year was the belief that she was part of some magnificent experiment in justice, that what she and her judge were doing with *In re Turbo XL Tire Litigation* might have a profound impact on the way courts in the future would handle mass tort litigation.

And in her defense, she was not alone in that conviction, or in casting McCormick in the role of judicial visionary. Peterson Tire Corporation's legal predicament had been at the heart of the transformation of Brendan McCormick's judicial stature. The reputation he'd earned as a state judge—pro-government in criminal cases, pro-defendant in civil cases, lackluster in all cases—remained constant during his early years on the federal bench. But six years ago, the federal multidistrict panel consolidated 114 separate lawsuits and class actions from around the country arising out of the Peterson Turbo XL tire scandal and assigned the colossus to Brendan McCormick. His critics predicted disaster, but he surprised them by seizing control of the massive case and its bickering hordes of attorneys. Within a year, and just a few months before Judith's clerkship commenced, he'd hammered out a comprehensive dispute resolution procedure governing more than a thousand wrongful death and personal injury claims arising out of accidents allegedly caused by tire-tread separations. Under the procedure, Peterson Tire Corporation admitted liability, the plaintiffs waived all claims for punitive damages, and all parties submitted to a procedure whereby each claim for compensatory damages would be resolved in a one-day, nonjury mini-trial before the judge. During the last four years, McCormick had heard and resolved more than six hundred claims under his innovative procedure. His handling of the case had garnered praise from the *Wall Street Journal* (in a three-part series entitled "Taming the Ravenous Plaintiffs Beast") to the *New York Times* (in a Sunday magazine story entitled "The Judge Who Balances Tires") to *Business Week* (in a cover story entitled "Running a Courtroom Like a Business").

By the end of her first year, Judith's commitment to the case had become almost religious in its fervor. In more than one of her research memos on issues before the court, she would base her recommendation on what was, in her words, "more in harmony with the McCormick vision." In her Hearing Notes and Chambers Notes, admiring adjectives and adverbs began appearing in her descriptions of McCormick's actions. He was "forceful" and "skillful" and "cogent" and, Hirsch couldn't help but smile, "eloquent." In one of her Chambers Notes, she recounted the judge's attempt to resolve a dispute over certain expert witness testimony. Hirsch would have labeled the judge's ruling "confusing" and "short-sighted." She called it "Solomon-like." In one of her Court Notes, she used the words *decisive* and *innovative* to describe a pair of evidentiary rulings that Hirsch would have characterized as, respectively, "ludicrous" and "clear reversible error."

Hirsch had no trouble imagining how Brendan McCormick would have relished having this adoring young acolyte in his chambers. He could visualize McCormick performing for her on the bench, preening around her in his chambers. He also had no trouble imaging how tempted McCormick would have been to take advantage of her. Back in their days together at the U.S. Attorney's Office, McCormick used to brag about the postgame parties at

Mizzou featuring freshman girls eager to provide sexual favors for the varsity football players. McCormick's conquests during his prosecutor days included several female interns from the local law schools.

Hirsch read through her memos carefully, trying to read between the lines, trying to detect whether her relationship with the judge went beyond professional, whether McCormick had added her to his list of conquests.

He couldn't tell.

But her devotion to her judge was obvious. Tracking the create dates on the document profile sheets, he learned that during her first year on the job she spent several weekends ghostwriting speeches and articles for McCormick, all on the glory and genius of *In re Turbo XL Tire Litigation*. As pointless as it seemed all these years later, he found himself angered at the thought of Judith devoting, for example, an entire weekend in June ghostwriting an essay on alternative dispute resolution procedures for the *Journal of the American Bar Association* while the putative author of that article was no doubt spending that same weekend on the golf course with his buddies or down in Bermuda with his latest girlfriend.

And then he found it.

A Chambers Notes dated November 12. Approximately thirteen months before her death.

He thought at first that it was just another one of the dozens and dozens of Chambers Notes he'd already read. The first two pages summarized an afternoon meeting in the judge's office with a lawyer for Peterson Tire and two lawyers on the plaintiff's steering committee. The purpose of the meeting was to schedule a pair of hearings on the admissibility of a new area of expert testimony. Later that same afternoon, the judge's secretary summoned her to his office again. When she arrived, he was studying what appeared to be a financial statement. He was upset about something on the statement. Her memo continued:

> The Judge told me that he needed some information about the Sanderson claim. He said he needed to know the dollar amount of what Sanderson's lawyers had presented as their damages claim at the hearing and the amount that he had actually awarded. He told me he needed it ASAP.
>
> I hurried back to my office to review my files. The Dorothy Sanderson matter had been heard on October 7. I was able to confirm that the damage award had been $1 million even. I recalled that Mrs. Sanderson's attorneys had asked for more than that, but I couldn't remember how much more. As I was reviewing my notes of the hearing, I received a telephone call from Ada Hershey, one of the paralegals at Emerson, Burke. Imagine my surprise when she asked me the very same question that the Judge had asked! She told me that her records indicated that the Judge's award to Mrs. Sanderson had been $1 million but that she needed to know what the plaintiff's final demand had been. Of course, I didn't dare tell her about the coincidence, but I did ask why she needed to know. She told me that Mr. Guttner was upset and demanding to know the answer. I told her I was taking care of something else at the moment but would check my notes and get back to her later.
>
> Very weird, I thought as I hung up.
>
> Anyway, I was relieved to find in my notes that Mrs. Sanderson's lawyers had put on evidence to support a claim for $1.4 million. I hurried back to the judge's office and told him what I found. He started laughing. He told me I was the most wonderful law clerk he'd ever had. He said I was literally worth my weight in gold.

I was floating on Cloud 9 on the way back to my office, but my good mood was shattered when Ada Hershey called to tell me that I didn't need to bother looking because she'd found the answer. Acting innocent, I asked her what she'd found. She said that Mrs. Sanderson's lawyers had demanded $1.3 million. I told her I thought it was $1.4 million, but she said that she'd checked with one of the paralegals for the plaintiffs who'd explained that the original demand had been $1.4 million but that due to the exclusion of one item of damages at the hearing, the final demand was $1.3 million. I asked her if she was sure and she said she was positive.

I felt totally terrible. I rushed back into the Judge's office to confess my mistake. He was standing by the window on the phone, his back to me, holding that financial statement in his hand. I realized that he was talking to Mr. Guttner about the Sanderson claim. I was so upset, but I didn't want to disturb him, so I stood there hoping that he would turn around. Maybe it was because my emotions were so intense or maybe it was just because of what he was saying, but I wrote it all down from memory when I got back to my office. He said:

"Don't try that bullshit, Marvin. My law clerk confirmed the number. They asked for one point four. I gave them a mil. Do the math. Fifteen percent is thirty-nine. I've got the statement in my hand and guess what? The number I'm looking at starts with a two. Huh? No way, pal. My girl said one point four, and my girl's never wrong. Hey, Marvin, these aren't the Brookfield warehouses. These numbers are final. What's done is done, pal. Oh, yeah? Well, listen carefully. You ever try to fuck me again and I'll fuck you and your client into bankruptcy. Guaranteed. You understand?"

I backed out of the Judge's office and walked back to mine in a daze. I didn't understand what I'd just heard, but I sure didn't like the way it sounded. After I wrote it down, I stared at my legal pad, trying to make sense out of what I'd heard.

> Twenty minutes later, the Judge called me back into his office and told me that from now on he wanted me to keep a chart showing for each claim the exact amount the claimant sought at the hearing and the amount that he awarded. He wanted me to keep the chart current and give him a copy each Friday. I told him I would.

And she did, as Hirsch confirmed by flipping through the next hundred or so documents. On the Friday of each week that included claims hearings in *In re Turbo XL Tire Litigation*—usually two weeks each month—she created a document entitled Award Grid. The format was the same for each one. For example, the Award Grid dated Friday, December 11, apparently summarizing that week's proceedings, read as follows:

CLAIMANT	CASE NUMBER	CLAIMANT'S AWARD	CLAIM
Alvey	44782	$1,650,000	$1,200,000
Annis	34267	$950,000	$925,000
Kalinowski	49024	$1,200,000	$950,000
Gerber	33165	$575,000	$450,000

He studied the grid, trying to make sense out of it. He turned back to her Chambers Notes and read again her rendition of McCormick's phone conversation with Guttner.

He took out his calculator and ran the numbers on the Sanderson case. He could not find a way to make fifteen percent of anything come out to a number beginning with thirty-nine. Fifteen percent of $1.4 million was $210,000.

Fifteen percent of $1.3 million was $195,000. Fifteen percent of one million was $150,000. He subtracted one million from $1.4 million, took fifteen percent of the remainder, and came up with $60,000. He tried the reverse. If thirty-nine was thirty-nine thousand, than it was fifteen percent of $260,000, but he couldn't figure out how to come up with $260,000 from the other numbers.

He stood and stretched. The two cleaning women had come through more than an hour ago. The offices were completely empty now.

He looked down at the stack of unread documents. Still about a third of the pile to go. At least another two hours of reading. He massaged the back of his neck with his right hand and yawned. He checked his watch. 10:52 P.M. He looked back at the stack of documents.

Oh, well.

30

HE finished the last of Judith's documents around three that morning. Yawning, he stood up and stretched and checked his watch. He padded down the darkened hallway in his socks, flicked on the light in the small lunchroom, refilled his mug with the remaining coffee in the pot, and turned off the coffeemaker.

On the way back down the hall, he took a sip of the coffee, which had been sitting on the warmer for more than two hours. It tasted as harsh and burnt as it smelled. Still, it was coffee and it was hot.

Tilted back in his chair, his feet resting on top of his desk, he sipped the bitter coffee as he mulled over what he'd discovered and tried to formulate his next move. Although the pace of Judith's document creation gradually declined after her November 12 Chambers Notes memo describing the overheard telephone conversation, the complexity, and subtlety, of what followed increased. Certain basic documents were not affected. The Award Grid, which commenced the Friday after her November 12 memo, continued through the rest of her clerkship. So, too, various administrative documents, mostly based on forms she'd created during her first months as a clerk, continued as before.

The most immediate change was the tone of her Hearing Notes and Chambers Notes. Gone was the animated style sprinkled with flattering references to McCormick. Subsequent Hearing Notes and Chambers Notes were written in a passive, bureaucratic voice shorn of praise or other editorial comment. He read every one of them, but the dead prose offered no glimpse into Judith's concerns.

Not so, however, with what she had previously labeled Research Memos. Before November 12, those memos consisted of summaries of her legal research or summaries of her investigations into the factual issues raised by various motions. There were still some of those after November 12 as well, but now there was also a new subspecies. Though still entitled a Research Memo, these new ones—there were five in all created over the next eleven months—focused on different aspects of what Hirsch came to think of as the aftermath of the November 12 memo. Each of these five aftermath memos marked an important phase in what appeared to be Judith's ongoing efforts to make sense out of that November 12 telephone call.

The first one described her follow-up conversations with Ada Hershey, the paralegal from Marvin Guttner's office that she'd spoken with about the Sanderson case. Judith called Ada, ostensibly trying to organize the court records on the costs to be awarded the prevailing party at the conclusion of each damages hearing. Since there was a hypothetical possibility, albeit remote, that Peterson Tire could be the prevailing party at one of the damages hearings, Judith told Ada that she was trying to get a handle on the types of costs Peterson Tire was incurring in defending each claim.

Take the Sanderson case, for example, she told Ada. The

damage award entered by the judge included an award of Mrs. Sanderson's costs. The bill of costs that Mrs. Sanderson's lawyers filed included a court filing fee, photocopying charges, court reporter fees for various depositions, and two expert witness fees (one for the doctor who testified about Mrs. Sanderson's injuries and one for the economist who testified about her damages).

But what if Peterson Tire had prevailed, Judith asked. *What kinds of costs would Peterson Tire have included in its bill of costs?*

Ada promised to look into it and get back to her. She called the next day and said that the answer was more complicated than she'd realized. In most lawsuits, she explained to Judith, her law firm advanced all litigation costs and then included the disbursements on the client's monthly bills. Thus, for example, a court reporter would send the firm a bill for transcribing a deposition, the firm would pay the bill, and then the firm would put that disbursement on the client's bill for reimbursement directly to the firm. But with Peterson Tire, the only costs the firm paid were internal ones, such as photocopying costs, long-distance charges, and computer research fees. All other costs were billed directly to Peterson Tire by the vendor, and Peterson Tire paid the bill directly to the vendor.

Was there any record of the costs that Peterson Tire paid directly? Judith asked.

Presumably there was, Ada told her, but the law firm didn't have a copy.

Could she get a copy?

Ada told her that she'd already asked Mr. Guttner that very question. Mr. Guttner told her in no uncertain terms that in the highly unlikely event that court costs would ever became an issue, all necessary information would be disclosed. Until that happened, no such information would be made available to anyone.

Judith asked Ada about her call on November 12 seeking the amount of Mrs. Sanderson's final demand at the hearing. Ada confessed that she wasn't sure why it had become an issue. However, now she was under orders to keep track of that information in the form of a grid for each claim showing the amount of the claim and the amount of the award. She told Judith that she had to send one copy of the grid memo to Mr. Guttner and fax one copy to Donald Foster, the CFO of Peterson Tire. Mr. Guttner hadn't told her why, she said, but she was guessing that maybe he wanted that information to show the client how much money they were saving them, since often there was a several-hundred-thousand-dollar gap between what the claimant sought at the hearing and what Judge McCormick actually awarded.

Below that statement, Judith had added a final sentence: *I hope she's right.*

Judith wrote the next aftermath memo a little over a month later, in December—indeed, almost a year to the day before her death. At first, it seemed an ordinary Research Memo. The topic was Peterson Tire's responses to various discovery requests served on it by the plaintiffs. Hirsch had seen other such memos from Judith in connection with the many discovery motions filed by the parties. The format was fairly consistent: she would review the contested discovery response, examine other relevant information provided by the objecting party, research the pertinent case law, and conclude with a recommendation to the judge and a proposed order. This Research Memo started out in the same way, but by the second page Hirsch realized that there was no reference to any pending motion. Instead, the memo appeared to be a compendium of interrogatory answers, responses to document requests, and deposition excerpts on one topic: the identities and job descriptions of all employees at Peterson Tire's corporate headquarters in Knoxville. Judith didn't yet have all, or

even most, of the names on the chart. Instead, her Research
Memo set out a strategy for compiling that information
from the various discovery requests in the case.

Hirsch didn't make the connection until the last paragraph of the memo, which mentioned that she had re-
quested floppy disks containing the discovery database put
together by Drahner Cortez LLC. The date on the Research Memo confirmed the connection. Missy Shields
and Judith had first met toward the end of November. By
the middle of December, according to Missy; Judith had
asked for a copy of her firm's discovery database.

Another one of the aftermath memos, dated in April of
the following year, was the follow-up memo to the December one. This memo filled in most of the blanks in the chart
with names, job titles, home addresses, and home phone
numbers (all with the 423 area code). Hirsch confirmed
from his copy of Judith's phone bills that many of those
phone numbers had shown up on her phone bills from that
April through July. According to the document profile
cover sheet, Judith made numerous edits to this memo
from April through the last week in August.

Of particular interest on this memo were the entries under the name Donald Foster, chief financial officer of Peterson Tire. In the version of the Research Memo that had
been printed out, which, according to the document profile,
had last been edited on August 24 of Judith's final year, the
CFO's secretary was identified as Marcella Vitale. There
was an asterisk after her name, and at the bottom of the
page the following note appeared:

Ms. Vitale started her job on July 15. She was formerly
a secretary at the Allstate Insurance regional claims office in Knoxville. Mr. Foster's prior secretary, Ruth
Jones, apparently resigned earlier in the summer and
moved to Chicago. According to sources, she had been

with Foster for many years. Her new address and phone number are presently unknown. *Need to find her. Must talk with her!*

If she ever found Ruth Jones, there was no mention of it in any of the rest of the documents he read that night.

There was another aftermath memo dated in March of that final year. It was basically a bullet-point outline devoted to Judith's efforts to make sense out of McCormick's reference to the Brookfield warehouses, which apparently were involved in a pair of condemnation cases dating back sixteen years earlier. The cases had made it into the newspaper, and Judith's memo cited three articles from the *St. Louis Post-Dispatch*. She also had the name and phone number of Patrick Markman, the reporter on the stories. She had apparently gone out to the St. Louis County courts to review the files in the cases. She had learned that the government entity was something called the Brookfield Shopping District Redevelopment Corporation; its attorney was Mitchell Monroe, identified as the city attorney of Brookfield, Missouri; the property owner was Eagle Valley Storage Corporation; and its attorneys were Emmanuel Castleman and Marvin Guttner. Both cases went to trial during the same summer, and both were tried in Division 25 of the Circuit Court of St. Louis County. The trial judge for both cases was St. Louis County Circuit Judge Brendan McCormick.

No commentary from Judith. Just the facts—one by one in bullet points down the page. Both cases were the subject of posttrial motions. Both cases settled prior to the hearings on those motions.

The fifth and final aftermath memo was dated September 17—just three months before her death and about a week after her trip to Knoxville. There was no mention of the trip in the memo. Instead, the topic hearkened back to the claim at the center of the November 12 memo and of the memo on the follow-up conversation with Ada Hershey. This final aftermath memo read, in its entirety, as follows:

According to internal company records, the following are the costs incurred by Peterson Tire Corporation in connection with its defense of the claim of Dorothy Sanderson:

Boudreau Court Reporting (transcripts)	$2,552.29
Metro Region Orthopedics (medical expert)	$11,400.00
Pembris-R Productions (video depositions)	$875.00
Felis Tigris LVII, Ltd. (litigation support)	$25,500.00
St. Martin's Radiology (X-rays)	$2,225.50
Klingel & Craven, P.C. (economic expert)	$9,500.00
Kwik Copy Services (photocopies)	$784.25

All amounts paid by check or wire transfer out of the CFO's office.

No commentary, no questions, no speculations. Just the facts.

He searched back through the documents to the November 12 memo. He read again the excerpt from McCormick's telephone conversation with Guttner:

"They asked for one point four. I gave them a mil. Do the math. Fifteen percent is thirty-nine. I've got the statement in my hand and guess what? The number I'm looking at starts with a two."

He stared at the column of costs, and then he reached for his calculator.

31

"OH, yes," Cassie Markman said with a smile. "Pat was impressed with that little gal. Told me more than once that she could have been one heck of an investigative reporter. 'Far better than me,' he used to say. 'Far better than me.'"

"Did your brother say why?" Hirsch asked.

She frowned as she thought back. "I can't say for sure. I just know he was real taken with her." She placed her hand on her chest. "He was just devastated when that poor girl died. He went to her funeral."

They were in the small living room of Cassie Markman's bungalow on the far south side of St. Louis, just a block or so off Gravois. She'd grown up in that bungalow—she and her older brother Patrick, the two of them raised by their mother, who'd been widowed when her fireman husband died fighting a three-alarm factory fire. Cassie's brother was just eight at the time. She was five.

Like her bungalow, Cassie Markman was small and

neat. She was in her late sixties, barely five feet tall, trim, close-cropped white hair, keen eyes, high cheekbones. Her face and hands were weathered, no doubt from spending the summer months outdoors tending the gardens that took up most of her front yard and painting the dozen or so urban landscapes that hung on the walls of her house, all signed *C Markman*. She wore a simple, freshly starched white blouse, a long navy skirt, sturdy brown shoes, no jewelry, and man's wristwatch.

"More tea?" she asked, reaching for the teapot on the coffee table.

"No, thanks."

He waited until she refilled her teacup. The scent of chamomile filled the room.

So far he'd learned that Cassie's brother had joined the army after high school. His sister stayed put, taking a sales job at a department store. Patrick returned home after his honorable discharge and took a job as a police beat reporter with the old *Globe-Democrat*. When their mother died of cancer at the age of forty-six, Patrick moved back into his old room. The two siblings, bachelor and spinster for life, lived together in the family home for nearly forty years until his death.

"How did your brother meet Judith?" Hirsch asked.

"I think she actually called him up. Out of the blue. Said she was interested in some stories he'd written many years ago. He was a reporter, you know."

"I do," Hirsch said.

"And a darn good one, rest his soul."

Markman had died less than two months after Judith. He was a special assignment investigative reporter with the *Post-Dispatch* by then. According to the obituary Hirsch read on microfilm earlier that afternoon, he was killed in a one-car accident late at night on his way home from Jefferson City, where he'd gone to investigate a story on government corruption. The medical examiner said he'd apparently fallen asleep at the wheel and driven into an embankment.

"She called him about a court case he'd covered," Cassie continued. "I remember meeting her. A little thing. Even smaller than me. She came by one night to drop off some papers for Pat. As best I recall, they were copies of some court files."

"Did they involve any Brookfield condemnation cases?"

"Brookfield," she repeated. "Now that does sound familiar."

"I've reviewed her papers," Hirsch said. "In one of them she mentioned some articles that your brother wrote on the Brookfield warehouse condemnations. I found the articles on microfilm this afternoon and made copies." He reached into his briefcase and handed her copies of each.

He watched as she read them, one by one.

The first article, five paragraphs on the second page of the Metro section, ran under the headline: $3.75 MILLION AWARDED IN BROOKFIELD CONDEMNATION CASE; CITY OFFICIALS EXPRESS SURPRISE OVER AMOUNT. The story explained that a St. Louis county jury had awarded the owners of a pair of warehouses on the south side of Bulger Road $3,750,000 for the properties, which had been condemned as part of the city's proposed redevelopment plan. What made the case noteworthy, and the city officials concerned, was that the verdict exceeded the city's appraised value of the property by more than a million dollars. The article quoted the city's attorney, Mitchell Monroe, as "evaluating the possibility of an appeal." The successful property owner's attorney, Marvin Guttner, told the newspaper that his client "is quite satisfied with the verdict and believed that justice has been bestowed." The article closed by noting that the same parties would be back in court in two weeks for the trial of the condemnation of the two remaining warehouses on the north side of Bulger Road.

Patrick Markman was there when they returned to court for that case, and his story made it onto the first page of the Metro section under the headline: BROOKFIELD OFFICIALS FEAR SECOND MULTIMILLION-DOLLAR VERDICT ENDANGERS REDEVELOPMENT PLAN. The story opened:

> A surprisingly acrimonious condemnation trial ended this afternoon with a multimillion-dollar jury verdict that one Brookfield city official labeled "the death knell" for his town's ambitious redevelopment project.
>
> A St. Louis County jury awarded Eagle Valley Storage Corporation $4.1 million as compensation for the taking of a pair of warehouses on the north side of Bulger Road. The warehouses are located on a parcel of land that Brookfield city planners hope will one day be the site of a restaurant, theater, and shopping complex. The properties had been condemned under eminent domain authority by the Brookfield Land Clearance Redevelopment Authority, a municipal authority established by the city as part of its ambitious plans for transforming its aging industrial park into an entertainment and shopping district.
>
> The award exceeded the city's appraised value by $950,000, making it the second time in less than a month that Eagle Valley Storage Corporation has obtained a jury verdict for Brookfield warehouse properties that significantly exceeded the city's valuation of the properties.

The article quoted a Brookfield alderman who claimed that the combined jury verdicts had so far exceeded the city's condemnation budget that the entire redevelopment project was in jeopardy. There were several paragraphs describing the origins of the redevelopment project, the performance of similar projects in the region, and the use of eminent domain powers to achieve those goals. More interesting for Hirsch was the description of certain courtroom events:

> Courtroom observers noted that the most critical portion of the trial took place outside the hearing of the jury. Attorney Guttner objected to the testimony of appraiser Lawrence Gallagher, the city's expert witness on valuation of the properties. Judge McCormick excused the jury and conducted a mini-hearing on the admissibility of Gallagher's opinions. In a ruling mirroring his ruling in the prior condemnation case, he excluded large portions of Gallagher's testimony, including the expert's opinion as to the valuation of the properties.

> As a result, the jury heard valuation testimony only from the property owner's expert, Harlan Reston. Moreover, Monroe's cross-examination of Reston was severely restricted when the judge sustained objections to several of Monroe's questions.

> After the jury verdict, an obviously frustrated attorney for the city, Mitchell Monroe said, "This is a verdict that cries out for reversal on appeal."

The last article ran three weeks later. It described a hearing before Judge McCormick in which attorneys for the city and the property owner announced that they had worked out a global settlement of both cases for a compromise amount. The resolution, according to the city's attorney, would save the redevelopment project. The article quoted both attorneys on the subject of their clients' satisfaction with the results, and also quoted the mayor of Brookfield, who said he was thrilled that the project could once again move forward. But it was the final sentence of the article that caught Hirsch's attention: "The good spirits seemed to be shared by everyone in the courtroom except the judge, who angrily chided attorney Guttner for 'wasting the court's time with matters that should have been settled before trial' and then abruptly left the bench."

Hirsch had pondered that final sentence. In his experience, a judge was often the party most satisfied by a lawsuit settlement. The plaintiff might feel he'd settled for too little, the defendant might believe he'd overpaid, but the judge was always delighted, since it meant another case off his docket. Hirsch thought back to McCormick's comment in Judith's November 12 memo: "Hey, Marvin, these aren't the Brookfield warehouses. What's done is done."

The comment still made no sense.

Cassie looked up from the final article and nodded. "I think these were the cases she was interested in."

"Do you remember why?"

"Oh, my." She closed her eyes as she tried to remember. "The best I can recall," she said, eyes still closed, "is she wanted to know about the relationship between the judge and one of the lawyers."

"Which lawyer?"

She opened her eyes and shook her head. "I don't recognize any of the names in the article."

"Do you know what kind of relationship she was interested in?"

Cassie gave him a puzzled look that faded into an amused grin. "I've never been an investigative reporter, Mr. Hirsch, but I did spent four decades living with one. You pick up a few things over time, and one of them was that when someone came to see my brother about a relationship between a government official and a lawyer, there's only one kind of relationship they're talking about."

"Had he ever talked to you about that judge?"

She glanced at the article. "McCormick? Not specifically."

"What do you mean not specifically?"

"The name doesn't ring a bell." She paused. "These articles you copied, that was back when my brother was covering the county courts for the *Post-Dispatch*. I've heard things have changed out there since then. Changed for the better. But back then, well, my brother had a pretty low opinion of some of those judges. Real low. He told me a joke among the lawyers back then. It went like this. What's the definition of an honest judge in the circuit court of St. Louis County?"

"What?"

"When you fix him, he stays fixed." Her smile faded. "He may have met a lot of bad men over the years, but he never did lose his sense of humor."

They talked some more about the articles and the condemnation cases, but it was clear that she didn't remember any of the specifics.

She did recall that Judith met several times with her brother, sometimes during the day, once or twice at night. And she was certain that Judith had "passed the test."

"What test?" Hirsch asked.

Cassie Markman smiled. "He gave her a tour of the pyramid. My brother was a tough judge of people, Mr. Hirsch. If he gave that little gal the tour, it meant she was special. It meant she was okay in his book."

"I'm afraid I'm lost," he said. "What pyramid are you talking about?"

She stood up. "Stay there. I'll be right back."

She headed toward the back of the house and reappeared carrying a quarto-sized book entitled *An Illustrated Journey to the Seven Wonders of the Ancient World*. She opened the book on her lap and looked up at him.

"Do you know where the word *mausoleum* comes from?" she asked.

"No idea."

"From a king named Mausolus. He was one of the provincial kings of the ancient Persian empire."

She started leafing through the book as she spoke. "He had a small kingdom along the Mediterranean coast. He ruled over it from the city of Helicarnassus." She looked up. "It's called Bodrum today. It's on the Turkish coast. Mausolus had a queen named Artemisia, who happened to be his sister, too."

She gave him an impish grin.

"Sounds weird, I know, but my brother assured me it was the custom for kings in that region to marry their sisters. He claimed the marriage was purely ceremonial, and he better have been telling the truth, because he nicknamed me Artemisia. Especially after I started showing my paintings." She gestured toward the paintings on the wall. "He used to call me the Artist Artemisia."

She smiled at the memory. Her eyes seemed to go distant, but only for a moment.

"Anyway, when King Mausolus died, his sister was heartbroken. She decided to build her brother the most splendid tomb in the world. She brought in the top artisans from Greece. The result was a spectacular tomb on a hill overlooking the city. What's sad is that Artemisia never lived to see it. She was killed in battle before the tomb was completed. The city buried her and her brother side by side inside it. The tomb of Mausolus became the most famous one in the ancient world—so famous that all fancy tombs came to be called mausoleums in honor of Mausolus."

She handed him the open book. "Take a look. Tell me if it looks at all familiar."

He stared at the artist's rendering of the Tomb of Mausolus at Helicarnassus. It consisted of a Greek temple topped by a stepped pyramid topped by a sculpture of a four-horse chariot holding a man and woman standing side by side.

Hirsch looked up with a tentative smile. "The Civil Courts Building?"

"Very good, Mr. Hirsch. My brother was an ancient history nut. That's why he had a special place in his heart for that crazy building. Especially after he got back from Turkey the first time."

"Is the tomb still over there?"

"Wouldn't that be divine? I'm afraid not. An earthquake knocked it over in the thirteenth century. Then an army of crusaders called the Knights of St. John built a fortress on the spot. They used materials from the tomb as building blocks. The fortress is still there—right out on that same finger of land in the bay. You can actually see the polished stone and marble blocks from the tomb inside the castle walls. That's all that's left of it in Turkey. The rest is in the British Museum. It's all on display in the Mausoleum Room. My brother was there." She pointed to the book. "Turn the page."

He did. The next page had photographs from the British Museum, including sections of the friezes that had decorated the walls of the structure, fragments of the colossal sculptured chariot and horses from the roof, and the damaged statues of the king and queen, each in tunics.

"They didn't completely duplicate the tomb when they built the City Courts Building," she said. "They left off the horses and chariot and statues. Even so, Pat said they did a pretty fair job."

She stood. "Come on back. I'll show you his photos."

He followed her down the short hall to a room on the right. She opened the door and turned on the light.

"This used to be Pat's room. I've changed it around some, but I left his photos on the wall."

He stepped into the small bedroom, which looked more like an artist's workroom. There were art supplies arranged on wall shelves, three paint-splattered easels neatly stacked against the near wall, a bookcase filled with art books, a desktop with papers, pencils, and pens in tidy order, and a daybed against the far wall.

Framed and hanging in a row above the bed were three twelve-by-sixteen black-and-white photographs of the Civil Courts Building, each taken from a different angle. The photographer shot the first one at street level from about a block away. In that shot, the Greek temple, topped by the four-sided pyramid, loomed high atop the massive structure. In the second photo, taken with a telephoto lens from several stories aboveground, the Civil Courts Building dominated the left foreground, the Old Courthouse just to its right and centered beneath the parabola of the Arch, the left leg of which disappeared behind the temple portions of the tomb, the whole scene foreshortened by the telephoto lens. The third photo had been shot from above, perhaps from a helicopter. It was a bird's eye view of the tomb replica with an excellent view of the sculptures of the two sphinxlike figures seated back to back atop the stepped pyramid.

He leaned in close, squinting. "What's on the chest of those things?"

"That's the fleur-de-lis of St. Louis."

Hirsch stood back. "These are remarkable photos."

"Pat took them."

"Really?"

"Oh, yes. Photography was his hobby, and that building was his favorite subject. He took dozens and dozens of photos of it. These were his three favorites." She smiled at the memory. "My goodness, he just loved going up there. If he thought you were special, he'd take you up there for a tour."

"I didn't realize they gave tours."

"Oh, they don't. But he knew how to get in."

"Did he ever take you?"

"He sure did. We went up there one beautiful spring day, climbed up those zigzag ladders inside the pyramid and out onto the roof. It was quite a view."

"You said he took Judith on the tour?"

She nodded. "He told me how much she enjoyed it." Her smile faded. "He was a good man, my brother. He had a fine opinion of your client."

FIFTEEN minutes later, he started the car engine and pulled away from Cassie Markman's house. As he glanced in his rearview mirror, he saw a pair of headlights come on farther down the street on the opposite side.

The route back to Highway 40 included several side streets and a main boulevard. He kept checking the rearview mirror as he drove. The same set of headlights was behind him the whole way, although by the time he reached the highway entrance ramp the headlights were three cars back.

When he pulled into the flow of traffic heading west on the crowded highway and moved into the center lane, the several sets of headlights in his rearview mirror all looked the same.

He gripped the steering wheel, his thoughts racing.

32

NEVERTHELESS, they met as planned at nine that night at Dulcie's office at the law school. Now that she was out of the closet, so to speak, there didn't seem need for a clandestine meeting. Indeed, with her semiofficial role in the case, any effort at concealment might actually create suspicion, especially, as Hirsch realized, if there was a factual basis for his sudden paranoia.

He described his meeting with Cassie Markman earlier that night.

When he finished, Rosenbloom said, "I'd say the fix was in on those warehouse cases."

"Does Monroe agree?" Hirsch asked.

"Monroe?" Rosenbloom snorted. "The guy is a *schlemiel*."

While Hirsch had been meeting with Cassie Markman, Rosenbloom had met with Mitchell Monroe, the former Brookfield city attorney. Their professional paths had crossed occasionally over the years, and they vaguely knew each other. Monroe, now in his late sixties, shared a suite with several other attorneys in a suburban office tower.

"What did he say?" Dulcie asked.

Rosenbloom shook his head. "He remembered the cases, of course. You don't forget that kind of ass whooping. But he mainly remembered the happy ending. I asked him about McCormick's exclusion of all of his evidence. He thought the rulings were wrong, but he said it wasn't the first time he'd had things go wrong in one of those cases."

"That's all?" Hirsch asked.

"That's all. He's fucking clueless. I asked him whether he thought there was anything funny going on in the case, and he gives me this baffled look and says, 'What do you mean by funny?' " Rosenbloom shook his head in disbelief. "Talk about your *goyishe kup*."

Rosenbloom reached for another biscotti and took a bite. Dulcie had brought a tin of homemade biscotti and a large thermos of coffee for the meeting. Rosenbloom closed his eyes in bliss as he crunched away.

He gestured toward Dulcie. "My God, Samson, this woman is unbelievable. On top of everything else, she's a gourmet pastry chef. If I ran this law school, I'd give her tenure based solely on these biscotti."

Dulcie laughed. "Let's hope they make you dean. More coffee?"

"Sure." Rosenbloom held out his mug. "And while you're at it, how about marrying me?"

"I don't know, Seymour. I'd always wonder if you were marrying me only for my pastries."

"I may be shallow, my dear, but I'm not that shallow. Rest assured that I'd be marrying you for your body as well. I'll even swear out an affidavit to that."

"Such a romantic." She turned to David with the thermos. "Coffee?"

He was smiling. "Sure."

Dulcie asked Rosenbloom, "Did you give Monroe a reason for why you were asking him about those old cases?"

"I gave him some bullshit story about representing the owners of one of the restaurants out there who were getting hassled by their lender over the value of underlying property. I told him I was trying to use those two verdicts to justify a higher value. He seemed to buy it, but that *schmendrick* is so clueless I could have told him I was representing an equity investor from the planet Neptune. We're talking about a guy who spent his career as a city attorney. That puts him one step up the evolutionary ladder from a Shetland pony."

"If the fix was in," Hirsch said, "it certainly gives McCormick and Guttner an interesting prior connection."

Dulcie asked, "But how can you fix a *jury* verdict?"

"Actually," Hirsch said, "it's easier and safer than fixing a judge's verdict."

"How so?"

"Fixing a jury trial is like fixing a basketball game," Hirsch explained. "You don't need to corrupt everyone. All you need is the key player. In a jury trial, the key player is the judge."

Rosenbloom said, "The judge can have a huge impact on the outcome of a case merely by what evidence he lets the jury hear."

Hirsch nodded. "And there are other ways he can influence the outcome. Judges will make comments about certain witnesses or certain evidence or even certain lawyers. Happens all the time, and often in ways that are invisible."

"Invisible?" she asked.

"Juries pay special attention to what the judge says, and they're very attuned to tone of voice. But trial transcripts don't pick up tone of voice. Especially sarcasm. As a result, the transcript reads one way, but the jury hears it another way. All of which means that fixing a jury trial is less risky than fixing a bench trial."

"Absolutely," Rosenbloom said. "Remember, people have no trouble believing that juries do wacky things. So if one jury happens to come in at four million instead of three in a condemnation case, who's gonna raise an eyebrow when the week before another jury awarded some douche bag twenty million dollars because he claimed McDonald's french fries made him fat?"

"If that's so, though," Dulcie asked, "how are you going to prove anything?"

Rosenbloom smiled. "Good question, Professor."

"We'll just keep digging," Hirsch said. "We've made some progress. We've found a few pieces of the puzzle."

"Or what you hope is a puzzle," Rosenbloom added.

"Or what you hope are pieces to the same puzzle," Dulcie said.

Hirsch nodded. "All we know for sure is that Judith thought she found something troubling, and whatever that was, it all started on the afternoon she overheard her judge's telephone conversation with Guttner."

"Speaking of Jabba," Rosenbloom said, turning to Dulcie, "tell us about your settlement meeting today."

"He's quite good at what he does," she said.

"How so?" Hirsch asked.

"Start with the meeting place. He insisted on coming out here to the law school."

"Nice show of deference," Rosenbloom said.

Dulcie nodded. "Exactly. More important, he'd done his homework, or he had someone do it. He knew about my relationship with Judith. He knew about her volunteer work at the clinic. He knew about her rocky relationship with her father, and how guilty her father must have felt about her death. And he knew all the right buttons to push with me. At one point during our discussions, he suggested that as part of the settlement his client might be willing to make a donation to the clinic in Judith's name."

Rosenbloom whistled in appreciation. "He's a slick bastard."

"Did he seem suspicious?" Hirsch asked.

"He pretended he wasn't," she said, "but he was. He has this laid-back manner when he asks certain questions; but you can tell it's all a facade. He asked me when I first heard about the lawsuit. He wanted to know whether I'd known either of you before and how you selected me as the additional attorney."

"What did you tell him?" Hirsch asked.

"I kept it general enough to be truthful without telling him anything important. I said I found out about the lawsuit when you came to talk to me about Judith. I told him we'd never met before. I told him on the morning of the competency hearing I received a phone call from one of you. I couldn't remember which. I said whoever called asked whether I'd be willing to enter my appearance as an additional attorney to give the court some comfort about Mr. Shifrin's representation. He wanted to know what our financial arrangement was on the case and I told him we hadn't discussed it yet."

"Was he satisfied with your answers?" Hirsch asked.

"He acted like he was." She paused, shaking her head. "Who knows? Marvin Guttner is a formidable adversary. He can do the soothing voice and the pleasant smile and the cozy manner, but he can't do anything about those eyes."

Hirsch nodded. "Ice cold."

Rosenbloom said, "Enough with the psychoanalysis. Do we have a settlement?"

"We might be close," she said. "I went through the whole routine and told him I couldn't see recommending a settlement for less than six figures. He winced and pretended that it might be difficult to get his client to go that high. I told him I'd seen better acting in my son's junior high school play."

"Nice," Rosenbloom said, grinning. He winked at Hirsch. "This woman is good."

"I warned him that we'd need more than money to settle. We'd still need some form of vindication."

"And?" Rosenbloom.

"That's when he suggested the contribution to the clinic. I told him it was a nice gesture, but that we needed something more direct. He told me that an admission of liability was out of the question because it could hurt him in other cases. I suggested an apology. He thought that might be tough to get for the same reason, but he said he would talk to his client. I told him I would talk to you."

Hirsch glanced over at Rosenbloom, who shrugged and said, "Works for me."

"One more thing," Dulcie said. "He told me that once the case settled, all work had to stop. He said that you two would have to sign an agreement to cease all work on any personal injury matter having to do with Peterson Tire and you'd have to turn over your entire investigation file to him."

"You got to be shitting me," Rosenbloom said.

"Did he say why?" Hirsch asked.

"He said Peterson Tire didn't want plaintiffs' lawyers out there drumming up new cases based on what they'd learned in a prior case or peddling their files to other personal injury lawyers. He told me it was nonnegotiable. He said that every settlement agreement had to include that provision along with a clause requiring the lawyer to pay Peterson Tire a sum equal to one-half the settlement amount as liquidated damages for a breach of that provision."

Hirsch looked at Rosenbloom. Neither said a thing. Hirsch turned back to Dulcie.

"Anything over a hundred grand is fine on the money," he told her. "We'll want some form of an apology. I also like the idea of a donation in her name."

"How much?" she asked.

"Whatever you think is fair."

"Okay," she said. "But what about that attorney provision?"

"I'll sign it," Hirsch said.

Dulcie frowned. "Are you sure?"

"I'm no longer investigating a wrongful death case involving Peterson Tire. I'm investigating a wrongful death case involving Brendan McCormick."

"Speaking of which," Dulcie asked, "has your friend Jumbo been able to find Judith's e-mails?"

Hirsch said, "I haven't heard from him since he left St. Louis. I hope he's still looking. I really want that one from the file clerk in Peterson's legal department. What was her name?"

"Carmen Moldano," Dulcie said.

He turned to Rosenbloom. "She's the one Judith visited in Knoxville. About a week later, she sent Judith an e-mail with a new address and phone number for Ruth Jones."

"Whose last name may no longer be Jones," Dulcie said.

The two men looked at her.

Dulcie said, "Carmen said the reason Ruth moved to Chicago was to get married. That's where her fiancé lived. She doesn't know his name, though. Unfortunately, she doesn't have access to any current information on Ruth because Carmen doesn't work at Peterson Tire anymore."

"When did you learn all this?" Hirsch asked.

"Today."

"You talked to her?"

"I didn't."

"Who did?"

Dulcie gazed at him. "Your daughter."

ROSENBLOOM tapped his horn once and waved to them as he pulled away. They waved back, standing side by side in front of the law school.

The night was clear, and there was a half moon overhead. Their breath vapored in the chilly March air as they watched the black Cadillac drive off.

Hirsch had been too upset to respond to the news of his daughter's involvement. Rosenbloom jumped into the awkward silence by claiming he had to get home for something. Hirsch wasn't listening. It was all a flurry, and now he was gone.

Dulcie turned to Hirsch. The moonlight highlighted the curls in her hair.

"How?" he said, trying to keep his voice calm.

"She asked if she could help."

"How did she even—"

"She asked me what I was doing in the case. I told her."

"How much?"

"Just the wrongful death part."

Hirsch's thoughts roiled as he walked her toward her car.

"What did she think was the purpose of calling that woman in Knoxville?"

"I told her you were trying to put together a list of former employees who might be worth interviewing if the case didn't settle. I told her that Ruth was an ex-employee we were having trouble locating. I explained that we didn't want anyone at Peterson Tire to know that we were looking for her. I had her pretend to be the younger sister of an old friend of Ruth. It went fine."

"Dulcie, I don't want Lauren involved in this."

"She wanted to help you, David."

"I understand. Look, I'd love *any* good excuse to work with my daughter. But not this case, Dulcie. It isn't what she thinks it is. I'm not even sure I know what it is."

"She wants to make a connection, David. She's an adult."

"She's also my daughter."

"Exactly. Where's the harm?"

"You don't understand my point. She's my daughter. That's the point. I don't want my child involved in this case. And after the settlement, I don't want you involved, either."

"What's that supposed to mean?" There was an edge in her voice.

"It means I don't know where this case is headed anymore. I thought the stakes were high enough when we were dealing with just a possible homicide, but now—"

He shook his head. "Now they seem even higher. This case was my responsibility at the beginning, and it still is. It isn't yours, and it isn't Lauren's."

"All because of an unidentified set of headlights?"

"Yes," he said, surprised by the force of his voice.

Dulcie studied him.

"Look," he said in a softer voice, "I've hurt my daughters more than enough for one lifetime. What's done is done, and I can't undo it. But I can try to prevent any further harm. If there's even a slight chance that someone is out there following me, I don't want Lauren—or you—anywhere near this case. I don't want either of you at risk."

She smiled as she reached into her purse for the car keys. "Our protector."

"More like your endangerer."

She looked up at him for a moment. Then she stood on her tiptoes and kissed him gently, slowly, on the lips.

"You can be my protector," she whispered.

He'd been imagining that kiss almost from the moment he saw her enter the coffeehouse that first afternoon. It was even better than he'd imagined.

She leaned back, the moonlight shimmering in her dark eyes.

"That was nice," she said.

He stared into her eyes, unable to talk, not sure what he was doing, knowing that they hadn't resolved what they needed to resolve.

But none of that mattered. He leaned forward to kiss her. Her eyes closed as their lips touched. They kissed, no part of them touching except for their lips.

The kiss ended.

Her eyes opened. She smiled.

Silently, they turned toward her car. She opened the door and looked back at him.

"Good night, David."

"Good night, Dulcie."

The idiocy of the kiss struck him as he was watched her drive off.

What was he thinking?

Or not thinking?

He scanned the parking lot. There were about two dozen parked cars scattered around the lot. He scrutinized them one by one as he walked toward his car. He didn't see anyone in any of the cars, but it was hard to be sure in the dark. Someone could have been ducking down inside one of the cars.

He got in his car, started the engine, and drove toward the exit, all the while glancing in his rearview mirror, watching the parked cars, watching for movement. He stopped at the exit and turned around, scanning the lot again, looking for the sign of exhaust vapor. He didn't see any.

He faced forward, checked the traffic, glanced again in his rearview mirror, and pulled out of the parking lot.

33

THEY waited in silence as Judge Ann Burke read through the settlement papers. Ken Felts and Dulcie Lorenz stood at the podium—Dulcie on the left, Felts on the right. She stood almost a head taller than Felts. Hirsch stood to Dulcie's left. Arrayed on the other side of Felts were Marvin Guttner and then Jack Bellows and then Elizabeth Purcell. They were a trio of contrasts: Purcell earnest and attentive and oblivious to the real drama; Bellows tense and struggling to suppress his irritation; and Guttner tranquil, heavy-lidded eyes half-closed, liver-colored lips sagging open, as if he'd just finished eating a particularly tasty young associate.

Two weeks had elapsed since Dulcie's first settlement meeting with Guttner. They'd met again five days later—the day *after* the parties and the court received the report from Dr. Nemes, the examining physician. The doctor had run a battery of tests on Abe Shifrin and concluded that his Alzheimer's disease had progressed to stage five, which rendered him unfit to live alone. Hirsch had no basis to challenge the doctor's opinion. In truth, he'd been relieved to be able to get his client into an assisted-living environment under the watchful eye of professional caretakers. He and Dulcie arranged for Shifrin to be moved that weekend to a room at the Jewish Center for the Aged, which is where he now resided.

With Shifrin medically eliminated from the settlement loop, Dulcie quickly hammered out a deal. The judge seemed pleased with her results.

"So you will wire-transfer the settlement payment?" Judge Burke asked.

Guttner nodded, his lower jaw disappearing into the ample flesh of his double chin. "Promptly upon the Court's approval, Your Honor."

Judge Burke looked at Dulcie. "You've agreed on one hundred and twenty thousand dollars."

"We believe that is a fair amount," Dulcie said to her, "especially given some of the other settlement terms."

The judge nodded. "Such as the fifty-thousand-dollar donation to your family justice clinic."

"Actually, it's a grant, Your Honor. We will use the money to establish the Judith Shifrin Internship. The principal should generate enough income to fund an annual summer internship for a law student at the clinic."

The judge nodded again, clearly pleased.

Dulcie said, "In addition, Your Honor, you will note that paragraph eight of the settlement agreement includes an expression of sorrow and regret by Peterson Tire for the death of Ms. Shifrin."

"I did read that, Ms. Lorenz. I confess that I've never seen such a provision."

"Nor have I," Dulcie said. "Our challenge was to craft a settlement that reflected Mr. Shifrin's stated purpose. When he originally retained David Hirsch to file the lawsuit, he told him that his purpose was to find a way to preserve his daughter's memory, both in the minds of the defendants and in the minds of others. Although two of the defendants refused to participate in that portion of the settlement, Peterson Tire stepped forward. Mr. Guttner was quite helpful in that regard."

She gestured toward Guttner, who acknowledged it with a magnanimous nod.

"As a result," Dulcie continued, "we have been able to reach a settlement of the lawsuit that I believe comes as close as possible to achieving Mr. Shifrin's original purpose in filing it. I strongly recommend its approval."

The judge turned to Felts. "And your client's response, Mr. Felts?"

"My client has nothing to add regarding this matter, Your Honor," he murmured, suddenly as deferential as an Elizabethan manservant.

"That wasn't my question, Mr. Felts. Does your client support the settlement?"

"My client defers to the judgments of the attorneys for the litigants in that case." He bent at the knees and leaned forward in a semi-curtsey. "If they are satisfied, Your Honor, so is my client."

"Very well, Mr. Felts. The Court has reviewed the settlement agreement and sees no reason not to enter an order approving its terms. You may draft the order, Mr. Felts. The Court will be in recess."

GUTTNER approached him in the hallway outside Judge Burke's courtroom.

"David," he said, reaching out a hand, "I hope you are as pleased as I am that we've been able to bring this unfortunate matter to a final resolution."

Hirsch shook his hand. "I'm glad it's over."

"It is more than over. That professor of yours negotiated an excellent settlement for you."

Hirsch nodded. "The endowment was a nice touch."

"That it was. Yes, indeed. A veritable living memorial to Judith. I have been told that the clinic does good work."

"They represent women who've been physically abused by men," Hirsch said.

"Do they really? Good for them, eh?"

Hirsch turned to peer through the window of the courtroom door. Dulcie was still in there with Felts, who was drafting the order approving the settlement. He turned back to Guttner. Waiting off to the side was Guttner's associate, a thirtysomething woman in a conservative gray suit and dark flats. She stood rigid, face blank, eyes straight ahead—a lawyer robot waiting for the master's next command. Down the hall, Jack Bellows and Elizabeth Purcell were boarding an elevator. Bellows had been the first one out of the courtroom, leaving without a word and heading straight toward the elevator bank, where he'd waited impatiently, tapping his foot. Purcell had paused briefly in the hallway to ask Hirsch how his client was doing at the nursing home, and then she hurried on toward the elevator bank as the down light flashed above the middle elevator.

"So is it back to bankruptcy for you, David," Guttner asked, "or have you developed a hankering for personal injury cases?"

"Hard to say," Hirsch replied, unwilling to offer the fat man any opening.

"Speaking of which," Guttner said, forcing a chortle, "we need to take care of that settlement provision regarding the turnover of your investigative file. I can send someone by your office to pick it up. How about later this afternoon?"

"We won't have it ready by then."

"Tomorrow?"

"I don't know."

"Just have your girl call my girl."

Hirsch nodded. He'd already put together a "file" for Guttner. It contained more than ten thousand pages of documents that his paralegals had gathered for him during the initial phase of the lawsuit, back when he thought it was just another accident case. There were copies of court filings and deposition summaries and hearing transcripts and interviews and expert witness reports from dozens of other accident cases involving Ford Explorers or Peterson tires. Enough documents to fill six bankers boxes. Enough documents to allay any concern Guttner might have as to Hirsch's compliance with his obligations under the settlement agreement.

"The sooner the better, David. Now that we've got the case settled, we need to make sure we tie up all the loose ends."

Hirsch gazed at him and nodded. "That's my thought exactly."

34

DUSK faded into night as Hirsch sat in his car, which was idling at the curb in front of Abe Shifrin's house. His mood felt as empty as the house.

He'd driven out to the nursing home after court to share the news of the morning's settlement hearing. He'd found Abe in his room, seated in the armchair watching television. He was wearing a white shirt speckled with food stains, wrinkled gray slacks, brown slippers. The stubble on his face suggested that he hadn't shaved for several days.

Hirsch couldn't tell whether Abe recognized him. The old man had smiled and waved him in when Hirsch had knocked on the open door to his room. He'd nodded pleasantly when Hirsch explained that the judge had approved the settlement.

"Does that makes you happy?" Shifrin had asked.

"It makes me happy if it makes you happy."

Shifrin smiled. "Then let's both be happy."

The old man turned his attention to the television program, which appeared to be a rerun of a show called *The Wonder Years*. A show, Hirsch thought to himself, about memories. Ironic. They watched together in silence, Hirsch on the bed, Shifrin in the easy chair.

During a commercial break, Shifrin turned to him. "Have you seen her?"

"Who?"

"My Judith."

He sorted through possible responses. "No."

"She's been a good wife to me."

Hirsch nodded.

"I've not always been an easy man to live with. You may find that hard to believe, sir, but it's true." He frowned. "Where could she have gone. Have you seen her?"

"I haven't."

Shifrin pulled up the left sleeve of his robe and glanced at the back of his wrist, as if he expected to see a watch.

"Hard to keep track," he mumbled, more to himself. He let the sleeve slide back into place.

Something on the television caught his attention, and he settled back in his chair to watch. Hirsch waited a few minutes and then stood up.

Shifrin turned to him, puzzled. "So soon, Mr. Hirsch?"

Hirsch was heartened by Shifrin's use of his name. Pockets of memory were still intact.

"I'll come back next week, Mr. Shifrin. And then next month, when we set up the endowment for Judith's internship, I'm sure there will be a nice ceremony at the law school. You'll be a guest of honor."

"Guest of honor?" he repeated, pleased. "At my age, eh? Will Judith be there?"

"She'll be there in spirit."

"Ah, well." He appeared to think it over, and then he nodded. "If you see her, Mr. Hirsch, be sure to tell her I love her. Would you do that for me?"

Hirsch nodded. "I will."

"I've not always been an easy man to live with. You may find that hard to believe, sir. Still, I have always loved her. You be sure to tell her that."

Those words echoed in Hirsch's mind as he gazed now at the dark house. The nursing home visit had been just one more downer in a week of downers that began on Monday afternoon, when an exasperated Jumbo Redding had called to tell him that he wouldn't be able to retrieve any of Judith's e-mails. He'd been working on the problem for more than a week, trying to figure out what had happened to all of the e-mails in the system prior to June 12 of last year. Eventually, by snooping around in related government networks, he'd been able to piece together the answer. A nasty computer virus struck the district court's computer network on June 7 of last year, causing the system to crash within hours. The feds flew in an information technology SWAT team from D.C., who determined that the virus had entered as an infected attachment to an e-mail, which had replicated itself at an exponential rate by grafting itself onto e-mails throughout the user network. The tech guys tried several cures before taking their drastic final step on June 12.

"Dumb bastards purged every goddamn e-mail in the system. Every last one. I'd like to know who the hell was running that operation? Homer Simpson? I wish I had better news for you, Rebbe, but it looks like the damn memory for those years is just gone."

More missing memory. Of course.

And then yesterday afternoon, Rosenbloom's longtime secretary Evelyn had hurried into Hirsch's office, closed the door, and leaned back against it.

"Oh, David," she'd said, fighting back tears, "please go help Seymour."

He had hurried down the hall to Rosenbloom's office,

where he found him at his desk, head down. For one terrible moment, Hirsch thought he was dead, but then he saw that his shoulders were shaking.

"Sancho," he said, closing the door behind him.

Rosenbloom looked up, eyes red, face contorted.

Hirsch understood immediately. "Again?"

Rosenbloom lowered his head.

Hirsch found a blanket to place over his lap and quickly wheeled him out of the office. He got him home to his apartment and helped him remove his urine-soaked clothing, clean himself up, and put on fresh clothes. He tried to get him back to the office, but Rosenbloom refused to go. When Hirsch said good-bye, Rosenbloom was slumped in his wheelchair in front of the picture window.

It was the second time in as many weeks that he'd lost control of his bladder—both times during heated telephone calls with opposing counsel.

The first time, Hirsch had tried to cheer him up by making light of it. "Now that's what I call getting pissed off, Sancho."

And Rosenbloom had smiled that time, in spite of himself.

But not this time.

What had never happened since his toddler days had now happened twice in two weeks. The second time made it different. Hirsch knew, and he knew that Rosenbloom knew, what incontinence signaled. Hirsch had read up on multiple sclerosis. He had learned that it was a disease that progressed in starts and stops, with the victim descending from plateau to plateau, sometimes slowly, sometimes abruptly.

Twice in two weeks signaled an abrupt descent.

Twice in two weeks meant adult diapers from now on.

Twice in two weeks meant worse symptoms were edging closer. It meant that a remarkable life force known as

Seymour Rosenbloom was starting toward the exit. It meant that a powerful light in Hirsch's world was beginning to dim.

All in all, a lousy week.

He tried to be upbeat about the resolution of Judith's case, but he'd been through too much over too many years to match Dulcie's enthusiasm for the settlement agreement. The money was okay, but as Abe Shifrin made clear that morning in the synagogue parking lot last December, it wasn't about the money. The endowment for the internship was certainly worthwhile, although he knew that it was mostly eyewash for Peterson Tire, a way for the company to get some added public relations bang for a modest buck. Better than nothing, of course, but he'd been around long enough to see through the vanity of trying to buy immortality with your name on an endowment or a building.

The expression of sorrow was even less meaningful. Sorrow without responsibility. Lots of people were sorry about Judith's death. Peterson Tire's expression was little more than a Hallmark sympathy card pulled off the rack and sent three and a half years too late. Worse yet, as Hirsch suspected, it was probably a sympathy card from a party that had little to do with her death.

But, as he reminded himself again, it was a settlement agreement. A compromise. Nothing more, nothing less.

Ironically, there was plenty there for a decent publicist to spin into gold. The settlement money, the endowment, the expression of sorrow—the mix had all the makings of a David and Goliath story for some credulous reporter.

Even Rosenbloom had mentioned it, pointing out that a well-placed blurb could be a nice career boost. "With a real David in the role of David. Could be a helluva way to let the world know that you're back on top."

Alone in the car, Hirsch shook his head. He had had enough press releases for one lifetime. He'd been famous, and he had relished the perks. And then he'd been infamous, and suffered the consequences. And during his years in prison, reading and rereading Jumbo's copy of *Meditations*, he'd learned a lesson from Marcus Aurelieus. He'd copied it onto a sheet of paper and taped it to the prison wall. And when he left, he took it down from the wall and folded it up and put it in his wallet. He still carried it with him, even though he'd long since committed it to memory:

> The man whose heart is palpitating for fame after death does not reflect that out of all those who remember him every one will himself soon be dead also, and in the course of time the next generation after that, until in the end, after flaring and sinking by turns, the final spark of memory is quenched. Furthermore, even supposing that those who remember you were never to die at all, nor their memories to die either, yet what is that to you? Clearly, in your grave, nothing; and even in your lifetime, what is the good of praise—unless to subserve some lesser design? Surely, then, you are making an inopportune rejection of what Nature has given you today, if all your mind is set on what men will say of you tomorrow.

But what exactly had Nature given him today?

Maybe the settlement agreement was all he would ever achieve for Judith. Maybe this was it.

The end of the line.

He gazed at the front of Abe Shifrin's house. The streetlights barely illuminated the small front porch. From where he sat, the porch seemed almost a stage set. He could imagine the scene. Almost see it. First night of Hanukkah. It would have been dark then, too. Dark when Judith stepped up to the porch. He could almost make out her small figure in the dim light. With her armful of containers, including one with home-made *latkes* and one with applesauce. He could see her take a deep breath and reach for the doorbell, her finger hesitating just a moment before pushing the buzzer. She moved back two steps. Waiting in the dark, her breath visible in the cold air. The porch light came on. The front door opened. There they stood, the two of them, staring at one another from opposite sides of the storm door—the father grim, the daughter with a tentative smile. Seconds passed. No words. No gestures. And then the father stepped back and closed the door. The porch light went off. Judith standing there. Standing there alone. A lone silhouette in the dark, head lowered.

Hirsch closed his eyes and rested his forehead on the cold steering wheel.

35

THE men rose for the *Aleinu,* the final prayer before the
mourner's *Kaddish.* Pinky Green had described it as
the national anthem of Judaism, a prayer thanking God for
giving the Jewish people a unique destiny. Tradition
teaches that the author of the *Aleinu* was Joshua himself,
who composed it shortly after leading the Hebrews across
the Jordan River and into the Promised Land.

The men bent their knees in unison and bowed as they
chanted, *"Vah-ahnach-nu koh-reim ooh-mish-tah-cha-vim
ooh-moh-deem lif-nay melech . . ."*

*We bend our knees and bow, and acknowledge our
thanks before the King of Kings . . .*

The *minyan* was smaller this morning. Only eleven. Sid
Shalowitz, a member of the *Alter Kocker* Brigade, was
back in the hospital for more heart tests. One of the two
regular Friday volunteers, Jerry Tennenbaum, was missing.
Jerry was an occasional handball opponent of Hirsch's,
and they'd played a match last night. In the locker room af-

terward, he told Hirsch that he wouldn't be at services in the morning because he was on a 6:15 A.M. flight to Detroit. Hirsch had done the head count before going to bed and confirmed that there'd be at least ten for the morning service.

He glanced back. The last row on the other side of the aisle was empty, as it was most mornings. Staring at the far back seat, he thought again of that morning last December when he'd turned to see Abe Shifrin sitting there. He remembered the distracted look on Shifrin's face, the prayer book closed on his lap. That was the last time Abe Shifrin had attended a morning service at Anshe Emes.

The prayer ended. The men took their seats.

The rabbi led them in the recitation of the short reading between the *Aleinu* and the *Kaddish*—a passage composed of snippets from Exodus and Proverbs and Isaiah. Hirsch followed along in English as he moved up the aisle toward the podium:

> Do not fear sudden terror, or the holocaust of the wicked when it comes. Plan a conspiracy and it will be annulled; speak your piece and it shall not stand, for God is with us. Even till your seniority, I remain unchanged. Even until your ripe old age, I shall endure. I created you, and I shall bear you. I shall endure, and I shall rescue you.

Mr. Kantor tipped his hat. "And a good day to you, *Gabbai*. I shall see you tomorrow morning bright and early."

Hirsch held the door for the old man and then followed him out of the shul. Mr. Kantor turned left toward the handicapped spaces in front of the building. Hirsch turned right toward the parking lot, his mind already shifting from religious to legal mode, from prophets to profits, from chapter seven of Leviticus, with the bloody ritual of the guilt offering touched upon that morning by Rabbi Saltzman, to chapter seven of the Bankruptcy Code, with the bloodless ritual of the debtor's offering to be touched upon later that morning by Judge Crane.

His stride slowed as he looked up. Standing at the end of the walkway was his daughter Lauren. The chilly April breeze ruffled her curly red hair. She had on a cable-knit sweater, jeans, and suede clogs. Her hands were in the front pockets of her jeans.

His delight was tempered by a rush of anxiety. He scanned the parking lot as he started toward her, looking for, well, for anything that seemed suspicious.

Nothing.

"Hey, Peanut," he said, trying to stifle his concern.

She smiled. Peanut had been his nickname for her going all the way back to nursery school. He called her that until the day they led him off to prison.

"Hi, Big D." Her nickname for him.

"What are you doing here?"

"I asked Professor Lorenz if there was something else I could do to help with your case. She said she didn't think so." She shrugged. "I just wanted to make sure."

He glanced around again. "Do you have a few minutes? We could get some coffee, maybe a bite to eat?"

Her smiled broadened. "Sure."

She followed him in her car to Companion Bakery in Clayton. He got them each a cup of coffee and a pumpernickel bagel. Just like old times, he thought as they carried their trays to an empty table. They had been the pumpernickel pair. Lauren's older sister and her mother preferred poppy seed. He remembered those Sunday morning runs to Pratzel's bakery—milling in front of the display cases with the other dads, nodding at a familiar face, exchanging a few words with an acquaintance, waiting for his number to be called, picking out his mixed dozen (four pumpernickel, four poppy seed, four sesame), and then heading back to the smell of fresh coffee and the sight of his beautiful wife and his pajama-clad daughters waiting in the breakfast nook for their daddy.

As Lauren spread cream cheese on a bagel half, he explained to her that the case was basically settled and thus there was nothing further she could do—or that anyone else could do, for that matter.

She looked up at him with those earnest blue eyes. "I think it's terrific what you did for that poor girl."

"Dulcie is working out the final terms. She gets the credit."

"That's not what she said, Dad."

He felt a pang when she said *Dad*.

Hirsch sipped his coffee and watched his child eat her bagel. He wanted this to be a special time, but he couldn't hold back his unease. Ever since spotting those headlights in his rearview mirror, he'd worried that he'd become a danger to his daughter and to Dulcie. He'd talked to Dulcie about it. He'd called her, in fact, the same night of their kiss in the parking lot. He'd told her his concerns and explained that they should avoid any non-lawsuit-related contact until after the settlement had been approved and consummated. She'd accepted good-naturedly, telling him that his advanced years were rendering him hopelessly paranoid.

Rosenbloom told him the same, although in coarser language, when Hirsch explained why he felt they shouldn't go to Dulcie's house for the *seder*. So instead, the two men celebrated the first night of Passover at Rosenbloom's apartment. They did so in strict accordance with Rosenbloom's Rules, which included a reading from *Don Quixote* in lieu of the Four Questions; a tasty selection of Spanish tapas and a seafood paella instead of the standard gefilte fish, matzo ball soup, and overdone brisket; a full-bodied Paternina Tempranillo Rioja from Spain in place of the Mogen David Concord Grape; and a ceremonial fourth cup of wine poured in honor not of the Prophet Elijah but of Don Miguel de Cervantes Saavedra, whose grandfather Rosenbloom claimed was a *converso* who'd secretly practiced Judaism after escaping the flames of the Spanish Inquisition.

But now the settlement was approved. The funding would be complete by the end of next week. The defendants were supposed to wire the $120,000 settlement payment into a court-supervised trust account by Tuesday, and Peterson Tire was scheduled to deliver the $50,000 check to the law school in a special ceremony at the end of next week, by which time the school's lawyers would have finalized the paperwork for Judith's endowment fund.

And the investigation was dead in the water. He'd been up late last night paging through his notes, trying to figure out a new angle. He'd failed. There was no new angle. Judith's deleted e-mails haunted him. They were the key, the secret map through the forest, and they were gone forever.

"It's so sad about her father," Lauren said.

"Pardon?"

"Mr. Shifrin."

Hirsch nodded. "He has no one left."

"He has you."

"That's not much." He took a sip of coffee, wanting to change the subject. "Tell me about you, Lauren."

He listened as she told him about her apartment and her roommates and her classes and her plans for the future, which didn't extend beyond her summer clerkship with a Chicago legal foundation that specialized in family law. It was a conversation he'd dreamed about for years. Nothing epic. Nothing dramatic. Just the two of them talking about everyday things over coffee.

She glanced at her watch. "Whoa. My Con Law class starts in eight minutes."

He walked her to her car.

She turned to him. "Well."

"Thank you, Lauren."

"Sure."

"I mean it. This is the best breakfast I've had in more than a decade."

She giggled. "Oh, Dad."

"The case will be over soon. We'll get together after that. I'll have you over for dinner."

"That would be awesome, Dad."

He kissed her gently on her forehead. "I love you, Peanut."

"I love you, Big D."

He waved to her as she drove off.

ALL *those years*, he thought as he turned on the ignition and put the car in Reverse.

All those years, and what had the two of them ever really done together? What experiences had they actually shared as father and daughter?

An afternoon at the zoo.

A father-daughter Girl Scouts banquet.

A few of her soccer games. He mainly recalled standing along sidelines and talking business on his cell phone—so distracted that he missed her one goal that season, not even realizing he missed it until she asked him about it after the game, asked him softly as he started the car engine, wanting to bask in the glory of her father's praise but not wanting to ask for that praise. He had barely picked up the cue in time, telling her how proud he was, trying to make it sound like he'd actually seen her goal.

Could that really be all? His own child. His own blood.

He shook his head.

You could never rectify something like that. He knew men his age, successful lawyers and doctors and businessmen, men like him who had allowed their ambitions to destroy their first marriages. Nasty divorces, strained, distant relationships with their children. They were all on their second wives now. The trophy wife. And their second round of children. Bragging that they were going to get it right this time. That they were going to make time to coach the Little League team and be at the birthday party at Chucky Cheese, and help with the homework.

Kidding themselves.

As if getting it right this time would expunge the first time. As if the wreckage they'd walked away from hadn't involved real consequences, including their own children.

As if there were do-overs in this life.

Hirsch shook his head.

There were no do-overs. No rain checks. Once you fucked up a life, you couldn't unfuck it. Anyone who thought otherwise was deluding himself.

Time moves in one direction only. It doesn't slow down and it doesn't circle back and whatever it passes once it passes forever. Your child grows up only once. You miss that childhood and you miss it forever.

IT was not until he turned onto the entrance ramp for the highway downtown that he remembered. He looked in his rearview mirror, but it was too late. There was no way to tell whether any of the five cars following him up the ramp were actually following him.

"Damn."

36

"THERE'S a Mr. Redding for you on line four."

Hirsch smiled as he reached for the phone. A welcome break from preparing for tomorrow's round of Chapter Thirteens.

"Jumbo?"

"Hey, Rebbe, how's it hangin'?"

"Good. What's up?"

"Found something."

"Where?"

"In that network. Been rummaging 'round in there like one of them old codgers with a metal detector."

"And?"

"Found y'all some loose change."

"E-mails?"

"Wouldn't that be nice? Naw, them e-mails is gone for good, thanks to those government imbeciles. But there's this other feature in Outlook called Notes. Lets you type out little reminders and comments, sort of like a computer version of them yellow Post-it thingies. Some folks use 'em, others don't. I never do, but that little gal of yours sure did, and I think I found most of hers."

Hirsch leaned forward and reached for a pen. "Anything important?"

"Hard to say. Nothing jumped out and bit me on the nose, but I'm not up to speed on that case of yours."

"How many of her notes did you find?"

"There's a bunch."

"Can you send them to me?"

"Done that already, Rebbe. Check your e-mail in-box."

He did. There were three new e-mails. One from a lawyer for GMAC in one of his Chapter Sevens, one from the clerk of the bankruptcy court of the Southern District of Illinois regarding a new hearing date on a Chapter Thirteen, and one from Harry and David Fruit-of-the-Month Club announcing a special discount on an attached coupon.

"Hasn't arrived yet," Hirsch said.

"Don't you be dissing my Royal Rivieras."

"You're kidding."

"Don't call me Ishmael, Rebbe. Call me Harry."

"I'm impressed, Harry."

"Don't want any of them nosy bastards tracing this stuff back to me. All you got to do is double-click on that coupon."

He did, and watched the screen view transform.

"Jumbo, you're a genius."

The big man chuckled. "Happy hunting, Rebbe."

THERE were forty-seven notes in all, displayed on his computer screen in chronological order like a fanned stack of playing cards. Each bore the date and time (down to the minute) of its creation. The notes spanned the entire time of Judith's clerkship.

Most were commonplace—the type you would expect

to find on anyone's computer. Birthday reminders. Confirmation numbers for mail-order items from J. Crew, Lands' End, Nordstrom. Contact information (name and phone number) for an auto mechanic and a tire center and an electrician and a hair stylist. Various to-do lists and notes of telephone calls, all related to court matters.

But four notes stood out. None fit neatly into any of the usual categories. All four were created during the last few months of her life:

10:42 a.m.—Sept. 9:	R—(847) 878-3080
1:27 p.m.—Oct. 12:	SWIFT Code— HBTLBMHM
2:18 p.m.—Nov. 9:	Right after prehearing conf in J's chambers—men joked re notorious Victoria's Secrets TV show last night—on way out of chambers, J aside to G: "We've got our own Victoria's Secret"—both laughed
7:38 p.m.—Nov. 30:	G safe: 8-25-5-13

Hirsch read through the four notes a second time. He leaned back in his chair and stared out his window.

Eight-four-seven.

And look at the date.

It wasn't much, but it just might be enough.

"Judith," he said aloud, "we're back in the hunt."

Part Three

———

Oh, what'll you do now, my blue-eyed son?

"A HARD RAIN'S A-GONNA FALL"
BY BOB DYLAN

37

SIX-thirty A.M.
  Evanston, Illinois.

Hirsch was seated in the rental car on the east side of Asbury, across the street and four doors down from the red-brick home of Mr. and Mrs. Jason Ruggeri.

He'd been there now for almost an hour.

He'd made the connection, or at least the possibility of a connection, the moment he read Judith's note of September 9. That was the one with the letter *R* followed by a telephone number with an 847 area code. The area code reinforced the connection, since 847 was one of the metropolitan Chicago area codes. The date did as well. Judith's aftermath memo on the names and job titles of the Peterson Tire employees, the one last edited on August 12 of that same year, had included a footnote on the importance of finding Ruth Jones, the CFO's longtime secretary who'd resigned earlier that summer. The same Ruth Jones who had moved to Chicago.

He'd logged on to a reverse telephone directory site on

the Internet, typed in the telephone number from Judith's note, clicked on the Search icon, and waited. A moment later, the screen displayed the names *Jason and Ruth Ruggeri* with an address in Evanston, Illinois.

He'd flown up to Chicago that evening, rented a car, and spent the night in a Lincolnwood motel. He had no plan beyond trying to identify Ruth and trying to come up with a nonthreatening way to make contact.

He checked his watch. Six forty-three A.M.

It was a beautiful April morning in Chicago—blue skies, light breeze, temperature already in the mid-fifties. He rolled down his window and could hear birds chirping and the distant growl of a locomotive.

This was, he thought to himself, what fictional private eyes called a stakeout. He shook his head with amusement. He should have remembered to do what Spenser and Lew Archer and the rest of them did for their stakeouts, which was to bring along a thermos of coffee and a sack of doughnuts. A cup of coffee sounded awfully nice about now.

Maybe next time.

Let's hope there is no next time.

The first commuters began emerging from their houses around seven o'clock. Some in cars backing down the driveways, others walking out the front door. Those on foot headed south down the street to the corner, passing his parked car on the way, and turned left at Noyes. From the map of the area he'd printed out yesterday afternoon, he knew there was an el station a few blocks east on Noyes.

At seven twenty-two, a woman came out the front door of the redbrick house of Jason and Ruth Ruggeri. She paused on the porch, turning to call something back inside. Then she closed the door, stepped down from the porch, and moved briskly toward the sidewalk. He slid down in his seat as she walked past him on the other side of the street.

As soon as she disappeared around the corner, he got out of the car and grabbed his briefcase. Glancing back to make sure no one else had emerged from the redbrick house, he jogged to the end of the street and walked briskly until he was about thirty yards behind her.

Ruth Ruggeri was wearing a conservative dark pant-suit and white tennis shoes. Commuter footwear, he recalled from his summer job at a Wall Street firm during law school. Her office shoes would be in the large shoulder bag.

Two blocks ahead, a southbound el train pulled into the elevated platform at the Noyes station. The crowd of commuters started filing into the train when the doors opened. Just moments after that train pulled out, a northbound train rolled in from the opposite direction.

He kept his distance from Ruth as other commuters turned onto Noyes from side streets. Mostly men and women in business attire, most with briefcases. He had dressed to blend in this morning—gray pinstriped suit, white shirt, dark tie, black shoes, briefcase. He might be ten years out of that life, but it wasn't hard to walk the walk and dress the part.

As he entered the el station, he saw her going up the stairway toward the platform. He bought a token, straining his ears for the sound of an approaching train. Pushing through the turnstile, he hurried up the stairs, two at a time, slowing as he reached the top, pulling the sunglasses out of his suit pocket and slipping them on.

She was standing just ahead along the southbound side of the platform. He strolled by her and stopped about fifteen yards farther up the platform. She turned to look past him, squinting up the track for a sign of an incoming train.

He studied her from behind his sunglasses. Ruth Ruggeri was in her early forties. Dark hair cut short, thick

wire-rimmed glasses, large nose. She was tall and a little
gangly. In her free hand she held a copy of the *Sun-Times*.
Must have bought it in the station.

A few minutes later, a four-car southbound train rum-
bled into the station and came to a halt with a metallic
grunt. He was near the rear doors to the third car. She was
facing the rear doors to the second car. The doors to all
cars clattered opened. He stepped in and moved through
the crowd to the front of the car, positioning himself so that
he had a view through the front window of his car into the
car ahead. She'd taken an aisle seat three rows from the
back of that car.

The doors closed. The train lurched forward and accelerated along the curving tracks.

Ruth read her paper and didn't look up as they came to
each stop.

Foster.

Davis Street.

He gripped the handhold and swayed as they moved
along the curving tracks through Evanston, rumbling past
buildings at the second-story level.

Dempster.

Main.

South.

As the train pulled into the Howard Street station, the
conductor announced that everyone had to get off. Hirsch
stepped out of his car. Ruth was up ahead, walking briskly
down the tracks toward a waiting train with its doors open.
She stepped into the forward door of the second car. Hirsch
ducked into the rear door of the same car. She took a seat
next to a window near the front. He sat three rows back on
the other side of the aisle.

The conductor announced that this was the Evanston
Express. First stop Belmont.

She rode the train all the way downtown to the Monroe Street stop.

He followed her across the Loop and into the lobby of a familiar sixty-story office tower. Back when he traveled to Chicago for depositions and joint defense counsel meetings in the huge antitrust and securities cases of his former life, this tower was known as the First National Bank Building, a proud symbol of a proud Chicago institution. Now it was the Bank One Building.

While they waited with the crowd for the next elevator, Ruth glanced once in his direction without any sign of recognition. An elevator arrived. They squeezed in with about a dozen other people. He saw her press the button for the forty-ninth floor. Others pressed buttons for floors above or below that. Two people got off at the forty-fourth floor, one at forty-six, four at forty-eight. The doors opened at the forty-ninth floor, and she got off with another woman. On the opposite wall he saw the words *Sidley Aus*—before the doors closed.

He knew the name. Sidley Austin Brown & Wood.

He'd been there many times and knew many of the firm's partners, or at least did back when the firm was Sidley & Austin.

He rode the elevator the rest of the way up and then all the way back down to the lobby.

WHEN Ruth Ruggeri stepped off the elevator into the lobby at noon, he was waiting over in a corner by the newsstand. She was carrying a brown lunch bag in one hand and a paperback book in the other.

Perfect.

After he'd ridden the elevator back down to the lobby that morning, he mulled over how and when and where to make contact with her. He'd almost called her on the phone, but held off, concerned that a first contact by telephone might scare her away. He sensed their first communication needed to be in person.

And thus as the hour approached noon, he'd returned to the lobby of the Bank One Building, hoping that the nice weather would lure her outdoors, praying that she would come out alone.

And she had.

She exited the building on the Dearborn side and paused to gaze around the Bank One Plaza. The plaza was a large semicircle facing the building. It descended in tiers to the fountain, which was running that day—nine columns of water, all at different heights at the moment, moving up and down in patterns. The water sparkled in the bright sun.

There were dozens of office workers scattered on different levels around the plaza, some seated alone, others in small groups, some with homemade lunches in brown paper bags, others with take-out sacks from McDonald's and SUBWAY and Taco Bell. The sun was high, the sky a clear blue. At various spots around the plaza young women leaned back on their elbows, faces toward the sun, using the lunch hour to get a head start on their summer tans.

Ruth took a seat on an empty cement bench in the shade near the massive Chagall mosaics. He strolled toward the Chagall as he watched her unpack her lunch—a meat sandwich on white bread, a bag of chips, an apple, a can of Diet Coke, a paper napkin. She spread the napkin on her lap and lifted her sandwich. As he came around the near side of the mosaics, she was munching on a potato chip and reading her paperback book.

He took a seat to her right at the other end of her bench, outside her personal space but close enough to be noticed. She glanced over at him—no sign of recognition—and returned to her book.

He waited a few moments and then said, "My name is David Hirsch."

She gave him a puzzled frown and then looked down, concentrating on removing two more potato chips from her bag.

He stared straight ahead. "I represent the estate of Judith Shifrin."

She stopped, the chips in her hand.

He glanced around, trying to see whether anyone was watching him. As he turned away from her toward the right, he slid his left hand across the bench and let the business card in his palm drop onto the bench by her paper bag. As he turned back he saw her slide the card under the bag.

"I'm investigating Judith's death." He was still scanning the crowd, not looking at her. "I know she came to Chicago to visit you. Twice. I know you gave her some important information. Perhaps even deadly information."

She hadn't moved.

He glanced over.

"I need to know what you told her, Ruth."

She flinched at the sound of her name.

"But not here," he said.

He leaned forward and gazed down the tiers toward the fountain. He rubbed his upper lip with the index finger of his left hand, screening his mouth.

"And not at your home in Evanston. I don't want anyone to know you're talking to me."

He looked down at the cement between his feet, his hand still screening his mouth. She was silent, tense, waiting.

"You work at Sidley Austin. As I recall, they use the top floor as their conference room center. I can meet you up there this afternoon. At two o'clock. Reserve a conference room. For you and a Mr. Peterson. I'll show up at two. I'll tell the receptionist up there that my name is Mr. Peterson. You and I will meet in the conference room. We'll talk for a few minutes, and then I will leave. You will never hear from me again. I promise. No one will know we met."

He gave her a moment to absorb that information.

"Otherwise," he said, "you will leave me no choice but to serve you with a subpoena. Then it all becomes public. I would rather keep this confidential. I would rather keep this just between you and me. That way I can can keep your name out of it."

He sat up and shaded his eyes from the sun.

"This is for Judith, Ruth. It's more her case than mine. She did most of the work. I'm just trying to wrap it up for her. I need you to help me do that for her, Ruth."

He stood. "I'll see you at two o'clock."

He lifted his briefcase and moved off in the direction of the Daley Center.

He didn't look back.

38

THE Hispanic receptionist gave him a perky smile. "And your name, sir?"

"Peterson."

She looked down at the schedule sheet and nodded. "Here we are."

She pressed some buttons on her telephone console and then spoke into the headset. "I have Mr. Peterson here. Okay, I'll send him right back."

She smiled at him again and pointed down the hallway. "You're all set, Mr. Peterson. The third conference room on your right."

The door to the small conference room was open. He paused in the doorway. Ruth was seated on the far side of the round table, her hands clasped in front of her on the table. She looked at him and lowered her eyes. He closed the door behind him.

"Thank you, Ruth."

She nodded, eyes still averted.

He took the chair across the table from her.

He said, "Tell me about your contacts with Judith."

She looked up. "What do you mean?"

"What did she want from you?"

She stared at him. The thick lenses of her glasses magnified her eyes.

"Did they kill her?" she asked.

"They?" Hirsch said.

"Peterson Tire."

"What makes you think that?"

"Tell me."

"I don't know."

"They said it was a car accident."

"That's the official version."

"But it wasn't, was it?"

"I don't think so, but I don't know for sure. That's part of why I came to see you."

"I don't know whether it was an accident." She shook her head defensively. "I don't know anything about that. Why do you think I would know anything about that?"

"I don't. But if it wasn't an accident, if she was killed, then you might know why she died."

She frowned and looked down.

"What did she want from you, Ruth?"

After a long silence, she looked up. "She wanted me to tell her about the money."

"What money?"

"The payments. The ones for litigation costs. She knew I handled the wire transfers."

"You worked for Donald Foster, right?"

She nodded.

"He was the chief financial officer?"

"I was his assistant."

"What did Judith want to know about the costs?"

"How they were calculated."

"What do you mean?"

"Most of the companies invoiced us for costs," she explained. "Court reporters, copying companies—that kind of stuff. But one company didn't send us any invoices. She wanted to know about that one."

"Do you remember which one it was?"

She frowned. "It had a foreign-sounding name."

He flipped through his file to Judith's memo summarizing the costs incurred by Peterson Tire Corporation in connection with its defense of the claim of Dorothy Sanderson.

"Boudreau?" he asked.

She shook her head. "I don't think so."

"Pembris?"

"No."

"Felis Tigris?"

She nodded. "That's the one."

"You say that company didn't send Peterson Tire invoices for its services?"

"Yes. Judith wanted to know how I knew what amounts to pay them."

"What did you tell her?"

"I explained that we paid them a fee based on a percentage."

"A percentage of what?"

"The difference between the final court award and another number we were given. It was a complicated formula."

"What was the other number?"

"It varied for each claim."

"Where did you get it?"

"From the law firm."

"Emerson, Burke and McGee?"

"Right. They were our lawyers in the St. Louis case."

"Marvin Guttner?"

Her upper lip curled in disgust. "Yes. Him."

"His law firm supplied you with the numbers?"

She nodded.

"Where did they get the numbers?"

"I'm not sure. I think it had something to do with the total damage amount the plaintiff had asked for. It was all on a fax they would send us for each case."

"What would you do with the numbers?"

"I'd do the calculation and then wire transfer the money. I'd always include the case number on the wire transfer form."

"Where did you transfer the money?"

"I don't know the name of the bank. I just know it was overseas."

"Why do you say that?"

"It had a Swift code."

He recognized the word. He leafed through his documents until he found his printout of Judith's Outlooks Note.

"What is a Swift code?" he asked.

"It's like a bank routing number, except it's used by banks outside the country."

"Swift?"

"It's an acronym." She squinted her eyes in concentration. "Society for Worldwide . . . uh . . . S-W-I-F . . . Worldwide Financial Transactions. Something like that. I've done some of those transfers here, too. I'm in the firm's accounting department. We make international wire transfers to banks with Swift numbers."

He looked at his notes. "What else did Judith want to know?"

When she didn't answer, he looked up. She had her arms crossed over her chest and she was staring at the framed railroad poster on the side wall.

"Ruth?"

She turned to him.

"She wanted to know what I'd heard."

"About what?"

"About that company. That Felis outfit."

"What about them?"

"About why we were paying them. About what they were doing. About what their role in the case was."

"What did you tell her?"

She stood up and walked over to the window, which looked south beyond the Loop toward the Field Museum and the Shedd Aquarium and the waters of Lake Michigan. She stared out the window, her arms crossed below her chest.

He waited.

Still facing the window, Ruth said, "She knew."

"She knew what?"

She turned to face him. "That's why she came to see me. She knew there was something wrong."

"Did she know what it was?"

"She had a pretty good idea."

"What did she think?"

"That someone was getting paid off. She thought the money I was transferring to that overseas company was part of a kickback scheme. She was pretty sure, in fact. But she needed proof. That's why she came to me."

"Did she want you to testify?"

"Oh, no. Never. But she hoped I could help point her to the evidence."

"What did you think of her theory about the wire transfers?"

She turned toward the window. "I thought she was right."

"Why?"

"Because everything about it felt wrong. Especially all the hush-hush. I remember back at the beginning I once asked my boss about it."

"Donald Foster?"

She nodded, still facing the window. "Mr. Foster told me it was strictly confidential. He told me I should never ask about it again. That I should never talk to anyone about it. He said that any disclosure by me was grounds for termination."

"Did he tell you why?"

She snorted. "Of course not. All I knew was that the whole wire transfer arrangement was set up a few weeks after my boss attended this secret meeting with the general counsel and our CEO and Mr. Guttner. It was all top secret."

"What kind of evidence did Judith hope you could help her find?"

"Evidence of the wire transfers."

"Why did she think you could help her with that?"

Still facing the window, her back to him, she shrugged. "I'm not sure. She'd already talked to other people who used to work at Peterson. I think some of them may have told her I was unhappy when I left."

"Were you unhappy?"

She nodded.

"Why?"

She turned to face him. "Because I knew there was something wrong with those wire transfers."

"How did you know that?"

Her face was flushed with emotion. "Because everything about them felt wrong. When I tried to ask my boss, all he told me was to mind my own business."

She shook her head angrily.

"Mind my own business. That's exactly what I was doing. I was the one they were using to carry out their plan. I was the one calculating the amounts and wire transferring the money. But I didn't know why. I didn't know whether we were breaking the law or cheating someone or what. All I knew was that I was part of something that didn't seem right. I started having trouble sleeping. I was getting depressed. I talked to my priest. I decided enough was enough. I quit."

"Did they ask you why?"

"I told them my boyfriend was in Chicago and we were getting married."

"That was Jason?"

She shook her head. "There was no one. I invented a fiancé for the story. I just wanted to get out of there. I thought it sounded better, less suspicious, if I was moving because I was engaged. I had a sister in Chicago. I moved in with her. I didn't meet Jason until a few months later."

"Does Jason know?"

She shook her head. "No. And he never will. That part of my life is over, Mr. Hirsch. No one knows. Except Judith. And now you."

He let her final words linger as he skimmed through the notes on his legal pad.

He asked, "What about the evidence Judith was looking for?"

"I'd made copies before I left the company. Secretly, of course. I brought them with me when I moved here. I put them in a safe-deposit box."

"What were they?"

"I made copies of the wire transfers and the confirmations. I also made copies of the faxes from Mr. Guttner's firm with the numbers that I used to calculate the amounts of the transfers."

"You had them in your safe-deposit box?"

She nodded. "Judith wanted to see them. I told her I'd have to think about it. We communicated some more after she left, mostly by e-mail. I finally decided to let her see them. She came back to Chicago. I took a day off work. I went to my bank and got the documents out of my safe-deposit box. I gave them to her."

"What did she think of them?"

"We went back to her hotel room. I took her through them, one by one, explaining how they worked. She was real excited. She already had other documents from the case. They all seemed to fit together, she said. She told me my documents were the key."

"Did she tell you why?"

Ruth shook her head. "I told her not to. I told her I didn't want to know. I'd closed off that part of my life. Permanently. I told her I never wanted to hear about it again. And I still don't."

"Was that your last contact with Judith?"

Her eyes suddenly welled up with tears. She looked around the room and went over to the side table, where there were glasses and coasters and napkins. She grabbed a napkin and held it in her clenched fist.

He said nothing.

She came back to her chair and sat down. She pressed the napkin against the bottom of her nose.

He waited.

"She sent me a Christmas card," she said, almost in a whisper.

"Judith?"

She nodded.

"When?"

"It arrived three days after she died."

He waited.

"She included a message," she said.

"What kind of message?"

She looked up, her eyes red. "About what she was doing. I didn't know she was already dead when I got her card. I had no idea. I didn't hear anything else from her.

Not from her or from anyone else. I didn't find out that she had died until February, and by then it was too late."

"Too late for what?"

"For him. He was dead, too."

"Who was dead?"

"The reporter. The one she wanted me to give the message to. My God, I didn't know what to do then. I just hoped it would all disappear. That I'd never hear anything about it again. And I didn't. Until today. Until you."

"Do you remember the name of the reporter?"

She shook her head.

"Markman?" Hirsch asked. "Peter Markman?"

"Yes." She nodded. "Markman. That's him."

"What did she tell you about him?"

"Not much. When she came back to Chicago that second time, she told me that a reporter was helping her investigate the story. She never told me his name, though. Not until she sent me the Christmas card. Even then she didn't say he was the reporter."

"How did you know he was?"

"I put two and two together. I knew she was working with a reporter, and she said something on the card about him and a Pulitzer, so I assumed he was the one."

"Do you remember what she said about a Pulitzer?"

"No." She paused, staring down at the table. "I still have the card."

"Where?"

"In my safe-deposit box."

"What about the documents you gave to Judith? Do you still have copies?"

"No." She shook her head. "I gave her my copies. I trusted her. I told her that I never wanted to see them again or hear anything about them again. Ever. I made her promise."

"She took your only copies?"

Ruth nodded.

Hirsch felt a wave of frustration.

"But I still have her Christmas card," she said.

"Right."

"I can send it to you."

He gazed at her, trying to hide his disappointment. "That would be nice."

"Maybe it will help."

"Maybe."

"I liked her."

He nodded.

She stared at him, her eyes no longer red. "She had a lot of guts."

"That she did."

"A lot more than I did." She took a deep breath and exhaled slowly. "They killed her, didn't they?"

"That's what I'm trying to find out, Ruth."

Her expression darkened. She stood up.

"You need to leave now."

As he gathered his notes, she turned and stepped to the window again.

He closed his briefcase and watched her for a moment as she stared out the window, her back to him.

"Thank you, Ruth."

She didn't turn around. "Please go now."

He gathered his stuff, opened the door to the conference room, and stepped out. As he started to close the door, she turned toward him.

He waited in the doorway.

After a moment, she shook her head.

"Just go," she said.

39

As he watched from the back row of the classroom, Hirsch couldn't help but ask himself again why he'd given up his Friday afternoon handball game to attend this ceremony.

The answer should have been Judith, but it was probably Dulcie. He'd put their relationship under enough strain already by insisting they have no social contact until his investigation was complete.

He'd told Lauren the same thing, although without giving her the real reason. He had called her two nights ago. It had been almost a week since their pumpernickel bagel breakfast, and he was acutely aware of his promise to get together for dinner after the case was over. With each passing day, that promise weighed heavier on his thoughts. He knew that she'd know about this afternoon's ceremony. It was at her law school, after all. She'd thus know the lawsuit was officially over. But what she didn't know was that the lawsuit had become the least important, and the least hazardous, aspect of the case. So he told her on the phone that he was working on a new matter that involved people who might try to harass anyone with a personal connection to him. He told her that he ought to be able to wrap it up in a week or so, but that until that happened he didn't want to endanger her by making any contact, especially at something as public as the ceremony at the law school. Lauren had been fine with it. Indeed, she'd sounded impressed, apparently willing to believe that her father was still important enough to be involved in matters that required him to protect those in his inner circle.

Dulcie, however, had not been impressed. The more accurate term was annoyed.

"You should be there," she'd told him over the phone. "Dammit, David, she was your client. I don't care what you think about the people involved. This is in her honor, not theirs. You should be there."

A good argument, although perhaps not as persuasive as Rosenbloom's.

"Are you out of your mind, Samson?" He'd shaken his head in disbelief. "She wants you there. She'll be happy if you're there. She'll be unhappy if you aren't. So let's ask ourselves whether she is someone you want to make happy? Let's examine that weighty question, shall we? Item one: She's bright. Item two: She's funny. Item three: She's totally gorgeous. Bright, funny, totally gorgeous. Does that sound like someone you want to make happy?" He slipped into his Mister Rogers voice: "Kids, can you say, 'Fucking aye'?"

So he agreed to come to the event, although he insisted that no speaker mention his name or his involvement in the lawsuit or the settlement.

The ceremony was held in one of the large classrooms at the law school. It consisted of several curving rows of table desks arranged in descending levels around the instructor's stage below. The room was filled for the event—

mostly professors and students. Lauren wasn't among them, thank God. The dignitaries were seated down below in a row of chairs facing the audience. Standing off to the right side were a local TV reporter and her cameraman, a husky guy with a videocam on his shoulder. On the side were three press photographers and a newspaper reporter. The reporter was scribbling in his notepad as the dean of the law school gave his introductory remarks.

"We live in an era," Dean Miller was saying, "where corporate America is too often and too easily accused of caring about profits and not people, of focusing on the bottom line of the balance sheet instead of the bottom part of society. We read in the papers and hear on the news . . ."

Hirsch watched the dean perform with mild amusement. Once upon a time, Arnold Miller had treated him as a fellow member of the elite, although their kinship had in truth extended no further than their Supreme Court clerkships—Hirsch for Justice Potter Stewart, Miller for Justice Lewis F. Powell Jr. And one possible additional connection. Although Miller had the perfect WASP facade, right down to the horsy wife nicknamed Bunny, Hirsch had heard from others that only one generation back the family name had been Milkovitz.

He was struck by how much Miller had aged during the past decade. The goatee had once been dark and sharply trimmed, adding a European intellectual flair to Miller's features. Now those same features had faded and sunk, as if from erosion, and the goatee, gray and bushy, seemed little more than a vain old man's ploy to hide a receding chin line.

Hirsch shifted in his seat, trying to focus on the dean's opening remarks. He was introducing someone.

"—one of our own esteemed alumni," the dean said, his reading glasses perched on the end of his nose.

The bigwigs down below included three middle-aged

white guys in suits and Dulcie, who looked stunning in her simple black matte jersey dress and gold necklace, her curly hair cascading to her shoulders. The tableau could have been the stage set for the beautiful young queen and her senior advisers. Treacherous advisers, though. To her right sat Marvin Guttner, his girth spilling over the sides of the chair. He resembled a cross between a corporate lawyer and a sumo wrestler. To his right sat a short balding man in his late fifties with droopy eyes and a droopier gray mustache. He was, according to the program, Donald Foster, chief financial officer of Peterson Tire Company. To Dulcie's left was the dean's empty seat, and to the left of that sat the featured speaker, Judge Brendan McCormick, nattily attired in a dark suit, white shirt, and striped tie.

"A gentleman," the dean continued, "who is now a senior partner in a prominent law firm with headquarters in this fine city. He has represented the Peterson Tire Company for years, and through his good services has been instrumental in making the arrangements for today's most generous gift."

Guttner, Foster, and McCormick—quite a rogues' gallery, Hirsch thought. All gathered on stage to bask in the glory of a donation that represented, at best, a fraction of the revenues that Peterson Tire would earn during the length of this ceremony.

"Without further ado, it is my great pleasure to present a distinguished attorney and graduate of our law school, Mr. Marvin Guttner."

As the applause began, the dean turned to Guttner with a smile. The fat man heaved his bulk out of the chair, adjusted his suit jacket, and stepped to the podium, pausing to shake the dean's hand.

To his credit, Guttner kept the proceeding moving. At ease in the role of master of ceremonies, his voice in full mellifluous mode, he gave the audience a brief summary

of Judith Shifrin's life and her "tragic and untimely death."
With an acknowledgment to Dulcie, he spoke of Judith's
involvement in the legal clinic and Peterson Tire's desire to
pay tribute to that commitment. That was the segue to Donald Foster, who Guttner motioned to join him at the
podium. He also summoned Dulcie and the dean to the
podium.

"We are honored today," Guttner continued, "by the
presence of a top officer of Peterson Tire Corporation, who
has traveled to St. Louis for this special ceremony. What
makes his appearance here especially noteworthy is that
thirty-nine years ago, he earned his bachelor's degree from
this university. So without further ado, I am pleased to
introduce a fellow alumnus of Washington University and
the chief financial officer of Peterson Tire Corporation,
Mr. Donald Foster."

Foster acknowledged the applause with an awkward
wave as he removed an envelope and a folded sheet of paper from the inside pocket of his jacket. He put on his reading glasses, unfolded the sheet on the podium, and cleared
his throat.

"Thank you, Mr. Guttner." He had a high-pitched twang.
He glanced up briefly and then returned to the written text.
He acknowledged the dignitaries and greeted the
audience—eyes focused on the text, voice close to a mon-
otone.

"On behalf of the Peterson Tire Corporation," he read,
"I am pleased to present to the law school this check"—
and here he held up the envelope stiffly—"in the amount of
fifty thousand dollars, to be used for establishment of the
Judith Shifrin Memorial Internship at the law school's
Family Justice Legal Clinic."

He looked up from the text with a squint and turned toward the others gathered around the podium, still holding
the envelope at an odd angle. The dean stepped forward to

take it from him, placed a hand on his shoulder, and gently turned him in the direction of the photographers. The two men posed side by side, the dean smiling and holding the envelope in front of them waist high, Foster looking down at the envelope, his bald head shining in the glare of the overhead lights.

Once the others had returned to their seats, Guttner placed a hand on either side of the podium and waited until there was total silence.

"For the final two years of her life," Guttner began, "Judith Shifrin served as a law clerk to the Honorable Brendan McCormick of the United States District Court for the Eastern District of Missouri. They shared a special professional relationship, this tall federal judge and his diminutive law clerk. For those of us who appeared in Judge McCormick's courtroom, it was clear that the Judge and his Judith were the dynamic duo. The mutual respect was obvious. Alas, Judge McCormick was the last person to see Judith alive. We are honored today that this busy jurist has made time in his schedule to help us mark this special occasion with some of his memories of Judith Shifrin. Ladies and gentlemen, please join me in giving a warm welcome to the Honorable Brendan McCormick."

Hirsch leaned forward as the judge stepped to the podium. McCormick looked vigorous and imposing in his dark suit and deep tan. Hands holding the edges of the podium, he gazed around the crowd, pausing for a nanosecond as he made eye contact with Hirsch, acknowledging him with a tiny nod.

"I miss Judith," McCormick said.

He paused. The room was silent.

"I miss her energy. Her insights. Her commitment." He smiled. "I even miss her stubbornness. There was nothing halfway or halfhearted about Judith Shifrin. She was a believer, and she acted on her beliefs. I saw it every day in my chambers and in my courtroom. If she disagreed with a decision of mine, she'd let me know it. Politely, of course. But persistently, too. She was walking determination. What did she do for a living? She made things better. That was her job in life. From what I've heard today from those involved with the Family Justice Law Clinic, she made that a better place, too."

Another pause, a sadder smile. "And she made me a better judge. Unfortunately, I still had a long way to go when she left us. But Judith never gave up. She kept working on me up until the very end. The very end."

He looked down, apparently overcome. Hirsch watched, fascinated. He'd forgotten what a consummate showman McCormick had been back in his prosecutor days. The courtroom audience for his closing arguments invariably included a handful of prosecutors and defense lawyers who just happened to drop by for the show. Although Assistant U.S. Attorney Brendan. McCormick rarely had a good grasp on the law or the facts, he always had a total grasp on the jury.

And like those juries back then, today's audience was rapt. The only noise was the occasional click of a camera shutter.

McCormick resumed, his voice filled with emotion. "This is a wonderful tribute to a wonderful person. To those of you who made this possible, including those too humble to allow their names to be mentioned here today, I thank you on Judith's behalf. Those of you who knew Judith know that she was far too modest in life to have been anything but embarrassed by all this attention. I'd like to think, though, that she's smiling down at us from somewhere up above. Maybe blushing, too. But smiling nonetheless."

He glanced heavenward and then nodded. "We salute you, Judith Shifrin."

He stepped away from the podium.

The audience remained silent for another two beats and then erupted into applause.

40

"DAVID!"

Hirsch had reached his car in the parking lot. He turned to see McCormick striding toward him.

"Not staying for refreshments?"

Hirsch shook his head. "I have another appointment."

"I thought it was a nice ceremony."

Even in the parking lot, he could smell McCormick's cologne.

Hirsch said, "The audience liked your speech."

"What about you?"

"What about me?"

"What did you think of my speech?"

"I thought it was effective."

"Effective, eh?" McCormick grinned. "I suppose that qualifies as a compliment. Especially from you, David." He bowed. "I thank you."

"You're welcome."

McCormick's smile faded. "I think her father would be pleased."

"I hope so."

"I didn't see him there."

"He wasn't."

"Nursing home?"

Hirsch nodded. "But the press was at the ceremony. I'll bring her father a copy of the article when it's published."

"I bet he'll like that."

"What do you want, Brendan?"

McCormick held up his hands. "No hidden agendas here, David. Just wanted to tell you how much I appreciate what you've done for Judith. I still remember when you and I had our first meeting about the lawsuit. Back in January. We both knew back then it was going to be a tough case, and that was before we even knew who your opponents were. Marvin Guttner is no teddy bear, and Jack Bellows is a genuine son of a bitch. But you took 'em on, all of them, and look what you accomplished. And in just a few months. You did a helluva job, David."

Hirsch waited.

"So how's it feel?" McCormick asked.

"How's what feel?"

"To be done with the case. To finally be able to move on to something else."

If McCormick was fishing, he wasn't going to get a nibble.

Hirsch checked his watch. "I need to go, Brendan."

"Sure. I do, too."

"Court?" Hirsch asked, trying to end the conversation on a neutral note.

"Well, in a way. Tennis court. And golf. I've had a crazy couple of months. I've decided to take a few days of R and R."

"Bermuda?"

"Actually, yes."

"You have a place there?"

"A little cottage. Up on a hill overlooking the ocean. You ever been to Bermuda?"

"No."

"Beautiful island. First time I saw it was on my honeymoon." He chuckled. "That was about my last good memory from that marriage, and just about the only thing she didn't take in the divorce. That bitch got everything but the place in Bermuda. Oh, brother." He shook his head at the memory.

Hirsch took out his car keys. "Have a good time, Brendan."

"Thanks. And thanks again for your work on the case. Judith deserved the best, and you gave it to her."

They shook hands again.

He watched as McCormick headed down the row of parked cars toward his black Mercedes. He waited until McCormick had pulled out of the parking lot, and then he dialed the office on his cell phone.

"This is David. Is Cheryl there?"

"I'll ring her office, Mr. Hirsch."

She answered on the second ring. Cheryl Jaspers was one of the firm's paralegals who'd been helping him on the Judith Shifrin case.

"I'm not having much luck on that Swift code," she told him.

"I have a different idea," he said. "Can you get me a list of the banks in Bermuda?"

"I can try. Why?"

"Just a hunch."

"Shouldn't take too long. Do you need it today?"

It was Friday afternoon. He checked his watch. Too late to drive back downtown and get anything done before sunset.

"No. I'll be in the office Sunday. If you find anything, just leave it on my desk."

"Sure thing."

41

SUNDAY morning.

Hirsch was seated at the conference table in his office, a legal pad on his lap, court papers spread across the table. For the last hour or so he'd been reviewing the file in one of his contested bankruptcy matters. It was set for a confirmation hearing Monday morning.

He stifled a yawn and tossed the pad onto the table. He stood and stretched his back, hands on his hips as he twisted his upper torso first to the left and then to the right. As he did, he glanced over at his desk and saw a stack of papers in his in-box. The papers reminded him of his conversation on Friday afternoon with his paralegal. He went over to his desk. Sure enough, the top document in the in-box was a two-page memo from Cheryl Jaspers. He picked it up and carried it over to the window:

Per your request, I was able to find five banks in Bermuda, all listed on the next page. As you will see, I

even found the Swift codes for two of them! Please let
me know what else you need me to do. Hope you have a
nice weekend!

He turned to the listings on the second page:

Bank of Bermuda Limited
6 Front Street
Hamilton, Bermuda

Bank of N.T. Butterfield & Son Ltd. (Swift Code
BNTBBMHM)
65 Front Street
Hamilton, Bermuda

Bermuda Commercial Bank Ltd. (Swift Code BP-
BKBMHM)
43 Victoria Street
Hamilton, Bermuda

Capital G Bank Limited
21-25 Reid Street
Hamilton, Bermuda

Hamilton Bank & Trust Limited
32 Victoria Street
Hamilton, Bermuda

He went over to the desk and flipped through his Shifrin
folders until he found the printout of Judith's computer
note with the Swift code: HBTLBMHM.
He compared it to the two codes on Cheryl's list.
No match.
Of course.

His eyes moved down the list to the last bank. Hamilton Bank and Trust Limited. One of the two banks on Victoria Street. The other one, Bermuda Commercial Bank Ltd., had a nonmatching Swift code.

He repeated the bank's address aloud as he found his printout of the Outlooks Note that Judith had created on November 9, just a little over a month before her death. That was the one that quoted some banter between "G" and "J" after a prehearing conference in "J's chambers." The men joking about a controversial Victoria's Secret show on television the prior night. The Note ended with the "aside" by J to G:

"We've got our own Victoria's
Secret"—Both laughed.

Victoria's Secret.
Victoria Secret.
They would have sounded the same to someone overhearing the conversation.

His eyes drifted back to his in-box. There were several documents in there—office memos, court filings, unopened envelopes. He sorted through the items and came to a five-by-seven manila envelope with his name and address printed in ink. No return address. A Chicago postmark over the two stamps.

He cut through the flap with a letter opener. Inside was a green envelope about the size of the ones sold with greeting cards. The envelope was addressed to Ruth Ruggeri at her Evanston address. The words and numbers were written in dark blue ink, as was the return address centered on the flap on back:

J. Shifrin
256 Lincolnshire, Apt. 5E
St. Louis, MO 63105

The green envelope had been sliced open neatly, probably with a letter opener. Inside was a Christmas card with an old-fashioned winter-in-New-England illustration of a horse-drawn sleigh carrying two laughing, rosy-cheeked woman, each bundled in a sweater, scarf, and gloves. They were emerging from a red covered bridge capped with snow.

He opened the card. The preprinted message inside offered "Warm Wishes for a Happy Holiday Season and a Joyful New Year." Below that, Judith had added her own message:

Dear Ruth:
Thank you so much. I know how difficult it was for you. I pray I can make it worth your effort. Tonight is the night! Cross your fingers. If anything goes wrong, be sure to tell Pat Markman that his Pulitzer is chilly but safe with Sadie the G.

> Your friend (and ally),
> Judith

He reread her message.
Tonight is the night.
He looked at the front of the red envelope, at the canceled stamp. It was postmarked on December 18 three years ago.

Judith Shifrin died on December 18 three years ago.

42

LOGISTICS were an issue. He needed to show the Christmas card to Carrie Markman, but not at her house. If he had really been followed the last time—and he still didn't know—he'd be putting her at even greater danger by going back. Carrie Markman was the quintessential innocent bystander, the sister of someone who may have learned something nasty about someone who may have killed someone else whose death was now being investigated by yet another someone who had dropped into her life unexpected and uninvited.

But perhaps not unobserved.

As for the challenge of arranging a safe rendezvous, well, he had never faced that problem before. Eventually, he turned to vaguely recalled scenarios from movies he'd seen, hoping he could cobble together a Hollywood scene that would hold together in the real world.

And thus at three forty-five in the afternoon of that same Sunday, barely four hours after he'd read Judith's Christmas card message to Ruth, he pulled his car into a space in the underground garage of the Plaza Frontenac shopping mall in suburban St. Louis. Four others boarded the garage elevator with him. Two were middle-aged women who'd apparently arrived together, since they were talking about someone named Nancy. The other two were men—one slender and tall in his fifties, the other burly and average height in his thirties. Neither acknowledged the other or Hirsch as the elevator doors slid closed. The taller man had gray hair and angular features. He was dressed country club casual in a red blazer, white shirt, yellow slacks, and penny loafers without socks. The younger one had a broad nose and curly brown hair and wore khakis, running shoes, and a light blue windbreaker zipped over a white turtleneck.

The elevator doors slid open on the first floor. All got off.

Hirsch wandered through the mall, working his way north toward Saks Fifth Avenue, which he entered at a few minutes after four. Along the way, he'd passed both men from the elevator. Once inside Saks, he meandered toward the main entrance at the north end of the mall. At four-fifteen P.M., he pushed through the front doors of Saks just as the Yellow Cab he'd ordered pulled up in front. He got in the cab, told the driver the destination, and turned to watch the Saks doors as the cab pulled away.

He expected to see someone—probably the burly guy from the elevator—burst through the door, spot the cab, and start charging after it as his right hand reached inside his jacket. Just like in the movies. Instead, an elderly woman with a hatbox stepped out and peered in the opposite direction.

The cab dropped him off at the Cheshire Inn. The clerk at the front desk gave him the key to room 204 and told him that the lady had already arrived. He couldn't tell whether the clerk gave him a wink or just had an eye twitch. It was only as he headed down the hall toward the room that he realized that the way he'd made the room arrangements earlier that afternoon, telling the clerk he only needed a room for a few hours and that the other guest would arrive separately, was subject to varying interpretations. Poor Carrie, he said to himself, imagining the desk clerk's X-rated speculations when she had asked for the key to room 204.

He knocked on the door and called her name. He made sure he was standing where she could see him through the peephole. She opened the door, smiled, waved him in, and closed it behind her.

He could see from the hollow in the bedspread that she'd been seated on the bed watching the television while she waited. A gourmet cooking show was on. She clicked it off and turned to him with a curious look.

"You have me quite intrigued, David." She sat down on the edge of the bed. "I feel like a secret agent."

"I hope this rigmarole was unnecessary. I just want to make sure no one knows about your connection."

"What exactly is my connection?"

He pulled the chair away from the desk and turned it so he could sit facing her.

"When we met at your house," he said, "you told me that your brother had helped Judith Shifrin with an investigation. You didn't know the details, or even the identities of the people she was investigating, except that you thought they might include a lawyer or a judge."

"That's right. Have you found something?"

"I think your brother was helping Judith even more than you or I realized."

"Really? What makes you think so?"

"Judith died three years ago on the night of December eighteenth. Earlier that same day, she mailed a Christmas card to a woman in Chicago who was also helping her with the investigation. Here's that card."

He handed her the envelope and watched her remove the card inside. She studied the front, opened it up, and read Judith's inscription. As she did, she put her hand up to her mouth.

"Oh, my," she whispered.

When she looked up, there were tears in her eyes.

He waited.

After a moment, she nodded for him to proceed, blinking back tears.

"That woman—her name is Ruth—she never contacted your brother. She didn't find out about Judith's death until months later. By then, your brother had died as well. Ruth didn't know what to do at that point. She kept the Christmas card in her safe-deposit box. I met with her last week. Afterward, she sent it to me."

Carrie looked down again at Judith's words and then raised her eyes to Hirsch's.

"She left something for him." Her voice almost a whisper. "Something important."

"But I don't know where."

Her eyes narrowed. "I do."

Hirsch could feel the adrenaline rush. "Tell me."

"Do you remember those photographs of the Civil Courts Building? The ones in my brother's bedroom?"

"Sure."

"Remember those two strange beasts on top of the pyramid?"

"I do."

Hirsch recalled them from the aerial photograph—the sphinxlike creatures seated back to back, one gazing out toward the Mississippi River, the other in the opposite direction.

"During construction, the workers nicknamed them Sadie and Sue. I don't recall which is which, but Judith seems to have left him something in the one called Sadie."

"Can you actually get inside them?"

"Oh yes. They're hollow. Made out of cast aluminum. Patrick took me in one of them. You get inside from an opening in the ceiling below, like a trapdoor." She frowned as she tried to remember. "Patrick must have taken me inside Sue."

"Why do you say that."

"I didn't see any safe."

"Safe?"

As he said the word, he remembered Judith's other computer note, the one from seven thirty-eight P.M. on November 30: *G safe: 8-25-5-13*.

Carrie said, "Patrick told me that they installed a safe up there during construction. I don't remember why. Maybe for secret court files. Who knows? He told me that no one had used it in years."

"How did he know?"

"He found the combination somehow. Probably while digging through old papers on the building. He was a brilliant investigative reporter, God bless him. He told me he opened the safe. He said there was nothing inside." She glanced down at Judith's inscription again. "But he didn't tell me enough."

"What do you mean?"

"Look at her note. She left something for him inside that safe." She shook her head. "He never told me the combination."

"But he told her."

Her eyes widened. "And you found it?"

"She saved it on a note that referenced something she called the 'G safe.'"

"'G' safe?"

Hirsch smiled. "Those strange beasts on top of the building—they're called griffins, aren't they?"

She nodded. "They certainly are."

* * *

THE exit plan was for him to leave first and catch a cab back to the shopping mall. Carrie would wait an hour before leaving. He called a cab from the hotel room. The dispatcher told him it would be in front of the hotel in five minutes.

Carrie walked him to the room door.

"You must let me know if you find anything," she said.

"I will, but we need to be careful. Don't call me. I'll contact you when it's safe to. But not until then. Okay?"

She was staring up at him, her lips quivering.

"They killed my brother, didn't they?"

He sighed. "I wish I knew, Carrie. Your brother must have been privy to a lot of what Judith knew. Did someone else find that out? Someone with a reason to kill him?" He shrugged. "I don't know."

She was blinking back tears. "He was a good man, my brother. A little rough on the outside, but a good heart. He loved Judith in his own way—like an uncle, or a guardian. You can't imagine how upset he was when she died."

She paused, staring up at him.

He nodded.

She said, "If she really left him something worth a Pulitzer prize—"

She was crying now. He leaned down to give her a hug. Holding her against his body, he was surprised how frail she seemed. With all her feisty determination, it was easy to forget that she was just a little old lady.

"Find it," she whispered. "For both of their sakes."

"I will, Carrie."

43

THIRTEENTH floor.
   The elevator went no higher.
   The bell dinged, the doors slid open, and he stepped out into the foyer of the law library of the Civil Courts Building. Directly ahead was the librarian station, a rectangular enclosure in the center of the room with a counter, two desks, and various equipment. Inside the enclosure, a heavyset black woman was seated at a computer terminal. The ceiling above was two stories high with a mezzanine overhang filled with stacks of books.
   He'd dressed for court today, the better to fit in. Dark suit, white shirt, striped tie, large trial briefcase. No briefs in the briefcase, though. And no yellow legal pads or pleading binders or photocopies of cases or outlines of cross-examinations. Nothing in there but a flashlight and a half-sized pry bar, both purchased that morning at Home Depot. The pry bar was his backup safecracking plan. He couldn't be certain that Judith had correctly written down

the combination, or that it would still work more than three years later. Thus the pry bar.

He would never have gotten that tool past security at the federal courthouse, but this was the Civil Courts Building, where the security guards treated attorneys with a quaint level of deference, requiring only a display of a Missouri bar membership card to be waved around the metal detectors and X-ray machine. Indeed, the elderly guard had nodded at his large briefcase and wished him good luck in court.

Hirsch moved around the main level of the library. He hadn't been up here in maybe twenty years. The place had a threadbare feel, as if it hadn't been renovated since the building opened in the 1930s. The carpets were faded, the woodwork was dull and scratched, the lighting uneven. Visible through the windows on all sides were the bottom halves of the massive Ionic columns that ringed the Greek temple structure, eight to a side. He moved down a long row of stacks to the window, which looked out between two of the fluted columns. He turned his head sideways to peer up, unable to see the tops of the columns.

The elevator bell dinged, and he turned with a frown.

He moved back through the stacks toward the front area, but by the time he reached that area there was no one nearby except for the librarian at her computer terminal. Perhaps someone had departed.

Perhaps.

He walked around the perimeter of the first level. He counted five people in addition to the librarian. Two were elderly attorneys in baggy suits and large ties. They were seated on opposite sides of the same rectangular table— one hunched over a law book with a magnifying glass, the other reading a newspaper attached to a bamboo pole. He saw two men, both in their thirties—a skinny guy with blond hair in a brown suit, and a husky guy in a dark gray blazer and khaki slacks. They were seated at small tables on opposite sides of the room. Each had casebooks piled on his table. The skinny guy was taking notes on a laptop computer. The burly guy had an open yellow legal pad at his side. Both looked vaguely familiar, although he couldn't place either. Lastly, there was a woman in her twenties, casually dressed and seated at a carrel with a casebook open in front of her, taking notes as she read.

He took the stairway up to the mezzanine level and walked around the perimeter. From the windows up there you could see the tops of the columns, which meant that the pyramid portion of the roof was directly overhead.

The only person he found on the mezzanine level was a middle-aged woman in a pants suit seated in a carrel. She was writing notes on index cards as she perused an unwieldy volume of what appeared to be zoning regulations or municipal ordinances dating back several decades. She didn't look up as he passed.

Moving around the mezzanine, he noted two exit doors along the walls, each bearing a stairway symbol stenciled in red. He confirmed that both doors were screened from view from the first floor. One was tucked around the corner at one end of the mezzanine. The other, though, was in the sight lines of the woman in the carrel.

He meandered back toward that far exit door, pretending to be searching for a book in the stacks. When he reached the door, he paused—right hand on the knob, left holding the briefcase—and looked back.

No one could see him.

He took a breath, turned the knob, and ducked inside, gently closing the door behind him.

He was on a stairwell landing. The stairs went up and down. At the top of the stairs was a metal door with the words *No Admittance* stenciled in black. As he started up the stairs he could hear rumbling mechanical noises from the other side.

He tried the door at the top of the stairs. It was unlocked. He pushed it open and stepped inside.

He wasn't sure what he was expecting to find up there inside the pyramid. Something exotic, perhaps. A hint of Arabia. But what struck him first was how absolutely ordinary it all seemed. And how familiar. This was hardly his first time on the top floor of a tall building—the real top floor, that is, instead of the top button on the elevator. He'd been on top floors in connection with various construction lawsuits over the years—up there maneuvering between massive heating, ventilating, and air-conditioning systems; walking around the elevator equipment; following paths to other machinery and supply areas that typically occupied the top level of tall buildings.

Including the Civil Courts Building.

No mummies or hieroglyphics up here. Just a dusty obstacle course of heavy equipment and storage sheds. Noisy, too. Just like other tall buildings. There was the deep thrum of the HVAC system and the whine and grinding clatter of elevator motors and cables. All familiar.

Until he looked up—up into what was unmistakably the inside of a stepped pyramid. The four walls slanted inward and met near the top. The interior space overhead was a warren of anchored ladders and screened catwalks that reached up to just below the rectangular ceiling. He estimated that the ceiling was fifty feet long and twenty-five feet wide.

He checked his watch: one forty-seven P.M.

He moved cautiously around the entire floor, using the large equipment as a screen, trying to determine whether any of the maintenance staff was up there.

He saw no one.

About twenty feet out from the wall near him was a perpendicular metal ladder that joined a catwalk overhead. Hirsch ran his eyes up the rungs to the catwalk and then looked down at his briefcase. He tried to gauge the added difficulty of climbing up the pyramid ladders with one hand while lugging a large briefcase with the other. It wasn't worth it. If she'd really hidden papers up there, they were likely to be inside some sort of container. A file folder, perhaps. Or even a shoe box. He could carry that down without the briefcase.

He knelt, opened the briefcase, and removed the pry bar and the flashlight. As he stood, he scanned the area for a place to hide the briefcase. Off to his right was a clothing rack on which hung about two dozen green maintenance jumpsuits. He turned off his cell phone, put it inside the briefcase, and stashed the briefcase against the wall behind the rack.

He slipped the flashlight into the left side pocket of his suit jacket and the pry bar into the right pocket. He had prepared for just this contingency by cutting through the bottom seams of both pockets, thereby adding just enough additional room to allow the flashlight and the pry bar to slide all the way inside.

He scanned the area again and then clambered up the first ladder, feeling exposed and vulnerable the whole way. He crouched on the catwalk and surveyed the floor area below.

Still no one.

He moved down the catwalk to the next ladder, and then up that ladder to the next catwalk. By the time he reached the uppermost catwalk, which was directly below the ceiling, he was breathing heavily. There were two short ladders on this level, each leading up to a small trapdoor in the ceiling.

Sadie and Sue, he thought.

Three and half years ago, Judith had been up on this same catwalk with a package of valuable documents to hide. Which ladder had she chosen?

He decided on the nearest one. He climbed up the short ladder and pushed up on the trap door, which opened with a loud creak. He climbed through the opening.

He was inside one of the griffins. Just enough light slanted in from what was presumably its head to dimly illuminate the space, which appeared to be about the size and shape and height of a bedroom—albeit a windowless bedroom with aluminum walls and ceiling.

He took out the flashlight and moved the beam across the floor and walls. No safe.

That meant this was the same griffin that Patrick Markman had taken his sister inside. The griffin named Sue.

He climbed through the trapdoor and down the ladder to the catwalk. He moved over to the other ladder, climbed up to the trapdoor, and pushed.

It didn't open.

He moved his legs up another rung and pressed his back against the trap door. He braced himself on the ladder. Using his legs for extra power, he pushed up.

Nothing.

Harder.

It wouldn't budge.

He went down the ladder and up the first one again—up through the trapdoor and into the griffin. He moved the flashlight beam slowly across the walls until he spotted a half-sized door in the far wall. It had a metal latch handle. He yanked up the handle and pushed on the door. It squeaked open. The room filled with light and the whistling of wind.

He bent low and stepped through the door onto the roof of the Civil Courts Building. He straightened and looked around, getting his bearings. He was standing atop the pyramid on a small platform between the two enormous griffins seated back to back.

He leaned over and looked down the pyramid—down ten stepped ledges, each about four feet wide with a four-foot drop to the next ledge. Far below, the base of the pyramid sat on a limestone platform at least ten feet thick. The bottom of the platform nestled inside a parapet wall on top of the Greek temple. Perched on each of the four corners of the parapet wall was a concrete eagle.

The sky had been partly cloudy when he entered the building nearly an hour ago. Now it was a solid gray. There was a heavy scent of rain in the air. As he turned back toward the griffins, a gust of wind flapped his suit jacket and snatched his kippah. He reached up too late and watched it sail away, jumping and swooping in the wind, quickly shrinking to a dark speck in the distance.

He turned his attention to the other griffin and spotted a similar small door on the beast's backside. He yanked up the handle, pulled the door open, and ducked inside. The interior was identical to the other.

Completely identical.

No safe.

He moved slowly around the room, studying the floor and walls for any evidence that a safe, or any heavy object, had been removed. He saw nothing.

He went outside and into the first griffin and performed the same inspection. No sign of removal there, either.

Back out on the platform, he stood between the two griffins as he thought it over. Inside a griffin had seemed the logical place for a safe—hidden, protected from the elements, easily accessible in all weather.

But then again, there was nothing logical about that roof.

Carefully, he moved along the ledge around the outside of the first griffin, the one facing east toward the Mississippi River. The ledge was narrow, with about a two-foot drop to the top level of the stepped pyramid. He saw no indication of a safe along the body of the griffin.

When he came again to the rear of that griffin, he moved over to the periphery of the ledge and stared up at the back and the wings and the head of the beast, trying to imagine how he could climb up there to inspect the top. He might be able to get a handhold on one of the wings and then hoist himself up, but it would be precarious work. And even if he could, how would a much shorter woman have done it on that cold day in December?

He'd worry about that later, he told himself as he started edging around the other griffin.

He almost missed it as he moved past the front of the beast. He stopped and knelt down between the front paws. He stared in amazement at the small safe nestled down at the base, almost shielded from view and from elements beneath the fleur-de-lis of St. Louis emblazoned on the chest of the beast.

He straightened up and looked around. The only taller building nearby was the United States Courthouse. It was two blocks to the south—a twenty-nine-story mix of pinkish columns and domes and dark expanses of glass. It towered overhead, its steel dome a dull gray beneath the overcast sky. Gazing up at the tall banks of windows, he wondered whether anyone inside that courthouse had noticed a man in a business suit on top of the Civil Courts Building.

He took out Judith's note with the combination and knelt in front of the safe. The sheet of paper fluttered in the wind.

The dial was rusted and needed lubrication, but he was able to make it turn.

Eight to the right.

Twenty-five to the left.

Five to the right.

Thirteen to the left.

He pulled on the little handle. The door squeaked open.

He leaned down and peered inside. Wedged in there was a thick manila envelope. He pulled it out slowly. From the heft, he guessed there were at least a hundred pages of documents inside. Printed on the front of the envelope in familiar handwriting was a message:

FOR PATRICK MARKMAN
STRICTLY CONFIDENTIAL

He stared at the handwriting, his heart racing as he shook his head in wonder.

I found it, Judith. Right where you left it.

He turned the envelope over. It was sealed with several layers of packing tape.

Just as well, he told himself as another gust of wind snapped at his suit jacket. He'd open the envelope later.

He closed the safe door, turned the dial once, and got to his feet. The wind had picked up. He heard thunder in the distance. Time to get off the pyramid.

He moved carefully around the outside of the griffin, watching his steps along the ledge.

As he came around the corner, a male voice said, "Whatcha got there, old man? A present for me?"

44

THE speaker was the burly guy he'd seen in the law library. He'd shed his gray blazer and yellow legal pad and replaced them with a black handgun and a blue windbreaker—the same windbreaker he'd been wearing when he boarded the garage elevator at Plaza Frontenac yesterday afternoon.

The man gestured toward the envelope with the gun. "I asked you a question. What's in there?"

"Papers. Who are you?"

"Your worst nightmare. So was it that old broad? Was she the one who told you what was hidden up here?"

"What are you talking about?"

"That Markman broad. The one you met at the hotel yesterday." He grinned. "Jesus, I sure hope you didn't go there to fuck her. I wouldn't fuck that dried up cunt with a rented dick."

Hirsch said nothing.

"You thought that cat-and-mouse routine of yours at the

mall actually fooled us?" He laughed. "Like I'd tail you alone?"

"What about now?"

"What?"

"Are you alone?"

"Alone?" The man looked down at his gun. "Boys, say hello to Mr. Hirsch. Mr. Hirsch, say hello to Mr. Smith and Mr. Wesson."

The wind was blowing harder now. Hirsch felt a drop of rain hit his cheek, then another on his forehead.

"Hey," the man said, gesturing toward Hirsch's head, "where's your beanie?"

Hirsch studied him. Assume he had a partner. Where was he? Most likely waiting down below. Up here, the man appeared to be operating alone.

So what was their plan?

It was possible, Hirsch told himself, that he only wanted the envelope. Take the envelope and leave Hirsch alive.

Possible.

But not probable.

The more likely scenario included his death. The proverbial two birds with one stone. That scenario made far more sense. Especially now that the man had followed him to the perfect spot to dispose of the body. It could take months, years, before someone discovered a corpse inside Sadie.

That had to be the plan, Hirsch told himself. Grab the envelope, shoot the lawyer, stash the body inside the griffin.

Hirsch glanced at the gun, his thoughts racing.

"Hand over the envelope, old man."

Think, dammit.

"Who hired you?" Hirsch asked.

An idea had begun to form.

"This ain't a courtroom. You don't get to ask questions up here, old man. You just get to follow orders."

A long shot, he conceded.

But it might work.

They were standing on the platform between the two griffins, about an arm's length apart.

And if didn't work? He'd be dead.

Hirsch said, "You think they'll still protect you once you're exposed?"

So what? He'd be dead if he just went along. Better to die trying.

"Exposed?" The man chuckled. "What the fuck you blabbing about?"

Hirsch shrugged and turned slightly away from the guy. "I assume you have a record."

"So?

Hirsch's eyes never left the man's face as he reached his right hand into the pocket of his suit jacket. He wrapped his hand around the pry bar.

Hirsch said, "That means the FBI will be able to identify you once they have a good photo."

"FBI my ass."

Hirsch was holding the envelope in his left hand. He pointed the envelope toward the United States Courthouse.

"You see that building?"

As the man glanced toward the courthouse, Hirsch slid the pry bar out of the jacket pocket and lowered his hand until it was against his right hip. He turned a little more to make sure the pry bar was screened from view.

The man looked back at him. "Yeah?"

"That's the federal building."

"So what?"

"Courts, prosecutors, FBI."

When the man turned toward the building again, Hirsch

tightened his grip on the pry bar and shifted his stance for better balance.

He waved the envelope toward the building. "Let's give them a good shot."

The man frowned at the envelope and then at Hirsch.

"What the fuck you talking about?"

Hirsch pointed with the envelope. "You see that bank of windows facing us on the top floor? Right beneath the dome? There are two FBI special agents up there with a telephoto lens. You don't think I'm crazy enough to do this alone, do you? Smile for the camera."

He bent his knees slightly, muscles tense, pry bar clenched in his hand, pretending to smile toward the court-house windows, all the while watching the man out of the corner of his eye.

The moment the man looked up at the windows, Hirsch whirled and slammed the pry bar into his throat.

The blow knocked the man backward two steps. He gagged, his eyes squeezed shut, reaching for his throat with his free hand, the gun dangling in the other. His hand clutched at his throat. He made choking, gargling sounds as he took another step back.

The man opened his eyes, his shock turning to rage. His breath rasped in his throat. Weaving slightly, his eyes widening, he staggered back another step as he raised the gun, trying to aim. Hirsch ducked to the side behind the griffin. The man fired as he toppled backward.

The bullet clanged off the griffin.

Hirsch waited.

No sound but the wind.

Hirsch poked his head around the griffin. The man was nowhere in sight. Hirsch dashed over to the edge of the pyramid.

The man had tumbled down two tiers. He was on his back staring up at Hirsch. There was a gash open on his forehead and the right side of his throat was caved in. He'd lost the gun in the fall.

Slowly, the man rolled off his back and struggled to his feet, clearly in pain, one hand on his throat, the other touching his forehead. He looked around and spotted his gun one level down. He glanced back at Hirsch and then started to climb down to the next level.

Hirsch scrambled down after him, jumping from tier to tier. As the man bent for the gun, Hirsch jumped on top of him and knocked the gun farther down the pyramid.

The man grabbed for Hirsch as they rolled off the tier. They turned in the air as they fell and landed with a thud. Hirsch was on the bottom, the wind knocked out of him. The man was straddling him, wrestling for the pry bar, garbled noises coming from his mouth.

Hirsch tried to punch him in the neck with his left fist, but the angle was bad. The blow glanced off his shoulder.

The two of them grappled for the pry bar, the man still on top. With each gasp he sprayed a mist of blood. Blood from the gash on his forehead ran down the side of his face. He tried to gouge Hirsch's right eye with his other hand. Hirsch grabbed at his arm, trying to pull it away from his face, trying to turn his head way.

The man wrenched the pry bar free and swung it down hard. Hirsch blocked the blow with his left forearm.

A bolt of pain shot through the length of his arm.

The man raised the pry bar again, gargling sounds coming from his throat. Hirsch pressed his legs against the back of the pyramid step and pushed hard. The force sent them tumbling over the edge. He spun out from under the man as they fell and kicked him in the stomach when they landed. The blow knocked the man onto his side.

Hirsch clambered on top and punched him in the head. He punched him in the neck.

Gasping for breath, his left arm throbbing, he grabbed

the man's hair, raised his head, and slammed it down hard enough to make the aluminum reverberate.

The man was still clutching the pry bar but seemed too groggy to do any with it. Fighting back the pain in his left arm, Hirsch yanked the bar out of the man's hand and raised it over his head like a hammer. The man tried to cover his face and turn away. He moved almost in slow motion.

Hirsch stared down at him, his chest heaving. Blood was streaming down from the gash in the man's forehead, and more blood was leaking out the side of his mouth. A puddle of red was spreading beneath his head. The caved in part of his throat had turned blue. The man's breath rasped.

Hirsch struggled to his feet, swaying slightly, trying to clear his thoughts. He looked down at the man and then at the pry bar. He turned and heaved it over the edge of the pyramid. It disappeared, and a moment later it clanged onto the parapet below.

He tried to focus. They were two levels up from the pyramid's base, which rested inside the parapet. Maybe there was a doorway down there. A doorway somewhere along the inside wall of the parapet.

He leaned over the man, grabbed him by the front of his windbreaker, and pulled him up.

"Let's go."

As the man staggered to his feet, there was a flash of silver in his right hand. Hirsch tried to spin away, but the knife sliced into his left hip.

"Fuck you," the man said in a gargled whisper.

Hirsch stared down at the knife sticking out of his left hip, the blood already running down his leg. The man was grinning at him.

Fury exploded inside Hirsch as he punched him in the

nose. The blow knocked the man backward over the edge. He seemed to crumple as he fell—eyes rolling up, arms flopping outward, legs going limp. He landed at a downward angle, the back of his neck smacking the edge of the tier. The force snapped his head backward.

His body twitched once, and then it was still.

Hirsch stood one level above, leaning over, right hand on his knee, left arm hanging limp.

Dizzy.

Panting.

He stared at the body below. The only movement now was the dribble of blood from the man's open mouth.

Hirsch looked down at the knife sticking out of his left hip. His left arm was useless. He reached around with his right hand, grabbed the handle, held his breath, and yanked hard. The knife slid out. He stared at the blood-smeared blade and then tossed the knife aside.

Woozy, he sat down on the edge of the tier. The pain in his hip had grown worse. His left forearm was throbbing now. So were the knuckles of his right hand. He stared at the back of that hand and tried to make a fist. The knuckles were too swollen to let him completely close his hand.

Raindrops.

Pattering his shoulders and head.

Slowly at first, like the steady beat of a metronome. Then faster. Even faster.

Rain snare-drumming along the aluminum tiers of the pyramid.

He forced himself to stand, his legs unsteady. Turning, he gazed up the side of the pyramid, up toward the platform on top, shading his eyes from the rain. He had tossed Judith's package to the side after hitting the man with the pry bar. He needed to get back up there. Had to retrieve the envelope before it got too wet.

He felt as if he were staring up at the south summit of Mount Everest. Swaying slightly, he tried to gather his energy for the climb.

He turned for a last look at the body below. Splayed legs and outstretched arms palms up. Head hanging over the ledge at that terrible angle. Open eyes and open mouth, as if he were staring up in awe at the flash of lightning above.

Thunder crashed as Hirsch began his ascent.

45

FERNEL was gaunt and stooped and dressed in funeral black. It took him a moment to recognize the customer as the same one from yesterday afternoon. Then again, the version of Hirsch standing before him today was far different from the version yesterday.

Fernel glanced at the cast, smoothed his hand over his angular bald head, and gave Hirsch a rigid smile. The same smile, in fact, that he'd given him yesterday.

"Oh, my. Looks like we have had ourselves a bit of an accident, eh?"

"I need to get into my safe-deposit box again."

"Certainly, Mr. Hirsch. Please follow me."

Hirsch had made this same trip down this same bank corridor yesterday afternoon, although today he was wearing a suit and tie. Yesterday, he'd had on a green maintenance crew jumpsuit and was carrying a toolbox.

The events of yesterday seemed surreal. Less than twenty-four hours ago, he'd been climbing up the side of a pyramid in a fierce thunderstorm, a dead man sprawled below. A man he had killed. When he had reached the top of the pyramid, he'd located Judith's package, lowered himself through the trapdoor in the griffin, and worked his way down the network of ladders and catwalks inside the pyramid to the floor. He'd limped over to the rack of maintenance jumpsuits where he'd stashed the briefcase and cell phone. That's when he caught a glimpse of himself in the mirror above the sink near the rack.

The blood from the knife wound had stained the entire left leg of his pants crimson. His suit jacket was soaked through with rainwater and torn in several places. His shirt was smeared with blood and grime. There were red scratches on his face and blood oozing from a cut over his right eye. To say the least, he'd be conspicuous on the elevator and down in the lobby—and even more so if word of the pyramid battle had spread to the security guards. That's when he recalled that the dead man probably had a cohort waiting somewhere below. That cohort would have no trouble picking him out of the crowd even if he'd emerged unwrinkled and unscathed. But stepping off the elevator in his current condition would have been the equivalent of emerging with bull's eyes pasted on his chest and back.

So he'd gone to the sink where the maintenance crew changed and washed his face and his hands and daubed up the blood with paper towels. He took off his suit jacket. Using just one hand, he'd somehow gotten himself into one of the baggy green maintenance crew jumpsuits. He found a toolbox, emptied its contents, stuffed his suit jacket and Judith's manila envelope inside, made sure his briefcase was empty of any identifying materials, and then called a cab on his cell phone. With the toolbox in one hand and the briefcase in the other, he'd taken the stairway down to the library, stashed the briefcase under a table near the back, and boarded the elevator. He got off on the first floor, walked across the lobby with his head lowered, and hurried down the front steps into the waiting cab.

When the driver reached the bank, Hirsch had asked him to wait. Inside, he'd met Cecil Fernel, who had scrutinized his picture ID and made him wait several minutes while he confirmed from bank records that the limping, disheveled man in the maintenance jumpsuit was in fact attorney David Hirsch.

Yesterday, Hirsch had simply placed the package inside the safe-deposit box, set the toolbox on the floor, and walked out with nothing in his hands. His main goal had been to find a safe place to store the package until he could review its contents. His other goal had been to leave the bank conspicuously empty handed. In the cab on the way to the hospital, he had called Rosenbloom to tell him the bank name and the safe-deposit box number.

"What's this about?" Rosenbloom had asked.

"I found something Judith hid a few days before she died. I put it in that safe-deposit box. If anything happens to me, Sancho, you need to get the FBI to drill the box."

"If anything happens to you? What are you talking about? What the fuck is going on?"

"I don't have time to explain. Just promise me you'll do it. I'll talk to you later."

He'd had the cabdriver drop him off at the hospital emergency room after first stopping to let him toss the green jumpsuit into an alley Dumpster. He had explained to the emergency room personnel that he had slipped on the wet pavement and fallen over a retaining wall. Three hours later, he'd emerged with a cast up to the elbow on his left arm, eleven stitches in his left hip, three butterfly stitches over his right eyebrow, a tetanus shot in his arm, and a bottle of painkillers in his pocket.

Later that night, he had watched the ten o'clock news, waiting for the report on the body found atop the Civil Courts Building. But there was no report. He had listened to the local news on the radio before going to bed. Nothing again. He had gotten up early, picked up the *Post-Dispatch*, and searched through the front page and then the Metro section. Nothing. Same with the local news on TV.

He'd had a Chapter Seven hearing in federal court that morning. After court, he took the elevator up to the twenty-eighth floor of the courthouse and found his way through a back corridor to a north window with a good view of the Civil Courts Building two blocks away. He'd stared down at that weird tableau—at the back-to-back griffins atop the stepped pyramid, at the base of the pyramid nestled inside the parapet on the roof of the Greek temple. He'd stared down in disbelief.

No corpse.

No knife.

No pry bar.

No sign of a fight.

As if the thunderstorm had washed it all away.

For one eerie moment, he'd wondered if he'd dreamed the whole thing. But then he glanced down at the cast on his left arm. He had tapped it against the window to be sure.

"Okay, Mr. Hirsch."

Fernel was bending over the safe-deposit door and inserting the second key. He turned them both and pulled the safe door open. Reaching in, he slid out the covered metal box and turned to Hirsch.

"I can put you in a private room back here, sir."

Hirsch followed him around the corner to a small room. Fernel placed the metal box on top of the table and gestured toward a button on the wall near the door.

"Just press that buzzer when you're ready to go, Mr. Hirsch."

* * *

INITIALLY, it was just a bunch of documents with a jumble of numbers. It took more than an hour to figure out the scam. But when he did, he was astounded.

The materials that Judith had hidden inside the griffin consisted of dozens of photocopies of three types of documents.

> Monthly "status reports" from Guttner's law firm faxed to Donald Foster, CFO of Peterson Tire, at the company's headquarters in Knoxville, Tennessee.
>
> Monthly wire transfer instructions from Peterson Tire to its bank for the transfer of specific sums of money to an account for Felis Tigris LVII at a bank in Bermuda whose Swift code Hirsch recognized as the same one on Judith's Outlooks Note; and
>
> Confirmations of those wire transfers.

The status reports from Guttner's firm were generated the third day of each month. They summarized the results of the *In re Turbo XL Tire Litigation* mini-trials the prior month. Each case was identified by case number. The report separately stated the damage amount sought by the plaintiff in that case and the actual amount awarded by the judge. Thus the status report for the month of March during Judith's final year contained the following information:

Case No. 99-32482 (Embry, Harry)
    Plaintiff's Demand: $1,250,000
    Amount of Award: $1,050,000

Case No. 00-43193 (Zircher, Louis)
    Plaintiff's Demand: $1,955,521
    Amount of Award: $1,300,000

Case No. 99-13115 (Brown, Roberta)
Plaintiff's Demand: $1,115,000
Amount of Award: $1,115,000

Case No. 01-22145 (Ramallo, Maria)
Plaintiff's Demand: $975,000
Amount of Award: $845,000

Case No. 01-12449 (Cannis, Michael)
Plaintiff's Demand: $2,251,750
Amount of Award: $1,885,000

Case No. 02-24512 (Schenker, Merle)
Plaintiff's Demand: $1,450,000
Amount of Award: $1,350,000

The wire transfer instructions for that same month referenced most, but not all, of the same cases:

Case No. 99-32482—	$11,250.00
Case No. 00-43193—	$68,995.34
Case No. 01-22145—	$4,875.00
Case No. 01-12449—	$21,236.25

Two of the six cases were not referenced in the wire transfer instructions: Roberta Brown and Merle Schenker.

He compared status reports and wire transfer records for other months and turned up a similar pattern: not every court award had a matching wire transfer. He sorted through the documents, trying to figure out what was going on.

He recalled Judith's memo on the telephone call between McCormick and Guttner regarding the Sanderson case. McCormick had told Guttner, "They asked for one point four. I gave them a mil. Do the math. Fifteen percent is thirty-nine."

Hirsch borrowed a calculator from a bank employee and

went back through the documents, trying to find a match between a wire transfer amount and fifteen percent of any number in the status reports.

No matches.

He set aside the numbers and pondered the issue. Under the consolidated proceedings, Judge McCormick was deciding damages in mini-trials for each of the more than one thousand cases. If Peterson Tire's goal was to reduce the damages on a case-by-case basis, what was an effective incentive system with the judge? The most straightforward one, of course, was to give him a percentage of the difference between the plaintiff's demand and the actual award. Thus if plaintiff's expert witness testified that the damages were one million dollars and the judge awarded only nine hundred thousand dollars, he'd receive a percentage of the difference. In that example, fifteen percent would equal fifteen thousand. Peterson would pay the judge fifteen grand and still pocket a savings of eighty-five thousand dollars.

But what if Peterson Tire was a tough bargainer? What if they took the position that a plaintiff always asks for more than he's entitled to? What if they said that your fifteen percent kicks in only after a certain threshold?

Hirsch fiddled with the numbers, trying to concoct a more sophisticated formula for a kickback scheme. And suddenly it clicked—not the actual formula, but the basic concept.

He flipped back to the March numbers. There was no wire transfer on two of the cases. In the Roberta Brown case, the plaintiff's demand was $1,115,000 and the award was the same amount. No revelation there. But in the Merle Schenker case, the demand was $1,450,000 and the award was $1,350,000. A difference of one hundred thousand dollars, but no wire transfer.

In the Maria Ramallo case from the same month, the award was $130,000 less than the demand, but that was enough of a difference for a wire transfer of $4,875. If the operative percentage was fifteen, then what was $4,875 fifteen percent of?

He did the calculation.

Thirty-two thousand five hundred dollars.

Fifteen percent of $32,500 equaled $4,875.

But where did the $32,500 come from? Presumably, it was the difference between the award and some greater number, which in the Ramallo case would be $845,000 plus $32,500 equals $877,500. But what was the relationship between $877,500 and the plaintiff's demand of $975,000?

He tried the same approach with the numbers in the Sanderson case, which had been the subject of the overheard conversation in Judith's memo. There the award was four hundred thousand dollars less than the $1.4 million demand. The wire transfer amount was $39,000. Thirty-nine thousand dollars was fifteen percent of $260,000. Thus what was the relationship between $1,260,000 and the plaintiff's demand of $1,400,000?

Presumably, that relationship was the same as in the Ramalla case, and in every case where a damage award resulted in a wire transfer.

He stared at the numbers. He punched a few into the calculator.

And finally, he saw it.

He tried it first with the Sanderson case. Ninety percent of the plaintiff's $1.4 million demand was $1,260,000. The actual award was one million dollars. The difference between one million and $1,260,000 was $260,000, and fifteen percent of that was $39,000.

Ninety percent of the $975,000 demand in the Ramalla case was $877,500, which was $32,500 more than the award. Fifteen percent of $32,500 was $4,875, which was the amount transferred to the Bermuda bank account.

He did the numbers on the Merle Schenker case. The demand was $1,450,00. Ninety percent of that was $1,305,000. But the award was $1,350,000—that is, more than ninety percent of the demand. No money wire transferred.

He flipped through the other status reports and wire transfers, doing random calculations. Every single one of them conformed.

The scam was simple. Simple and brilliant. Peterson Tire paid McCormick a kickback equal to fifteen percent of the difference between the actual award and ninety percent of the plaintiff's demand.

He stared down at the numbers on his yellow legal pad, struggling to grasp the economic impact of the scam.

Approximately seven hundred of the thousand cases had been resolved so far. If McCormick was shaving roughly $125,000 off each damage award—and that was a conservative estimate—the total savings to Peterson Tire already topped eighty-seven million dollars.

Eighty-seven million dollars.

Stated differently, Peterson Tire and the judge had cheated the plaintiffs out of eighty-seven million dollars of compensation for their injuries.

Eighty-seven million dollars.

And still three hundred mini-trials to go. The final number would easily exceed a hundred million dollars.

He did the other calculation—the fifteen-percent-of-ninety-percent formula. He punched in the numbers and pressed the Equal button on the calculator. He stared at the result. The kickback scheme had already funneled into the offshore bank account of Felis Tigris LVII more than nine million dollars.

HE pushed the buzzer. A few moments later, a young woman in a conservative skirt and blouse appeared at the door.

"Can I help you, Mr. Hirsch?"

He held up the full set of papers. "I need to have a copy of these made and hand-delivered to someone downtown. I'll pay all the charges."

She reached for the papers. "I can make the copies now. I'll bring you back a form to fill out for the delivery. If we hurry we might still be able to get them delivered today."

"No. I'd actually prefer to have them delivered tomorrow. If you have a sheet of paper, too, I'd like to write a note to include with the documents."

"No problem, sir. I'll have these copied right away and bring you some paper."

"I'd appreciate that. One more thing. I have the Swift code for a bank in Bermuda but I'm not sure of the bank's name. Would you be able to look that up for me?"

"Certainly, Mr. Hirsch. We have a Swift code directory online. I can get you that bank's name in a jif."

THE digital clock on the nightstand read 2:18 A.M. Just over three hours before he had to wake for morning services.

He stared at the clock as it changed from 2:18 to 2:19 to 2:20.

At 2:21 A.M., he threw back the covers and got out of bed. In his T-shirt and pajama bottoms, he padded into the small living room. The streetlamp outside the window faintly illuminated the room. He knelt in front of the book-case, found the thick dictionary, and carried it back to the bedroom. He clicked on the nightstand lamp, squinting in the sudden brightness. When his eyes adjusted to the light, he flipped through the dictionary to the "F" listings. He found the page and moved his eyes down the column of words:

felicity
felid
feline
feline distemper
fell
fellah

No felis tigris.

He read the definition of "felicity," which at least
sounded like felis. The etymological information in brack-
ets indicated that the word came from the Middle English
word *felicite*, which in turn came from a similar Middle
French word that in turn came from the Latin word *felici-
tas*, which in turn came from the Latin word *felix*, which
meant "fruitful or happy."

No help there.

He looked down the column to "feline":

fe-line *adj.* [L *felinus*, fr. *Felis*, genus of cats, fr. L. cat]
1: of or relating to cats or the cat family **2:** resembling a
cat: as **a:** sleekly graceful **b:** SLY, TREACHEROUS **c:**
STEALTHY—**feline** *n*—**fe-line-ly** *adv*—**fe-lin-i-ty** *n*

Thus "felis" was the genus of cats.

Felis tigris.

He stared at the second word, sounding it out.

He flipped to the *T* pages. He ran his eyes down the column until he found the word:

ti-ger *n, pl* **tigers** [ME *tigre*, fr. OF *tigre* fr. L *tigris*] **l:** a
large and powerful South Asian and East Indian carniv-
orous mammal (*Felis tigris* or *Panthera tigris*) of the cat
family having a tawny coat transversely striped with
black. When full grown, it equals or exceeds the lion in
size and strength **2:** a ferocious, bloodthirsty person.

46

"MR. Guttner on line three."
Hirsch stared at the blinking button on the telephone console, his lips pursed. He lifted the receiver and
pushed the button.

"What do you want?"

"I need to see you, David."

The normally soothing purr had some growl in it.

"Why?"

"Something quite important has come up."

"Oh? What?"

"I do not want to explain over the telephone."

"Why not?"

"Christ Almighty, David."

He waited.

At the other end, the sound of heavy breathing.

"Suit yourself, Marvin. Good-bye."

"Wait. Don't hang up. Please, David. Please. Hear me
out. This is of great consequence. Trust me."

"Trust *you*? Are you out of your mind?"

"Bear with me."

"Why should I?"

"Because this concerns someone special to you."

After a moment, Hirsch said, "Who?"

"Not over the telephone, David. We need to meet in person. As soon as possible. How quickly can you come to my office?"

"Why don't you come here?"

"That will not work. I need to show you certain items. I have them here in my office."

"Bring them along."

"I cannot do that."

"Why not?"

"You will understand when you see them."

Hirsch checked his watch. Almost a quarter after one. His meeting with the U.S. attorney was at four.

"I'll be there by two."

"Thank you, David."

"Not in your office."

"Pardon?"

"I'm not going any farther inside your law firm then the reception area. We can meet in that big conference room on the main floor. The one with all the glass. Just you and me, Marvin. You better be seated in there waiting when I arrive. If not, I'll get right back on the elevator and leave."

HIRSCH gestured toward the glass-walled conference room behind the receptionist.

"He's waiting for me."

"Then you must be Mr. Hirsch."

"I am."

She turned to look back. Marvin Guttner was seated at

the head of the conference table and gazing out the window as he talked on his cell phone. There was a large envelope on the table in front of him. He was drumming his fingers on it. Next to the envelope was what appeared to be a remote control device. Guttner swiveled back around, saw Hirsch, and gestured for him to come in.

"I guess you can go right in, Mr. Hirsch."

Guttner was folding up his phone and getting to his feet as Hirsch entered the room. The conference table seemed as a long as a bowling alley.

"Good heavens, David," he said as Hirsch approached, "what happened to your arm?"

"How 'bout we save some time and cut the crap, Marvin. You already know what happened to my arm."

Guttner frowned but said nothing. His gaze took in the bandage above Hirsch's eyebrow, the slight limp, and the gauze wrap on his right hand. Hirsch took a seat on the far side of the conference table. He was facing the reception area, his back to the outside window.

"I don't have much time," Hirsch said to him. "Tell me why I'm here."

"Fair enough, sir."

Guttner leaned forward and rested his massive arms on the table in front of him. "The people I represent have—"

"Who are they?"

"They wish to remain anonymous, David. At least for now. They have advised me that you are in possession of a packet of materials of great interest to them."

"What kind of materials?"

"Ah, I'm afraid they haven't provided me with those details."

"What makes them think I have this packet?"

"It seems that they have had you under surveillance. From what they have observed, you placed those materials in a safe-deposit box at your bank on Monday afternoon.

You inspected them again yesterday afternoon but left them there."

"How do they know that?"

"They informed me that you went into the bank with a, well, with what appeared to be a toolbox on Monday but left with nothing in your hands. You returned on Tuesday with no briefcase and left again with nothing in your hands. Unless you threw the materials out while you were at the bank, they should still be in there."

Hirsch kept his expression neutral. He'd planned his entrances and exits at the bank both days on the assumption that he was under surveillance. He'd hoped to increase his chances of survival if they thought there was only one copy of the materials, and that that one copy was still in his safe-deposit box.

"You have made no copy, correct?"

"Not as of yet," Hirsch said, spacing the words to make it sound like a warning.

"Excellent, David. That simplifies matters enormously. Do not make a copy. That is critical. The people I represent want those materials, but only if they have the sole copy. Otherwise, no deal. On that basis, they have asked me to negotiate the transaction with you. I can assure you that they are willing to pay you a handsome sum for those materials."

Guttner paused.

Hirsch said nothing.

"A very handsome sum, David. Seven figures is not out of the realm of possibility. Such a sum could be quite advantageous for someone in your position, especially with your not insubstantial financial obligations. I should think that the years since your release from incarceration have not been prosperous ones for you."

"The documents aren't for sale, Marvin."

Guttner smiled. "Ah, well. I suppose I am not surprised

to hear you say that. Puzzled perhaps, but not surprised. Indeed, I warned them that pecuniary incentives might have little appeal to you. I explained to them that you appear to have developed a most unusual obsession with matters surrounding the life and the death of one Judith Shifrin. So they suggested to me, in the words of Don Corleone, that I make you an offer you can't refuse."

Guttner leaned back in his chair and rubbed his chin as he studied Hirsch.

"Well, David, I believe I can make you such an offer. I propose to trade that packet of materials in your safe-deposit box for the reputation and the career and perhaps even the freedom of your dear friend and mentor."

"I'm not following you."

"I am saddened to report my discovery of some distressing evidence of professional malfeasance on the part of Seymour Rosenbloom."

"What are you talking about?"

"Are you familiar with the term *chaser*?"

"Somewhat."

"Then you know that chasers occupy a shady and unseemly niche in the personal injury practice. They literally chase the ambulances. They cruise the highways with police radios on, listening for accident reports, often arriving at the scene before the ambulance does. Other chasers lurk in the shadows of the hospital emergency rooms with handfuls of attorney-client agreements. Plaintiff's lawyers pay them a commission for every victim they get to sign one of those agreements. The practice is, of course, illegal, immoral, and in direct contravention of the rules of professional responsibility. Indeed, mere payment of a fee to a chaser is grounds for disbarment. Moreover, a pattern and practice of using chasers can result in criminal charges."

"What does this have to do with Seymour?"

"Everything, David. It grieves me to inform you that your mentor has at least two chasers on his payroll."

"He doesn't do personal injury work."

"Exactly. And that means that cruising the highways or trawling the emergency rooms is hardly an efficacious strategy for finding prospective bankruptcy clients. He chose another tack."

Hirsch watched as Guttner opened the flap on the manila envelope and slid out a three-page document.

"This is a photocopy of an affidavit by one of the managers of the credit union serving the local members of the auto workers union who toil away at the Ford and Chrysler assembly plants in town."

He slid the document across the table. "Most disconcerting."

Hirsch read through the affidavit of one Eugene Pruett, who identified himself as one of the loan managers of the credit union. Pruett stated that over the past eight years he'd referred close to two hundred auto workers experiencing financial problems to Seymour Rosenbloom. He further stated that he did so under an arrangement whereby Rosenbloom agreed to pay him one hundred dollars for every referral that resulted in the filing of a Chapter Seven or Chapter Thirteen proceeding.

Hirsch read through it again.

He looked up at Guttner. "How'd you get this?"

"How is not relevant here, David. The who and the where and the what are far more significant."

"Cash payments?"

"That is the gentlemen's testimony."

"Thus no record of the transactions." Hirsch gestured toward the affidavit and shook his head. "He could be making this up."

"I suppose one could raise that question if Mr. Pruett

were the only participant asserting such charges. Here, however, I have a second affidavit. This one is from the credit manager at one of the riverboat casinos. He attests to a similar financial arrangement with Mr. Rosenbloom. One hundred dollars per case appears to be his going rate. Would you care to see a copy of his affidavit?"

"No."

"Just in case you are still in doubt, David, we have obtained some additional corroborating evidence from Mr. Pruett. He was unusually accommodating. Apparently, he formed the belief that he was dealing with law enforcement agents. Accordingly, he agreed to wear a wire for his last monthly meeting with Mr. Rosenbloom. We have the entire transaction on videotape."

Guttner reached into the envelope and removed a video-cassette. He lifted the remote control device off the table, swiveled toward the wall behind him, and pressed a button on the remote. A panel in the wall slid up to reveal a television and a videocassette player. Guttner pushed another button and the television came on. All snow and static. He reached over and slid the videocassette into the player. He gazed back at Hirsch as the machine whirred and clicked.

"Let's have a look, shall we?"

The screen flickered several times before settling on an image of the front of the credit union. In the lower-right corner was a digital readout of the time and date. Approximately four weeks ago. A middle-aged man came through the front door of the credit union. He had on a winter coat and was carrying a briefcase. He glanced toward the camera once as he moved across the street to the parking lot. The camera panned with him, revealing in the process that the cameraman was seated in the front passenger seat of a car.

"That is Mr. Eugene Pruett," Guttner said.

Pruett emerged from the parking lot driving a Buick with a dented front fender. Guttner pointed the remote at the screen and pressed a button. The video jumped into fast-forward mode.

"The drive takes ten minutes," Guttner explained.

Hirsch watched the screen as Pruett's car careened from lane to lane on the highway and then jerked and lurched from stoplight to stoplight on the city streets. Guttner slowed the tape to normal speed as Pruett turned into the parking lot at a Home Depot. The Buick drove down to the far lane, moving away from the camera as the trail car held back. Pruett pulled the Buick into one of the empty spots along the aisle. The microphone on his body transmitted the noise of the engine cutting off followed by the sound of the car door opening and closing as Pruett got out. He placed the briefcase on the ground beside him and leaned against the car, waiting, his right hand shading his eyes form the sunlight.

A few minutes passed, and then he reached down for his briefcase and straightened up. A familiar black Cadillac was coming down the lane toward him. The car stopped alongside Pruett, who opened the passenger door.

"Howdy, Gene." Rosenbloom's voice. "How's it hanging?"

Pruett got in and closed the door. The Cadillac started down the aisle, as did the trail car with the cameraman.

"I'm doing just fine, Seymour." Pruett spoke with a nasal drawl. "How about you?"

"Other than having a terminal disease and having to wear adult diapers so I don't piss in my pants, I couldn't be better."

Gene gave a short laugh. "You sure haven't lost your sense of humor."

"Yeah, I'm hoping to land a gig at the hospice someday. Maybe they'll need a sit-down comedian. Don't know about my audience, but I'll sure be rolling in the aisles."

They were silent as Rosenbloom waited at the parking

lot exit for a break in the traffic, his left blinker on. The surveillance car was directly behind the Cadillac now. You could see the backs of Rosenbloom's and Pruett's heads through the rear window.

After Rosenbloom pulled out of the parking lot, he said, "You in the mood for some frozen custard? I'm buying."

"Sounds good to me."

They drove several blocks, turned into the parking lot of a Dairy Queen, and pulled into the line of cars in the drive-thru lane. The tail car pulled into the line directly behind them.

There was silence for a few minutes as the Cadillac inched up one space, then another. The camera zoomed in close. The backs of the men's heads filled the screen.

"You had a good month, Gene."

"Oh, yeah?"

"We were able to help out seven of your folks. Five Chapter Thirteens, two Chapter Sevens. We'll get them all back on their feet before too long. You earned yourself a nice fee."

They'd reached the order board. Rosenbloom rolled down the window, leaned toward the speaker box, and ordered them both a medium cone—a plain one for him, a chocolate dipped for Pruett. The female voice from the speaker box announced the total and told him to drive forward to the second window.

As the Cadillac moved forward, the trail car swerved out of line in a U-turn and pulled all the way around to the front of the Dairy Queen, the camera veering for a blurry shot of the cameraman's feet. From the microphone on Pruett's body came the sounds of the transaction at the drive-thru window.

The trail car followed them back to the Home Depot. The Cadillac stopped alongside Pruett's car. The trail car waited at least a hundred yards back. Even with the zoom lens, it was difficult to see what was happening inside the Cadillac.

"Here you go," Rosenbloom said.

"It's all in the envelope?"

"Count it if you'd like."

"No need to. I trust you."

"Keep sending those folks, Gene. We're here to help."

The sound of the car door opening.

"See you later, Seymour."

Pruett watched the Cadillac drive off. Then he unlocked his car door and got in.

"I am opening the envelope now," he said, his mouth closer to the microphone, his voice suddenly amplified. The sound of paper tearing.

"There is money inside. Looks like all fifty-dollar bills. Yep. Let's see what's here. Fifty, one hundred, one hundred fifty, two hundred, two hundred fifty—"

He counted aloud until he reached seven hundred dollars. A rustling noise, and then he started the car engine. The tape ended as he pulled out of the space.

Guttner used the remote to eject the tape and turn off the television. He removed the videocassette from the machine, turned back to the table, and slid the cassette into the large envelope.

He gazed at Hirsch as he closed the envelope and pressed down the clasps.

"Bad stuff, David."

"You call a hundred-dollar referral fee for a Chapter Thirteen case bad stuff?" Hirsch shook his head. "Come on, Marvin. You spend far more than that every time you take one of your clients to dinner and a ball game. I read about your law firm's golf weekend for clients last fall at that resort near Tucson. What does that cost come out per case? Five grand?"

"The cost for that does not matter one iota. You are

comparing apples to oranges, David, and you know it. That golf outing was a legitimate business expense, and, more-over, a perfectly proper one under the rules of professional responsibility that we all live by. The rules are the rules. I don't make them, and neither do you, but we both know that those rules prohibit your colleague's kickbacks to his chasers. If those transactions become public, he could lose his law license. He could even go to jail. Maybe the chaser fees aren't a big enough deal to interest the U.S. attorney, but think of Mel Browning."

Browning was the county prosecutor.

Guttner said, "That ambitious twit would jump on this case like a rat in heat."

Guttner was right, Hirsch thought. Maybe not about the criminal exposure, but certainly about the jeopardy to Sey-mour's law license. An all-expense-paid $5,000 golf outing with the in-house corporate counsel responsible for refer-ring his company's legal business to your firm was proper. A hundred-dollar referral fee for a bankruptcy case was improper. The lawyer with the golf outing got lots of lucra-tive new legal business for his extravagant investment. The other lawyer got disbarred for his modest one. As Guttner said, the rules were the rules.

"So," Hirsch said, "you called me here to propose a trade?"

Guttner gave him thoughtful nod. "I am prepared to agree to such a proposal."

"The only copy of my material is in the safe-deposit box." Hirsch gestured toward the envelope. "How do I know you won't keep an extra copy of these?"

"I suppose you will have no choice but to trust me."

Hirsch laughed. "Not in this lifetime, Marvin. You'll have to give me an affidavit at the time we make the trade. Your affidavit has to describe exactly what you're giving me, state that you've kept no copies, and further state that you're giving the stuff to me in exchange for the materials I'm giving you."

Guttner pursed his lips and mulled it over. "Only if you do the same concerning your materials."

Hirsch pretended to weigh the request.

"Well, okay," he said, feigning reluctance.

"How soon can we do this?"

"Tomorrow."

"Fine," Guttner said. "You can come over here."

"Oh, no. Never. I'll figure out a public place for us. Someplace where I can feel safe. I'll call you with the meeting place."

"Oh, come now, David. No cloak-and-dagger routines. We hardly need to go to those extremes."

"Yes we do." Hirsch held up his cast. "Someone's already tried to kill me for those documents, Marvin. For my own safety, I have to assume that you hired that thug. So from this point on, I only go to extremes."

47

HE called Russ Jefferson when he got back to his office.
"Is our meeting still on?" Jefferson asked.

"Definitely. We'll have plenty to talk about. But we have to assume that someone is following me. I don't think it's wise to meet in your office, especially after my meeting with Guttner. They still believe the only copy is the one in my safe-deposit box. They're going to question that belief if they see me walking into your office."

Jefferson mulled it over. "Do you have a credible reason to be in this building?"

"I'm in there all the time on bankruptcy matters. I was thinking maybe you could arrange for us to meet in one of the bankruptcy judge's chambers."

"I'll call down there and see whose office we can use. I'll get back to you in a few minutes."

Hirsch hung up.

"So?"

He turned. Rosenbloom was in his doorway.

Hirsch nodded. "Hi."

Rosenbloom had only the vaguest idea of what he had been up to the past week. That was by design. As the hazards of the investigation had increased, so had his determination to keep Rosenbloom out of the loop. And not just Rosenbloom. He'd done the same with Dulcie and his daughter. He hoped that the less they knew the less their risk.

Rosenbloom rolled into his office. "So what did Jabba want?"

Rosenbloom knew that he'd gone to meet with Guttner. Hirsch had told him he was. He'd also told him that Guttner had called the meeting and that he didn't know why Guttner wanted to meet. All true.

But the rest of what Rosenbloom knew, or thought he knew, was vague. He knew that Hirsch had found some important documents having to do with the Peterson Tire litigation. He also knew that the discovery of those documents had placed Hirsch in danger. But those were obvious deductions from Hirsch's terse call from his cell phone on the cab ride to the hospital. He didn't know what the documents were, or where Hirsch had found them, or why Hirsch had been concerned enough to put them in his safe-deposit box. To Rosenbloom's increasing exasperation, Hirsch had refused to answer each of those questions.

He also knew that Hirsch had broken his arm and banged up his head—as did anyone who saw Hirsch's cast and bandages. He wasn't buying Hirsch's story that he'd slipped as he got out of his car in the rainstorm, but he'd been unable to wheedle anything else out of him.

And now, Hirsch thought as he looked at his pal seated in the wheelchair, he certainly didn't need to know about the affidavits and the videotape and the other things he'd learned during his meeting with Guttner.

Hirsch said, "Guttner thinks I'm still working on the case. I told him I wasn't. He doesn't believe me. He said that if he finds out I'm lying, he'll file a claim under that provision in the settlement agreement. The one that requires me to pay back part of the settlement amount."

Rosenbloom frowned. "What makes him think you're still on the case?"

"He wouldn't say."

"Something else is going on. Something he's not telling you."

"Maybe."

"You think that bastard is having you followed?"

Hirsch shrugged. "Anything's possible."

"This is some serious shit, Samson. You got to let me back in this case. You can't keep fighting this battle alone. I can help."

"I know you can. Let's talk later. I have to go over to the courthouse."

"Now? For what?"

"I have a meeting with the U.S. trustee. He wants to talk about the IRS claims in a couple of our Chapter Sevens. I'll probably head home after that. We can talk tomorrow."

"Okay. But we *have* to talk tomorrow. We're a team, Samson. You and me. Don't forget that. You're not in this alone. I can help."

48

HIRSCH and the grizzly bear studied one another. Hirsch was leaning on the wood railing overlooking the bear pit. The grizzly was seated facing Hirsch, its back resting against the rock formation above the pool of water. Its companion paced back and forth along the back wall, head swaying side to side, never looking up.

The bear shifted its gaze as Guttner arrived at Hirsch's side.

"Interesting choice of venue, David."

Hirsch glanced over at Guttner, his eyes moving down to the briefcase in the fat man's left hand. Guttner had on a dark brown suit, white shirt, tie, and polished wingtips. He could have been standing before a judge in a court instead of a grizzly in a pit. Hirsch had a briefcase as well, but he was dressed more for the location in khaki slacks and a navy turtleneck.

A teacher ushered a class of elementary school children past them toward the polar bear pit. "This way, children. Over here. No pushing, Kevin. Hurry up, Lisa."

The kids chattered and laughed as she directed them toward the viewing area.

The zoo was a good choice for a Friday morning in late April. As he'd hoped, it was mostly empty. Other than a few groups of schoolchildren on field trips and a smattering of mothers and nannies pushing strollers, the usual zoo crowds, the ones that packed the place on spring weekends, were in school or at work or out running errands.

He turned to Guttner. "I'll need to see your affidavit before I give you the documents."

"Right here? In the open?"

Hirsch reached into his front pocket and pulled out two tickets. "On the train."

He gestured toward the main train station, which was beyond the bear pits near the entrance.

Guttner looked incredulous. "You actually want to accomplish this exchange on the zoo train?"

"We'll have plenty of privacy. No one rides it weekday mornings. We can exchange affidavits as the train passes through the woods beyond the children's zoo. If the affidavits are acceptable, we can trade the materials when we pass through the long tunnel after Big Cat Country. Let's go. I want to get this over with."

Waiting in the station was a zoo train, a miniature steam locomotive and three passenger cars. Each car consisted of several rows of bench seats beneath a canopy roof. Hirsch and Guttner climbed aboard and sat along one of the middle benches in the second car. Despite Guttner's bulk, the bench was wide enough for them both plus room in the middle for their briefcases.

Although Guttner seemed displeased by the prospect of a train exchange, he didn't seem suspicious. That's what Hirsch had hoped for. Among several possible exchange sites, he'd selected the zoo train on the assumption that Guttner was not a regular. He'd confirmed that the man's two children were teenagers and that he was not a member of any zoo board or committee. That meant it was unlikely that Guttner would know that the principal reason the zoo train was empty that morning was because it didn't run at that time of day during that time of the year. Nor was he likely to know that the man seated at the controls of the miniature locomotive was at least three decades younger than the usual zoo train engineers. Nor was he likely to know that the engineer himself normally took the passenger's tickets, and not the athletic young man in the conductor outfit.

The engineer blew the whistle twice, and the train pulled out of the station.

They sat in silence as the train clattered past the bear pits at maybe fifteen miles an hour. Several of the schoolchildren turned to watch. A few waved. Behind the children, one of the polar bears jumped into the water with a loud splash.

The train pulled into the little station near the children's zoo area. No one got off. No one got on. Two whistle blasts, and the train pulled out of the station.

The tracks curved around the children's zoo on trestles over the water and then entered the woods.

Hirsch said, "Let me have your affidavit."

Guttner gave him two stapled sheets of bond paper. "Let me see yours."

Hirsch unsnapped his briefcase and handed Guttner his six-page affidavit. He'd been careful to make sure that the description of the documents in his affidavit was detailed enough to eliminate any doubt as to Guttner's state of mind at the time he would receive the documents themselves. Moreover, he'd made sure that the description would leave Guttner with no doubt that Hirsch had figured out the entire scheme. Among other things, his affidavit states that the materials he'd found in the safe atop the Civil Courts

Building consisted of (a) monthly status reports from Guttner's law firm to the chief financial officer of Peterson
Tire Corporation summarizing for each resolved case the
plaintiff's demand and the actual amount awarded, and (b)
corresponding wire transfer records in which Peterson Tire
instructed its bank to transfer specified sums of money to
an account for Felis Tigris LVII at the Hamilton Bank &
Trust Limited in Bermuda. (His bank had matched the
Swift number with the Hamilton Bank & Trust, which was
the one on Victoria Street.) His affidavit further stated that
each wire transfer equaled fifteen percent of the difference
between the amount actually awarded and ninety percent
of the plaintiff's demand.

He watched Guttner as he read that page of the affidavit.
No change of expression.

Guttner's affidavit was much shorter. Just three one-
sentence paragraphs that identified the videotape and the
two affidavits plus a final paragraph stating that Guttner
was turning over the originals of each and had "personally
destroyed all extant copies of same to the best of his information and belief."

Hirsch's affidavit was somewhat vague on the subject of
copies. The final paragraph stated only that "I will turn
over the originals of the documents to Mr. Guttner and will
not retain a copy of them." Nevertheless, that appeared to
be sufficient to Guttner, who nodded and dropped Hirsch's
affidavit into his briefcase.

The train had now entered the River's Edge section of
the zoo. The still air was punctuated by an exotic bird call,
followed by a monkey's shriek. Hirsch looked up from his
briefcase. A pair of black rhinos stood motionless in front
of a waterfall. Two hippos paddled across a small river.

The train slowed as it arrived at the station near the
south entrance to the zoo. Up ahead was a waterfall and
pool of water. Hirsch had memorized the railroad map. He

knew the tracks looped behind the waterfall and into the first tunnel.

"Not this one," he told Guttner as the locomotive entered the tunnel. "Too short. The third tunnel is the longest one. That's the one we'll use."

They emerged from the tunnel. The tracks curved to the right along the pool of water and then looped into the woods behind the reptile and monkey houses. New leaves were on all the trees. A cardinal zipped by overhead and landed on a branch to the right. Hirsch looked back at the bird surrounded by green leaves. He stared at that red focal point, which grew smaller by the second, as he tried to maintain control of his emotions, of his anxiety.

He glanced over at Guttner, whose expression mainly evinced irritation and impatience. The man was oblivious to what lay just ahead.

"Not this one," Hirsch said as the train entered the tunnel behind the monkey house.

The train began to slow as it came to the end of the short tunnel and emerged into the light at the next train station. They were in the Big Cat Country now. In the grassy enclosure to their right, a large Bengal tiger was walking directly toward them. Somewhere beyond the tiger, a lion roared. The tiger turned as it reached the fence and strolled on past, ignoring them.

Felis tigris, Hirsch thought.

Four passengers boarded the train—three men and a woman. Two of the men took seats in the forward car. The other man and the woman took seats in the rear car. Guttner had his briefcase on his lap now. He was drumming the fingers of his right hand on the leather of his briefcase.

Two whistle blasts from the locomotive.

Guttner looked at Hirsch.

Hirsch nodded and unsnapped his briefcase.

"Get ready," he said. "We'll do the exchange as soon we enter the tunnel."

Guttner unclasped his briefcase.

The train started forward. As they entered the darkness of the third tunnel, Hirsch handed his package to Guttner, and Guttner handed his package to Hirsch. Each man closed his briefcase and straightened in his seat.

The tunnel was several hundred feet long. Hirsch peered into the darkness, watching, waiting. They passed a closed door on the right, then one on the left. The two men in the front car were looking back now. Hirsch glanced back, too. The tunnel entrance was no longer visible behind them.

The train began to slow down.

"What the hell?" Guttner muttered.

Hirsch turned forward. A man was standing in the middle of the tracks up ahead. He waved a powerful flashlight back and forth.

The train came to a stop, the engine rumbling.

"This is ridiculous," Guttner said.

The man with the flashlight started toward them. The beam illuminated a narrow pathway along the side of the track. As he drew near, three other men stepped out from the wall of the tunnel behind him and fell into line. Hirsch could hear the two passengers in the rear car getting off the train.

As the four got closer, details began emerging from the dark.

The man in front was wearing a suit. The three men behind him were in dark windbreakers.

The man in front was black. The three behind him were white.

The man in front was the United States Attorney for the Eastern District of Missouri. The three men behind him had yellow FBI logos on the fronts of their windbreakers.

Russell Jefferson stopped on Guttner's side of the car. The three FBI agents arrayed themselves behind him, joined now by the two men from the first car. The man and woman from the rear car took up positions on the other side of the car.

"What is the meaning of this?" Guttner said.

"Mr. Guttner, my name is Russell Jefferson and I work for the United States government. I have a warrant here for your arrest. These gentlemen and this lady are special agents of the Federal Bureau of Investigation. They are here with me this morning to take you into custody, sir."

"On what grounds?" Guttner demanded.

"On myriad grounds, sir." Jefferson enunciated each word clearly.

Hirsch climbed down from the train as Jefferson continued.

"My office has filed a criminal complaint against you, sir, and it sets forth more than one hundred counts. Those counts include bribery of a public official, obstruction of justice, conspiracy, mail fraud, wire fraud, bank fraud, and violation of the Racketeer-Influenced and Corrupt Organizations Act. The list goes on and on, sir. Now would you please step down from the train?"

One of the FBI agents stepped forward and grasped Guttner by the arm. "Let's go."

Guttner pulled back. "Wait a minute. You have made a terri—"

"Move it," the agent commanded and pulled him forward.

As Guttner lumbered down off the train, two agents stepped forward, pulled his arms together in back, and snapped a pair of handcuffs around his wrists.

Guttner was furious. "This is an outrage. Do you have any idea who you—"

Jefferson held up his hand. "I realize you are an attorney, Mr. Guttner, but I must remind you that you have the right to remain silent. Anything you say can and will be used against you in a court of law. You have the right to speak to an attorney, and to have—"

Guttner spun toward Hirsch, his face contorted by hatred and panic. "You miserable prick."

Hirsch gazed at him calmly. "Some free advice, Marvin. If you end up there, watch out for the second showerhead on the left. The hot water cuts out."

Guttner stared at him. "What? End up where?"

"Allenwood."

GUTTNER tried to reclaim his arrogance, and he almost succeeded. But not quite. And the collapse was fast and it was ugly.

Russ Jefferson had paused to allow Guttner to go ahead of him into the long passageway through the wall of the zoo railroad tunnel. Without even acknowledging Jefferson's presence, Guttner stepped through the entrance as haughty as a Roman emperor. With his entourage of federal law enforcement agents—half ahead of him, the other half behind—the only missing props were the toga, sandals, and garland of myrtle.

But the facade began splintering as they moved farther down the passageway. The first sign was the cursing. Under his breath, barely audible.

"Son of a bitch . . . double-crossing prick . . . bankruptcy scumbag."

The rage and the volume kept building.

"Fucking bastard . . . Going to set me up, huh? . . . Protect that cripple and try to screw me? In your dreams, asshole . . . I'll nail your fucking kike ass to the fucking wall you fucking motherfucker."

He spun around, craning his head, trying the find Hirsch

in the crowded passage, his face flushed and beaded with sweat.

"You hear me, you slimy Jew bastard?! You want me—"

One of the federal agents yanked him around and shoved him forward. "Shut up and keep moving."

By the time they reached the end off the passageway, Guttner was moaning.

"Oh, my God . . . oh, my God . . . oh, my God."

Hirsch's last view of Marvin Guttner was just after two agents pushed him up into the back of the government van. He'd collapsed into the seat and slumped forward, head down. Someone slammed the door shut. As the metallic reverberation faded, and just before the driver started the engine, he could hear the sounds of weeping.

49

IT was Tuesday. Four days later.

Hirsch was seated in the office of the United States Attorney for the Eastern District of Missouri. He leaned back in his chair and watched as the FBI agent ushered Jack Bellows out of the office and closed the door behind them. He turned back to Russ Jefferson.

Jefferson shook his head. "Not much help there."

Hirsch sighed. "Nope."

Even so, it had been a remarkable four days.

Guttner had vanished from public view late Friday morning when the unmarked van pulled out of the zoo's service entrance. The feds moved him to an undisclosed location, where he'd been ever since. The only people who'd seen him were his criminal defense attorney, three FBI special agents, Russ Jefferson, two of Jefferson's assistants, and a court of stenographer.

They allowed Guttner a telephone call to his wife Friday night to tell her that he'd been called out of town on an emergency and would be gone several days. The agent listening in said she hadn't seemed concerned. Hadn't even asked where he was calling from, or where he was going to, or when he'd return. He called her again on Saturday around dinnertime to say that he was still out of town and might not be home for a few more days. All business. No hint of intimacy between husband and wife.

Later that Saturday night, sometime between seven-thirty, when Jefferson left Guttner and his lawyer alone in the room, and eleven twenty, when Guttner's attorney stepped out in the hall to ask the FBI agent to summon Jefferson, Guttner finally acknowledged the gravity of his predicament. Each of the seven hundred secret payments to McCormick was clearly and incriminatingly documented on the papers that Judith had hidden in the safe. Each of those payments constituted no less than three and possibly as many as five separate federal crimes. A sentence of just one year per felony would yield a prison term spanning two millennia—and that didn't include the sentence-enhancing consequences of a finding that the bribery scheme constituted an "enterprise" under the Racketeer-Influenced and Corrupt Organizations Act.

All of which must have suggested to Guttner the prudence of exploring a plea bargain. The main obstacle was the person who'd be seated across the bargaining table. Even in a typical case, Russ Jefferson was no Monty Hall, and here he saw even less reason to deal. He already had enough evidence to render Guttner's pension plan irrelevant. Nevertheless, as Guttner's attorney finally got him to concede, in criminal conspiracy prosecutions the inventory-accounting rule known as FIFO—first in, first out—seemed to resonate with the judge at sentencing time. True, Jefferson responded, but the degree of resonance depended upon the quality and quantity of the goodies that the first one brought to the bargaining table. Guttner's attorney assured him that his client could deliver quality and quantity.

The court stenographer joined them at noon on Sunday. She stayed until six that night and returned the following morning. By the time she'd packed her equipment Monday afternoon, Guttner had given Russ Jefferson enough evidence to convict McCormick and the inner circle of executives at Peterson Tire and two other members of Guttner's law firm of enough crimes to ensure that the only way most of them would leave prison was at room temperature in the back of a hearse.

But Guttner's knowledge of criminal activities did not include the circumstances surrounding the death of Judith Shifrin. He readily conceded that he'd suspected from the outset that Judith's death was not an accident. Those suspicions had been heightened by McCormick's reaction to Hirsch's lawsuit. From the moment McCormick had learned of the case, he started pressuring Guttner to get it settled. He'd call Guttner several times a week for status reports, warning that an investigation of Judith's death could endanger them all. In short, Guttner believed that chance had nothing to do with Judith Shifrin's death. Unfortunately, he had no admissible evidence to back that up.

Nor had Guttner been involved in the hiring of whoever it was who tried to kill Hirsch atop the Civil Courts Building. His best guess was that McCormick handled that part on his own. Which was not to suggest that Guttner and his client were innocent bystanders, as Guttner conceded. Peterson Tire had arranged for the surveillance of Hirsch, which resulted in the report to Guttner on Hirsch's back-to-back visits to the bank. And Guttner himself had hired the investigator who'd turned up the chaser materials on Rosenbloom. But he swore, literally, that he had nothing on Judith Shifrin's death—or Markman's death.

That was Sunday and Monday. At Hirsch's urging, Jefferson turned up the heat on Jack Bellows on Tuesday morning. Two U.S. marshals accosted him in the parking garage of his office building as he arrived for work. Flashing their badges and escorting him to the back of a dark blue Ford with tinted windows, they whisked him out of the garage. By the time they opened the rear door of the Ford in the basement of the United States Courthouse, Jack the Ripper had become Jack the Pisser. The marshals tried to keep a straight face as they rode up the elevator with him, pretending not to notice the sharp odor or the dark stain in the crotch of his two-thousand-dollar suit.

Bellows had no knowledge, or even any suspicions, concerning any aspect of any of the crimes at issue. Hirsch wasn't surprised. He'd assumed that Bellows and his client had been completely out of the loop from the start. His hope was that Bellows had followed up on his boasts about retaining a top pathologist.

And he had. Two of them, in fact. And Bellows, frantic to cooperate, instructed his office to hand-deliver copies of both pathologists' reports to the U.S. Attorney's Office. While the feds waited, Jefferson's secretary located an old pair of sweatpants for Bellows to change into.

Hirsch had joined Jefferson while Bellows was in the men's room changing pants, and thus he was there when the reports arrived. Unfortunately, they were less conclusive and less incriminating than the oral report Hirsch had received from Henry Granger. Like Granger, both of Bellows's pathologists dismissed any contention that the decedent had suffocated against an inflated air bag. They also agreed from the X-ray evidence that Judith's spinal cord was intact, and thus not related to the cause of her death. Those two conclusions, however, led the experts down pathways of conjecture far different than Granger's.

One of them, an Ohio professor of pathology named Rupert Tomaso, speculated that Judith might have had a latent medical problem that could have been exacerbated by the sheer force of the impact. Perhaps a heart valve defect, he suggested, or maybe a severely weakened artery in her brain. But the existence of that causal link, his report explained, could only be confirmed through an autopsy.

The other pathologist, a former Detroit medical examiner named Dr. Johnny Hsieh, noted the same reference to petechial hemorrhages that had caught Henry Granger's attention and also noted the phrase *slight compression of soft tissue of neck*. But those observations generated an entirely guiltless hypothesis. Dr. Hsieh speculated that at the moment of impact the decedent could have had a large object in her mouth, perhaps an ice cube or a chunk of food. The force of the impact could have driven that object into her trachea, cut off the flow of air to her lungs, and caused her to suffocate. Dr. Hsieh surmised that the soft tissue compressions on her neck were caused by her own hands as she tried to dislodge the object that was choking her. But to confirm this as the cause of death, Dr. Hsieh stated in his concluding paragraph, one would need to perform an autopsy on the decedent.

After Hirsch and Jefferson finished reviewing the reports, Jefferson sent Bellows on his way with a stern warning about maintaining strict confidentiality concerning what had transpired. Bellows nodded submissively, avoiding Hirsch's eyes. Hirsch couldn't help but smile as he watched Bellows depart, the top half of him dressed for the boardroom in his expensive suit jacket, dress shirt, tie, and platinum cuff links, the bottom half in baggy, paint-stained sweatpants, one hand holding a calfskin briefcase, the other a plastic supermarket bag containing his damp pants and underwear. Arrogance was a tough attitude to maintain after pissing in your pants.

"Let's not lose perspective here," Jefferson said. "Thanks to your work, we will have plenty on Judge McCormick."

"But not for murder," Hirsch said.

"True. Unfortunate, but true. Still, Brendan McCormick is going to be behind bars for a long time. Probably the rest of his life."

"He killed her, Russ. He killed her with his bare hands. And he probably arranged for the death of that reporter, too."

"You could be right, David, but we can't prove it. Even so, he is still going to end up in jail for a long time."

"But not for murder."

"That is the way the system works. That is the way it has always worked. You know that. You worked in this office. Far worse men have gone to jail for far less. Let us not forget that when the federal government finally convicted Al Capone, the charge was income tax evasion. Think of it, David. One of the most notorious criminals of the twentieth century. How many men did Al Capone murder? How many lives did he destroy? How many serious crimes did he commit? But when he finally entered prison, it was for failure to pay the taxes on those ill-gotten gains. When Brendan McCormick enters prison, David, it will be for far worse crimes than income tax invasion. Although—" Jefferson smiled, "I suppose he'll go to jail for that as well. . . ."

"But he won't go to jail for her death."

Jefferson nodded. "But not for her death."

Hirsch stared at his former colleague. "Let me try, Russ."

Jefferson frowned. "Pardon?"

"Give me a chance to get him to incriminate himself."

"What are you talking about?"

"Put a wire on me. Let me meet with him. Let me talk to him. Let me see if I can get him to admit it."

"Don't be ridiculous, David."

"I'm serious, Russ. I know him. I know what buttons to push. Put me in there with him. Forget the wire. You've got more than enough probable cause to put a bug in his office. Any judge will sign that order. Let me give it a try. One meeting. What's the risk? You already have enough to convict him on scores of other crimes. If I strike out, it doesn't matter. But if I get him to admit that he killed her, well . . ."

Hirsch leaned back in his chair, overcome by emotion. He shook his head.

"Well what, David?"

Hirsch tried to organize his thoughts. "I don't represent the government here, Russ. I represent Judith Shifrin. When her father hired me, he told me he wanted one thing: justice."

Hirsch paused. "I don't think I'm sure what justice means anymore, Russ. Maybe it's a farce to have someone like me out there searching for it. All I know is that if Brendan McCormick killed her, if he grabbed her by the throat and choked her until she died, Russ, if he . . ."

He paused again, his voice trailing off. He stared down at his hands.

Jefferson was studying him, waiting.

After a moment, Hirsch looked up, his eyes intense. "If Brendan did that to her, Russ, then that's a crime he ought to be forced to answer for. Let me try to make him do that. Just give me one chance. That's all I ask."

Jefferson stared back, his arms crossed over his chest.

50

"*NU?*" Rosenbloom asked, his chopsticks poised over the half-empty carton of Szechuan beef. "How was it?"

"Low-key." Hirsch popped a piece of spicy broccoli into his mouth and crunched. "Jefferson had me walk the grand jurors through each piece of evidence—the key entries on her credit card and phone bills, the important notes and memos Jumbo retrieved from her computer, the documents she hid in the safe."

Rosenbloom nodded, chewing as he listened. "Think they understood?"

"They seemed to. Jefferson's people put together summary charts from the financial documents. That made it a lot easier for them to follow along."

"Are they finished with you?"

"I think so. At least for now."

They were in Rosenbloom's condo. Just the two of them. Rosenbloom had been out of the office at meetings all afternoon and was flying up to Chicago early in the morning for a bankruptcy seminar. The only time they could get together was tonight, so they agreed to meet for dinner. Hirsch brought dinner from his favorite Chinese take-out, and Rosenbloom supplied the beer.

Rosenbloom twisted off the cap from another Bud long neck and took a long sip. "So when does Jabba get to sing soprano before the grand jury?"

"They have him scheduled for tomorrow afternoon and all day Friday."

Rosenbloom chuckled. "Oh, to be in the room for that one. I'd love to watch that nasty prick squeal."

"He's looking pretty down these days."

"Reminds me of my favorite self-help book."

"What's that?"

"When Bad Things Happen to Nasty Pricks."

Hirsch smiled. "Haven't read that one."

"I'll lend you my copy. So tell me, Samson, where's the big soiree gonna be Saturday night?"

"I haven't decided yet. We'll meet at my apartment at six for drinks and appetizers. I'll find us a nice restaurant and make a reservation. Just the four of us—you, me, Dulcie, and Lauren." He took a sip of beer and smiled. "I'm looking forward to it. We can all finally relax, have a nice time, with this case finally behind us."

"Yeah. That will be nice."

ROSENBLOOM tired early these days. He didn't put up much of a fight when Hirsch insisted on cleaning up. He stayed at the kitchen table, slightly slumped in his wheelchair.

As Hirsch washed the dishes, he struggled with whether to tell Rosenbloom about tomorrow—and if so, how to even raise the subject.

Rosenbloom took care of that part. "Is there a Chapter Thirteen docket tomorrow?" he asked.

Hirsch nodded. "Judge Shea."

"You going to cover it?"

He glanced back at Rosenbloom. "I asked Barbara to cover it for me."

"How come?"

Hirsch thoroughly soaped and rinsed a glass and held it up to the light. He said, "I'm meeting with Brendan McCormick."

"You're what?"

"Russ and I talked it over. He agreed."

"Whoa. Back up a second. Why the hell would you want to meet with McCormick?"

"They're going to bug his office."

He shut off the faucet and turned toward Rosenbloom. He dried his hands with the dish towel. "I'm going to see if I can get him to admit that he killed her."

"What?" Rosenbloom almost came out of his wheelchair. "Are you out of your fucking mind? You can't let those government bastards use you like that."

"It was my idea. I had to fight Russ to get him to agree."

Rosenbloom was frowning. "I don't get it. Why?"

Hirsch came back to the table and sat facing him. "This is my last chance, Sancho. They arrest him tomorrow afternoon no matter what. They don't have enough to make a murder case. Not even close. And they never will once they arrest him."

"This is crazy."

"No, it isn't. Just think if I can get him to say something incriminating."

"What if you can't?"

Hirsch shrugged. "So be it."

Rosenbloom moved his head back and forth, mulling it

over. He suddenly looked up at Hirsch. "Hold on. Didn't you tell me he has a gun cabinet in his office?"

"Don't worry. The FBI is going into his office tonight to plant the bug. While they're in there, they'll make sure no gun is loaded."

"What if he goes berserk tomorrow? What if he attacks you?"

Hirsch smiled. "I'll whack him with my cast."

"I'm serious."

Hirsch sat down across the kitchen table from Rosenbloom. "The feds know what they're doing. We've gone over everything. Once I enter his office, two FBI agents will take up position right outside his door. If anything suspicious happens, they'll bust in."

Rosenbloom studied him. After a moment, he took a deep breath and exhaled slowly. "You don't need to do this."

Hirsch reached across the table and squeezed him on the shoulder. "I'll be fine."

Rosenbloom sighed. "When are you going to learn, Samson?"

"Learn what?"

"That it doesn't work this way."

"What doesn't?"

"Life. You don't get closure in the real world. No one gets to live happily ever after. That's how things work down here, *boychik*. Even if you nail McCormick tomorrow, it's not going to bring her back. It's not going to make her father a better person. Hell, it's not even going to remind him that he had a daughter."

Rosenbloom shook his head. "*Oy*, Samson. How can someone so smart be so dumb. So when exactly is this taking place?"

"Tomorrow at ten."

"Does he know you're coming?"

"I called his secretary this morning. I told her I needed to see him tomorrow. She called back to say he could meet with me at ten."

Rosenbloom shook his head. "What am I going to do with you?"

HIRSCH paused at the front door and called back, "So give me a buzz tomorrow night when you get back from Chicago. I'll come over and give you the blow by blow."

"Wait, David."

Hirsch turned.

Rosenbloom was wheeling himself down the front hall toward him.

"Thanks," Rosenbloom said.

"Hey, you supplied the beer."

"Not for that."

"What?"

"For letting me know."

"Letting you know what?"

"About your meeting tomorrow with McCormick." His eyes were moist. "You be careful, okay?"

Hirsch leaned over and kissed him on top of his bald head. "Get some sleep, Sancho. You're up early."

BUT he hadn't told Rosenbloom everything. As he rode the elevator down to the garage, he thought of what he'd left out. Of what he couldn't, and wouldn't ever, tell him.

One key term of his deal with Russ Jefferson was his promise to make sure that nothing came of the surveillance videotape and affidavits that Guttner had compiled on Rosenbloom. If any copies of the videotape or affidavits should surface in the future, Jefferson would say that Rosenbloom had been cooperating with the feds on a criminal investigation.

That had been the easy part of the deal, and, as Hirsch expected, Jefferson accepted immediately. Like any federal prosecutor, he was far more interested in getting access to key documents at the heart of a massive corruption of justice conspiracy than he was in pursuing a bankruptcy lawyer over some hundred-dollar referral fees.

The hard part of the deal, and the part that Hirsch agonized over before broaching with Jefferson, was how to let Rosenbloom know that someone out there had discovered what he was doing. Even though his conduct might seem penny-ante stuff in the world of crime, it was tainted conduct nevertheless. While a federal prosecutor might not bite, Rosenbloom's referral arrangement could still land him in a disciplinary proceeding before the Missouri Supreme Court. For Rosenbloom, that would be almost as painful as a criminal conviction.

Thus someone had to tip him off.

Hirsch couldn't bear the thought of being the one to tell Rosenbloom about Guttner's evidence. He knew Rosenbloom would be humiliated—and not just by Hirsch's discovery of his little secret. He'd be humiliated by the circumstances surrounding Hirsch's discovery, including the meeting with Guttner and the subsequent deal worked out with Jefferson. Hirsch loved Rosenbloom's wit and his bawdiness, but above all else he treasured the dignity beneath that bluster. It was, he understood, the core of their relationship. He would never do anything to damage that bond.

So he'd worked out another term of the deal with Jefferson, a provision to ensure that Rosenbloom would never know how or where Jefferson got the materials. The ploy was simple enough: a week or so after Guttner's arrest became public, Jefferson would summon Rosenbloom to his office. He'd show him the videotape and the affidavits and he'd explain that the FBI had discovered it while searching though Guttner's files. He'd give them to Rosenbloom, assure him that there'd be no reference to them in the investigative file, and let Rosenbloom deduce on his own his need to change his techniques for getting business.

That was the deal he'd worked out with Jefferson, and that was the deal he could never reveal to Rosenbloom.

HIRSCH stood alone in the center of his apartment. The place seemed even quieter than usual.

But quiet was okay for now. He had a long night ahead of him.

Over the span of his career, he'd made hundreds of presentations to judges. To trial judges, appellate judges, and even Supreme Court justices. Other attorneys liked to gather their minions a day or two in advance and run through a mock presentation with everyone firing questions and offering critiques. Not Hirsch. He'd found that the best time to prepare—to organize his points, to polish his words, to prepare for the tough questions—was alone on the night before. Even for his Supreme Court appearances. All three times, he'd done the final preparations into the wee hours in his hotel room. Alone.

And so it would be tonight. He checked his watch. Twenty minutes after nine.

But first things first. He needed to confirm the *minyan* for the morning service. He kept the list of phone numbers paper-clipped to the Jewish calendar hanging on the wall by the telephone. As he approached, he could see that tomorrow's date was printed in red. Red meant holiday. He looked closer. The fourth of May was also the fourteenth of Iyar. *Pesach Sheni*, or the Second Passover. The only "second chance" holiday in Judaism, as he recalled from Rabbi Saltzman's commentary last year. A special day for Jews who were unable to obey the commandment the first time around.

As he reached for the phone, he thought again of his telephone conversation with Dulcie that afternoon. He'd called to invite her to the dinner on Saturday night.

"Sounds great. How 'bout if I come by early? I'll help you set up the appetizers and drinks."

"You don't need to do that."

"My pleasure. By the way, Mr. Talmud, is it true that it's a *mitzvah* to make love on *Shabbat*?"

He'd laughed. "So the rabbis tell us."

"I don't know if I'm ready for such a big *mitzvah* yet, but my ex does have Ben for the entire weekend, and suddenly the thought of Saturday is making me feel a little more religious."

He was grinning as he punched in the first telephone number on the list. As the phone rang, he checked his watch again. In a little over twelve hours, he was scheduled to appear before the Honorable Brendan McCormick. Regardless of the outcome, he knew one thing for sure: This would be his final appearance before Judge McCormick.

51

As Brendan McCormick stood to greet him, his smile turned to a look of concern.

"What happened to your arm, David?"

"Why bother asking?"

"Why? Look at it. It's in a cast. What the hell happened?"

Hirsch took a seat facing the desk. "You already know what happened."

"I know?" McCormick gave him a puzzled smile as he sat down behind his desk. "I'm afraid I'm not following you."

Hirsch gazed at him. "Cut the bullshit, Brendan. Your guy did this to me."

McCormick leaned back in his chair and crossed his arms over his chest. His leather briefcase rested on top of the desk to his right. He was frowning at the brass clasps on the briefcase, as if confused by their mechanics.

"So," McCormick finally said, still staring at the clasps, "here we are. Together again, eh?"

Hirsch's gaze shifted to the framed photo of Mc-Cormick in his college football uniform. He gave a mordant smile as he stared at the number emblazoned on McCormick's jersey.

McCormick turned to see what Hirsch was looking at.

"What's so funny?"

"I forgot how much we have in common," Hirsch said.

"Football?"

"For starters. Both played linebacker. Both played on teams called the Tigers. Both wore the same number."

"Oh, yeah. That's right. You were fifty-seven, too."

"I didn't make the connection at first."

"What connection?"

"To you. The name and the number."

McCormick frowned. "What are you talking about?"

"Come on, Brendan. This isn't Romper Room. You were a Missouri Tiger, and that was your number. Tiger fifty-seven equals Felis Tigris L-V-I-I. I suppose it could have been me, too. We're just a pair of corrupt old tigers, eh? Except I'm not the tiger with the bank account in Bermuda."

"So?" McCormick forced a laugh. "I have a house in Bermuda. That's why. I used to have a bank account in Steamboat Springs when I had a condo there. It's convenient."

"Please, Brendan. I saw the documents."

"What documents?"

"The papers Judith hid in the safe. Bad stuff. All those wire transfers to your account at the Hamilton Bank and Trust. Each one tied to a damage award in the Peterson Tire case. Fifteen percent of the difference between ninety percent of the plaintiff's demand and the actual amount awarded. I did the math. Each transfer comes out to the penny."

McCormick was staring at him now.

"Millions and millions of dollars," Hirsch said. "Nice work if you can get it."

McCormick leaned forward, his face coloring. "Like Guttner didn't have his fat snout in the trough. Don't try any of that holier-than-thou bullshit with me, Hirsch. I know who you are. And I know exactly why you're here today."

"Is that so? Why am I here today?"

McCormick patted his hand on his briefcase. "This."

"What's in there?"

"What you came here for."

"Money?"

"Hush money, right? Or should we call it blood money? I figured you'd get around to it eventually. It's what makes your people tick."

"My people?"

"You heard me."

"What if I told you I wasn't here for the money, Brendan?"

He laughed. "Right. You came here to talk football. Linebacker to linebacker."

"What if I told you I couldn't care less about your kick-back scheme?"

"Sure. And there really is an Easter Bunny, too."

Hirsch stared at him. "I'm telling you the truth."

"You expect me to believe that?"

Hirsch shrugged.

"You're trying to get me to believe you're not here for money?"

"That's what I'm telling you."

McCormick frowned. "So what are you here for?"

"I think you already know the answer to that."

McCormick leaned back in his chair. He stared up at the ceiling and scratched his chin.

Hirsch waited.

McCormick lowered his gaze. "Judith?"

Hirsch nodded.

"That's what this is all about?"

"Yep."

McCormick shook his head. "I don't get it."

"Get what?"

"You didn't even know her."

"Not then. I do now. She was a remarkable person."

"I suppose."

"But easy to underestimate."

"You think so?"

"Come on, Brendan. You know that better than anyone else. Look what she did. She figured out what no one else had even suspected. She pieced together your entire scam. All on her own, too. Even traced it back to the origins— back to your kickbacks from Guttner in those warehouse cases."

McCormick was staring at him now, his jaws tensing.

Hirsch said, "But she had a tragic flaw, didn't she?"

"What?"

"Youth."

"What the fuck are you talking about?"

"She actually believed she could save you, didn't she? She believed she could get you back on the path of the righteous. Turn you back into the judge she'd once worshipped." Hirsch shook his head sadly. "So naive. She didn't understand that you were decades beyond redemption. Nor could she imagine how you'd react when she told you what she'd found."

McCormick was frowning again at the clasps on his briefcase.

Hirsch leaned forward, his anger beginning to build. "So that's why I'm here today. I don't care about your kickback scheme, and I don't care about your money. I want only one thing from you."

McCormick look at him. "What?"

"The reason."

"What reason?"

"Why you killed her."

McCormick laughed. "Come on, David. We both know the accident killed her."

"Actually, Brendan, we both know the accident didn't kill her. She was dead before that SUV left your driveway."

"Good God, David. Listen to yourself. Dead before the SUV left my driveway? What are you smoking, pal?"

"You weren't listening to me, Brendan. I didn't come here to find out *how* she died. I already know that. You strangled her. Murdered her with your own hands. I've tried to visualize it, Brendan. Where'd you do it. In your den? Or was it in the breakfast room?"

McCormick stared at him.

"It's a nasty image, Brendan. You're more than a foot taller than she was right? You must have outweighed her by a hundred and fifty pounds." Hirsch grimaced and shook his head. "Like choking a child. And then you put her in the car and faked the accident. I assume that part was improvised. Not bad, either. You fooled the medical examiner that night. Still, it was a close call, and you knew it. You learned your lesson, though."

"What lesson is that?"

"To hire professionals. That's what you did the second time, right?"

"Second time?"

"That was a professional job."

"What are you talking about?"

"The reporter."

McCormick stared at him but said nothing.

"You remember Patrick Markman, Brendan. Died in a one-car accident driving back from Jeff City. Fell asleep at the wheel. How convenient. Were they the same folks you hired to stop me?"

"I'm not telling you a goddamn thing."

"Forget about Patrick Markman, Brendan. Forget about me, too. I didn't come here for that. I'm here only for Judith. I know you didn't set out to kill her that night. You may be dumb, but you aren't that dumb. Did you even suspect why she wanted to talk with you that night? That must have been a shock, eh? Your cute little law clerk had you by the short hairs, didn't she. Is that why?"

"Why what?"

"Is that why you killed her?"

The room was silent. McCormick was staring at the clasps again.

Hirsch waited.

McCormick raised his eyes and met Hirsch's gaze.

"Why should I tell you anything?"

Hirsch thought of his conversation with Rosenbloom. "Closure."

"What's that supposed to mean?"

"Time to wrap up the case and move on. I filed it as a wrongful death case, Brendan. I've established the wrongful part, but I haven't established the reason."

McCormick forced a laugh. "You forgot your first lesson as a prosecutor, David. You don't need to establish a reason. The law doesn't care why you robbed that bank. It only cares whether you did it."

Hirsch said, "You forgot the second lesson. The law may not care why, but the jury does. I'm the jury here. I care, Brendan."

McCormick leaned back in his chair and stared up at the ceiling tiles. After a long pause, he said, "I couldn't sleep that night."

"What night?"

"The night after you filed the lawsuit. I'd had that date

marked on my calendar for three years. The first months after she died were rough. I kept waiting for someone to file suit."

"Why?"

"Why?" McCormick lowered his gaze to Hirsch. "Think of who the defendants would be. Big corporations with deep pockets. Plenty of money to spend on medical experts and plenty of incentive to find a different cause of death. Those first six months I had one of my clerks check the court files once a week. I viewed her father as my best hope. The old bastard hated lawyers. Especially plaintiff's lawyers. And he hated personal injury cases. I'd touch base with him every month or so. See how he was doing. See whether he'd changed his attitude. Tell him how much I admired the way he was sticking with his principles. Even in the face of his own daughter's death. Gradually, a lawsuit seemed less and less likely. I contacted her father after the second year, and he was still against it. Last December eighteenth was my finish line. Once I crossed that line, the race was over. What was that word you used? Closure? That was going to be my closure. I sent one of my law clerks over on the morning of the nineteenth to confirm that it was over. I had my ticket for a flight to Bermuda that afternoon. Man, I was ready to celebrate. And what happened? He came back carrying a copy of your fucking lawsuit." McCormick grimaced. "What a cluster fuck that was."

"You did a good job of acting at our first meeting."

"Obviously not good enough."

"You had me fooled."

"Oh? So what happened?"

"Exactly what you feared."

"A pathologist?"

Hirsch nodded.

"I knew it." McCormick shook his head. "Shit."

"You still haven't told me."

McCormick frowned. "Huh? Oh, right. Not much to tell. You think it was one of those haunting Greek tragedies? Some big Hollywood ending?" He chuckled and shook his head. "Sorry to disappoint you. I lost my temper and grabbed her. Freaked out. Don't even remember what happened after that."

He paused, the hint of smile on his lips. "But you are right about one thing. I learned something important that night."

"What?"

He contemplated Hirsch for a moment. "I'll show you."

He reached for his briefcase and unsnapped the clasps.

"I don't want your money," Hirsch said.

McCormick stood and opened the lid of the briefcase. "I have something better than money."

Hirsch got to his feet. "What?"

"Relax, David. I'm going to show you what I learned. It all relates to Judith's death."

The open lid of the briefcase screened its contents from Hirsch's view.

"You were right," McCormick said. "She caught me by surprise that night. It taught me the value of preparation. I'd hoped you were coming here for money. Money's easy. But you want something more than money. Well, guess what? I'm prepared this time."

"What are you doing?" Hirsch said, more for those listening in. The equilibrium had shifted. Everything felt wrong.

"I brought a present. Something better than money. See if you can guess what it is. Catch."

McCormick tossed something metallic at him.

Hirsch caught it. A handgun.

He looked up.

McCormick was pointing a gun at Hirsch's chest. He grinned as he gestured toward the gun in Hirsch's hand. "I call it evidence of self-defense."

And then he pulled the trigger.

The blast knocked Hirsch backward over the chair.

He heard shouts as he fell.

Then gunshots. Four of them.

Then shattered glass.

Then nothing.

He was on his back gazing up at the ceiling tiles. At the thousands of little black holes in white tiles.

He was gazing up at a negative of the night sky.

All those stars.

Was that Orion over there?

A face blocked his view. A face up close. A frown. Worried eyes. Hand touching his neck. Mouth moving.

But no words.

No sound.

The face gone now.

The stars blurring overhead.

And then a voice.

"Don't die, your grace."

A familiar voice.

"Take my advice."

What?

"Live a long, long time, because the worst madness a man can fall into in this life is to let himself die for no real reason."

He recognized the words.

"Don't be lazy, my grace. Get up from there. Let us go out to the fields together dressed as shepherds. Just the way we decided we would. Who knows? Maybe we'll find your fine lady out there waiting for you behind some bushes."

Dressed as shepherds.

He smiled. He knew who it was.

The sky was dark now; the stars blinking out one by one.

Yes, he thought, *let's go out to the fields, Sancho.*

Just the way we decided we would.

Epilogue

THE twenty-eighth of Kislev fell on a Saturday that year, which partly explained why the main sanctuary of Anshe Emes was nearly full for the morning *Shabbos* service. But many in the crowd were not members of the congregation, and many of those were not even Jewish, including Channel Five's Michelle Warner, who was standing along the side wall, and *Post-Dispatch* columnist Mitch Ryan, who was seated in the back row with a steno pad open on his lap. Michelle and Mitch and the other visitors had come to Anshe Emes on this chilly December morning because the twenty-eighth day of Kislev was also the fourth *yahrzeit* of Judith Shifrin.

Much has changed since this day last year, when barely a *minyan* gathered in the small shul down the hall. The scandal of *In re Turbo XL Tire Litigation*, which the media christened TurboGate, stayed on the front page and in the evening news throughout the summer. And with good reason. TurboGate is now the largest corruption-of-justice scandal in the nation's history. Criminal fines and restitution judgments levied against Peterson Tire, its various top executives, and the Emerson, Burke & McGee law firm exceed seven hundred million dollars. To that sum one must add at least a billion dollars in damage claims in pending lawsuits filed by a who's who of the nation's class-action lawyers.

Op-ed pundits and editorial cartoonists have had a field day with Marvin Guttner and Brendan McCormick and the top brass at Peterson Tire. So have the newsweeklies. Guttner appeared on the cover of *Newsweek*. Other key players, including Judith Shifrin, made it onto the covers of *Time* and *U.S. News*. Perhaps the most memorable was McCormick's computer-altered cover appearance on *Forbes*— a black patch over one eye, a skull-and-crossbones on his black robe, a cutlass in one hand, a fistful of cash in the other, under the caption: "The Blackbeard of American Justice."

Marvin Guttner did indeed seek the advantage of FIFO accounting by being the first of the defendants to plead guilty. Although his prison sentence was the shortest, it could hardly be called short. District Judge Maxwell Harper heard Guttner's guilty plea and lived up to his nickname at the sentencing. Thanks to Maximum Max, Guttner won't be able to savor his beloved chocolate cheesecake at the Saint Louis Club until after he turns eighty—and even then he'll need to cadge money to pay for it, since the government seized all of his personal assets, including the hidden ones McCormick alluded to during Hirsch's final appearance before him. That Guttner is serving out his term in the same correctional facility that once housed his nemesis is particularly galling, especially whenever he feels that sudden blast of cold water from the second showerhead on the left.

Maximum Max also presided at the trials of two of the

top three officials of Peterson Tire. If either of them lives to be one hundred, he'll enjoy his centennial birthday cake in the prison dining hall. Perhaps Guttner takes some comfort in that. And perhaps he feels some remorse over the fate of his two loyal lieutenants at the law firm, both in their thirties, both married, both fathers of small children. Neither will be eligible for parole until after his youngest child graduates from high school.

Guttner's most important client may soon vanish as well. Peterson Tire staggered through the summer months and into the fall buffeted by grand jury subpoenas and besieged by plaintiffs' lawyers. By September, its stock was trading in numbers normally associated with drill bit sizes. Two weeks before Halloween, it sought refuge under Chapter Eleven of the bankruptcy code. Few expect it to emerge.

Had Brendan McCormick survived Hirsch's final appearance before him, he could have been the first federal judge in American history to receive the death penalty. Although his strangulation of Judith Shifrin might not have qualified as first degree, his murder-for-hire of Patrick Markman most surely would have, as the prosecutors learned in October when a death row convict named Albert Fondella cut his deal with the State of Missouri. In exchange for getting his death sentence commuted to life in prison, Fondella gave detailed sworn testimony about the eight-thousand-dollar fee McCormick paid him to make sure Markman died in an "accident."

The two FBI special agents who burst into McCormick's chambers that last morning spared the judge the final indignity of a lethal injection on a prison gurney. They also spared him the pain and suffering he'd inflicted upon Judith Shifrin. According to the audiotape, the agents fired a total of four bullets in 1.3 seconds. Although the three that pierced his upper torso would not have been instantaneously fatal, the one that entered through his right eyeball and ricocheted inside his cranium would have turned out the lights pretty fast.

And as with most major criminal investigations, there were a few loose ends, including one the investigators will never connect to their investigation. In late May, about two weeks after McCormick's death, the Coast Guard fished a bloated floater out of the Mississippi River about ten miles south of St. Louis. The decomposed corpse appeared to be the remains of a burly Caucasian male in his late thirties. The medical examiner determined that the cause of death was acute spinal cord damage resulting from the fracture of the C-2 vertebra, apparently caused by a severe blow to the back of the neck. Any hope of fingerprint identification had been stymied by the catfish and turtles of the Mississippi River, who'd nibbled off all flesh on both hands, along with the dead man's tongue, eyeballs, and genitalia. The morgue eventually disposed of the remains as unclaimed and unidentified.

IN the main sanctuary of Anshe Emes, the service is nearing its end. Rabbi Zev Saltzman moves up to the podium and waits for the hum of Hebrew prayers to fade.

"This is the time in our service," he announces, more for the benefit of the visitors than the regulars, "when we pause to remember those of our loved ones who have died this year, and those who died at this time in years gone by."

He gazes out at the audience, at the familiar *Shabbos* faces and at all the new ones.

"Before I ask our mourners to rise, I want to extend an invitation to all gathered here today to join us down in the social hall after the service for a delicious *kiddush* luncheon presented by a friend of our congregation, Mr. Seymour Rosenbloom. He offers the luncheon in memory of an extraordinary young woman who died on this day four years ago."

The rabbi smiles down at Rosenbloom, who is seated in his wheelchair in the center aisle next to the sixth row of seats. Those who haven't seen Rosenbloom for a few months note that he has lost more weight. He doesn't seem to sit up quite as straight as before, and the bags under his eyes look darker. Those seated closest to him can see the tremor in his hands. But even from afar, his broad grin is as hearty as ever, and his eyes sparkle with gusto.

"Will the mourners please rise."

The rabbi waits as many in the audience get to their feet.

"I now call to the *bima*," he says, "a special member of Anshe Emes. Although he prefers the humbler title 'sexton,' to those of us who make up the weekday *minyan* each morning, he is our *gabbai*. We now call upon our morning *gabbai* to lead us in the mourner's *Kaddish*."

The *gabbai* is seated next to the aisle, with Rosenbloom on his right and Dulcie's son, Ben, on his left. As Ben stands and helps him to his feet and hands him his cane, the rabbi begins reading the names of the dead.

". . . Saul Birnbaum . . . Eugene Chosid . . ."

The *gabbai* makes his way slowly up the aisle. The bullet had punched through his lower chest, splintering two ribs and deflecting at an angle through his abdomen before lodging in his spinal canal between two lumbar vertebrae. He spent eight hours on the operating table the first time as the surgeons stitched his insides back together and, after much deliberation, decided that the risks of removing the bullet outweighed the risks of leaving it there. After another operation, two more weeks in intensive care, and several months of rehabilitative therapy, the *gabbai* can walk with a cane, his right leg in a brace.

One day at a time, his physical therapist always reminds him.

". . . Stanley Fink . . . Samuel Gilberg . . ."

He takes the three steps up to the *bima*, one by one, carefully.

"Get up!" a stern voice hisses.

The *gabbai* turns toward the familiar voice. Mr. Kantor is standing in the first row and glaring down at Abe Shifrin, who had been gazing ahead with a vacant smile. Shifrin looks up at Mr. Kantor with a puzzled expression.

"Now, Abe! Up."

Shifrin gets to his feet.

". . . Shirlee Kahn . . . Mikhail Lenga . . . Zvi Naiman . . ."

The *gabbai* is at the podium now. He looks around the sanctuary. Dulcie and his daughter, Lauren, stand side by side in the row he just left. Lauren leans against Dulcie and uses a handkerchief to wipe her eyes. Dulcie strokes Lauren's hair as she smiles at Hirsch. Scattered through the sanctuary are other women he knows, including several paralegals and secretaries from his office. Over near the left side stands Carrie Markman, frail but determined.

Down in the second row are the five remaining members of the *Alter Kocker* Brigade, all staring up at him with genial expressions. The sixth, Saul Birnbaum, passed away just last month. Along the side wall on the right stands Russ Jefferson, dressed in a dark suit and gray fedora, arms clasped in front of his hips. Seated near him are several of the FBI agents and assistant U.S. attorneys who worked on the TurboGate prosecutions. Standing in the back row like some massive sentry is Jumbo Redding. He'd driven from Tennessee last night, but only after extracting a promise that they'd all go out for sushi tonight. Dulcie had made reservations at Nobu for a party that would also include Lauren, Ben, Rosenbloom, Carrie Markman, and Russ Jefferson and his wife.

". . . Harold Rosenthal . . . Peggy Strauss . . ."

The rabbi had told him before the start of the service that he should take this occasion to say something about Judith. And now, as he listens to the names of the dead, he thinks again of what he could say to those gathered in the sanctuary, to those who've known her, to those who've only read about her, and to the man in the front row who no longer remembers her.

He'd given eulogies in the past—dozens during his glory years. He knew the language and the rhythms of tribute. He knew how to touch hearts and moisten eyes, how to make the audience sigh with grief and smile through tears. He knew the drill. It was, after all, not so different from a closing argument to a jury.

". . . and finally—"

The rabbi pauses.

"Judith Lynn Shifrin."

The rabbi nods toward him and steps back from the podium.

The *gabbai* looks out at the crowd.

Yes, he thought, there were things he could tell them about Judith, about her determination and her efforts to stop an injustice, about her faith and her sorrow, her courage and her solitude. They were all true, these things he could say. But the words were eulogy words, dulled by overuse.

He lowers his gaze to Rosenbloom, and their eyes meet. They stare at one another in the silence of the sanctuary.

After a moment, Sancho gives him a wink.

And that is when the *gabbai* realizes that the best words today are the same words his people have recited on this occasion for centuries—in the Sinai desert and in the Spain of Maimonedes, in the Polish shtetls and in the Park Avenue co-ops, in the Prague ghetto of the fourteenth century and the Warsaw ghetto of the twentieth, in the Jerusalem of

Herod and the Florence of the Medicis, in the valleys and on the mountaintops and in river cities just like this one in the heart of America.

And so he says, "Please join me in the words of the *Kaddish* in memory of all of these good people."

And they did.

Akediah Hebrew word for "binding"; refers to the scene in the Bible where Abraham binds his son Isaac to the altar to sacrifice him. The *Akediah* is the point in the morning service when the *minyan* remembers Abraham's supreme act of self-sacrifice in obedience to God's will.

Aleinu A prayer recited near the end of every Jewish service.

aleya ha'sholem "May she rest in peace."

Alter Kocker an old man

bar mitzvah The coming-of-age ceremony marking the fact that a boy has reached the age of thirteen and is thus obligated to observe the commandments.

bima the pulpit

bobba grandmother

boychik young boy (term of endearment)

bupkes something of no value (literally: beans)

chumash The compilation of the first five books of the Bible and readings from the prophets, organized in the order of the weekly Torah portions

gabbai the sheriff of the congregation who chooses who is to be called up to the *bima* to receive an *aliyah* (the honor of reciting a blessing over the Torah) or to read from the Torah; a position of great honor and respect within the congregation

goniff thief

goyishe kup used to indicate a person who is not smart or
shrewd: goyishe=non-Jewish; kop=head. Opposite is a *yid-
dishe kup.*

Kaddish The prayer associated with mourning and recited by
the mourner for eleven months after the death of a loved
one and then on each anniversary (*yahrzeit*) thereafter

Kiddish A prayer recited over wine at the beginning of a fes-
tive meal on the Shabbat or other holiday; shorthand for
the luncheon held in the synagogue after Shabbat services.

kippah skullcap, yarmulke

latkes traditional potato pancakes served on Chanukah

mensch term of respect for a special person ("He's a real
mensch.")

minyan quorum (generally ten men) required for praying as
a "community," or for the public reading of the Torah, or
for reciting the Kaddish or other ritual matters of special
holiness

mitzvah a good deed (literally, a command of God)

oy an expression of dismay, astonishment, concern, or pain

pushke little charity box for coins

putz a jerk (slang word for penis)

schlemiel an inept person, a fumbler

schmendrick a stupid person

schmuck derisive term for a man (slang word for penis)

schvartza a black person

Shabbas Sabbath (also, Shabbat)

shammas the sexton or beadle of the congregation, the person
who takes care of the physical plant

shanda shame or disgrace

Shemoneh Esrei A prayer that is at the center of every Jewish
service and consists of nineteen blessings

shiva mourning period of seven days observed by family and
friends of the deceased

shtupping sexual intercourse

siddur Jewish prayer book

tallit a prayer shawl worn during morning services with tzitzit (long fringes) attached to each of the four corners

tefillin phylacteries, i.e., leather pouches containing scrolls with passages of scripture, used to fulfill the commandment to bind the commandments to your hands and between your eyes

tsouris trouble, suffering

yahrzeit the anniversary of the death of a close relative

zayde grandfather